SUSAN MALLERY

Three Sisters

MIRA®

ISBN-13: 978-0-7783-1814-9

Three Sisters

Copyright © 2013 by Susan Macias Redmond

Recycling programs
for this product may
not exist in your area.

For questions and comments about the quality of this book, please contact us at CustomerService@Harlequin.com.

www.MIRABooks.com

Printed in U.S.A.

Dear Reader,

I've been honored by the way book clubs have embraced *Three Sisters*. The reader reviews are amazing and mean so much to me! I'm delighted that it's now being reissued in mass market paperback so it can start conversations with a whole new group of readers. If your book club has selected *Three Sisters* and you'd like to chat with me about the book, please visit the Book Clubs page at blackberryisland.com for information on how to set up a phone call or Skype chat. I'd love to hear what you think and to answer your questions about the book and my writing process.

This spring, I'll launch a brand-new women's fiction series with the release of *The Girls of Mischief Bay*. Mischief Bay is an eclectic beach town on the California coast. Like *Three Sisters*, *The Girls of Mischief Bay* features three friends who are each at a turning point in her life. Nicole's husband quit his job to write a screenplay, leaving Nicole to support the family and care for their young son. Shannon rose through the ranks in her company and is proud of her career success, but somewhere along the way, she forgot to get married and have kids. Pam never had much of a career. But now that the kids are grown, she needs to figure out what comes after life as a stay-at-home mom.

If you enjoy *Three Sisters* and want to read more from me, please sign up for my mailing list at susanmallery.com so I can pop you an email when I release a new book.

Happy reading!

Susan Mallery

Three Sisters

One

Being left at the altar is not for sissies. Aside from the humiliation and hurt, there are actual logistics to worry about. Odds are if a guy is willing to leave you standing alone in front of three hundred of your closest friends and relatives, not to mention *both* your mothers, he isn't going to sweat the little stuff like returning the gifts and paying the caterer. Which explained why three months after going through that exact experience, Andi Gordon was putting her life savings into a house she'd only seen twice, in a town she'd only visited for seventy-two hours.

Go big or go home. Andi had decided to do both.

After signing the final paperwork and picking up the keys, she drove up the hill to the highest point on Blackberry Island and stared at the house she'd just bought. It was known as one of the "Three Sisters." Three beautiful, Queen Anne–style homes built around the turn of the last century. According to the Realtor, the house on the left had been restored perfectly. The ice-cream colors reflected the style and fashion of the year it was built. Even its garden was more traditionally English than casual Pacific Northwest. A girl's bike leaned against the porch, looking modern and out of place.

The house on the right was also restored, but with less period detail. The slate-gray trim framed stained-glass windows and there was a sculpture of a bird taking flight in the front yard.

The house in the middle still had a For Sale sign planted in the unkempt grass. While like the others in style and size, the house she'd bought had little else in common with its neighbors. From the roof, with missing shingles, to the peeling paint and broken-out windows, the house was a testament to neglect and indifference. If the building hadn't been historic, it would have been torn down years ago.

Andi had seen the seller's disclosure—listing all the problems with the house. It was pages long, listing every major issue, from an electrical upgrade done twenty years before to lousy and nonfunctioning plumbing. The building inspector Andi had hired to look over the place had given up halfway through and returned her money. Then her agent had tried to show her a lovely condo overlooking the marina.

Andi had refused. She'd known the second she saw the old place that it was everything she'd been looking for. The house had once been full of promise. Time and circumstance had reduced it to its present condition—unloved and abandoned. She didn't need a degree in psychology to understand she saw herself in the house. She understood the pitfalls of believing if she fixed the house, she would also be fixing herself. But knowing and doing, or in this case not doing, weren't the same thing. Her head might be busy pointing out this was a mistake of mammoth proportions, but her heart had already fallen in love.

Given her recent, very public broken engagement, falling for a house seemed a whole lot safer than falling for a man. After all, if the house abandoned her at the altar, she could simply burn it down.

Now parked in front of the three-story disaster, she smiled. "I'm here," she whispered, offering the promise to both herself and the house. "I'll make you whole again."

The past three months had been a nightmare of logistics and recriminations. Buying one of the "Three Sisters" had given her something else to think about. Emailing documents for her loan was a lot more fun than explaining to her second cousin that yes, after dating for over ten years, Matt really had left her at the altar. He had actually said their decision to marry had seemed sudden and that he'd needed more time. And yes, he had run off to Las Vegas two weeks later, marrying his receptionist. She refused to think about the conversations she'd had on the subject with her mother.

But knowing that she would soon be leaving Seattle for Blackberry Island had kept her going. She'd focused on her escape. Then she'd packed up her place in the city and headed north.

Andi squeezed the keys her real estate agent had handed her, feeling the metal dig into her skin. The pain brought her back to the present, to this moment where there were only possibilities.

She got out of her car and stared at the broken house. But instead of boarded windows and a sagging porch, she saw what it would be. New. Shiny. A home people would admire. Not a castoff. Because when the house was restored, Andi could call her mother and talk about that. It would be a far better conversation than listening to the woman list everything Andi had messed up in her life. Like not allowing Matt to guide her into changing herself and how she'd foolishly let a good man get away.

Andi turned to admire the view. On a clear day the water of Puget Sound sparkled. Granted, clear days were relatively rare in this part of the country, but Andi was okay with that. She liked the rain. The gray, drizzly sky, the squish of her boots against the sidewalk. All that gloom made her appreciate the sunny days.

She turned west, looking out over the sound. The houses had a perfect view. They'd originally been built by sea captains, oriented to watch the ships sail in. In the late 1800s, seafaring had still been important to the area, not yet overtaken by the lure of logging.

This was right, she thought happily. She belonged here. Or she would belong, with time. If the renovations started to get to her, she would simply look at her view. The dance of the water, the peninsula beyond were far different from the high-rises of downtown Seattle. The city might only be a couple of hours away by car, but it was another planet when compared to the small town that was Blackberry Island.

"Hello! Are you the one who bought the house?"

Andi turned and saw a woman walking toward her. She was of average height, with long dark red hair that flowed halfway down her back. She wore jeans and clogs, with an ivory cable-knit sweater that just grazed her hips. Her face was more interesting than pretty, Andi thought as she approached. High cheekbones and large green eyes. Her pale skin was probably a result of both genetics and a complete lack of sun exposure since the previous September.

"Hi. Yes, I am."

The woman smiled. "Finally. That poor place. It's been

so lonely. Oh, I'm Boston. Boston King." She pointed to the house with the sculpture of the bird on the lawn. "I live there."

"Andi Gordon."

They shook hands. Weak sunlight broke through the clouds and highlighted what looked like a dark purple streak in Boston's hair.

Andi fingered her own dark hair and wondered if she should do something as dramatic. The most she'd ever managed was a trim.

"Any relation to Zeke King?" Andi asked. "He's the contractor I've been emailing about the house."

Boston's expression brightened. "My husband. He and his brother own a local firm here on the island. He'd mentioned he'd been in touch with the new owner." She tilted her head. "But he didn't say anything about you, and I'm dying to know the details. Can you spare a few minutes? I just put on a fresh pot of coffee."

Andi thought about the cleaning supplies in the back of her SUV. With the moving van arriving in the morning, she had plenty to do to get the place ready. But there were only three houses on the small cul-de-sac, and getting to know one of her neighbors seemed just as important.

"I'd love a cup of coffee," she said.

Boston led the way across the ragged grass to her own yard, then up the steps to the front door. Andi noticed the boards that made up the porch floor had been painted dark blue, and there were stars and planets scattered around. The front door was dark wood with stained-glass panels.

The eclectic mix of traditional décor and whimsy continued in the foyer. A Shaker-style bench stood by a coat-rack. On the wall was a mirror framed by silver squirrels and birds. The living room to the left had comfortable sofas and chairs, but there was a huge painting of a naked fairy over the fireplace.

Boston led the way down a narrow hallway, painted bloodred, and into a bright, open kitchen. There were cobalt-blue-painted cabinets, sleek, stainless appliances and a gray-and-blue marble countertop. The smell of coffee mingled with fragrant cinnamon and apples.

"Have a seat," Boston said, pointing at stools pulled up against the breakfast bar. "I just heated a couple of scones. I have cinnamon apple butter I made last fall."

Andi thought of the protein bar and cup of coffee that had been her breakfast and heard her stomach growl. "That sounds great. Thanks."

She took the offered seat. Boston opened the oven and removed a cookie sheet with two large scones on it. The apple butter was in a glass jar. Boston put the scones on a plate and passed one over, then poured coffee.

"Just black for me," Andi told her.

"Ah, a true coffee drinker. I have to conceal my caffeine in hazelnut and vanilla."

She got the flavored creamer from the refrigerator.

Andi glanced around. There was a big window over the sink and another in the corner eating area. A large pantry took up most of one wall. While she could see the original molding and beadboard by the back door, the rest of the kitchen had been updated.

"I love your space," Andi said. "I'm not sure my kitchen has seen so much as a coat of paint in the last sixty years."

Boston collected two knives and handed her one, then cut open her scone and smoothed on apple butter. As she worked, several silver charm bracelets clinked together.

"We saw your place at the open house. The kitchen was very 1950s."

"I don't mind the retro look," Andi admitted. "But nothing works. I have a thing about turning on a faucet and having hot water come out. And I'd like a refrigerator that keeps food cold."

Boston grinned. "So you're a demanding sort."

"Apparently."

"I know Zeke's been drawing up plans. I haven't seen all of them, but he and his brother do beautiful work."

Andi looked at her kitchen. "Did he update your house?"

"About six years ago." Boston picked up her coffee. "Where are you moving from?"

The island was small enough that Andi wasn't surprised Boston assumed she was from somewhere else. "Seattle."

"Big city, huh? This is going to be a change."

"I'm ready for a change."

"Do you have a family?"

Andi knew she didn't mean parents and siblings. "No."

Boston's expression registered surprise. "That's a big house."

"I'm a doctor. A pediatrician. I want to use the main level for my practice and live upstairs."

Boston's shoulders seemed to tighten. "Oh, that's clever. You'll avoid the hassle of commuting." She glanced out the window over the sink toward Andi's house. "There's plenty of space for parking and I can see how the conversion wouldn't be difficult."

"The biggest modification will be moving the kitchen upstairs. I was going to have to gut it anyway, though, so it won't add much more to the bill." She reached for her scone. "How long have you lived on the island?"

"I grew up here," Boston told her. "In this house, actually. I've never lived anywhere else. When Zeke and I started dating, I warned him I came with about three thousand square feet of baggage." Her smile faded a little. "He said he liked that about me."

Andi chewed the vanilla-flavored scone, enjoying the tart apple and cinnamon spread, then swallowed. "Do you work outside the home?"

Boston shook her head. "I'm an artist. Mostly textiles, although lately…" Her voice trailed off and something dark entered her eyes. "I sometimes do portraits. I'm responsible for most of the strange things you see around here."

"I love the porch."

"Do you? Deanna hates it." Boston wrinkled her nose. "She would never say anything, of course, but I hear her sighing every time she steps on it."

"Deanna?"

"Your other neighbor."

"Her house is beautiful."

"Isn't it? You should see the inside. I'm sure she'll invite you over. The front rooms are furnished true to the time period. The historical societies love her." Boston glanced out the window again. "She has five daughters. Oh, customers for you." She frowned. "Or is it clients?"

"Patients."

Boston nodded. "Right. The girls are very sweet." She shrugged. "And that's the neighborhood. Just the three of us. I'm so happy someone is going to be living in the middle house. It's been empty for years. A vacant house can be sad."

Although nothing about Boston's tone had changed, Andi felt a shift in the other woman's energy. Even as she told herself she was being what her mother would call "weird beyond what we consider normal," she couldn't shake the feeling that her neighbor wanted her gone.

She quickly finished the rest of her scone, then smiled. "You've been more than kind. I really appreciate the jolt of caffeine and the snack. But I have so much I have to do."

"Moving. I've heard it's tough. I can't imagine living anywhere but here. I hope you're happy here on our little street."

"I'm sure I will be." Andi rose. "It was nice to meet you."

"You, too," Boston told her, walking her to the front door. "Please stop by if you need anything. That includes a shower. We have a guest bath, you know, in case the water gets turned off."

"That's very nice of you, but if the water gets turned off, I'm moving to a hotel."

"I like your style."

Andi waved and stepped out on the porch. Once the front door closed behind her, she paused for a second, looking at her house from her neighbor's perspective. There were several cracked windows on this side, and part of the siding was hanging down, loose and peeling. The yard was overgrown.

"Talk about ugly," she murmured, returning to her car.

Not to worry, she told herself. She'd gone over the plans for the remodeling and would be meeting with Zeke first thing Saturday to finalize their contract. Then work would begin.

In the meantime, she had to get ready for the movers

who would arrive in the morning. She'd identified an upstairs bedroom where she would store the majority of her furniture. While the construction was going on, she would live in two small attic bedrooms. They were ugly, but serviceable. The bigger of the two would serve as a living room and pseudo kitchen. If she couldn't heat it in a toaster oven or microwave, she wasn't going to cook it.

The tiny attic bathroom had a shower obviously built for those who didn't hit the five-foot mark and fixtures dating back to the 1940s, but everything worked. Zeke had promised to rig up a hot water heater right away.

She had what she would need to survive the three months of construction. Although she'd told Zeke she wanted everything done by early July, in truth she was planning to launch her practice September first, giving her a nice buffer. She'd seen enough shows on HGTV to know there were often problems and time delays in re-modelings.

Andi collected the supplies from the back of her SUV. She needed to clean the room that she would be using for furniture storage, then tackle the bathroom she'd claimed. After that, she was going to reward herself with a pulled-pork sandwich from Arnie's. Her real estate agent had promised the food was great.

Andi carefully walked up the front stairs. Two of the eight steps were loose. She put her key in the front door and jiggled to make the lock turn. Then she stepped into the foyer.

Unlike in Boston's place, there was no eclectic array of charming furniture, no window coverings and nothing that looked remotely livable. The smell of decay and dirt mingled with the stench of former rodent inhabitants.

Wallpaper hung off water-stained walls, and plywood covered several of the living room windows.

Andi set down her bucket filled with cleaning products and a bag full of rags and paper towels, then put her arms straight out and spun in a circle. Anticipation had her giggling as she faced the three-dimensional disaster that was her new home.

"You are going to be so happy," she whispered. "I'm going to make you sparkle." She grinned. "Well, me and a construction crew. You'll see. When it's all done, we'll both be better."

By the time the house was finished, she would be settled here on the island. Her ex-fiancé would be little more than a cautionary tale and she would have the beginnings of a thriving practice. She would no longer be the family screwup or the woman who had been stupid enough to give ten years of her life to a man who had tried to change her before dumping her and marrying someone else two weeks later. She wouldn't have to worry about not being good enough.

"We won't be as perfect as that house on the left, or as artistic as the one on the other side, but we'll be just right. You'll see."

The words were like a promise. And she'd always been good about keeping her promises.

Two

Deanna Phillips stared at the photo. The girl was pretty—maybe twenty-five or twenty-six, with dark hair. It was impossible to see her eye color, because of the pose. The young woman had her arms thrown around a man, her lips pressed to his cheek. He was facing the camera, and the girl was facing him.

The snapshot had caught a happy moment. The man was smiling, the young woman leaned toward him, her knee bent, one foot raised. Everything about the picture should have been charming. Aspirational, even. Except for the fact that the man in question was Deanna's husband.

She stood in the bedroom, listening to the sound of the shower. It was barely after six, but Colin had been up since five. First he went for a run; then he ate breakfast; then he showered. He would be out the door by six-thirty. From there he went to the office and then on the road. Colin traveled for work, and she wouldn't see him again until the end of the week.

A thousand thoughts flashed through her mind. He'd cheated. He'd been stupid enough to keep a picture on his phone. He'd cheated. Who else had there been? How many others? He'd cheated. Her stomach pitched and rolled like a ship in a storm. Had she eaten anything, she would have vomited. As it was, she shivered, her skin breaking out in goose bumps, her legs trembling.

"Get it together," she whispered. She didn't have much time. In less than a half hour, she had to get the girls up and ready for school. She was expected at the twins' classroom that morning. She had to go to work after that. There were a dozen details, a thousand chores and jobs and responsibilities. None of that stopped because Colin had betrayed her in the worst way possible.

Her eyes burned, but she refused to cry. Tears meant weakness. Still clutching the cell phone, she debated what to do. Confront him? It was the logical decision. She should say something. Only she didn't know what. She wasn't ready. Wasn't—

The shower went silent as Colin turned off the water. Deanna shivered, then quietly set the phone back on the dresser, next to her husband's wallet and car keys. She'd only picked it up to check the photos from the last softball game. She'd wanted a couple of pictures to update the family's Facebook page. What she'd found instead was betrayal.

She needed time, she realized. Time to sort out what was happening. What it all meant. Her next step. Was there a next step?

She grabbed her robe and pulled it on, then hurried downstairs to the study. Once there, she turned on her computer. She noticed her fingers trembled as she pushed the button on her laptop. She sat in the big leather chair and wrapped her arms around herself. Her feet were cold, but she wasn't going to go back to the bedroom for her slippers. She couldn't. She was going to fly apart, she thought, her teeth chattering. If she wasn't careful she would explode into a million pieces.

The computer hummed and chirped as it booted. At last she saw the wallpaper picture come into focus. It showed a perfect family—father, mother, daughters. All blond, attractive, happy. They were on the beach, all wearing ivory sweaters and jeans, a jumble of arms and legs, the twins ducking, the older girls behind them. Colin had his arms around her, Deanna thought. They were laughing. Happy.

What the hell had happened?

"Are you all right?"

She glanced up and saw her husband standing in the doorway. He wore a suit, the dark blue one she had picked out for him. The man had hideous taste in clothing. She didn't love the tie, but so what? Did that really matter today?

She studied him, wondering how other women saw him. He was handsome, she acknowledged. Tall, with broad shoulders and blue eyes. He kept himself fit. She'd taken pride in that, in having a husband who still looked great in jeans and a T-shirt. Unlike a lot of men his age, Colin had avoided a beer belly. He would turn forty next year. Was that what the other woman was about? Dealing with middle age?

"Deanna?"

She realized he was staring at her. "I'm fine." She wasn't sure she would be able to speak, but somehow managed the words.

He continued watching her, as if expecting more. She licked her lips, unsure what to say. Time, she thought desperately. She really needed time.

She tucked her hands under the desk so he wouldn't know she was shaking.

"My stomach's bothering me a little this morning. Must have been something I ate."

"Are you going to be all right?"

She wanted to scream at him that of course she wasn't going to be all right. How could he even ask? He'd taken everything they'd had together and destroyed it. Destroyed her. Everything she'd worked for, everything she wanted was gone. She was going to have to leave him. Become one of those desperate single mothers. Dear God, she had five children. Five daughters. She couldn't manage that on her own.

"I'm okay," she told him, anything to get him to leave. She had to have time to think, to breathe, to understand. She had to have a moment to stop the bleeding.

"I'll be back on Thursday," he said. "I'm going to be in Portland."

He always told her stuff like that. Details. She never listened. She and the girls had their routine. They were used to Colin being gone during the week.

Now he might be gone forever, she realized. Then what? She worked part-time in a craft store. She taught quilting classes and scrapbooking. Her salary paid for things like vacations and dinner out. She couldn't support a tank of fish, let alone five girls, on what she made.

Panic curled through her, twisting around her heart until she thought she would die right there. She forced herself to keep staring at her husband, desperate to remember what normal was.

"I hope it's warm," she said.

"What?"

"In Oregon. I hope the weather's good."

He frowned. "Deanna, are you sure you're all right?"

She knew trying to smile would be a disaster. "It's just my tummy. I think I'd better make a run to the bathroom. Drive safe."

She rose. Fortunately, he stepped back as she got close and she was able to slip by him without brushing against him. She hurried up the stairs and ran into the bathroom. Once there she clutched the marble vanity and closed her eyes against the pale, stunned face she saw in the mirror.

"Mom, you know I hate this bread. Why do you keep making it?"

Deanna didn't bother looking up. She simply placed the sandwich she'd made the night before into the lunch cooler. Baby carrots were next, then the apple and the cookies. Flaxseed, she thought as she picked up the recyclable container filled with small cookies. They were made with flaxseed. Not the girls' favorite, but healthy.

"Mom!" Madison stood with her hands on her hips. At twelve she'd already mastered a contemptuous glare that could shrivel the sturdiest of souls.

Deanna recognized the look and knew the cause, mostly because she'd felt exactly the same way about *her* mother, all those years ago. The only difference was Deanna's mother had been a nightmare, while Deanna couldn't figure out what she'd done to make her oldest daughter loathe her so.

"Madison, I can't deal with this today. Please. Just take the sandwich."

Her daughter continued to glare at her, then stomped off muttering something that sounded suspiciously like "You're such a bitch." But Deanna couldn't be sure, and this morning that was a battle she couldn't take on.

By eight, all five girls were gone. The kitchen was the usual disaster, with bowls in the sink, plates on the breakfast bar and open cereal boxes on the counter. Lucy had left her lunch box by the refrigerator, which meant another stop for Deanna later. And Madison's coat still hung over the bar-height chair.

Lucy's absentmindedness wasn't anything new and certainly not personal, but the same couldn't be said for Madison and the jacket. Her oldest had hated the waterproof red coat forty-eight hours after insisting it was perfect and that she *had* to have it. Since that late September shopping trip, she and Madison had battled about the garment, with her daughter insisting a new one be purchased. Deanna had refused.

Sometime in October, Colin had said they should get her a new coat—that it wasn't worth the fight. Lucy liked the red one and would probably be in it by the fall. If Madison wore it all year, it would be too battered to be passed down.

Just one more time where Colin hadn't supported her, Deanna thought bitterly. One more example of her husband siding against her with the girls.

Deanna crossed to the sink and turned on the water. She waited until it was the right temperature, then carefully pumped the soap three times and began to wash her hands. Over and around, again and again. The familiar feel of warm water and slick soap comforted her. She knew she couldn't let herself continue for too long. That if she wasn't careful, she would go too far. Because of that, long before she was ready, she rinsed, then opened the drawer by the sink and pulled out one of her cotton towels and dried her hands.

She walked out of the kitchen without looking back.

She would deal with the mess later. But instead of climbing to the second story and the master bedroom, she sank onto the bottom stair and dropped her head into her hands. Anger blended with fear and the sharp taste of humiliation. She'd done her best to be nothing like her mother, yet some lessons couldn't be unlearned. The familiar question of "What will the neighbors think?" lodged in her brain and refused to budge.

Everyone would talk. Everyone would wonder how long the affair had been going on. Everyone would assume he'd been cheating for years. After all, Colin's job was on the road. While she would get the sympathy, the solicitous attention of their friends, the other wives would take a step back. They wouldn't want a divorced woman hanging around. The husbands would look at her and wonder what she'd done to make Colin stray. Then they would ask her husband for the wheres and hows, living vicariously through his adventures.

Deanna longed to crawl back in bed and restart the morning. If only she hadn't gone looking for that picture, she thought. Then she wouldn't have to know. But time could not be turned back, and she had to deal with the reality of Colin's treachery.

She stared down at the wedding ring set on her left hand. The large center stone glinted, even in the dim light. She was so careful to get the rings cleaned every three months, have the prongs checked to make sure nothing was loose. She'd been so careful about so many things. She'd been a fool.

Deanna tugged the ring off her finger and threw it across the hallway. It bounced against the wall and rolled to the center of the polished hardwood. Then she covered her face with her hands and gave in to tears.

* * *

Boston King arranged the tulips on the small hand-painted table she'd brought in from the spare bedroom. The top of the table was white, the legs a pale green. Years ago, she'd stenciled tulips around the sides, a perfect echo of the flowers she now moved around, trying to find the right air of casual disarray.

She positioned a long dark green leaf, shifted a petal, moved the yellow tulip closer to the pink one. When she was pleased with what she'd done, she picked up the whole table and carried it so that it sat in a shaft of bright sunlight. Then she settled on her stool, picked up her pad and began to sketch.

She moved quickly, confidently. Her mind cleared as she focused on shapes, contrasts and lines, no longer seeing an object, but instead the parts. Pieces of the whole, she thought with a smile. She remembered one of her teachers who would remind her, "We view the world on a molecular level. The building blocks, not the end results."

The first of the flowers grew on the page. Impulsively, she reached for a piece of chalk, thinking she could capture the purity of the yellow petal. As she guided it to the paper, her charm bracelet provided a familiar melody. Her eyes drifted closed, then open again.

Gray. She'd picked the gray, not the yellow. The darker of her grays, nearly black, but not quite. The piece was stubby and worn, but sharp. She always kept it sharp. Then her hand was moving again, faster than before, the lines so comfortable, her movements almost habitual.

What had been a flower became something much more beautiful, much more precious. A few more strokes and she was staring at the face of an infant. Liam, she thought, running her hand across the picture, smudging and softening the defined lines until they were as sleepy as the boy.

She drew in a few details of background, then studied the result. Yes, she'd captured him, the curve of his cheek, the promise of love in his half-closed eyes. Her best boy.

She put her initials and the date in the bottom right-hand corner of the paper, then tore it from the pad and set it on top of the others already there. After picking up her mug of white tea, she walked to the window and stared out at the rear garden.

Spruce trees lined the edge of the property. In front of them, Pacific wax myrtle swayed in the afternoon breeze. They'd all survived last winter's big windstorm. The last of her tulips danced, their promise of spring already met. Over the next week or so, she would plant the rest of her garden. She enjoyed the fresh vegetables, although she didn't share her neighbor Deanna's rabid obsession with growing her own food whenever possible.

She was aware of the silence, feeling rather than hearing the steady beating of her own heart. That's what she experienced these days. Silence. Not quiet. Quiet had a restful quality. In quiet, she could find peace. In silence, there was only an absence of sound.

She turned and walked to the front of the house. The big moving van in Andi's driveway rumbled to life. It had been there since early morning. Zeke had told her about Andi's plans to store most of her furniture in an upstairs bedroom and live in the attic during the remodeling. Boston didn't envy the movers the work of hauling heavy furniture up the narrow stairs.

As if her thoughts had conjured him, her husband drove his battered red pickup around the retreating moving truck and up toward their house. She watched him park, then get out and walk toward the side entrance.

He moved as easily and gracefully as he had the first time she'd seen him. She'd been all of fifteen—a new sophomore at the mainland high school. It had been the first week of classes and she'd clung to her friends like a motherless monkey abandoned in the jungle. He'd been a senior. Handsome. Sexy. On the football team. Despite the heat of the September afternoon, he'd proudly worn his letterman jacket.

She'd taken one look at him and had fallen deeply in love. She'd known in that instant that he was the one. He liked to tease that it had taken him longer. That it was only after he'd been talking to her for ten minutes that he'd accepted his fate.

They'd been together ever since. Married when she was twenty and he was twenty-two. Their love had never wavered and they'd been so happy together that they'd put off starting a family. She had her career to establish, and he'd been busy with his business. There had been the world to see. Their lives had been perfect.

"Hey, babe," Zeke called as he walked in the kitchen door. "Our neighbor moved in."

"I saw."

He came out of the kitchen and walked toward her, his brown eyes affectionate, as always, but now also wary. Because in the past six months, they'd seemed to stumble more than they got it right.

It all came down to blame, she thought, tightening her hold on her mug of tea. In their heads they knew neither was at fault, but in their hearts... Well, she couldn't speak to his heart, but hers had turned into a void. Lately she'd started to wonder if it was possible for love to live in a black hole.

"Her remodeling is going to have a serious effect on our bottom line this year," Zeke said. "You be friendly, you hear?"

She smiled. "I'm always friendly."

"I'm just saying you might want to put off talking about the power that flows from the earth until we cash the checks."

Boston rolled her eyes. "I only celebrated the summer solstice once and that was just to be nice to my friend from the art class I was teaching."

"You can be plenty weird without blaming other people."

"Redneck."

"Flake." He kissed her on the cheek. "Let me go get my stuff."

He walked back outside to his truck. Boston glanced at the clock and saw it was too early to start dinner. With the weather so nice, she was thinking they would just barbecue burgers. Their first of the season. Zeke had pulled out the high-tech stainless monstrosity the previous weekend and was itching to fire it up.

She could make a salad, she thought. Maybe invite Andi over. She had to be exhausted after a hard day of moving, and Boston knew there wasn't anything remotely close to a working kitchen in her house.

Zeke returned, his arms full of plans and contracts. He had his lunch box in one hand and a small box in another.

She smiled. "Is that for me?"

"I don't know. I bought it for the most beautiful girl in the world. Is that you?"

Whatever else might go wrong, Zeke always tried,

she thought. He was a thoughtful guy, regularly bringing her little presents.

The gifts themselves weren't expensive. A new paintbrush, a single flower, an antique pin for her hair. For all the years they'd been married, he'd always gone out of his way to let her know he was thinking of her. That she was important to him. It was part of the glue that held their marriage together.

She reached for the box, but he turned, keeping it out of reach. "Not so fast, young lady."

He put his paperwork down, then slowly held out the box. She took it, letting the anticipation build.

"Diamonds?" she asked, knowing they weren't something either of them would be interested in.

"Darn it. Did you want diamonds? Because it's a new truck."

Despite the tease, something in his voice sounded different. When she looked up, she saw the hesitation in his eyes. Boston opened the box slowly. Her gaze settled on the tiny pink booties.

They had been knit in the finest gauge, with a little crocheted lace trim and delicate ties. Lovely and girly. Staring at them made her chest tighten. She couldn't breathe. Her body went cold and the box with the booties slipped from her grasp.

"How could you?" she asked, her voice barely a whisper. Pain shot through her, slicing and cleaving. She turned away, determined to keep the monster that was her pain firmly in its cage.

Zeke grabbed her arm. "Boston, don't block me out. Don't turn way. Give me something, hon. We have to talk about it. It's been six months. We could still have a family. Another baby."

She jerked her arm free and glared at him. "Our son *died*."

"You think I don't know that?"

"You're not acting like it. You say six months like it's a lifetime. Well, it's not. It's nothing. I will never get over him, you hear me? Never."

She watched the affection fade from her husband's eyes as something much darker took its place. "You keep doing this," he told her. "Shutting me out. We have to move on."

"You move on," she told him, the familiar numbness settling over her. "I'm staying right where I am."

Resignation settled into the lines around his mouth. "Like always," he said. "Fine. You want more of the same, you can have it. I'm leaving. I don't know when I'll be back."

He hesitated before turning, as if waiting for her to ask him not to go. She pressed her lips tightly together, wanting, no, *needing* to be alone. He was off to get drunk and she was fine with that. She got lost in her painting and he got lost in his bottle. It was how they got through the pain.

He shook his head and stalked out. A few seconds later she heard his truck start up.

When the sound of the engine had faded away, she walked back to her studio. As she stepped inside, she didn't see the light spilling in through tall windows, the hand-built shelves, carefully constructed to her specifications, the easels and empty canvases awaiting their destiny. Instead her gaze fell on the pictures of Liam. Her son.

Tiny sketches and life-size portraits. Drawings and watercolors. She'd used every material, every medium. She had created hundreds of pictures, maybe thousands.

Since they'd buried him, he was all she could draw. All she wanted to create.

Now, her heart still pounding, her body still cold, she picked up a sketchpad and a pencil. Then she settled onto her favorite stool and began to draw.

Three

Deanna sat in her car in the parking lot. Spring had come to the Pacific Northwest. New leaves reflected sunlight and buds covered the bushes. The municipal park had soft green grass that had yet to be trampled by the children who would soon come to play.

She reached for her take-out coffee, only to realize she was shaking too hard to hold it, let alone guide it to her mouth. She'd spent the past two days shaking. Shaking and not eating and trying to figure out how to salvage the shattered remains of her once perfect life. She'd alternated between blaming herself and wanting to kill Colin. She'd cried, screamed and when the children were around, pretended absolutely nothing was wrong. Then she'd come up with a plan.

On the passenger seat next to her were several sheets of paper. Notes she'd made, phone numbers and statistics. She had all the girls' paperwork and copies of her and Colin's joint bank statements.

Her options were limited. The bottom line was, she didn't want a divorce. Being married was part of her identity, part of what she'd always wanted, and Colin wasn't going to take that from her, too. So she was going to explain that while she might forgive, she wasn't planning on forgetting. That he would have some serious work to do if he planned to win her back.

She had several weapons she was willing to use. The girls, of course. His standing in the community. Colin loved the island, but if he didn't come around, he would find himself ostracized.

In the back of her mind, a voice whispered that maybe he didn't want to give up the other woman. Maybe he wasn't interested in his family anymore. And by family, she knew the voice meant *her* because no one could doubt Colin's love for his girls.

She ignored the voice, knowing it came from a weaker part of herself. Strength was required, and she would be strong. She knew how. She'd survived so much worse than this.

She drew in a breath and steadied herself enough to pick up her coffee and take a sip. Once Colin agreed to end the affair, she was going to insist on couple's therapy. She would casually mention that she had the names of several good lawyers. Lawyers who weren't sure a straying father deserved much time with their children.

The house wasn't an issue, thank God. It was in her name and would be until the day she died. A few times over the years, she'd thought about putting his name on the deed, but never had done it. Now she was grateful.

She glanced at her watch. About an hour ago, when she'd known he was close to home, she'd sent Colin a text saying that she knew about the other woman and telling him to meet her at the park. This conversation needed to be conducted in private, and with five girls in the house, privacy was rare. Madison was with a friend, and Deanna had hired a sitter to stay with the other four.

Colin's battered sedan pulled next to her SUV. Deanna put down the coffee and reached for the folders. As her fingers closed around the door handle, anger flooded her. Cold, thick fury that made her want to lash out, to cut and wound. How dare he? She'd spent her life in service to her family and this was what he did to her?

She sucked in a breath, trying to calm herself. She had to keep her mind clear. She had to be able to think. She had to stay in control.

Colin got out of his car and looked at her across the roof. He was still in his blue suit, although he'd changed his shirt and tie. Buoyed by the righteousness of her position, she opened her door.

"Hello, Deanna."

Hello? Not "I'm sorry"? She pressed her lips together and nodded, then led the way to a bench on the grass. She sat on the side with a view of the sound. It would give her something to stare at as he groveled.

He sat across from her. His blue gaze settled on her face. She waited, prepared for the explanation, the apologies. She hoped to see a little fear in his eyes. No, she thought grimly. A lot of fear.

But it wasn't there. If anything, he looked as he always did. Tired from his trip, of course. If she had to pick a second emotion, it would be resignation. She would almost say he looked determined, but that didn't make sense.

He nodded at the folders she held. "You came prepared."

"I did."

He leaned toward her, resting his elbows on the table. "I'm not having an affair. I've never had an affair."

"I saw the picture."

"You saw *a* picture."

She drew back and squared her shoulders. "If you're going to play word games, we're not having this conversation."

"I'm saying you saw a picture of me with a coworker. The whole office was celebrating. Val had just gotten engaged. A few weeks ago, her boyfriend was acting strange. She thought he was trying to end things, but I told her to hang in there. It turns out he was preparing a romantic weekend away so he could propose. The picture is her thanking me."

"With a kiss?"

"On the cheek, Deanna. She's a kid. I'm not cheating."

She saw the truth in his eyes. Colin had never been much of a liar. A good quality in a husband, she thought, as relief replaced fear. The folders she held suddenly felt heavy and obvious.

"You could have said something," she murmured, aware she owed him an apology.

"So could you." He straightened and studied her. "I'm sorry you think I'm the kind of man who would cheat on you."

"I didn't know what else it could be," she admitted, uncomfortable being in the wrong. "Your work life is separate from us. You were kissing another woman and you're gone all the time."

"Your misinterpretation isn't my responsibility," he told her.

"I know."

She was an idiot, she thought. She had to explain and admit fault. It's how these things went. "I just…" The words stuck in her throat.

"No," Colin said suddenly when she didn't continue. He stared at her. "No, that's not good enough."

"What?"

"You not apologizing. Again."

She stiffened. "Colin!"

"I'm sick of it. Of you, of us. I'm not happy with our marriage. I haven't been for a long time."

She blinked, the words hitting her directly in the chest. Her mouth opened, but she couldn't think of anything to say.

His expression tightened. "I'm tired, Deanna. I'm tired of dealing with you. You don't care about me or our relationship. I'm not sure you care about anything except getting your way and how things look to other people. You sure as hell don't seem to want me around. You want my paycheck and then you want me to get out of your way."

Heat burned on her cheeks even as fear froze her chest and made it impossible to breathe.

"You think I don't notice how impatient you are with me every time I try to do something with the girls? You make all of us feel like unwelcome visitors in our own home. Nothing is good enough for you. We certainly aren't. You're constantly riding the girls and you can't stay off my ass. The house is your domain and you make it damn clear I'm not welcome there."

"I don't know what you're talking about," she whispered, battered by the unexpected attack. "None of that is true."

"Really? You actually believe that? Then we have a bigger problem than I thought." He was quiet for a moment. "I thought it would get better. That you'd see what you were doing. But you haven't and you won't. Maybe

I've been afraid of the consequences, I don't know. Regardless, I'm done waiting."

He stood and looked down at her. "I'm sure you've got all kinds of information in your folders there, Deanna. I don't know if you planned to try to scare the crap out of me or tell me to get out. So my bottom line won't have the same details as yours, but here goes anyway. I want a real marriage. I want to feel like I'm welcome in my own home. I'm tired of you calling all the shots and treating our daughters like they're dogs to be housebroken rather than children to be nurtured. Things are going to change, starting now, or our marriage is over."

He might have said more. She wasn't sure. All she knew was that she was cold and couldn't breathe and her stomach hurt. She tried to stand and couldn't. The folders fell onto the ground. Papers scattered everywhere.

He was wrong. He was wrong! The words repeated over and over again. Wrong and cruel. She hated him, hated this.

She managed to stand. Once she'd stepped out from the bench, she turned to tell him that, but he was already gone, his car driving away. She watched him disappear around a curve, and then she was alone.

Boston plunged her hands into the cool soil and moved her fingers through the loose dirt. Seedlings lined up beside her, delicate wisps that would grow into sturdy plants. While she planted most of her garden directly with seeds, the past few years she'd been experimenting with starting a few vegetables as seedlings. Zeke had built her a small greenhouse just for that purpose. Last year she'd had success with her tomatoes. This year she was adding broccoli and cabbage to the mix.

She reached for the first plant, then sat back on her heels when she heard a truck pull into the driveway. Not her husband, she thought. Her brother-in-law, Wade. Most likely here to plead Zeke's case. Once a big brother, always a big brother. Wade could no more help himself from stepping between Zeke and trouble than he could change his eye color or height.

She shifted so she was sitting cross-legged on the grass and waited. About thirty seconds later, Wade walked around the corner of the house and spotted her.

"I figured you'd be in your garden," he said as he approached.

Boston stared up at him. The brothers were around the same height, six-two, with dark hair and eyes. They were strong, easygoing and loyal to a fault. They were also driven by demons neither would admit to and shared a passion for sports that she had never understood. All she knew was that she held a small private celebration every year when football season was finally over.

Wade settled next to her, his long legs stretched out in front of him. He had on jeans and worn work boots, a plaid shirt. No jacket. The King brothers were tough and barely bothered with any kind of outerwear until it hit near freezing.

She'd known Wade nearly as long as she'd known his brother. If she remembered correctly, Zeke had taken her home to meet his family after their second date. Over salad and spaghetti he'd announced he was going to marry her one day. She had to give his parents credit. Neither had blinked at the statement. Probably because they'd assumed that young love didn't have much of a shelf life.

"He thinks you're pissed," Wade said, his tone conversational.

"Shouldn't he be having this conversation with me?" she asked.

"You know Zeke hates confrontation."

"And you don't?"

Wade gave her a familiar grin. "You like me too much to yell at me. Besides, I'm the innocent bystander."

"I love Zeke and I'm very comfortable yelling at him."

"Sure, which is why I'm here instead of him. He doesn't know how to reach you. He says it's like you're not even there some days."

An accurate assessment, she thought, knowing that every spare corner of her heart was filled with pain. There was so much of it, she couldn't feel anything else. And because the pain consumed her, she deliberately chose to feel nothing at all.

She missed her beautiful baby boy in perfect solitude, in an emotional vacuum, where he was always smiling and happy and only slightly out of reach.

She poked at the turned earth. "This isn't your fight, Wade."

"Tell me he can go home. I'm tired of him sleeping on my couch."

"He never had to leave."

Wade raised his left eyebrow.

She sighed. "It's not my fault he'd rather run than fight. I'm willing to take him on."

"Are you? He says the problem is you don't fight." Concern darkened his eyes. "You already lost Liam. Don't lose each other."

Boston managed not to flinch at the sound of her son's name. "I can't be lost," she said, doing her best to keep her voice steady so Wade wouldn't guess the truth. "I will love Zeke until I die. As to the rest of it, did he tell you what he said?"

Wade looked at her. "He's not wrong, Boston. Having another baby..."

She scrambled to her feet and shook her head. "Stop it. You don't get to say that. You have a daughter. She's beautiful and healthy and you don't get to tell me when I should be ready." She took a step back, then another.

Wade held up both his hands. "I'm sorry. You're right. I don't get to say. I shouldn't have mentioned it."

She drew in a breath. Wade moved close and wrapped his arms around her. She settled into the comfort—a silent acceptance of his apology. Her brother-in-law kissed the top of her head.

"Don't be mad at him. He loves you. I love you, too. Just, you know, not like that."

It was an old joke—a familiar one. Comfortable. She closed her eyes and nodded. "I don't love you like that, either. Send him home. It's fine."

"You sure?"

"If he's here, I can torture him more thoroughly."

"That's my girl." He released her. "I'm taking over the Gordon job."

"The house next door? Not Zeke?"

"He and I decided I was more suited to the project."

She looked up at Wade and raised her eyebrows. "Of course you did. I'm sure it was a long, thoughtful conversation and had nothing to do with the fact that Andi Gordon is pretty, single and has a great butt."

"My work is pain. I do what I can."

"You're a complete and total dog."

"Not really, but I do want to check out the new neighbor." He winked. "I have an appointment first thing in the morning. Wish me luck."

"No, and send my husband home."

Wade waved his agreement and started toward his truck. Boston returned to her planting.

Zeke would return and they would talk and life would go on. At some point he would have to accept that she wasn't ready for the next step—that her heart had been torn in so many pieces it might never be whole. People healed in different ways and at different speeds. She was fine with him having already moved on. She almost wished she could be like him. Almost. Because the truth was, not letting go allowed her to keep her baby close. In her pain, Liam was always with her. Exactly where he belonged.

Deanna wasn't sure how long she sat in the park. When she finally forced herself to move, she was shivering. Perhaps from the cooling temperatures or perhaps from something deep inside herself.

Colin's words continued to batter her. As she stood, she felt blood seeping from wounds no one else could see.

He was wrong, she told herself as she made her way back to her SUV. How could he think that about her? She loved her children. She devoted her life to her family. She had nothing for herself. She was defined by her relationships, by her love for them.

She started the engine and slowly drove back to her house. As she made a turn, the folder slipped off the seat and papers scattered on the passenger-side carpet.

She'd been so sure, she thought bitterly. So prepared. She'd known what she was going to say, going to demand.

Now she was left scrambling, unable to figure out what exactly had gone wrong.

Humiliation seared through her, making her skin burn. Had he talked to the girls about this? Did they all know what had happened? She would expect Madison to be gleeful, but the other girls, the younger ones, the twins, they were her babies. They loved her. She was their mother.

But Deanna realized she was less sure than she had been an hour ago. It was as if someone had picked up her entire world and shaken it before putting it down again. While everything was where it was supposed to be, the seams weren't straight and the edges didn't line up.

She turned at the corner and started up the last hill. The three houses, the Three Sisters, came into view. The sight of hers, so beautifully restored, usually calmed her, but not today. Not now.

Apparently she hadn't sat in the park as long as she'd thought because Colin was still in the driveway. All five girls crowded around him, hugging and talking, each struggling to be the one who carried his suitcase.

She slowed, then came to a stop in the street and watched as her children smiled at their father. They were so happy to see him. She could hear their excited voices and their laughter. They practically danced for him.

A few days ago, the scene would have filled her with contentment and pride. So many fathers weren't interested in their children, but not Colin. He'd always been involved with the girls. Now she understood that he'd had a plan all along. A desire to take everything from her. To hurt her.

Deanna waited until they'd all gone inside, then parked next to his car and went into the house. Loud conversation came from the kitchen as each of Colin's daughters vied for his attention. She took the stairs up to their bedroom and closed the door.

She leaned against the sturdy wood and struggled to keep breathing. She wouldn't cry, she told herself. Wouldn't let him know he'd gotten to her.

She crossed to the bed and grabbed one of the corner posts. She held on, gasping for air.

The unfairness made her want to scream. She'd sacrificed everything for Colin. Had created this perfect life he now complained about. She was a good mother. She was! How dare he judge her? He got to leave every week. She took care of all the details, she had to manage every crisis, while he got to come and go as he pleased. He was always the returning hero. She was the parent who reminded the children to brush their teeth.

Bitterness rose like bile in her throat. She hung on to the carved wood with both hands, digging her nails into the varnished surface. Hatred filled her. Resentment and anger blended into a poison.

Damn him, she thought viciously. Damn them all.

Four

Andi stood in front of the coffeepot. "Come on," she murmured. "Hurry. I'm seriously desperate."

Water gurgled over grounds, then dripped out as dark, magic elixir. Andi held her mug where the carafe usually sat and waited until the cup nearly overflowed, then expertly put the carafe back in place and took her first sip.

Life, she thought happily, the hot, caffeinated liquid slipping down her throat. Life and promise and a gradual easing of the sleepy dullness blanketing her brain.

She pushed her hair out of her face and tried to remind herself that she loved the house. She'd uprooted her life for a reason that had seemed very compelling at the time.

"More coffee," she said aloud. "Then I'll remember why I thought this was a good idea."

She crossed the attic floor and stared out the window. She might be living in tight quarters, but she sure couldn't complain about the view. From up here, she could see across the whole west half of the island. Beyond that the sound sparkled in bright morning sun. Right now, coffee in hand and nothing horrifying dive-bombing her head, she could see the potential. At three in the morning, not so much.

A truck pulled into her driveway. She glanced down, wondering who could be visiting her at eight on Saturday morning. It wasn't as if…

"Crap," she said, putting her coffee on the windowsill and glancing down at the oversized T-shirt she slept in. "Double crap."

Zeke, her contractor. They had an appointment. Something she would have remembered if she'd had more than four hours of sleep in the past three nights.

She ripped off her T-shirt, pulled on jeans and fastened up a bra. After grabbing the same shirt she'd worn yesterday, she shoved her feet into sandals and hurried down the stairs. She paused at the second-story landing long enough to pull the shirt on and smooth it into place.

Aware that she hadn't showered since she'd arrived and that her hair looked like something out of *Halloween 5,* she was grateful she'd at least brushed her teeth. Civilization required standards. Hers might not be especially high, but at least she'd kept some.

She jumped down the last three stairs and headed for the door at a run. She pulled it open just before Zeke knocked.

"Seriously," she said with a laugh. "You drove? You live—"

Next door. The words stayed on her tongue as her jaw dropped open. Because the guy standing in front of her wasn't Zeke King, her contractor and neighbor.

Zeke was tall, with dark hair and a nice smile. Good looking, she supposed. But even if that exact description could be used for the man standing in front of her, nothing about them was the same.

While his height was probably within a half inch of Zeke, he looked taller. His hair was darker, his smile brighter. Sexier, she thought, carefully closing her mouth and wishing desperately she'd showered and put on makeup. Maybe that great suit that made her look as if she actually had curves and hey, boobs.

"Morning," the man said, his voice low and smoky.

Her unpainted toes curled ever so slightly.

"You must be Andi Gordon. I'm Wade King. Zeke's brother."

Zeke had a brother?

There were a few lines by Wade's eyes, and the planes of his face were more sculptured. She would guess he was older than Zeke by a couple of years. If she hadn't spent the past decade getting her heart trampled by a no-good jerk who'd left her at the altar and then had married his secretary two weeks later, she just might have wondered if Wade was single.

"Andi?"

"What? Sorry." She shook her head. "I'm not all here. Come on in."

She stepped back to allow him entry into the house.

"Where are you?" he asked.

"Excuse me?"

"You said you're not all here."

"Oh, right. Lack of sleep. I have bats."

Wade laughed.

She suddenly found him slightly less sexy. "I'm not kidding. I have bats and no hot water. When I'm awake I'd say the lack of hot water is the bigger problem, but flying rodents are keeping me up at night."

He dropped his worn backpack onto the dusty floor. "You really hate bats."

"I hate anything that flies into my hair at three in the morning. I've been beating them back with a broom."

"I'd pay money to see that."

"I'd pay money to get them gone. Do you know the percentage of bats that carry rabies?"

"No."

"It's really high."

His mouth twitched. "As long as you have the actual number."

She put her hands on her hips. "Why are you here?"

"I'm your contractor. Wade King. You really *are* tired."

"I remember your name. You're Zeke's brother. You work together?"

"Yes. King Construction. No relation."

"What?"

"King Construction. The Kings of California?" His tone was helpful. "They're a big deal in— Never mind. Zeke and I work on all the jobs together. We'll be in and out here, but I'm going to take point." He pulled on his backpack. "I have the plans with me. Are you up to looking at them? I know you met with Zeke right after you made your offer, but I want to confirm everything before we get started with the demolition on Monday."

"Can I have hot water and no bats?"

He flashed her a grin that made her knees go weak. "Sure. I'll take care of both before I leave."

"Then I'm happy to look at plans."

Shortly after ten, Andi stood under a spray of hot water and decided that she was never going to ask for anything or complain, ever again. Her shower was heaven. She rinsed the lather out of her hair, then reached for her birthday-cake-scented shower wash and squeezed a generous dollop into her palm. The sugary fragrance surrounded her, chasing away the last of her exhaustion. As long as she had hot water and coffee, she could be a happy person.

Twenty minutes later, she had dressed in clean clothes and combed out her wet hair. She followed the sound of cursing to the third floor and stood watching as her very hunky contractor discovered she hadn't been lying about the bats.

"See?"

"This is not a good time to be smug," he told her, waving what looked like a butterfly net toward a dark corner of the space she'd claimed as her living room.

"Sure it is. You didn't believe me. Oh, and I wasn't kidding about the rabies, either. Don't let them bite you."

He gave her a quick glance. "Not getting bitten was the plan."

Something dark swooped from the rafter. Wade swung the net and snagged the shadow before it could retreat behind the large armoire against the wall. Andi had to admit she was torn between his impressive eye-hand co-ordination and the ripple of muscles she'd seen under his worn T-shirt.

The bat fluttered in the net. Wade held the opening against the wall, so it couldn't get out.

"Grab this, please."

She took the handle while he pulled on gloves. "You're not going to kill it, are you?"

"No. I'm going to take it out to the trees and let it go. I could only find this one, so once it's gone, you should be fine."

"Good." She shivered. "I hope it doesn't attack you."

One eyebrow rose. "Me, too."

She watched from the window. Wade appeared on her

patchy lawn and walked toward a grove of trees. Seconds later, something fluttered in the leaves and he was heading back for the house.

Impressive, she thought, wishing she'd called after the first night. She could have been bat-free that much sooner.

She poured them each a cup of coffee, then settled at the small table. Wade joined her and pulled the plans out of his backpack.

They were close enough that she could inhale the clean smell of soap and fabric softener. His dark eyes were made up of a thousand shades of brown with tiny flecks of gold. Her gaze settled on his mouth as she wondered if he was a good kisser. Not that she would be able to judge. She'd been kissing Matt for a decade and look where that had gotten her.

"Here's the plan for the main floor."

He pushed the paper toward her and oriented it so the front door was closest to her. She leaned in and traced the various rooms. Waiting area, front reception desk, back office, lunch room, three treatment rooms, supply space.

He talked about windows and light, the materials they would use. Decisions would have to be made on paint colors and fixtures.

"We did the remodeling at Doc Harrington's office a few years back," he told her. "Have you met him?"

"Yes. I'll be working there until my office is done. I start Monday."

"Look around when you get a chance. We did some custom built-ins the nurses love. We can do them for you, too."

She looked at Wade. "The most important thing to remember is that I'm dealing with children. I want them to be comfortable. Bad enough if they're sick—the environment shouldn't scare them, too. So bright, friendly colors."

He leaned back and grinned. "Now you sound like my sister-in-law." He motioned to the house next door. "Boston."

"Oh, right. Because Zeke is her husband. I met her earlier this past week. She's nice."

"She is. And an artist. Maybe the two of you can talk about what makes one color more friendly than another."

She studied him, aware that his eyes had crinkled in amusement. "You're mocking me."

"Some. We've got a little time until we're ready for paint."

"I'll be sure to get my decision made in the next couple of weeks."

They talked logistics—what walls would be torn down, how messy everything would be. Wade assured her she could live in the house through all the construction, and she nearly believed him. She confirmed delivery dates for various pieces of equipment and gave him a list of the fixtures and appliances she'd already picked out.

"I'll give you an update most evenings," he told her. "I'm generally the last guy out at the end of the day."

"A boss who works," she murmured. "Impressive. But aren't the long hours hard on your family?"

"They're used to it."

She sighed silently. So much for subtly trying to get information on whether or not he was married. The average sixteen-year-old had more dating experience than her. All she wanted to know was if Wade was as good as he looked. Oh, and if he was married, of course.

Not that she wanted a relationship. Or anything else. She'd moved to the island with the idea that she would spend the rest of her life celibate. Eventually she wouldn't miss being with a man. After all, how could she long for what she'd never really had? She and Matt had never had what could be called a wild sex life, although right now something other than lights-out, every other Saturday night, sounded kind of fun. Not that she was going to say that out loud. Or even think it. That part of her life was over. She'd moved on. Like to a higher spiritual plane.

"Andi?"

She blinked and realized Wade was staring at her. "Hmm?"

"You okay?"

"I'm fine. A little punchy from my nights with a bat."

"A challenge for anyone." He rose. "Come on. I'll show you where I was thinking we should put the kitchen."

Sadly, that was the most exciting invitation she'd had in recent memory.

Sunday morning, Deanna paused at the top of the stairs. She could hear the laughter and conversation coming from the kitchen. It was always this way. No matter his work schedule, Colin made sure he was home on Sunday. He got up early and made breakfast for the whole family. Sometimes it was omelets and other times pancakes. Once he'd made scones from scratch.

The girls joined him, sitting at the stools by the counter, talking about their weeks. Madison and Lucy helped with the preparation, and Audrey kept track of the twins.

Deanna had never been a fan of the Sunday ritual. She didn't like Colin cooking. He always made such a mess. The man used every pot and pan they owned. There were splatters and spills, dishes piled in the sink. But what she disliked most was the way the morning felt like all of them against her. Despite the fact that she was the mother and the one who cooked every other meal, she'd never felt comfortable in her own kitchen on Sunday morning.

Now she hovered, not sure whether to join them or not. She and Colin had been avoiding each other for the past two days. He'd slept on the couch, a fact that annoyed her. She'd so wanted to be the one to kick him out of their bedroom, but he hadn't given her the chance. Now he was acting as if nothing else had changed.

She supposed for him it hadn't. He'd delivered his ultimatum and then had walked away, abandoning her.

She rubbed her fingers together, aware of her dry skin, the cracked knuckles. She was washing her hands too much. Worse, it wasn't helping. The familiar ritual provided no comfort at all.

Shame crawled over her. Shame for being weak, shame for not being in control of her family and her husband. If people knew, they would laugh at her. She wouldn't belong anywhere.

That wasn't going to happen, she told herself. She was strong and determined. She'd survived more difficult circumstances than this. Somehow she and Colin would come to terms. They always had in the past. He was in one of his moods. He would get over it. As for the girls, she was their mother and nothing would change that.

She raised her chin and started down the stairs. As she approached the kitchen, the voices got louder. There was a burst of laughter. Deanna faked a smile, then walked in through the wide doorway.

Colin stood at the stove. The twins and Audrey were at the counter. Lucy was pouring juice and Madison stood by her dad.

As one they all turned to look at her. The three younger

girls' happy faces took on an expression of guilt. Lucy looked as if she wanted to crawl into a cupboard while Madison glared at her. Colin was impossible to read.

Silence pushed out the laughter. Deanna glanced from one daughter to the other, not seeing any sign of welcome. Her fingers curled into her palms as she told herself to stand her ground. Colin turned his attention back to the stove and flipped several pancakes.

"These are almost done," he said.

"I'll get the syrup," Madison told him.

Deanna stood in the doorway, invisible and unwanted, as memories of previous Sunday mornings crowded her vision. It was always like this, she thought, shocked by the realization. The silence when she walked into the room. The obvious signs that she should simply go away. That she didn't belong.

Tears burned. She blinked them away, turned on her heel and walked out. In the hallway, she paused, not sure where she should go. Her chest tightened and she hurried up the stairs. Once in her bedroom, she carefully closed and locked the door, then retreated to the bathroom, where she turned on the hot water and reached for the soap.

Sunday afternoon Andi sat on her battered and slightly dangerous front porch. She was careful to avoid loose boards and splinters, but the day was too beautiful to stay inside. Plus, she'd run out of things to do in her tiny living space. She was unpacked, bat-free and waiting until she started work in the morning.

Boston rounded the corner of her house, saw her and waved. Andi waved back.

"How's it going?" Boston asked, her hair flashing with purple highlights in the sun.

"Good." Andi stood and walked down the stairs. "I'm settled. Construction starts tomorrow."

Boston shook her head. "Enjoy this last day of normal, then. I know demolition is important, but it's hard to watch."

"Fortunately I'll be gone most of the day. I'm working with Dr. Harrington temporarily. It gives me a chance to meet potential patients."

"He won't mind you poaching from his practice?"

Andi grinned. "Not at all. He's told me he's pleased to have a pediatrician in the area." She glanced around and then lowered her voice. "I think he's tired of dealing with the little kids and babies. They tend to have more emergencies. Ear infections, that sort of thing."

Boston nodded, even as her gaze slid away. "Right." She crossed her arms over her chest. "Wade mentioned something about a bat. Is it gone?"

"It seems to be." Andi studied her neighbor. She would swear something had just happened, but she had no idea what. Before she could figure out a way to ask, the front door of the house on the other side opened and an attractive blond woman stepped out onto her porch.

"Your other neighbor," Boston murmured. "Deanna Phillips. She's the one with five girls. I should probably introduce you."

Andi was about to agree when Deanna raised her hand to her cheek and swiped her skin. They were too far away to see actual tears, but the movement was unmistakable.

"Another time might be better," Andi said, turning away.

Boston nodded, her eyebrows drawing together.

"Deanna's always so together. I can't imagine her crying. That would require a break in her perfect facade." She grimaced. "Sorry. That came out bitchier than I meant it to."

"No problem," Andi said, realizing life on their little street might not be as calm and simple as she'd first imagined.

Five

Monday morning Andi parked behind the low one-story building and got out of her car. Deep in her stomach, butterflies flew in formation. She knew that physiologically she could detail an explanation of synapses and adrenaline, along with other chemicals brought on by anticipation of a potentially uncomfortable event, but butterflies were a better visual.

She'd dressed carefully for her first day of work. A tailored blouse tucked into black trousers. Low-heeled, comfortable shoes. She'd pulled her long, curly hair back into a braid and added a light touch of mascara. She'd debated over lip gloss, but that had seemed too fancy for a workday, so she'd settled on a clear lip balm and had called herself presentable.

She collected her purse, medical bag and the white coat with "Dr. Andi" stenciled on the pocket. Some of her patients found the white coat intimidating, so she'd had a bright pink caterpillar embroidered on the pocket, as well. The combination of the nearly fluorescent color and purple high-heeled shoes on the bug had the desired effect. She went from scary to funny in a glance. A relaxed patient usually made for a better outcome, and Andi was all about helping her kids.

She walked around to the main entrance and went inside.

The waiting area had been done in a soft beige. There were plenty of sofas and chairs, lots of magazines and a view of the strip mall across the street. Typical medical office, she thought, crossing to the reception desk.

The woman sitting there was in her mid-fifties, with flame-red hair. She was tall, even sitting down, with flashy rings on several fingers and the longest lashes Andi had ever seen. She doubted they were any more natural than her hair color. But her smile was warm and Andi remembered her being friendly.

"Hi, Laura," Andi said.

The other woman looked up and then jumped to her feet. "You're here. We're all so excited you're starting today. You already have appointments, if you can believe it. When word got out a pediatrician was moving to the island, we started getting calls. Families are so excited."

Laura motioned for her to come back. Andi walked through the door in the reception area and found herself in a long hallway.

The medical offices had once been a sprawling private residence. Bedrooms had been converted to examination rooms and offices.

"Everyone should be here already, so you can meet the staff. Dr. Harrington said he wanted to spend a few minutes with you before you get started."

Dr. Harrington ran a family practice on the island. There was an urgent-care clinic open on weekends, but otherwise residents had to go to Dr. Harrington or visit the mainland to seek medical care. Given the demographics of the place—lots of families and within a couple of hours of Seattle—Andi had seen the need for a pediatrician. Now she was going to find out if she'd been right.

A pretty blonde with long, straight hair stepped out of one of the exam rooms. Andi recalled meeting her when she'd visited the island and had spoken with Dr. Harrington about working in the practice for a few months.

"Nina, right?"

The woman, in her early thirties and wearing light blue scrubs, smiled. "You remembered. Welcome, Dr. Gordon."

"Andi, please."

"Sure. Andi."

Laura touched Nina's arm. "We thought it would be easier for you to have one nurse assigned to you. Nina volunteered."

"Ask me anything," Nina told her. "I can tell you everything from where we keep the alcohol wipes to the best dry cleaner in town."

"I'm going to need both," Andi said.

Laura introduced her to the other nurses, then led her back to what would be her temporary office. It was a small windowless room with a desk and a computer.

"I know it's not much," Nina began.

"Not to worry," Andi told her. "I won't be here for very long. Anywhere to update my charts is fine."

"And maybe a little internet shoe shopping while on break?"

Andi grinned. "Absolutely. So far I love everything about the island except the lack of retail."

"If you want a magnet in the shape of a blackberry, I can get you a great deal."

"Right now I don't have a kitchen, so that will have to wait."

"Just let me know when you're ready."

"I promise," Andi told her.

She dropped her purse into the bottom drawer of the metal desk, then followed Nina across the hall to Dr. Harrington's office.

The older man rose as she entered. "Thanks, Nina. Andi, so nice to see you again."

"Nice to see you, Dr. Harrington."

The gray-haired man shook her hand. "Ron, please." He winked. "My father is Dr. Harrington."

She took the seat on the visitor side of his desk while he settled back in his chair.

"My staff is getting you settled?" he asked.

"They are. I even have appointments."

"You'll be kept busy, that's for sure. There's enough work for all of us."

"I appreciate you letting me work here through the summer."

"I'm happy to have the help." His blue eyes twinkled behind his glasses. "At least until my son joins me in September." He leaned back in his chair and smiled. "My son, the doctor. That has a nice ring to it."

"Yes, it does."

"Did I mention Dylan graduated at the top of his class in medical school?"

Only about fifteen times, Andi thought as she smiled. "Did he? You must be so proud."

"I am, as is his mother. He's a smart boy. And a doctor."

His pleasure in his son's accomplishments was a good thing, Andi told herself. Some parents were thrilled when their children became doctors. For her, the path to being a pediatrician was slightly more treacherous. It wasn't that her parents had a problem with the medical profession. They felt that her choice had been a waste of talent.

Why bother with "scraped knees and vaccinations," as her mother had put it? Her mother, the cardiothoracic surgeon, felt Andi should have picked a more challenging specialty. Her father, the neurosurgeon, agreed. Andi's brother was also a neurosurgeon and her sister was doing medical research that would probably cure cancer. Andi was considered a disappointment—a screwup, rather than the child who had lived up to her potential.

She shook off the voice of her mother and returned her attention to Ron, who explained how the practice worked.

"Nina will go over the schedule," he was saying. "If you don't mind, we'd like you to work a Saturday every three weeks. You'll get a compensating day off."

"That won't be a problem," she told him. "I know a lot of parents work, so getting to the doctor midweek can be difficult."

"Good. Then Nina will show you where we keep everything." He rose. "I thought you and I could go to lunch today. I can answer any questions you have." He winked. "Show you pictures of my son's graduation."

"I'd like that."

"Good."

He shook her hand again. "We're happy to have you, Andi."

"I'm excited to be here."

Nina was waiting in the hallway.

"All your appointments are routine," Nina told her as they walked toward the rear of the building. "A physical for camp, a few vaccinations, a well-baby visit."

"Sounds like my kind of day."

Nina motioned for her to enter the door on the left. It was the break room, with several lockers, a table with six chairs around it. A window looked out onto the rear parking lot. But what had Andi feeling all warm and fuzzy inside was the bouquet of flowers next to a cake with the word *Welcome* spelled out in pink icing. All the nurses and staff were gathered around, waiting for her.

"Welcome to the island."

"We should take you to lunch."

The last statement came from Laura, the receptionist.

"I'd love that," Andi said. "You don't have to take me, but it would be fun to go as a group."

The other women all looked at each other. Nina glanced at her. "Really? Because we weren't sure. What with you being a doctor and all."

"I still like lunch," Andi said with a smile. "And company. I'd enjoy the chance to get to know all of you."

"Then it's a date," Laura said firmly, reaching for a knife. "Tomorrow. I know Dr. H is taking you out today." She cut the first piece of cake and slid it onto a plate. "God, I love it when my day starts with a really big sugar rush."

By five minutes to nine, Andi had finished her slice of cake and a second cup of coffee. She was already on her way to a very nice caffeine-sugar buzz. Not exactly the breakfast she would recommend to her patients, but this was a special occasion.

Nina stuck her head in the office. "Carly and Gabby Williams are in exam room four. That's the one you'll mostly be using."

Andi stood and smoothed the front of her white coat. "I'm ready," she said, reaching for the chart.

Nina walked with her. "Gabby's ten, in good health. She's going to summer camp in a few weeks, and the camp requires a current physical."

"Okay." Andi stopped in front of the closed door and drew in a breath.

Nerves danced in formation while she told herself that she would be fine. Her patients were the best part of her day. She knocked once, then stepped into the examination room.

"Hi," she said. "I'm Dr. Andi Gordon." She smiled at the mother and daughter. "Nice to meet you both."

"Carly Williams," the mother said.

"I'm Gabby."

They were both blondes, with dark blue eyes and similar shapes to their faces.

Andi turned to the girl. "I'm going to guess you're the mom?"

Gabby grinned. "I know you don't think that."

"Don't I?"

Gabby shook her head. "You can't. You're a doctor and doctors are really smart."

"I've heard that, too." Andi sat on the stool. "So, I understand you're going to camp." She glanced at Carly. "This is about your daughter going, right? Not you."

Carly laughed. "I would love to spend a month away from my life at camp. But I don't think I fit the age requirement."

Gabby giggled.

Andi leaned toward her. "So, tell me about this camp."

"It's gonna be great. It's in the mountains and there's horses, but the best part is I get to help write a real play and then we perform it and everything."

"Wow. I want to go, too."

"I'm very excited," Gabby confessed.

"I'm getting that." Andi pulled her stethoscope out of her pocket. "Do you ride horses?"

"I'm gonna learn."

She started the exam, working slowly, making sure Gabby was still talking about camp rather than worrying about whether or not anything was going to hurt. When mother and daughter left the room, she made a few notes on the chart and then sighed. This was going to be a good day.

Monday night Deanna loaded the last two pictures onto the family's Facebook page, then scanned her latest entry. It was an update on how the girls were doing in school. She was less concerned about spelling and grammar than tone. She didn't want anyone reading the words to guess there was something wrong.

Keeping up the facade of "Gee, of course I'm fine. Why do you ask?" was exhausting. Or maybe it was the lack of sleep. She spent most nights lying awake in the large bed, wondering how everything had gotten so messed up and trying to figure out why she was the bad guy.

If she were like her mother, she would understand Madison's resentment and Colin's horrible accusations. But she wasn't. Her house was clean, she prepared meals, gave them positive attention. No one found her drunk, unconscious in her own vomit. She'd never once raised a hand to her children, let alone beaten them. They didn't flinch when she walked by.

But they didn't adore her—not the way they adored their father. They didn't run to her or light up when she walked into a room, and for the life of her, she couldn't figure out why not.

She tried telling herself it was because Colin was gone so much. He was less accessible than her. But she wasn't sure she could believe that reasoning. So it had to be something else. If only she knew what.

She rubbed her temples, wishing her eyes didn't burn so much.

"I'm leaving tomorrow."

Deanna looked up and saw Colin walking into the study. They'd barely spoken since his verbal attack in the park on Friday, and she sure didn't want to speak to him now. But there were logistics to be worked out.

"When will you be back?" she asked.

"Thursday." He closed the study door behind him and walked toward the desk. "Have you thought about what we talked about last week?"

She stood so she could glare directly at him and not have to look up. "We didn't talk. You told me everything I'm doing wrong and then you left. That's not a conversation."

He studied her. "You're right. So let's talk now."

"I've spent my life taking care of you and the girls and all I get is accusations and bitterness."

"You're expecting gratitude?"

Of course. She'd been a damn good mother and an excellent wife. Not that any of them appreciated her. "I don't want to be your punching bag."

He raised his eyebrows. "That's extreme."

"What would you call it? You say those things, and then you turn my children from me." Her throat tightened, but she refused to show weakness. "I don't know what you want from me. I don't have anything left to give."

"Then we have a problem, because I do want more. I want to be a part of things." He shoved his hands into his jeans pockets.

"What does that mean?"

"That means you lighten up a little. There are dozens of rules for everything the girls or I do. You want to be in complete control of where we go, what we wear, what we eat."

"I cook dinner and make lunch. That's not control." The unfairness stung. "I keep a calendar of activities so I know who has to be driven where. Why are you twisting everything I do?"

She wanted to tell him if he was so unhappy, he could leave. Only she wasn't ready for that. To be left.

"You're making me sound like a monster and I'm not."

His expression tightened. "Tonight at dinner, Audrey asked for a second helping of lasagna and you told her no."

"She'd had enough."

"How do you know? She told me later that she'd dropped her sandwich on the floor in the cafeteria, and one of the teachers had thrown it out. She didn't have any money, so she couldn't buy lunch. Your daughter had eaten only an apple for lunch and was starving."

Deanna felt herself flush. "She should have said something."

"And risk you yelling at her? It was easier to go hungry."

"I don't yell." She didn't yell. She spoke firmly and reasonably.

"You scare her. Hell, you scare me."

"I wish that were true."

He shook his head. "I know you mean well, Deanna,

but you're not easy. I was raised to think that as our children's mother, you knew best. I don't believe that anymore. I think there are issues from your past that—"

She slapped her hands on the desk and glared at him. "You leave my mother out of this, you hear me?"

He raised both arms in a gesture of surrender. "Fine. You don't want to talk about it? We won't. Here's what I know. I'm spending more than half my life on the road. I'm missing my children growing up. I'm not here for them and I want to be. I understand that I make more money on the road, but we're going to have to learn to get by on less. I want to be here. I want to go to games and performances. I want to take them to their various play dates. I want to meet their friends."

Leaving her with what? Deanna wondered. He was trying to push her out of her own life.

"The second thing I want is to understand what you think of me. Of us." His mouth twisted slightly. "I doubt you still love me and I'm not sure you even like me. I suspect you're a lot more fond of our lifestyle than our marriage." He shrugged. "I'd like to be wrong, but I don't think so."

He glanced past her, then returned his gaze to her face. "Was it ever about me or was I a means to an end?"

The insults burned to her bones, while fear held her in an icy grip.

"How dare you?" she said, her voice low and angry.

"Right. How dare I? It's only my marriage, too."

She wanted to throw something. To hit him and hurt him the way she'd been hurt. Hatred burned bright, but not bright enough to make her forget what divorce would mean.

"Don't even think about coming back to our bed," she told him.

Colin nodded, then actually smiled, even if it was ugly. "Sure. No sex. It's not like that will be a change."

With that he turned and walked away. Deanna stared after him for several seconds, before collapsing back into her chair and covering her face with her cracked and raw hands. She waited for the tears, but they didn't come. She was too empty, too broken. Everything was wrong and she didn't even know where to start to fix something that had become impossible to understand.

Six

The Blackberry Island Inn's restaurant looked out over the water. The lunch crowd was a combination of business people, tourists and ladies who lunched. Andi studied the menu, trying to decide between the soup and sandwich of the day and the quiche special.

Nina glanced up at her. "Seriously, you have to try the chicken salad on focaccia bread. It's so good, it's practically a religious experience."

"She's right," Laura said, adjusting her reading glasses. "I swear I could eat a big ol' tub of it every day. Of course then I'd get fat and Dr. H would lecture me on my blood pressure and cholesterol." She put down the menu. "I do adore working for the man, but he is obsessed with health."

Andi did her best to hold in her laughter. "It's, um, probably an occupational hazard."

"You're right. I was offered a job with a dentist years ago, but I knew I couldn't stand the sound of that drilling. We can see subatomic particles, but we can't make quiet dental drills? We're spending money on the wrong kind of research."

Everyone chuckled at that. Andi leaned back in her chair and listened to the conversation flow around her. She'd survived her first day at work and was well into her second. She was out to lunch with the office and nursing staff. That morning, she'd left a half dozen burly men ripping up the inside of her house. There weren't any more bats, she had hot water and basically life was pretty good.

Dawn, one of the nurses, picked up her iced tea. "I can't believe you moved here on purpose," she said. "I've lived here all my life. I've barely been out of the county. I used to dream of moving to Seattle."

"Then you got married and had kids and now you're stuck," Misty said cheerfully. She was the office manager-bookkeeper and the person who kept everything running smoothly.

Laura sipped her diet soda. "She's just complaining. Don't listen to a word Dawn says. She loves it here on the island. We all do."

"So you were all born here?" Andi asked.

"I moved here when I was five," Laura said. "Which is practically the same thing." She leaned toward Andi. "You know all the good men are married, right?"

"There are a few single guys around," Nina said.

"Not many," Laura said. "As for the tourists, if you see a guy who isn't with a woman, don't get excited. Chances are he's not into your girly parts."

Misty poked Laura in the arm. "Behave. Don't frighten Andi her first week."

"Yes, please don't," Andi said with a laugh. "We'll want to wait and frighten me my second week. For what it's worth, I'm okay with the lack of men. I suspected as much when I moved here. I had a bad breakup and I'm giving up on men. At least for the next decade."

Although looking at Wade was a pleasant diversion. She wondered if her handsome contractor fell into the single category or not. Unfortunately, she couldn't think of a casual way to ask.

"You're so brave," Nina told her. "Starting over in a new place. You bought that beautiful house and now you're going to open your own practice."

Andi smiled, knowing that description sounded a whole lot better than the truth, which was she'd been running away and this was where she'd ended up.

Misty sighed. "I agree with Nina. I could never do what you did. Dr. H said to let you know that we'll help in any way we can with interviewing staff and helping you set up."

Andi was speechless for a moment. "That's very kind of all of you."

"He's a good guy."

"Obsessed with his son," Laura said with a sigh.

"My son, the doctor," they all said together, then broke into laughter.

Their server came by and took their orders. Andi decided to try the famous chicken salad sandwich.

"Have you started construction on the house?" Nina asked when the server had left. "That's got to be a big job."

"It is. Fortunately I don't have to do any of it." Andi shrugged. "I just walk through in the evening and pray for progress. They're pretty much gutting each floor."

"You're going to have your practice there?" Nina asked.

"On the ground floor. The plans are finalized. Wade showed them to me on Saturday."

"Oooh, Wade." Laura pretended to fan herself. "He's so hot."

"And a little young for you," Misty reminded her.

"Honey, I'm just looking, although if he offered a taste, I wouldn't say no."

Andi felt her eyes widen. "He's popular, then?"

"He's practically a god," Dawn admitted. "He and I went to school together. I had a crush on him from the time I was twelve. He never looked at me."

"His loss," Nina told her.

"I wish that were true. He's a good guy."

"Love his ass," Laura said, then glanced at Andi. "Have you seen it?"

"I, uh, hadn't really noticed."

"You need to. And just think. It'll be there at the end of every day. You're a lucky woman."

Andi didn't know what to say to that, which turned out to be a good thing because she'd suddenly had a moment of inspiration. "What does his wife think about all the women around here ogling her husband?"

The other four women glanced at each other. Misty raised her eyebrows. "He's not married."

"His wife died," Nina said. "Cancer. It was very sad."

"He has a daughter," Dawn added. "She's twelve. Carrie. A real sweetie. She and my daughter sometimes hang out, although her real best friend is Madison Phillips. The Phillips family lives next door to you."

There was another moment of the women looking at each other, followed by a second of silence.

"I'll say it," Laura announced. "Have you met Deanna Phillips? She owns the house beside yours. She's a complete and total bitch."

"I met Boston." Andi quickly calculated the relationship. "She would be Wade's sister-in-law and Zeke's wife? Do I have that right?"

"You got it," Nina told her. "And I'm not sure I agree that Deanna's a bitch. She's…intense."

"Sanctimonious, you mean," Laura said. "Those poor kids."

All Andi knew was that Deanna had been standing on her porch a couple of days ago, crying.

Dawn shook her head. "Deanna is one of those mothers who makes her own bread, only buys organic and doesn't let her girls watch TV unless it's educational. There's nothing wrong with that," she added quickly. "It's just…"

Laura chimed in. "She's always telling people how long that damn house has been in her family. She can't have a regular garden. No. Hers is in perfect keeping with the perfect style of her perfect house."

"Not that you're bitter," Nina said.

"I didn't have a lot of money growing up," Laura said. "I'm not going to say different. Deanna grew up just as poor as me, but to hear her talk these days you'd think she personally came over on the *Mayflower.* I worked with her once organizing a charity wine tour. I didn't like her."

"Really?" Misty said. "Because you can't tell at all."

"I haven't met her," Andi said, suddenly not anxious to do so. She was having trouble reconciling the information on Deanna with the sad woman standing alone in front of her house.

"She'll be nice to you," Nina told her. "She has five daughters, so she must be thrilled to have a pediatrician living next door."

"Built-in customers," Andi murmured. She cleared

her throat. "I met Boston last week and we talked this weekend. She seemed nice."

"She's great," Nina said.

"An artist," Laura added. "I have two of her paintings. So beautiful. She makes most of her money from hand-painting fabric for designers all around the country. But her true calling is portraiture. She does lovely work. My husband had her do a painting of our two children about ten years ago. Boston was barely out of art school. That picture still hangs in our living room. It's wonderful."

Misty nodded. "She and Zeke have been together since they were kids. True love. It's nice to see." Her eyes darkened. "It's too bad, what happened."

Everyone went quiet. Laura looked up at Andi. "She and Zeke had a baby about a year ago. He died when he was six months old. It was a heart condition. She was holding him and he just went. I couldn't believe it when I heard. They didn't deserve to lose their little boy."

"I didn't know," Andi murmured. While she'd never lost a child of her own, she'd been with parents who had. Their pain had stayed with her.

"We don't usually gossip this much," Nina said into the silence that followed.

"Yes, we do," Laura told her. "And more. We're being good because Andi doesn't know us very well and we want her to like us. You should see us after a glass or two of wine. We'll straighten that curly hair of yours."

Andi reached up and pulled one of her curls. "I wouldn't mind straight hair. When I was little, I read a book about a girl who got scarlet fever. They had to shave her head and her hair grew back curly. I used to ask my mom to take me to the hospital so I could find someone with scarlet fever and get their germs. I was hoping my hair would grow in straight."

Laura slowly shook her head. "I can't decide if that's the sweetest story I've ever heard or the saddest. Either way, it's good to know you're just as crazy as the rest of us."

"Why would I be spared crazy?" Andi asked with a grin.

"Excellent point, honey. Excellent point."

Andi arrived home at exactly five-fifteen in the afternoon. She might still be adjusting to island life, but she had to admit she was loving the work hours. She'd been home before five-thirty both days. She knew eventually there would be emergencies that kept her out later every now and then, but the pace of life was sure slower than in Seattle.

She parked in her driveway, next to a battered pickup truck. She recognized it from her meeting on Saturday morning and quickly checked her appearance in her rearview mirror. Not that there was much to do. It wasn't as if she was going to suddenly start wearing more makeup.

She smoothed her hair and made sure none of the mascara had migrated to under her eyes, then grabbed her purse and stepped out of her SUV. At least she'd showered and was dressed decently. The last time Wade had seen her, she'd been exhausted, scruffy and fleeing dive-bombing bats.

She walked up the stairs to her porch and went into the house. She needed to come up with a casual but charming greeting, she thought. Something funny that Wade would—

Andi came to a stop in the center of what had been

the entryway and stared. She was pretty sure her mouth had dropped open, but she couldn't confirm the reaction. The shock was too great.

She didn't have a house anymore. There were outside walls and a staircase going to the second floor, yet little else remained.

All the interior walls were gone. There were still a few studs in place, probably to keep the second and third floor from collapsing. There were a few windows, she noted, wondering if she should be grateful. She could see clear back through what had been the kitchen. The flooring was gone, as well.

"Don't panic."

She heard Wade before she saw him. He came around from behind the stairs and grinned.

"I swear, it's going to be fine."

"I think I'm more likely to faint than panic," Andi admitted. "I can't believe how much you got done in a day."

"Isn't it great? All our other jobs got delayed for one reason or another. Our entire team was here doing demo."

"Lucky me."

She was too shocked to do much more than take in his long legs and broad shoulders. The man looked good in jeans, she thought absently, telling herself she would appreciate his easy good looks later. When her heart had started beating again.

"I feel violated," she admitted. That morning, she'd had a house. Now there was little more than a frame. Where did it go?

He put his hand on her arm. "Think of it as a good thing. The sooner everything is gone, the sooner we can get it put back together. Isn't there a medical way for you to relate?"

"Only if we want to talk about my house in terms of it being an infection that has to be cut out."

He shook his head. "No, I don't think so."

"Yeah, that's not going to make me feel much better." Andi dropped her purse on the bottom stair. "Is there more ripping apart to be done?"

"Just the part of the hardwood floor that has to come up. We'll refinish it later."

Andi knew they'd talked about saving the floor and reusing it in the attic. "I'm glad I wasn't here to see the deconstruction."

"It was loud."

He sounded cheerful. It was probably easier when the home being destroyed wasn't your own, she thought.

"Come on," he said, motioning to the rear of the house. "Let me show you what we're thinking about for the employee break room. If you're still interested in the mini-kitchen."

She followed him, her gaze dropping to his heretofore-mentioned butt. Laura was right, Andi thought, her gaze lingering. Wade's was pretty darned nice. Must be all the physical labor he did in a day.

"We were thinking cabinets here, with a counter. Single sink, but a deep one, a refrigerator."

He indicated where each item would go.

"Lockers on this wall and more storage under the window. That would give you a second, long counter if you have buffet-style work parties."

"How do you know about work parties?" she asked, smiling at him. "Is there a lot of that in construction?"

"Sure. We like theme parties. You know, tropical getaway or a costume party at Halloween." He winked at her. "My foreman likes to dress up like Marilyn Monroe."

"Does he?"

Wade grinned. "We've done business remodelings before. It's always a good idea to keep the employees happy, and the mini-kitchens are usually well received."

"I like it."

"Good." He studied her for a second. "How are you settling in with Dr. Harrington? He driving you crazy talking about his son?"

"Does everyone know about that?"

"Pretty much. You should have seen the college graduation pictures from a few years back."

"I'm doing well," she said. "Everyone has been very friendly. I have lots of patients. There seems to be demand for a pediatrician around here."

"Lucky for you. Did you always want to be a doctor?"

She thought about her family and how there hadn't been much of a choice. "Pretty much."

"Your parents must be proud."

They were more disappointed than anything, she thought. But that was difficult to explain to people who didn't know how she'd grown up. Those who weren't acquainted with her family assumed that they thought she was smart and successful. She wasn't going to admit to hunky Wade that when compared with what her parents and siblings had accomplished, she was something of a slacker.

"My mother would have liked me to be a surgeon," she said, knowing that wasn't exactly the truth. Her mother would have liked her to specialize even more than that.

"Someone needs to talk to her about her standards," Wade said. "I have a daughter. She's twelve. Right now she has a different career idea every week, but not once has she mentioned being a doctor. I'd sure be thrilled if she did."

"She doesn't have to decide for a while."

"That's true. She's growing up too fast as it is." His dark gaze settled on her face. "What's it like to be the smartest person in the room?"

"I'm hardly that."

"You are right now."

She laughed. "You forget you rescued me from a wild bat. Being smart didn't help with him. Or her. I didn't get that close a look."

"Me, either," Wade said.

"Regardless, you're my hero for that."

"I like the idea of being someone's hero. Remember that tomorrow morning when you walk downstairs and see all this. It'll keep you from freaking out."

Andi was less sure about that, but she would make the effort.

He glanced at his watch. "I've got to get home, but I didn't want to leave until we'd spoken."

"Afraid I'd run screaming into the night?"

"Just trust me on this, Andi. It's going to get better. In a few weeks, you won't recognize the place."

"I do trust you," she said, caught up in his words.

Oddly enough, she did trust Wade. Which made her an idiot. She'd trusted Matt and he'd left her standing at the altar. Not that Wade was like her fiancé. Nor were they dating. He was her contractor and…

"Andi?"

She blinked. "Sorry. I drifted."

"I could tell. It's sort of charming. Just don't do it when you drive."

"I'm very focused behind the wheel."

He looked at her, as if he was going to say something else. "We should go out" would be nice. Or "I want to kiss you senseless and then make wild love to you" was an even better option, she thought hazily.

No, she reminded herself. She'd moved here to avoid the whole boy-girl disaster, remember? No men. Which meant no sex. Or at least no sex with anyone else. How depressing.

"I'll see you tomorrow."

He would what? Oh, right. "Sure. Tomorrow. Have a nice night."

"You, too."

He smiled and walked past her. She gave in to temptation and turned to watch him go. Yup, Laura had been right, she told herself. The man had a very fine butt. In fact, all of him was very nice.

Unfortunately, he had yet to show the slightest interest in her. Not even a flicker. Was it her? Matt had always been trying to change her. To get her to dress more sexy and act more wild. Should she have listened?

Did she have an aura only men could see saying she was boring? It wouldn't surprise her. She hadn't been very good at relationships back in high school. She'd struggled to maintain a straight-A average in college, which hadn't left much free time. Then she'd met Matt the week before she started medical school. She didn't exactly have a world of dating experience to fall back on.

Not that it mattered, she told herself, heading to the stairs. She was going man-free now. A single, self-actualized woman embarking on a bat-free adventure. That was her.

Still, she wouldn't say no to Wade on the kissing front. If he happened to ever ask.

Seven

Andi changed her clothes and went back downstairs to more closely inspect her naked house. The sun was still several hours from setting, and the air was stuffy. She opened the few windows that hadn't been boarded shut, then went out front and sat on the porch.

From her newly favorite spot to quietly think, she couldn't see the demolition. Instead she could imagine what it would be like when it was finished. The whole place painted, the yard restored... Both her neighbors had beautiful yards. She wasn't looking to compete, but she needed her place to not be an embarrassment to the tiny neighborhood.

She'd nearly summoned the energy to start doing some research when a very large cat came out from around the side of her house and strolled toward her.

"Hello," she said as the cat approached. "Who are you?"

The cat walked up the stairs and sat next to Andi, his or her expression expectant. The cat had on a collar. She reached for the tag.

"Pickles," she said as she read the single word. "Not exactly a clear statement of gender. Hello, Pickles."

She let the cat sniff her fingers, then stroked the animal's face. Pickles leaned into her touch for a few seconds, then collapsed on the porch, as if settling in for a long petting session.

"Obviously you're not afraid of people, are you?"

"That's our cat."

Andi glanced up and saw a girl standing by the stairs. She was probably nine or ten, with long blond hair and glasses framing her big blue eyes.

"Pickles?" Andi smiled. "That's a fun name."

"Madison named him, but she was just a baby. Mom says I was born then, but I don't remember. I'm Lucy."

"Hi, Lucy. I'm Andi Gordon. It's nice to meet you."

Lucy gave her a tentative smile as she eased forward. Andi shifted on the stairs to make room.

Andi remembered what she'd heard about Lucy's mother at lunch. No one seemed especially fond of Deanna, which made Andi uncomfortable. She didn't want to make assumptions about someone she'd never met. Maybe Deanna was just one of those prickly people with a good heart.

"I'm having a lot of work done on my house," Andi said, then wrinkled her nose. "I hope it's not too loud."

"I don't think so. My mom hasn't said anything." The girl glanced up at her. "I'm glad you bought the house. It's been lonely all by itself."

"That's what I thought, too. And the other houses are so pretty."

"It's hard to be in the middle."

"Are you in the middle in your family?"

Lucy nodded, keeping her attention on the cat. "I have

four sisters. I'm the second oldest. The youngest two are twins."

"Wow. That's a lot of girls. Twins can be a handful."

"That's what Mom says." Lucy looked up again. "Mom wanted a boy, but we got Sydney and Savannah instead. I don't think Daddy cared. He says he has the best girls."

Andi smiled. "I'm sure he does. Who wouldn't want a family like that?"

Lucy sighed. "My best friend moved away over spring break. Her dad got a job in Texas. She wants me to come visit this summer. Mom thinks I'm too young to go."

"I'm sorry," Andi told her. "It's hard to lose a friend." Especially in the middle of the school year, when all the social groups were already established. She wanted to say that Lucy would have an easier time in the fall, but to a girl her age, September must be a lifetime away.

Lucy nodded. She pushed up her glasses. "My mom's been crying a lot," she said in a low voice. "In her room, so we're not supposed to know."

Andi winced. "That must be difficult."

"It is. Madison says Daddy should leave her and take us with him, but I don't want that. I want to stay here. Like it is." She hesitated. "Maybe a little better."

Andi wanted to pull the girl close and hug her. Lucy was obviously going through a lot. But they didn't know each other, and she wasn't sure the show of support would be welcome.

"It's hard when moms cry," she said instead. "When my mom cried, I always felt anxious inside. Like my tummy wasn't right."

Lucy stared at her. "I know. It's almost like I want to throw up."

"Sometimes parents can work things out."

"I hope so." Lucy looked at her house. "It's going to be dinner soon and I can't be late." She scooped up Pickles and stood.

"Thanks for coming by," Andi told her. "Come over anytime."

Lucy flashed a smile that shifted her face from ordinary to luminous. "Okay. Bye."

"Bye."

Andi watched her go. When the girl disappeared around the corner, she turned her attention to the beautiful house. Every family had secrets, she thought. Some were scarier than others. She hoped that whatever Deanna and her husband had going on, they got it resolved before the situation put more stress on their girls.

Boston watched Lucy scamper back to her house, Pickles draped over her shoulder. That cat deserved a special reward in kitty heaven, she thought as she crossed the lumpy weed-filled lawn toward Andi's house. Not only did he let the girls drag him around like a rag doll, but he submitted to being dressed in ridiculous outfits. Hats, even.

"Hi," she called as she approached.

Andi turned and saw her. "Hi yourself."

Boston raised the basket she carried. "I heard the entire crew was in your house today, basically destroying it. I thought you might be traumatized."

Andi stood and walked down the stairs. "I am. Honestly, I'm a little afraid to go back inside."

Boston handed her the basket. "Comfort food. Mac and cheese, a green salad and a bottle of nice chardonnay." She grinned. "Personally, I'd start with the wine."

Andi glanced at the basket she held. "You didn't have to do this. Thank you. It's so nice."

"You're welcome. I'm excited to have a neighbor." Technically she and Deanna were neighbors, but they'd never been close. Or friendly. Now that she thought about it, she wondered why. They'd lived on the same street for years.

She supposed part of the problem was that Deanna made it clear she disapproved of Boston in nearly every way possible. For her part, Boston would admit to a little smugness where Deanna was concerned.

"I've lived through construction," Boston continued. "It's not fun. Just try to remember that it's worth it in the end."

"I will." Andi motioned to the porch. "I don't have much in the way of furniture. Want to have a seat here for a second or do you have to get back?"

"I'll join you for a bit. Zeke will be home soon and he always loves it when I make mac and cheese." She settled on a stair.

Andi did the same. "I was thinking about the yard," she said. "I've never been much of a gardener, but I guess I have to start soon."

"It's prime growing season," Boston told her. "There's a nursery in town. I can get you the name of a woman who works there. She does landscaping on the side."

"You and my other neighbor have set a pretty high standard," Andi said with a grin. "I don't want to let the neighborhood down."

"You won't."

Boston studied the other woman. Light and shadow played across her face, highlighting her bone structure. She was pretty, Boston thought, more interested in shapes and forms than what the world considered attractive. Andi's hair, a tumbling mass of curls, would be difficult to capture on canvas. But her eyes—a brilliant green—would draw people in.

"You wouldn't happen to know a reasonably priced decorator, would you?" Andi asked. "I'm going to need some help pulling together the office. I want bright colors and a welcoming space. Going to the doctor can be scary for kids. I want them to feel comfortable when they come to see me."

Boston thought about the floor plan of Andi's house and the plans Zeke had shown her for the remodeling. "A mural," she said automatically, seeing a jungle scene on the wall. "Bright colors that can flow through to the other rooms. Blues and greens with pops of reds and yellows. A jungle. Birds. Big parrots. Maybe fish in a river and large cats with eyes that glow."

She paused. "Sorry. I got carried away."

"Don't be sorry, I love it. I'm great with the medical end of things. I've ordered the equipment. What I don't know how to do is the waiting area and the front office. Also, there's going to be a long hallway."

"You could do a different animal on every door," Boston said, feeling a surge of creative enthusiasm. "Pick a flooring with a green tone to carry through the jungle theme. If you want to go that way."

Zeke's truck pulled into the driveway next door. Andi glanced at it, then back at her.

"I would love to talk about this some more, another time. Would you be open to that?"

"Sure. It would be a fun project. I can give you some ideas, maybe draw a few sketches."

"I don't suppose you'd be interested in giving me a

price for a mural?" Andi asked. "I've seen your work in your house and it's beautiful."

Boston hesitated. She hadn't done much more than a few textile projects in months. Her days were spent in other ways. Designing and then painting a mural would be a challenge. Zeke would tell her it would be good for her to get out of her rut. To let the project take her away.

"Let me think about it," Boston murmured, coming to her feet. "I have a lot on my plate right now."

A complete lie, but it offered her a safe retreat if the idea of the mural overwhelmed her. She knew if she accepted the job, she would have to see it through. That would be pressure, and these days she still felt breakable. That's what loss had done to her—left her as fragile as spun glass.

"Either way, I'm happy to talk about the color scheme for your office," she said.

"That would be great." Andi stood. "Thank you. And thanks for dinner."

"Enjoy." Boston went down the stairs and started for home.

Zeke stood by his truck, waiting for her. He smiled when he saw her.

"Making nice with the new neighbor?"

"I took her some dinner."

His brown eyes brightened with anticipation. "Mac and cheese?"

"Yes. It's in the oven."

He swept her into his arms and pulled her close. "This is why I stay married to you. For the pasta."

She let herself sink into him, into the familiar combination of strength and heat. In that moment, all was well and she could breathe. Could almost forget that she might shatter at any moment.

Then they would fight, because they fought often these days. Anger was Zeke's way of trying to get through to her. She wouldn't engage and he would leave. After he left, she would paint and eventually he made his way home. Their life had become uneven. Like a wagon with one square wheel. She was aware of the cycle, but unsure how to break it without destroying the only thing that held them together.

Deanna scanned the small paintbrush and then jabbed the quantity into the computer. The Wednesday shipment had been bigger than usual, with several special orders and an entire display of yarn for Christmas.

It was May, she thought as she picked up the second brush and scanned it. Did people really need to be thinking about Christmas now?

She knew the answer. Crafters started early and anyone looking to knit a sweater or scarf or whatever for the holidays would, in fact, be working on it over the summer. She usually liked how the inventory of Cozy Crafts heralded the coming seasons. In truth today, everything was getting on her nerves.

She hated Colin. That was the real problem. She'd spent most of the past two nights lying awake, mentally calling him names. She'd also made detailed lists of everything she'd ever done for him. Everything he never noticed or appreciated.

Like her weight. She weighed exactly what she had on the day they'd gotten married. Four pregnancies, five babies and not an ounce different. Unlike Boston, who'd put on thirty pounds over her pregnancy and had never bothered to take it off.

Deanna kept up on current events. She understood the oil crisis, could speak intelligently on current issues and attended local school board meetings. She was well read. She took excellent care of her house and her family. She baked bread, shopped organic and made nearly every damn bite of food they put in their mouths.

And her thanks for that? Rejection. Dismissal. Threats.

She finished adding the new delivery to inventory and set out the brushes. She sorted the yarn and quickly started a holiday display.

Cozy Crafts was on the west side of the island, next to Island Chic, a clothing store. The clientele consisted of both tourists and locals. Deanna taught scrapbooking, basic quilting and basic knitting. She coordinated the other instructors. She'd been the one to convince Boston to give an introductory painting class two years ago. The class that had led to an article in a national travel magazine. But did any of that matter to Colin?

She glanced toward the windows at the front of the store and thought briefly about tossing a chair through the glass. Not that the action would help her current situation, but she had to do *something*. Every part of her hurt. She was frustrated and scared and angry.

Divorce. The very thought of it made her whole body clench. She didn't want to be divorced. She didn't want the stigma, the struggle. She didn't want the pity or the gloating.

Without wanting to, she remembered her mother standing in the middle of the horrible little kitchen of their disgusting, dirty house.

"Make sure when you marry a man, you keep him,"

the other woman had said. "Ain't nothing worse than being without a man."

Deanna figured she'd been all of ten or eleven when that pearl of advice had been tossed in her direction. At the time she remembered thinking a man would be a good thing. Her mother didn't drink as much when she had a man. The beatings weren't as often or as vicious. The house was cleaner and there was food in the refrigerator.

Now she was thinking the advice was worth taking, but for different reasons. She didn't want to have to change her lifestyle or work harder. She didn't want to have to explain the whys to anyone. Damn Colin for turning everything around.

She crossed to the front door and flipped the sign to Open, then unlocked the door. She had a scrapbooking class at eleven. That was something to look forward to. Colin would be home tomorrow. Deanna dreaded his arrival. She didn't know what to say to him or how to act.

She shook off the depressing reality that was her life now and walked to the stack of Christmas yarn she'd left on one of the craft tables. She might as well get it put up front so they could start selling it. Doing well at her job mattered now more than ever.

A few minutes later, the front door opened and Boston walked in.

"Hi," she called when she caught sight of Deanna. Her gaze dropped to the red and green yarn. "Oh, no. Already? It's not even summer."

"That's what I was thinking, but knitting projects take time."

"I know, but I'm not ready."

Boston wore a long, colorful tunic over slim-fitting jeans. The shapeless shirt did nothing to disguise the roll

of fat spilling over her waistband. Her face had a round-
ness that bordered on puffy. As she passed through a
patch of sun, the light caught the deep reds and purples
streaked through her hair.

What on earth was that woman thinking? Deanna
wondered. She wasn't a teenager anymore—she should
stop trying to pass for one. But Boston had always been
eccentric. It was the artist thing. People found it charming.

"My entire circadian rhythm just tilted," Boston said,
then took a deep breath. "But I'm not going to let it get
to me." She smiled. "I need acrylic paints. One of those
sets you sell kids."

Acrylics? Boston? She special-ordered most of her
supplies from Europe. Deanna was forever placing internet orders to Italy and France, trying to figure out forms
printed in a foreign language.

"What for?"

Boston turned and headed for the paint supplies. "I'm
going to paint a mural." She shook her head. "I'm going
to *try* painting a mural. For Andi's waiting room. I'll start
with a few sketches on paper and then test some colors.
I don't know. It's a big project, but maybe I need that."

Deanna trailed after her. "I have no idea what you're
talking about. Who's Andi?"

Boston came to a stop in front of the small jars of
brightly colored paints. "Our new neighbor."

Deanna swore under her breath. "I haven't been over
yet." She vaguely recalled moving vans in front of the
horrible house next door and the sound of construction,
but hadn't internalized that she had a new neighbor.

Boston reached for a jar of red paint and held it up to

the light. "You have a lot to deal with. There's so much going on right now."

Deanna felt herself flush. "What is that supposed to mean?"

Boston looked at her, eyes wide, expression confused. "I was talking about the girls. All five of them in school. It's getting close to summer vacation. Doesn't that mean last-minute projects? Colin travels so much that you have to handle most of that on your own." She hesitated. "Is there something else?"

"No. Of course not." Deanna mentally slapped herself. She had to keep it together. Bad enough to worry that Colin was blabbing their personal business. Worse if she gave it away herself. "I'm tired. Sorry."

"No problem." Boston scooped up a half dozen containers in bright colors, then grabbed a couple of inexpensive brushes. "I'll take these."

They walked to the cash register.

"I'll go visit Andi over the weekend," Deanna said. "What's she like?"

"Nice. Pretty. I like her. She's a pediatrician. Right next door in an emergency."

"Great." Deanna punched in the codes for the paints.

A career woman, she thought grimly. Someone to be critical of her choices. Someone to point out that by having so many children, she'd chosen to be dependent on a man and had no one but herself to blame for her current situation. Not exactly a conversation she was looking forward to having.

She put the supplies into a bag and handed it to Boston. "Good luck with the new project."

"Thanks. I'm excited about it. I need something new. A distraction. It's the perfect time of year for a change."

With that, she waved and left.

Deanna stared after her. What a stupid thing to say. Change was good? The last big change Boston had faced was the death of her only child. What kind of person thought change was good?

Eight

Saturday morning Andi headed out early. The construction crew was going to work much of the day, and the last thing she wanted was to be stuck in the attic, listening to the irregular rhythm of pounding and power tools. There wasn't enough coffee in the world to turn that noise into something bearable.

The deconstruction of the first floor was complete, but progress was being made in ways not visible to the untrained eye. Wade swore that there were new pipes and electrical updates. As far as she was concerned, she was still lacking walls or anything else she could point to. Later she would be grateful for outlets and switches, but right now staring at a few wires dangling between studs wasn't exactly satisfying.

Next week an additional crew would come in and start on the second-floor remodeling. That meant ripping out more walls and the two bathrooms. Her poor house was going to be nothing more than a shell.

But that was for later, she told herself as she started down the hill toward town. Today she was going to explore the island. The skies were clear, the sun was warm and the day held promise. She'd slathered on sunscreen and signed up for a wine-tasting tour that started at eleven. Until then she had plans to walk along the boardwalk by Blackberry Bay and check out the center of town.

As she approached the water, she saw several stores and businesses on her left. Four women walked into a studio called Scoop and Stretch. Yoga and Pilates, the sign said.

Interesting, Andi thought. She'd tried a couple of yoga classes and had found that she was possibly the least bendy person on the planet. But a couple of her friends swore by Pilates. Apparently it was all about core strength, and who couldn't use a stronger core?

She paused long enough to enter the phone number into her cell phone, then continued her walk. She would call them later and find out about classes.

As she reached the main road that circled the island, she saw a sign for a farmer's market and turned in that direction. There were lots of people walking. Mostly families. A little boy held on to a massive golden retriever, and it was difficult to tell who was leading whom. Up ahead a retired couple held hands as they walked.

This was nice, Andi thought. The sense of community. Right now she didn't know anyone, but that would change. She could already see making friends with the nurses at Dr. Harrington's office.

A few minutes later, she walked into the farmer's market. It was set up in the parking lot of a church. Stalls offered some fresh produce, although it was still early in the growing season. There was plenty of asparagus along with fresh flowers, eggs and cheese. The scent of slow-cooking pork mingled with barbecue beef. At the end of one row, several Latina women were making fresh tortillas and tamales. Even though it was still early and she'd eaten breakfast, Andi felt her stomach rumble.

She walked by each of the booths. There were jars of regional honey, handmade soaps and organic lotions. She was tempted by several items, but didn't want to carry them on her wine-tasting tour. She also wasn't sure she had time to walk back to the house, then return down the hill. So she settled on window-shopping. By the time she headed over to the meeting place for her tour, she was feeling pretty perky.

A twentysomething brunette stood in front of the wine-tasting room wearing an *Island Tours* T-shirt. Andi walked over to her.

"I'm here for the wine-tasting tour at eleven," she said. "Andi Gordon."

"Great. I'm Beth." Beth scanned the list, then handed Andi a bright purple plastic bracelet. "You'll need to wear this at all times today. We have special pourings at each of the wineries, and your way in is that bracelet. Remember to pace yourself and drink plenty of water. Also, do eat the snacks provided." She flashed a smile. "We don't want our tourists driving drunk."

Andi thought about pointing out she wasn't a tourist, but realized that wasn't the actual point. "I'm walking," she said.

"Perfect. Then you can get as tipsy as you like." She paused expectantly, her pen hovering over the list.

"What?" Andi asked.

"The other name?"

"What other name?"

"Aren't you with someone?"

For the past decade, Andi had been able to say yes. Yes, she was with someone. Yes, she was with Matt. She was half of a couple. Part of a twosome. A duo. Maybe she hadn't felt wildly and madly in love, but being with Matt had been comfortable.

"It's just me today," she said.

Beth blinked. "Oh. Great. We have some fun people along. I'm sure you'll have a great time."

Andi wanted to point out that the world didn't cease turning on its axis just because a woman didn't have a date. But she didn't. After all, she felt awkward, too, albeit determined. She'd decided that one Matt-like fiasco was enough. She would embrace her new single life, accepting that happily-ever-after wasn't meant to be for her. She would self-actualize. She was woman and hadn't someone written a song about that, a long time ago?

"Hey there, are you the one who's alone?"

Andi turned and found an older couple standing next to her. They were both tall and thin, with gray hair and friendly smiles. Seventy, at least.

"Excuse me?"

The woman smiled. "I'm Betty and this is my Fred. We're on the wine tour, too. That nice little girl who's our guide mentioned you didn't have anyone." Betty lowered her voice. "We said we'd look out for you."

Andi held in a groan. She was well into her thirties, a doctor and more than capable of going along with a group on a wine-tasting tour that never strayed more than four miles from her house.

However, she had been raised to be polite, so she gave what she hoped was a sincere smile. "That's very sweet of you, but I'll be fine."

"It's no trouble," Betty told her, linking arms with her. "We have a daughter just like you. Pretty enough, but for the life of her, no one can figure out why she can't get a man. For a long time we thought she was a lesbian, but she swears it's not that. We'd love her the same, either way. Maybe there will be some nice, single men on the tour."

"I'm actually here to learn about the island and taste the wine."

Betty patted her arm. "You're so brave. That's inspiring. I tell my Fred all the time that he doesn't get to go first. I don't know what I'd do with myself. I've been taking care of him for fifty years. Don't you think being a wife and a mother is a woman's highest aspiration?"

Andi cleared her throat. "I think it can be satisfying, but…"

"You'll get there, honey. Now we're traveling with friends. Let me introduce you. Everyone's very friendly, but you be careful with Walter. He has a bit of a wandering eye and you're just his type."

Andi rubbed her forehead, feeling the beginnings of a headache.

"Everyone, this is Andi. She's by herself today. I said we'd help her out." Betty lowered her voice. "She'd appreciate any suggestions for single men you might know. Grandsons, grandnephews. Andi here is at the age where she really can't be picky."

Andi opened her mouth, then closed it. Honestly, what was there to say? The only happy thought was very soon, she was going to be in a winery. As of this second, she vowed she would taste every last sample offered and drink it to the very last drop.

Andi had never been one to get drunk, but during the wine tour, she'd made an exception. Betty and her friends had offered to drive Andi back to her place, but she'd declined the invitation. The walk would do her good. The

way her head was spinning, it needed a good clearing.
She had a bottle of water with her for hydration. She
would be fine.

She'd also refused several phone numbers of age-
appropriate relatives from the other seniors along.
Frankly, the descriptions of the single men in question
had terrified her.

There was Bea and Harold's oldest grandson who was
still living with his mother but had so many ideas for new
businesses he didn't know where to start. Jeff, a thirty-
two-year-old extreme sport athlete, whose last case of
STDs was clearing up nicely. Chase, who at thirty had
already been married three times because he couldn't
find "the one," and Derek, a writer, looking for a woman
with a steady job to support him while he wrote the great
American novel. Even Beth, the tour guide, had mentioned an ex-boyfriend who was going to be getting out
of rehab in a couple of weeks.

Andi had brushed off all offers to set her up on a date
and had promised to keep in touch. Yes, the wine tour
had been wonderful, but she was so ready to be anywhere but there. She made her escape and started back
toward her house.

Alone with her thoughts and a giant buzz, she did her
best to focus on staying on the sidewalk. Even though
that was harder than it should have been, thoughts still
intruded.

Granted, she hadn't been on a date since Matt had
abandoned her at the altar, but if those men represented
her choices, she was happy to be alone. She didn't want
to be anyone's mother, nor was she interested in being a
port in a storm. She wanted a good guy who was funny
and caring. Loyal and maybe a little sexy.

"Correction—no man," she said aloud, then had to look around and make sure no one was in hearing distance. She'd come to the island to be on her own. To start fresh and be man-free.

She paused at the bottom of the hill and glanced up at the road that led to her street. With her brain fuzzy and the afternoon temperature climbing, she was suddenly less sure she could make it back. And how pathetic was that?

She drew in a breath and resumed walking. One foot in front of the other, she told herself. All journeys began the same way.

As she climbed the steep street, she let her mind wander. The view got more spectacular with each step. The sound spread out before her, gloriously blue. She could see the peninsula and the strait leading to the Pacific. It would all be so much prettier if she could just focus better.

The scent of salt spiced the air. She drew in several deep breaths, hoping to clear her head, and kept walking.

Maybe she'd been hasty on the man thing, she thought. Maybe one bad experience shouldn't cause her to make a decision that affected the rest of her life. Of course her Matt experience was enough to set anyone back. And it wasn't as if there were any prospects. She'd just relocated to a tourist haven. Tourists weren't date material. She'd liked Betty and Fred just fine, but didn't want to date either one. As for the island residents, from what she'd seen so far, they were paired up. Two by two. Ark people, she thought with a giggle as she came around the corner and saw her house.

"Oh, pretty," she mumbled. So tall and, well, pretty.

Sunlight sparkled on the few windows remaining, and the unkempt yard looked less scary than it had before.

Instead of weeds, she should look for potential, she told herself.

"Potential," she said aloud, then laughed because it sounded funny. Oh, yeah, she was drunk.

At least buying the house had been the right choice. As for dating and men and…

Speaking of the opposite sex, one of them walked out her front door. He was tall and muscled, wearing a T-shirt and cargo shorts. He bent down, picked up several two-by-fours, slung them onto his shoulders as if they weighed nothing, then walked back into the house.

Andi staggered a little to the left as he disappeared inside.

Nice, she thought, recognizing Wade. Very nice. "Do you think he'd go out with me?" she asked no one in particular. "Or have sex?" Because the past few months with Matt had been of the sex-free variety, and while their time between the sheets hadn't been all that interesting, she missed orgasmicisms. Orgasms.

Wade was so tall and strong, with those big hands. As a medical professional she happened to know the big hand and feet rumor was a myth, but a girl could dream. Only if she was dreaming about hot, sweaty sex with her contractor, didn't that mean she wasn't as self-actualized on the single front as she would have thought? And if she wasn't ready to be a—a spinster for the rest of her life, didn't moving to the island seem like a really, really stupid idea?

Her vision blurred slightly and she realized she needed to get in out of the sun. Maybe drink some water. That's right. Hydration. She would have water and then figure out what she was going to do about—

Andi blinked and the thought was gone.

She managed to get up the street to her house, then staggered up the stairs. When she walked into the darker interior, she had to lean against the door frame until her eyes adjusted to the change in light. She glanced down at the bottle of water in her hands and wondered where it had come from.

"Hey, you're back. How was the wine tour?"

She looked up and saw Wade approaching. She smiled up at him.

"I was on a tasting tour."

"I know."

"There was a lot of wine."

His dark eyebrows drew together. "You're drunk."

She held up her hand, to show her thumb and forefinger somewhat close together. Only there was a bottle in the way. Huh. Where had that come from?

"Andi?"

She returned her attention to his eyes. Pretty, she thought, swaying a little. Like the house, only different.

"How much did you drink?"

"I have no idea. I was with Fred and Betty."

"Who are Fred and Betty?"

"Friends. Old friends." She giggled, realizing he would think she'd meant people she'd known a long time when she really meant people who were old. But explaining the joke seemed way too complicated.

"Okay, you're going to be hating yourself come morning," he told her. "Let's get this off you."

"What?"

He stepped close and removed the backpack she'd totally forgotten she'd been wearing. It felt as if the weight of the world was lifted off her shoulders.

"Whoa, how much wine did you buy?"

She stared at the backpack. Where had that come from? "There's wine?"

He hefted it in one hand. "I'd say about a case. Want me to take it up to your kitchen?"

"I have a kitchen? You built me a kitchen? That's so nice." Just this morning, she hadn't had one at all. Just an empty space.

Wade shook his head. "You're worse off than I thought. Come on. I'll get you upstairs. You can sit quietly until you're ready to start throwing up."

"I'm not going to be throwing up," she informed him with a sniff.

"You better hope you're wrong. Trust me, get rid of it fast and you'll feel a lot better in the morning. Otherwise, I sure wouldn't want to be you tomorrow."

She had no idea what he was talking about, but it didn't seem to matter because they were moving. Wade half propelled, half carried her up the stairs. One second it seemed as if she was in her empty shell of a house, and the next she was in her attic living room and Wade was settling her into a chair.

"I'm fine," she informed him.

He chuckled. "I can see that."

He put her backpack on the counter, collected ice from her tiny freezer and put it in a glass, then filled it with water and handed it to her.

"Drink," he told her. "I'll be back later to check on you."

Before she could tell him it wasn't necessary, he was already leaving. By the time he reached the bottom of the stairs, she was shoving the glass onto a table and clutching her stomach. Thirty seconds later, she was on her way to the bathroom to test Wade's theory that throwing up now would make her feel better in the morning.

Nine

Boston stared at the large piece of paper in front of her. In her mind, she could see the mural exactly as she wanted it to be. The sleek jaguar with the glowing eyes, the smiling, mischievous monkey in the bright green trees, the winking caterpillar. Usually seeing it was all she needed. Once the vision was clear in her head, her hand started to move. Just not this afternoon.

It was her third attempt to start sketching out ideas for Andi's waiting room. Working out of her comfort zone but without the pressure of having to come up with a design for four-hundred-dollar-a-yard fabric had seemed the perfect antidote for her recent artist lull. But despite what she saw when she closed her eyes, despite how much she desperately *wanted* to make her work come to life, she sat immobilized. Her fingers numb and uncooperative.

"Hey, babe."

The familiar voice, the familiar words, released her from her artist prison. She jumped to her feet and hurried out of her studio.

"You're home early," she said, stepping into the kitchen.

Zeke stood in the mudroom, unfastening his tool belt. "I had to get home to my best girl," he said with a wink.

She moved toward him. His tool belt hit the ground, and his arms came around her. She stepped into his embrace.

Everything was familiar. Comfortable and sexy at the same time. She didn't just know how Zeke's mouth was going to move against hers; she knew how that movement was going to make her feel. Anticipation blended with certainty to create desire.

Before six months ago, sex had never been an issue, she thought, leaning into him and enjoying the feel of his hands sliding up and down her body. After Liam's birth, she'd been ready to be intimate with Zeke long before being cleared by her doctor. Lately, though, Zeke had been the one who wasn't interested.

He deepened the kiss, moving his tongue against hers. He gripped her butt in his big hands and squeezed. She arched her pelvis against him, rubbing back and forth, waiting for the familiar ridge of his erection. Wanting to feel that hardness. She dropped her hands to his wrists, ready to pull his fingers toward her breasts, only to realize there was nothing there. No physical evidence that he wanted her at all.

He broke the kiss and gave her butt a final pat, then looped his arm around her shoulders.

"So, tell me what you got done today on the mural," he said, leading her toward her studio.

"There's nothing to see. I'm having a little trouble getting started."

"That's okay. I don't expect perfection. I'm just curious."

He sounded determined and she realized stopping him

wasn't an option. So she gave in to the inevitable and let him guide her down the hall.

The studio had been added on to the house shortly after she and Zeke had gotten married. It faced south, and had massive windows to let in light. There were custom cubbies and shelves for her supplies, holders for her brushes and pencils and specially designed expanding tables for her hand-painted fabrics.

Zeke released her and walked into the studio. Boston stayed in the hallway, already knowing what he would see. What she hadn't had time to hide. Because that's what she'd been doing for weeks now. Hiding the evidence.

Blank sketch paper sat on an easel. Every other surface, every inch of wall space was covered with pictures of their dead son. Pencil sketches, oil portraits, watercolors, pastels. Black-and-white, color, realistic, surreal. Every style, every pose, every position. She found the images comforting but knew Zeke did not.

He turned in a slow circle, taking it all in. Finally he faced her, his mouth tight, his body stiff.

"What the hell, Boston? You're still doing this? Where are you?"

She stepped into the studio and faced him. "I'm right here."

"No, you're not. You have to deal with your grief."

"I am."

"This isn't dealing. This is hiding. You think you can paint him back to life?"

"Not everyone wants to drown their sorrows in a bottle, Zeke."

"At least I'm feeling something. At least I'm crying about our kid. Are you? Have you cried even once?"

She could see the anger. It was bright and red—a cliché, but there it was. Shimmering. Sadness, too. More muted. India-green or mantis, she thought, aware of the swirling blend and how much easier it was to think of that than her husband's words.

"I'm dealing in my own way," she told him.

"You're not. You're getting lost." He took a step toward her. "Dammit, Boston, I can't lose you, too. But I feel you slipping away."

He motioned to the studio, to the paintings and sketches. "Do you know how much this scares me? Do you know what it's like to think about you painting Liam over and over again?" His fingers curled into fists. "Don't do this to me, Boston. Please. Go see someone. Go talk to a doctor."

"A psychiatrist, right? Because I'm crazy?"

She shook her head. She knew what would happen. How he or she would want to fix what was broken. Didn't anyone understand that being broken was all she had left? Without that, Liam was truly gone.

"I can't watch you do this," he told her. He walked past her and down the hall.

She let him go. She knew that he would leave now. That he might go to Wade's house or he might go to a bar. She supposed she should worry. Not about him cheating but about what was lost every time they did this. If love were a house, she would say their foundation was beginning to crumble. That at some point, the house simply collapsed in on itself.

She waited for the stab of pain, for the worry. It was purple. No. Wisteria and thistle. Yes, that was better.

She heard Zeke's truck door slam, then the sound of the engine. She walked over to the stool and took a seat, then picked up her pencil. Thoughts of a cartoon jaguar disappeared. Instead she saw a beautiful sleeping baby and began to draw.

Andi woke up with a killer headache and a heartfelt vow that she would never, ever get that drunk again. Her eyes felt gritty, her whole midsection hurt from the barfing and her skin was maybe two sizes too small. As a doctor, she could detail the process of getting the toxins out of her body. As the person going through it, she could only hydrate and wait for the hangover to pass.

She only had vague memories of the previous afternoon. She was pretty sure she'd spoken to Wade. She could only hope she hadn't said anything too stupid. Like asking to touch his muscles. Or if he would take his shirt off. Yes, her contractor was a good-looking guy, and yes, maybe she'd been a bit hasty in the "I'm so over love" department. However, she needed to think things through. Move cautiously. And perhaps wait to feel slightly less like roadkill before throwing herself at him. Besides, it wasn't as if he'd made a move toward her. Not by a blink of his long, dark lashes had he even hinted he saw her as anything other than a client. She'd already suffered through enough romantic rejection for one year, thank you very much.

After drinking two glasses of water and eating three soda crackers, she made her way downstairs. At least it was Sunday and she wouldn't have to deal with any pounding or sawing or even conversation. She could detox in peaceful solitude, then later maybe sip some soup.

The large open area that was her sad, naked shell of a house didn't improve her mood. She wanted walls and flooring. Windows instead of boarded-up holes. Okay, sure, it had only been a week, but still. She wanted visual progress.

Andi paused by what looked like very new, very tidy wiring and tried to get excited. There wasn't even a flicker. She was about to make her way upstairs to spend the rest of the morning lying down when someone knocked on her front door.

At least she assumed it was supposed to be a knock. In her present condition, it felt a whole lot more like a herd of Visigoths battering relentlessly both on the door and inside her head. She hurried over to make it stop.

"Yes?" she said as she stared at the pretty blond woman standing on her porch.

Her visitor was of average height, with blue eyes and pale skin. She was casually dressed, but in a pulled-together way that made Andi aware of her slightly worn and possibly stained T-shirt and baggy shorts. Not to mention her bare feet and uncombed hair.

Realization registered as Andi recognized her perfect neighbor.

"Hi," the woman said with a practiced smile. "I'm Deanna Phillips. I live next door."

Deanna wore a light jacket over a lacy shell. Her pants were tailored and the beaded necklace pulled the whole outfit together. She had on makeup and earrings. Andi tugged at the fraying hem of her T-shirt.

"Nice to meet you," Andi said, automatically stepping back to allow the other woman in. She belatedly remembered she didn't exactly have walls, let alone a place to sit. "Sorry. I'm still under construction."

House, she thought frantically. She'd meant the house. Not that she couldn't do with one of those lifestyle makeovers, but that was hardly Deanna's issue.

Deanna walked inside and looked around. Her delicate nose wrinkled slightly. "At least you're down to the studs," she said. "I'm sure the place is going to look lovely when it's done." She paused. "I'm sorry to be so tardy in stopping by."

She held out a casserole dish. "Welcome to the neighborhood. It's basically chicken and vegetables. Healthy, but I hope you like it."

"Thank you."

Andi took the dish, grateful to have her meals for the day taken care of. Assuming she ever felt like eating again. Honestly just the hint of the spices escaping from under the foil was enough to make her tummy turn.

Deanna turned slowly, taking in the boarded windows and the exposed subflooring. "I heard you're a doctor."

"A pediatrician."

"A career. Yes, that's what's expected these days, isn't it? Having it all. I wanted to be a mother and have a family." Her mouth thinned. "I defined myself that way. Old-fashioned, I know."

Andi wasn't sure if it was her hangover or the conversation itself, but either way, she was having trouble following exactly what was going on.

"I understand you have five daughters. That's pretty amazing. I've met Lucy. What a sweetie."

Deanna stared at her. "Yes, daughters. Five girls I'm responsible for." She shook her head slightly. "I'm sure you'll want to come see my house. The downstairs is perfectly restored. The main sitting room is furnished with a combination of antiques and reproductions that are appropriate for the age of the house."

"Um, that would be nice. Thank you."

Deanna nodded. "The house has been in my family

since it was built. Boston inherited hers as well, but her grandparents bought it from the original owners."

"Okay." Because whose family had owned the house the longest mattered?

Deanna offered another smile, this one flattening at the corners of her mouth. "Yes, well, I've kept you long enough. Welcome. We're very grateful to have someone living here. Whatever you do to the place will be an improvement."

With that, she turned and left. Andi stared after her, not sure what had gone wrong, but confident that Deanna Phillips was someone she could never like.

A week later Andi found herself just as out of sorts, but without the hangover from the previous Sunday. As she wandered downstairs, she admitted that she was absurdly lonely and that the day seemed endless. During the week she kept busy. She was getting plenty of patients, and the nurses were friendly. When she got home from work, she was pleasantly tired and ready to relax. She'd filled yesterday with errands, but today she had nothing planned.

Usually she and Matt had spent Sundays together. It was the one day of the week they were both off and rarely on call. Although with Matt's specialty—pediatric surgical oncology—he was never truly off duty.

Still, they'd done things together. Gone to museums, out to dinner with friends, visited his family, seen movies. They'd gone shopping, with him telling her what to buy. Her day had been filled, often with what he wanted to do. At thirty-two years old, she was uncomfortable to discover she didn't know what to do with herself for a single day.

She finished her coffee and rinsed the mug, then made

her bed. She was already showered and dressed. The day was sunny and warm, so she should take advantage of that. Maybe she could... What? Were there any museums on Blackberry Island? She didn't want to go to the movies by herself, and her friends were a couple of hours away in Seattle.

She looked out the small attic window and saw her neglected yard below. That was something she could do, she thought. Discover her outdoor space. She could walk around, get a feel for it. Maybe even take pictures. Then later this week she could ask Wade if he knew a landscaper who could help her get it in shape. Or get the name of the person Boston had mentioned.

She quickly slathered on sunblock, plopped a hat on her head, picked up her small, digital camera and headed outside.

The Pacific Northwest might have rainy, miserable weather in the winter months, but once the sun came out, there was nowhere as beautiful on earth. Andi took in the brilliant blue sky, the island below and the water beyond. She would swear she could almost see to the Pacific. There was a light breeze and warm temperatures. Summer had truly come to the island.

She walked around to the backyard and began taking pictures. There were already plant beds in place, although they were overgrown with a lot of tall, scraggly bush-tree things she didn't recognize. The grass was bare in patches. The only lush sections of lawn were the weeds. She took more pictures and wondered if she had anything like a sprinkler system. Or gardening tools. There was a shed in the far corner, but it looked ready to collapse and she was reasonably confident it was a well-populated spider condo.

After snapping more pictures of the side yard, she walked around front and continued to take photos. Looking through a lens brought home how truly hideous her yard was. She had to talk to Wade pretty soon about suggestions for landscaping. At the end of the day she walked inside and could pretend all was well. Her neighbors had to stare at her yard from their windows.

"Hi, Andi."

She turned and saw Lucy walking toward her, the family's faithful cat cradled in the girl's arms. Two smaller girls were with her. Identical twins, Andi thought, taking in the pale blond hair and big blue eyes.

"Hi," she said with a smile. "Nice to see you again."

"These are my baby sisters. Sydney and Savannah. Don't worry. You won't be able to tell them apart the next time you see them."

Andi laughed, then dropped to her knees and held out her hand. "I'm very pleased to meet you both."

Sydney and Savannah both shook her hand; then they looked at each other and giggled.

All three girls wore T-shirts and shorts. The twins had on identical shirts with ruffles on the hem. One was pink, the other yellow.

"I'm Sydney," the girl in yellow said.

Lucy settled on the grass and released Pickles, who immediately collapsed in a patch of sun and began to groom his fur. The twins sat next to their sister.

"What are you doing?" Lucy asked.

"Taking pictures of my yard. I'm going to talk to someone about fixing it up. It looks pretty bad right now."

Savannah nodded vigorously. "Mommy hates your house. She says it's a bly…" She glanced at Lucy, who shrugged.

"Blight?" Andi offered.

"Right. A blight."

Not exactly friendly words, despite their truth.

"The poor house had been empty a long time," Andi said. "I guess it was sad before, but it should be happy now."

"Houses can't be happy," Sydney told her.

"Why not?"

"Because they're not real."

Andi tilted her head as she studied her place. "It looks real to me."

"She means the house isn't alive," Lucy added. "But I know what you mean. I always thought your house was sad, too."

Sydney inched a little closer and gave her a big smile. "Did you want to offer us a cookie?"

"What?" Andi stared at her. Right. Refreshments. That's what the hostess did. "I'm sorry. I don't have much food in the house. I have an apple. We could share that."

"No, thank you."

Andi groaned. "I'll have cookies next time."

Sydney looked hopeful. "And lemonade?"

"Sure."

"That would be nice."

"We could have a pretend tea party now," Lucy offered. "We do it all the time. Pretend. Although Sydney always tells us there isn't really tea in our cups."

"She doesn't get pretend," Savannah said with a grin.

"I do," Sydney told her. "But pretend isn't real."

"It's still fun," Lucy said.

Sydney inched even closer to Andi. "Mommy wanted a boy, but she got us instead."

Andi suspected the comment was true. After three

girls, wanting a boy was hardly a surprise. But she was sorry the twins had heard their parents discussing the subject. That sort of information didn't need to be passed along.

"I think you're lovely," she said warmly. "I would be very lucky to have three girls like you."

She received three smiles in return. Lucy then took charge of their tea and passed out cups on saucers and an assortment of very fancy pretend cookies.

Boston caught sight of the girls as she dusted the living room. Zeke and Wade had driven into Seattle to catch a Mariners game, so she was on her own and restless. For once, her studio had seemed confining and she'd been unable to lose herself in her artwork. Housework had seemed like a cheerful alternative, which only showed how bad things were. No one she knew enjoyed cleaning—with the possible exception of Deanna, and Lord knew Deanna prided herself on being just a little better than everyone else.

Boston stopped dusting long enough to remind herself to be careful with her judgments. Not only wouldn't they make her feel better, but she was a big believer in karma. Better to remind herself that Deanna did her best to be a perfect mother and try to remember her good qualities. Although at the moment, she couldn't quite remember what they were.

She walked to the window and watched as three of Deanna's daughters sat in Andi's front yard, having what looked like a pretend tea. They were in a circle, the family cat in the middle of their group. Sunlight seemed to embrace them, both blessing and protecting the innocence of the moment.

The golds and yellows and hints of creamy white that made up the blond of the girls' hair, the flash of pink of Pickles's tongue as he meticulously washed his face. There were sharp angles of bony elbows and knees, the spiral of Andi's curls, the serrated edges of the grass.

An energy bubbled up inside Boston, then spilled over, filling her. She could see the picture and felt it, too. Knowing it was futile, yet unable to resist the need, she dropped the dust cloth onto the table, then hurried back to her studio. Once there, she grabbed a box of pastels and a small pad of paper, then detoured through the kitchen to collect a plate of chocolate mini-muffins. The latter was made with white flour and sugar, which would cause Deanna to have a seizure if she discovered her children indulging, but Boston didn't care. She needed the girls to stay in place for a few minutes longer, and muffins seemed the easiest bribe.

She tucked three juice packs into her shorts pockets, then hurried out front.

The quartet was still there. Pickles had finished his ablutions and lay stretched out on his side, his feline eyes closed as he dozed in the sun.

"I hope you don't mind me interrupting," Boston said as she approached. "I saw you having a tea party out here and couldn't resist inviting myself."

"You're more than welcome. I'm a terrible hostess, a flaw I will fix by next weekend, I promise."

The sisters quickly shifted to make room for her. Three pairs of blue eyes focused on the treats.

"Are those chocolate?" Lucy asked, her voice low and reverent.

"Yes. I made them myself."

"Mommy says homemade is best," Sydney offered.

Boston held out the plate. "I know how she feels about premade snacks, so you don't have to worry."

The twins glanced at Lucy, who pressed her lips together, then slowly reached out to take a mini-muffin. The second her fingers closed around it, the twins each grabbed one. Boston handed Andi the juice boxes to pass out, then picked up her pad of paper.

She hesitated before choosing a color, then picked the yellow, already seeing the seemingly random lines that would be their hair. Fear bubbled up inside her, making her tremble, but she ignored the slight tremor in her fingers and made the first stroke.

The second went more easily, as did the third. She dropped the yellow and reached for pale pink to outline their faces. Her hand moved faster and faster. She was aware of conversation flowing around her, of the girls giggling and the slurp of the last ounce being sucked from the juice boxes, but she could only see the outlines, the forms, the colors.

Pickles obliged and stayed still. She drew in the black of him and let the paper provide the white. Andi's long legs took shape, as did her curly hair. Boston's arm started to ache and she felt the telltale twinge of a cramp in her fingers but worked on. Sweat beaded on her upper lip and trickled down her back. She would swear she could hear the roar of the sea, or maybe it was simply the sound of her blood rushing through her ears.

She drew in the tree, then the front of the house. The pad dropped onto her lap and she looked up to realize the girls and the cat were gone and she and Andi were alone.

It was like waking up after an intense dream. She wasn't completely sure what was real and what wasn't. Or if she'd drooled or said something she shouldn't. For her, creating was personal. Intimate. She hadn't meant to get so…lost.

Yet the proof she had was in front of her. The sketch was primitive at best, unfinished, sloppy, but it captured the girls together. There was life, movement. And it wasn't Liam.

Confusion made her even more uncomfortable. She wanted to collect her supplies and run into her house. Only she couldn't seem to move.

"You okay?" Andi asked, her voice low and gentle.

Boston nodded. "Sorry. I got carried away."

"That was intense, but impressive. I can't believe how you did that so fast." She leaned over the drawing, her finger lightly tracing the curve of Lucy's cheek. "I can't conquer stick figures. Look at Pickles's ear and the house. It's what? Five or six lines and yet it's my house. I'd know it anywhere."

Boston felt emotion rush up inside her. Embarrassment. Pleasure. Uncertainty.

"I wish I had a tenth of your ability," Andi admitted. "I'm dreading picking out paint colors and fixtures. You have a real talent."

Boston flushed, then rubbed the color from her fingers. "It's a gift. I can't take credit for it."

"I think you get a lot of the credit. You've worked hard to perfect what you have. We're all born with something. Look what you did with yours."

Boston pressed her lips together, then looked at Andi and managed a smile. "You're very sweet and I appreciate it. This isn't very good," she said, motioning to the drawing. "But I'm glad you like it. I've been stuck for a while now and this…"

"If it's the mural, don't worry about it. I knew you

were an artist, but I didn't realize how brilliant you are. That project is obviously beneath you."

"No," she said quickly. "It's not that at all. I really want to work on some designs for you. But I haven't been able to. I haven't been able to do anything." She paused, then squared her shoulders. "Zeke and I had a baby a year ago. Liam. He was beautiful. So happy and bright and…" She swallowed against the tightness in her throat. Tightness, not tears. Never tears.

"He died nearly seven months ago. A heart defect. They said it was just one of those things. He'd been born that way and it was just a matter of time. It wasn't genetic or detectable. One day his heart simply stopped." She stared at the grass. "I was holding him. One second he was smiling at me and the next, he was gone."

Andi squeezed her hand. "I'm so sorry. Losing a child is a pain beyond description."

She probably did know, Boston thought, appreciating the kindness. In her work as a pediatrician, Andi would have suffered through a patient's death, through the parents' pain.

"I draw him," Boston whispered. "Over and over again. I draw him and it comforts me."

"I'm sure it's like he's with you. You created him in your body and now you re-create him in your heart."

Boston stared at her. "Yes. That's it. That's what I do." Something Zeke couldn't or wouldn't understand. "I haven't been able to do any other work since he died, so this—" She pointed to the drawing. "This was something of a breakthrough."

"I'm glad." Andi squeezed her fingers, then released them.

Boston knew she was far from cured, but she felt as

if she'd taken a first step. After months of merely stumbling, moving forward seemed a miracle.

"Maybe now I can get going on your mural."

"No rush and you can still turn down the job. I feel like I asked Picasso to help me paint the bathroom."

Boston laughed. The sound was a little rusty, but it felt good. "I would be happy to help you paint the bathroom."

"I'm going to let Wade and his men handle that." Andi paused. "Wade seems like a nice guy."

"He is. Have you met his daughter yet?"

"No."

"She's great. Twelve, which is supposed to be a difficult age. So far she's the same sweet kid she always was. I'm sure you'll meet her soon. She's best friends with Deanna's oldest."

Her gaze fell on the remaining mini-muffins. "I'd better get these inside before Deanna sees them and attacks me with a rake." She grinned. "She doesn't allow her children sugar."

"Seriously?"

"No sugar, nothing processed, very little she doesn't make herself."

"That's devotion."

"No one could deny that she's a devoted mother."

A mother who had five children, Boston thought, feeling the grayness return. How was that fair?

She scrambled to her feet. "Thanks for letting me crash your party."

"You're more than welcome," Andi told her. "I'm going to be prepared for company next time. Cookies and lemonade."

"The girls will like that. Just make sure Deanna doesn't see."

"She kind of scares me," Andi admitted.

"Me, too."

Boston picked up her things and started back toward her house. Her gaze fell on the picture. On the faces and the colors. What had seemed so healing just a few minutes ago was suddenly a betrayal. She rushed inside, dumped everything on the counter, then pulled the sheet of paper from the pad and carefully tore it into two pieces. Then four, then sixteen. When it was little more than confetti, she swept it into the trash.

Five minutes later, she was in her studio, pencil in hand. She drew without thinking, the side view of the sleeping baby quickly taking shape.

Ten

Anger turned out to be more of a companion than Deanna had expected. Colin had been on the road most of the past two weeks, and last weekend they'd barely spoken at all. She told herself she was getting used to what life would be like when they divorced, but knew it was a lie. She had the protection a husband offered, the paycheck. Should they split up, she would be truly on her own, damn him.

So she'd stayed mad. It wasn't difficult and was actually starting to make her feel better. As she let the rage build inside her, she realized she'd been angry for a long time. Years, certainly. Not just at Colin, but he was a comfortable target. He deserved it.

"I like her hair," Lucy was saying as she set the table. "She says she was born with curly hair. I wish my hair was curly."

Deanna had no idea what her daughter was talking about. Or who. Some friend at school, most likely. At least Lucy was making friends. That was something. Lucy had always been difficult. Quieter and those glasses. Still, she was too young for contacts and when Deanna had asked about Lasik surgery, Lucy's doctor had stared at her as if she'd suggested leeches.

No one understood, she thought as she checked on the two chickens she had roasting in the oven. Five children. What had she been thinking? Who had five children these days? Of course she'd only wanted two. One of each. But with each girl, she'd been determined to have a boy. Because that was what people did. Then the twins had come along and she'd given up.

She loved her girls. All of them. But now she had five, and every day she was more and more overwhelmed.

She reached for the glass of chardonnay she'd poured earlier. It was from a bottle she'd opened a few nights ago. She would finish it before Colin got home, then open a fresh one before dinner.

She took a sip and set down the glass, then glanced over at the sink. She desperately wanted to wash her hands, to feel the slick soap, the warm water. To wash away all the pain and uncertainty she had to deal with. Only her skin was already raw in patches, and her knuckles were cracked. Telltale signs, she thought. She had to be strong. She couldn't give Colin an excuse to take more than he already had taken.

Footsteps thundered on the stairs.

"Daddy's home!" Madison shrieked as she raced toward the front door. Her bedroom faced the front of the house, so she was always the first to know.

Lucy abandoned the flatware and raced after her sister. The other girls came from wherever they had been, bent on being out in the driveway first.

Deanna stood alone in the kitchen and reached for the wine. Her stomach was in knots, but she drank anyway. She drank because she couldn't do what she really wanted and wash her hands and because her daughters never came running for her.

"Good for you, Audrey," Colin said. "You studied hard. I'm proud of you."

Deanna clutched her glass as her middle daughter beamed with delight at the praise. So typical, she thought, glancing around the table. One word from their father and they were all preening. She'd also told Audrey that she'd done well on her spelling test and she'd barely gotten any acknowledgment at all. And it wasn't as if the eight-year-old had gotten every word right. She'd missed two of the twenty. Deanna had made her copy each of the missed words five times to help her remember them for the next test. But no doubt that would be twisted into some form of child abuse.

"What else has been going on?" Colin asked, then glanced at Deanna. "Did you meet our new neighbor yet?"

"Yes, weeks ago." Okay, only two, but close enough.

"She's a doctor?"

"Pediatrician," Madison said. "Carrie told me. Her dad is doing the remodeling. She's going to have her office on the first floor of the house."

"She's nice," Lucy announced, then pushed up her glasses. "Sydney, Savannah and I had tea with her last Sunday."

"It was pretend tea," Sydney told them. "But then Boston came by and…" She lurched as if someone had kicked her under the table.

Lucy shot her a warning glance. "She's really nice," she repeated quickly. "Her hair is so pretty. Long and curly."

"Is that who you were talking about before? The woman next door?" Deanna frowned at her daughter. "You're spending too much time with her. What is a grown woman doing hanging out with children?"

"If she's a pediatrician, it's hardly unusual," Colin told her.

"Why isn't she married? Why doesn't she have a family of her own? She's probably a lesbian."

Colin's eyebrows drew together.

The four younger girls looked confused, while Madison's expression turned angry.

"You always do that," her oldest told her. "You always say bad things about people when you don't know if they're true. Why do you have to think the worst?"

"What's a lesbin?" Sydney asked.

"Never mind," Colin told her, then turned to Deanna. "I agree with Madison. You do enjoy assuming the worst. I'm sure our neighbor is a very nice person. She's certainly a welcome addition to the community. Haven't you been saying how much you'd like a pediatrician on the island? Now we have one next door. But you have to make it more than that."

Stung, Deanna opened her mouth, but couldn't think of what to say. "I was kidding," she finally managed.

"Right. Because we all know you're a real kidder." Colin stood. "Come on, girls. We're going out to get ice cream."

All five girls stared at him with identical expressions that were two parts excitement and one part apprehension.

Deanna clutched her wine. "This isn't their night for dessert," she murmured.

"Tell me about it." He pushed back from the table and stood. "Because everyone knows having dessert once a week builds character, right? I'm taking my beautiful daughters out for ice cream, and then we're going to walk along the boardwalk so I can show the world what a lucky man I am to have such great children. Come on, girls."

They scrambled to their feet. Lucy and Audrey picked up their plates and quickly carried them to the sink, but the other three left theirs on the table and hurried after their father.

Bursts of laughter came from the hallway. The front door opened and closed; then there was only silence. Deanna sat alone at the table, in the mess that was her kitchen. By herself.

She was in the middle of a war, but she didn't understand the rules of engagement or how she was supposed to win. She didn't even fully comprehend why it had started or when she had become the enemy. She only knew that there wasn't a single person anywhere she could call. No one who would give her a hug and say it was going to be all right. Not one person who counted as a true friend.

"I'm here for the five o'clock class," Andi said happily.

She stood in front of the small, sleek reception desk at Scoop and Stretch, the Pilates and yoga studio in town.

The receptionist, a beautiful twentysomething brunette, glanced at her. "I don't have any privates scheduled."

"I'm here for the mat class. I called a couple of days ago and signed up."

"Did you say you were new?" The brunette gave her a smile. "We ask all our new clients to take at least one private lesson first, to make sure they're clear on how to do the exercises. We don't want you getting hurt."

"Oh, I thought I mentioned I hadn't been here."

Andi's good mood deflated. She'd rearranged her appointments specifically to get here on time. Another very long Sunday had reminded her that she had been the one to decide to live on the island. It was up to her to make a life for herself. Find friends and activities she would enjoy. Exercise had never been one of her favorites, but at least in a class she could speak to other people.

"Have you done Pilates before?" the receptionist asked.

"Not really."

A petite redhead with the body of a dancer walked toward the desk. "I'm Marlie. I'm teaching the five o'clock class. You're welcome to try it if you'd like, but with five other students, I won't be able to do much more than keep an eye on you. If you're okay with that, I am. Then you can get a feel for what we do here and decide if you want to continue."

"Sure." Andi was less confident now. She'd assumed a class meant a group. Not just six students.

"Problem solved," the brunette said with a smile. "You can drop your stuff over there."

She pointed to a row of open shelving with wire baskets. Andi placed her purse inside one.

The other students ranged in age from early twenties to a woman in her sixties. Nearly everyone was fit-looking, wearing black, with bare feet. Thinking she should have taken time to get a pedicure, Andi stepped out of her shoes and put them in the basket with her bag.

"Let's get started," Marlie said.

Andi followed the women to a row of mats up against the wall. Each one had a metal frame anchored into the wall and various springs and handles hanging. Everyone sat on a mat and faced forward. Andi took one on the end.

"We'll start with the hundred," Marlie said.

Hundred what? Andi saw the other woman lying down and reaching for a pair of handles. She did the same. She raised her legs like everyone else, tucked her chin into her chest and immediately felt a burning in both her stomach and the back of her legs. Were they going to hold this count for—

"And we pump. Inhale two, three, four, five. Exhale, two, three, four, five."

To Andi's horror everyone began pumping their arms up and down while keeping their legs together and raised at a ninety-degree angle.

"Heels together, toes apart," Marlie said as she walked by. "Chin to chest, Andi. Pull in your core."

By sixty, Andi's stomach was trembling. By a hundred, she knew she'd made a hideous mistake. Worse, it turned out doing the hundred was actually one of the easier exercises.

Fifty minutes later, she lay on the mat panting and unsure if she could stand. Despite having studied anatomy, she had muscles complaining in places she didn't know muscles existed.

Everyone else bounced to their feet and thanked Marlie for the class. Andi managed to get to her hands and knees, then stagger to her feet.

"What did you think?" Marlie asked.

"It was great."

"You did fine. Why don't you schedule a couple of private lessons to get to know all the different exercises, then try the class again? Everyone's so friendly here. It's a lot of fun."

Andi looked at the women chatting by the front of the studio. They were a little sweaty, but didn't look as if they'd been run over by buses. Even the woman in her sixties moved easily, as if the class hadn't been that much of a challenge.

"I'm not sure I'd use the word *fun,* but I think I would like to try again." When she'd recovered.

She made her way to her car and climbed inside. Her arm actually shook as she inserted the key, then started the engine. Good thing she wasn't driving a manual transmission. No way she could work a clutch in her present condition.

She was so sore that just driving up the hill to her house hurt. She'd never been one to exercise, and now she was paying the price. She wondered if she would even be able to move in the morning.

She parked in front of her house and for once, the sight of Wade's big truck didn't get much of a reaction. She was sweaty, red-faced and wearing very unflattering sweats and a T-shirt. If she continued to go to Scoop and Stretch, she was going to have to invest in some cute workout clothes. She wondered if there were exercise clothes with built-in shape-wear.

She dragged herself up the stairs to the front porch, then walked inside. Wade stood with a clipboard in his hands.

"I have something to show you," he told her, pointing to the back of the house.

She dropped her purse and tote with her work clothes on the bottom stair and limped after him. He paused in front of several pieces of wood.

"We finished most of the electrical and we're framing out the offices. By the end of the week, you'll see where the various rooms are going to be."

"Progress," she said, and tried to smile. "That's great."

He studied her for a second. "I have a few work orders

I need you to sign. For the fixtures and switches. Also, the medical supplier called and we're on target for the examination tables."

He went into more detail and she did her best to listen, but her heart wasn't in it.

This was her life, she thought, staring at the wood framing, the exposed floor supports. This house, this island. She really had moved away from all her friends, her routine, everything she'd ever known. She was starting over with nothing more than an old ratty house, a job she loved and very weak stomach muscles.

While having a career gave her a big jump up on a lot of people, it didn't keep her warm at night. She'd been so sure she was done with men, only she wasn't and now she was on the island. What was she supposed to do about dating here? Wade was the only single guy she'd met and he hadn't shown the slightest hint of interest.

"You don't like it," Wade said.

She stared at him. "Like what? Sorry. I disappeared into my head. Can you repeat that?"

"Sure, but are you okay?"

She opened her mouth, then closed it. "No, I'm not. I moved here without realizing what I was doing. Everyone is either in a family or a tourist. I have no friends, no hobbies, no bathtub. I deliberately cut myself off from the world and now I'm stuck. There are no single guys. At least none I've met and even if I do find one, I haven't been on a first date in a decade. I don't know if anything is different and I wasn't very good at it before. I doubt age has improved that. I'm alone, lonely and if anyone tells you about an exercise called stomach massage, don't think it's a good thing, because it isn't."

Wade looked at her for a long time, then cleared his

throat. "So we should talk about the light fixtures to-morrow?"

She didn't know if she should laugh or break into hysterical sobs. "Sure. Sorry. This isn't your problem. I love what you're doing with the house."

"Thank you."

He retreated so quickly she half expected to see skid marks on the subflooring. She went upstairs, showered and changed. When she came back downstairs, Wade was packing up for the night.

He walked to the front door, then glanced back. "It'll get better."

"You don't actually know that, but thank you for the optimistic take."

He chuckled. "You're a little ray of sunshine, aren't you?"

"I'm pragmatic."

"Don't worry about dating. It hasn't changed."

"I hope not."

"See you tomorrow, Andi." He gave her a quick wave, then left.

She sank down on the bottom stair and dropped her head into her hands. Yup, a complete lack of interest. She wasn't even surprised.

Eleven

Deanna sliced the bread she'd baked the previous week and collected what she needed to make sandwiches. Except for Madison, the girls were still in bed, which meant another few minutes of peace.

Just another hour, two at the most, she told herself. Then Colin would be gone and the girls would be at school. She glanced at the clock and abandoned the sandwiches. She had to get the girls up.

She climbed the stairs. As she walked down the hall, she heard voices coming from the master.

"Why?" Madison was asking. "Daddy, we need you here."

Deanna paused in the hallway.

"I know, baby girl. I want to be here, too. I'm working on changing things."

"Not hard enough. It's because of her, isn't it? She makes you go. I wish she would go instead."

Deanna felt the words stab through to her heart.

"You don't mean that." Colin's voice was quiet.

"I do," her twelve-year-old insisted. "I hate her."

Deanna flinched.

"Madison." Colin's tone warned. "You will speak of your mother with respect."

"I don't respect her and I don't like her. You can't make me like her. Why would I? Why would any of us? The twins are too young to know any better, but Audrey and Lucy feel the same way. She's horrible."

Deanna felt herself getting smaller and weaker by the second. She turned and quickly stumbled downstairs. Once she was in the kitchen, she pressed her hands to her belly and told herself to keep breathing.

This wasn't happening. It couldn't be. How could Madison say those things? She didn't know what a horrible mother was. She'd had it too easy. Somehow this was all Colin's fault. He'd done this.

A few minutes later, he walked into the kitchen. Deanna turned on him.

"So that's how it's going to be?" she demanded. "You're turning my own children away from me?"

He stood there in his suit, overnight case in one hand, briefcase in the other. "I didn't tell her what to say."

"No, but you encouraged it. You want to turn my children from me. You don't want me to have anything."

"I won't accept that," he told her. "Whatever you have going on with Madison is between the two of you."

"Sure. Take the easy way out. You always do." She slapped her hands on the counter. "If I'm so awful, why did you marry me? Why do you stay?"

He drew in a breath. "I loved you, Deanna. I thought we would be happy together. As to why I stay..." He shrugged. "Some days it beats the hell out of me. I suppose because of the girls and what you and I once had. I want to know if we have a chance together. I'm starting to think we don't." He started for the door. "I'll email you the details of my trip later."

And then he was gone.

Deanna drew in a breath. Hysteria was a heartbeat away. She could feel pain and anger building up inside her until all she wanted to do was scream. There were still the girls to get up and sandwiches to make and…

She couldn't do this, couldn't take it. She didn't have the strength or the will. She had to keep breathing, but she couldn't breathe. Her chest was too tight. She was going to pass out.

Moving at a run, she raced to the sink and turned on the water. Still gasping for air, she plunged her hands under the scalding water and let it flow over her already raw skin. Then she pumped soap into her hand and began to wash.

Andi stood in the middle of the perfect garden and glanced slowly from side to side. Boston hadn't been kidding when she'd said that Deanna's yard was a perfect complement to the house. The front yard was pretty, but the backyard was stunning. There were paths and trimmed hedges, herbs and flowers. Andi tried to find inspiration and instead felt only defeat. She didn't know a dandelion from a petunia and wasn't sure how to cultivate one while getting rid of the other.

If her own yard wasn't so hideous, she would tell herself to simply wait—tackling one project at a time. Only the dead grass and overgrown beds made her unhappy every time she saw them. Imagine what the ever-perfect Deanna must think. Looking at all that ugly might actually cause a medical condition.

She drew in a breath. She could figure out what to

do. Or hire a landscaper to do the figuring for her. He or she would be like Wade, but outdoors. Or maybe not like Wade, Andi thought grimly. She didn't want to find someone else she could basically throw herself at only to be ignored. Having that happen once every decade or so was enough fun for her.

With Matt it had been different, she thought. Not better, but different. Matt had decided everything. When they'd talked about their future, it had been in terms of what he wanted. He'd been on her mother's side when it came to Andi's career, pressuring her to specialize. He'd hated her clothes and her hair. He'd wanted her to get it cut and have it straightened.

She blinked several times. "Matt was a jackass," she murmured. "A complete and total egotistical, selfish asshole and I said I would marry him. Which makes me the real idiot."

The back door of Deanna's house opened and Deanna stepped onto the porch. "Andi?"

Andi felt herself flush. "Hi," she said, giving a weak wave.

"I heard voices. Is someone with you?"

Andi was in the middle of her neighbor's backyard, in the middle of the day, without an invitation. There really didn't seem to be a good explanation, except maybe the truth.

"Sorry for disturbing you," she said, speaking quickly. "I had a break in my schedule, so I came home. Only with all the construction, I didn't want to go into the house."

She also hadn't wanted to face Wade, but telling the truth and being brutally honest weren't the same thing.

"My yard is a disaster and yours is so beautiful. I was admiring it and then suddenly I was walking over and here I am." She held out both hands, palms up. "As for the talking, somehow I started thinking about my ex-fiancé and I realized he's a complete jerk. He tried to change everything about me and I let him. I guess I thought he was right."

TMI, she told herself, and cleared her throat. "Anyway, that's the conversation I was having. I didn't mean to scare you."

"You didn't." Deanna's slight distant expression softened. "It sounds like you're better off without him."

"I am."

"At least you didn't have children with him. That makes a breakup easier."

Andie thought about what Lucy had said before—that her mother had been crying. She took an instinctive step forward.

"All relationships have their rough patches," she said softly. "If there's anything I can—"

Deanna's expression iced over. "There isn't. If you'll excuse me." She stepped back and firmly closed the door.

Late that afternoon, Andi drove to her house, determined to erase memories from her emotional meltdown the day before. She was going to be mature, professional and poised. If that didn't work, she would deny her previous meeting with Wade had ever occurred. As far as she was concerned, denial was a perfectly sound coping device.

She got out of her car and squared her shoulders. Before she could figure out a charming, sophisticated opening line, the front door to her house opened and a tall, gangly girl bounced onto the porch.

Wade's daughter, Andi thought, taking in the same

dark hair and eyes. But what was sexy and intriguing on him was innocent and beautiful on his daughter. She would guess the girl was twelve or thirteen. If boys weren't lining up, they would be soon.

"I'm Carrie," the girl said with a happy wave. "My dad's been keeping me away because he says that some clients don't want a kid around. I told him you're a pediatrician and that you must like children or you made a seriously bad career choice."

Andi laughed. "You're exactly right and I love my job. Nice to meet you, Carrie."

"Nice to meet you, too. Are you excited about the house? I've seen the plans and it's going to be so cool. My dad does excellent work. I know you're thinking I have to say that, but he really does."

"I have every confidence in him." She moved toward the stairs.

"Good. You should." Carrie waited on the porch. "Are you loving the island? It's pretty cool here. Sometimes my friends and I wish for a mall and more places to go, but it's really okay the way it is." She wrinkled her pert nose. "That's not really cool, so you can't tell anyone I said that."

"Your secret is safe with me." She climbed the stairs and stood next to Carrie.

"Being a doctor is hard," Carrie said. "I asked my science teacher about it and he said you went to school for a really long time. After college, I mean."

"I did, but I started college early. That helped. After a bachelor's degree, I had to go to medical school, then study more in my specialty. Pediatrics."

Carrie's eyes widened. "That's a lot of studying. I

should probably stop complaining about my social studies report, huh?"

"I might not be as sympathetic as you'd like."

Carried nodded. "You don't have any kids, right?"

"No. Someday, I'd like to."

"Kids are really great. Especially twelve-year-old girls. We're actually the best."

Andi grinned. "I've heard that, but I appreciate the reminder."

Carrie laughed. "I'm going to go see my friend Madison. She lives next door. It was nice to meet you."

"You, too."

Carrie started down the stairs. When she reached the walkway, she turned back. "Oh, my dad has this idea for storage space. He's really excited about it. I don't know if it's what you need or not, but maybe you could pretend to be excited, too? Because he's really into what he does, you know?"

"You're a very good daughter, and I promise to be thrilled."

"Thanks."

Carrie waved, then walked toward Deanna's house.

Andi watched her go. What a great kid, she thought. Losing her mother explained the emotional maturity. She would automatically step into the emptiness the void created. But her personality was pure charm. Some of that was genetics, but a lot came from her environment. Apparently Wade was more than just a pretty face.

News she so didn't need, she thought as she walked inside. The man was tempting enough without finding out he was a great dad.

"You're here," Wade said as she entered. "I have this idea I want to talk to you about. For storage."

She thought of Carrie and grinned. "How amazing. It's like you read my mind. I was thinking we're going to have some storage issues."

"Not anymore. Let me sketch out what I had in mind."

Deanna turned left and then drove over Getaway Bridge. Five miles inland, charming suburban neighborhoods gave way to strip malls and big box-store plazas. She circled around the brand-new Costco and drove into what had been a run-down neighborhood dotted with tiny, broken houses decorated with graffiti.

She'd grown up here, in a one-bedroom shack on a street with cracked sidewalks and abandoned cars. She pulled in front of a newer condo complex, grateful the blight of her childhood had been replaced with something so normal.

But time and new construction couldn't erase the memories. Of the way her mother smelled after days without bathing. Of the clink of liquor bottles in the trash. Of the knot that always formed in her stomach when she knew a beating was coming.

Deanna tightened her grip on the steering wheel, ignoring the pain in her cracked and peeling fingers. Even without closing her eyes, she could see everything about that filthy house. She remembered telling herself not to be afraid of the rats and getting to school early so she could secretly wash in the sink in the girls' bathroom.

There had been days that weren't so bad. When her mother had been younger and managed to capture the attention of a man. The place was cleaner, there was food and the beatings were less frequent. But the men always left and then things got bad.

The worst had come when Deanna was ten. Lucy's age,

she thought absently. Her mother had gone on a bender that had lasted two days before she'd passed out. She'd come to in a rage fueled by a hangover and hopelessness. She'd gone after her daughter with all she'd had, finally blackening both eyes and breaking her arm. She'd screamed so much the police had shown up.

Drunk and smelly and ugly as she was, her mother had tried to flirt with the officer. He'd ignored her and taken Deanna into his car. From there she'd gone to the hospital. She still recalled how clean everything had been. How she'd been terrified the nurse would yell at her for dirtying the sheets.

Then Aunt Lauren had shown up. Her mother's older sister. It was as if Deanna's mother was the image in a warped mirror and Lauren was the real-life person. They were so alike, yet so different.

Lauren had stood at the end of the bed, her blue eyes dark with concern. "I heard what happened. I'm sorry for all you went through, Deanna. Your uncle and I are willing to have you live with us. But you're going to have to promise to be good. Do you understand?"

Good. She wasn't sure what it meant, but she told herself she would figure it out. She'd vowed to be all they wanted, because if she didn't mess up, they wouldn't send her back.

There had been rules, but rules were easy, especially when they didn't change every other day. Deanna had done her best and she'd learned quickly. Lauren had praised her, allowing Deanna to relax a little, but never fully let down her guard.

The house on the hill had become her home. She'd treasured every corner of the beautiful home, had learned its history, had taken pride in its appearance. Lauren often told friends that Deanna was the perfect daughter.

Perfection—that was the goal. Being perfect meant she could stay. Being perfect meant having nice things.

Being perfect meant people cared about her. At least it had before, Deanna thought, squeezing her eyes shut.

Twelve

The whine of saws cut through the afternoon. Andi sat propped up against a tree in her front yard, catching up on her journal reading. Every now and then her gaze slid toward the house. The windows were being replaced this week, which meant a view inside. Every now and then Wade walked by.

May had rolled into June, and the weather had changed accordingly. Mornings were cool and foggy, but the afternoons stayed sunny. Men who did physical labor often wore shorts and T-shirts with no sleeves. As a medical professional, she could appreciate the honed muscles of a healthy man. As a woman who thought her contractor was hot, she found herself licking her lips in a slightly predatory manner.

She returned her attention to the article on whooping cough—a serious illness, especially for infants. Last year there'd been a significant increase in the number of local cases. Several Washington counties had offered special vaccination clinics to prevent the spread. As a practicing physician, Dr. Harrington received updates from the CDC on outbreaks. Andi had already signed up herself to get them, as well. Thinking about keeping her patients safe was a lot better use of her time, she told herself, than staring at Wade King.

The saws kicked on again. The high-pitched scream of the wood made her shudder.

"Having trouble concentrating?"

She looked up and saw Boston standing in front of her. Andi grinned. "It's not exactly a restful noise."

"Tell me about it. Come on and take a break at my place."

Andi scrambled to her feet and followed her neighbor across two lawns and around to the back of the house. Boston wore a loose sundress that fluttered with each step. The sun caught the dark red streaks in her hair. They went into the mudroom and then on to the kitchen, which was just as eclectic and homey as she remembered.

Boston took a pitcher of tea out of the refrigerator, then filled two glasses with ice. There was already a plate of cookies on the marble countertop at the bar.

"I'll warn you, I'm experimenting with gluten-free," Boston told her. "Don't get too excited about the cookies."

Andi picked one up. "You or your husband have celiac disease?"

"No, I'm being trendy. Shouldn't I avoid gluten?"

"If you think you have a sensitivity, there are good diets to try. They eliminate gluten triggers. Then you add foods back slowly. You could also try a cleanse and then start adding back food." She grinned. "You want to do a cleanse when you don't plan to go anywhere and have lots of free time for the bathroom."

Boston laughed. "Thanks for the warning. I'm not exactly disciplined enough to do a cleanse." She grabbed the plate of cookies and moved them to the far side of the kitchen, then pulled out a plastic container. When she popped the top, the delicious scent of chocolate drifted to Andi.

She inhaled. "What are those?"

"Brownies."

"You're my hero."

Boston set down the iced tea, then took a seat next to Andi. She reached for a brownie. "I don't usually see you at home in the middle of the week."

Andi picked up a brownie. It was moist and heavy. She could see the walnuts poking through the thick layer of frosting. Her mouth began to water.

"I haven't been fired, if that's what you're politely trying to ask. I want to start a Saturday clinic once a month. For a lot of parents, weekday appointments are a challenge. I can do vaccinations and well-care visits."

Boston nodded. "That's thoughtful. I'm sure the parents will appreciate it. I'm spoiled with my work hours. I do what I want on my own schedule." She paused. "I'm going to have something to show you in the next few days. It's not a lot, just a few jungle animals and some ideas I have for the foliage."

"I look forward to it. As I said—I appreciate you sharing your talent with me. I'm not a very worthy client."

"Would you feel better if I said I was doing it for your kids?"

"Yes, I would."

Andi waited. Boston looked as though she was going to say more. Finally she shrugged.

"It's good to have a project," she admitted. "I've been in a rut lately, and this has forced me to take a look at how I'm spending my time. That's a good thing. Oh, that reminds me. Wait here a second."

Boston slid off the stool and hurried out of the kitchen. She was back quickly, a painting in her hands.

The frame was a simple whitewash. The picture itself showed all three houses nestled together. The details on the outside two were perfect. Deanna's seemed stiffer somehow, more proud. Tiny brushstrokes captured the curl of the railings, the texture of the siding. Boston's house was just as beautiful, but in a more relaxed way. The yard sculpture was front and center.

Andi's gaze settled on her house. The artist had been kind, filling in the lawn, adding windows where there had only been boards, brightening the paint.

"On the days when the construction starts to get to you," Boston said, "this will inspire you to hang on."

"I love it," Andi admitted. "And your timing. Because it's only week four and I'm so over the remodeling."

Boston laughed and settled onto a stool. "Sorry to tell you, there are many more weeks to come."

"Thank you so much for the painting."

"If not the news?"

Andi squirmed on her seat. "That's a little harder to get excited about."

"Do the hunky guys help?"

Andi picked up her iced tea. "They add to the ambiance," she admitted. "There is something about male muscles that gets my heart beating faster. But as I'm sure they're all married, I'm keeping my heaving bosom to myself."

Boston raised her eyebrows. "Wade is single."

Andi told herself to stay calm. Blushing and stuttering wouldn't inspire confidence or friendship. "I've heard that, and while he's the prettiest of the group, I get the impression he sees me as a client rather than a woman."

She gave what she hoped was a casual shrug. "We're working together. It makes the most sense."

Boston tilted her head. Her hair tumbled over her shoulder in a cascade of browns and blacks and reds. "Wade's a good guy. Cautious with women, because of Carrie. He doesn't want her hurt."

"Of course not. Any single parent would be wary, but with her mom gone, it's even more complicated. When parents are divorced, there's usually still a role model in place. Not always, but…" She trailed off as she realized Boston was smiling.

"I didn't say anything funny," she said, feeling the awkward come back.

"You're perceptive. Most of the time you hide it in regular conversation, but your mind is always working things through."

"I'm less intuitive about people than you'd think." Matt was proof of that.

"I'm not convinced. Is it a family trait?"

"I'm not sure. My relatives are more into education than intuition. Everyone's a doctor plus."

"Plus what?"

Andi picked up her glass. "My mother's a famous heart surgeon. My father is even more specialized. Let's just say in my world, being merely a pediatrician is a waste. My mother constantly hounds me for administering to skinned knees and vaccinations."

Boston winced. "I'm so sorry. That's horrible. You're a wonderful doctor."

"Kind of you to say, but you have no way of knowing if that's true."

"You're wrong. I've seen you in action. With Lucy and the twins. You were perfect with them. You talk to kids like they're people, not a subspecies. They love that. I'll bet your patients adore you. They trust you."

Andi felt herself flush with pleasure. "Thanks. You're very kind."

"I'm an artist," Boston said with a sniff. "My job is to observe the world. I know what I'm talking about."

Andi grinned. "Okay, then. You're the expert. So tell me why, after dating for ten years and then his leaving me at the altar, I only just figured out I'm better off without my ex-fiancé."

The words spilled out with no warning. Andi tried to suck them back, but there was no way.

Boston stared at her. "Oh, Andi. Is that what happened?"

She nodded, the humor long gone. "He didn't warn me. I thought everything was fine, right until my mother came to tell me that he wasn't there. He never showed, never sent a note. Later, when I finally talked to him, he said he wasn't ready. We'd been together a decade and he wasn't ready?" Her voice rose with the telling. "I was angry and humiliated. How could he not be sure? What was there left to know? And if he didn't want me, why didn't he just say so?"

She swallowed against the tightness in her throat. "He ran off with his receptionist a couple of weeks later. They got married in Las Vegas. He'd known her three months. The worst part is I've only just figured out he was always trying to change me. He didn't like my clothes or my condo. He hated my hair."

"I love your hair."

"Thanks. Why did he bother? Why did I? I'm glad we didn't get married, but why didn't I see all this before?"

Boston put her hand over Andi's and squeezed. "I'm sorry. He sounds like a total asshole."

"He is. A complete shit." She stared at her new friend. "You know what really sucks? I miss being a couple more than I miss him. Which means I didn't love him. I loved what we were together. So getting married would have been a mistake. I see that and appreciate it. I just wish I'd figured all this out nine and a half years ago. I feel like I wasted a decade of my life on him."

"It helps to believe in karma."

"I'll give that a try. Wishing him to be run over and devoured by a wayward gang of cockroaches isn't helping much."

"Is he why you bought the house and moved to the island?"

Andi nodded. "I wanted a clean break." She gave a strangled laugh. "I knew this was the land of families and tourists. That I would be cutting myself off from a normal dating scene. I thought that's what I wanted. To be one of those cool single women who are so capable. They don't need a man. Only, I might have acted a little hastily."

Boston squeezed her fingers, then released her hand. "Leaving you stuck here with not a single man in sight."

"Something like that." She sipped her tea. "I do like the island and I know I'll settle in. I want to open my own practice, so that's all good."

"Wade's a great guy," Boston told her.

"A great guy who isn't the slightest bit interested in me."

"How can you know that?"

"If he's suffering from unrequited love, he's doing a great job of keeping it a secret." She shrugged. "It's fine. I understand there's a busload of seniors coming up for the weekend. There have to be at least a couple of single men in the group. Maybe I'll make a play for one of them."

Boston giggled. "You'll be a trophy wife for sure."

"Lucky me."

Boston leaned toward her. "Wade's careful, because of Carrie. He mostly dates off-island, if you get my drift."

"No complications, no explanations?"

"Exactly. So don't give up on him just yet. I've seen his brother naked, and if they're anything alike, he'll be worth the wait."

Andi laughed. "If it's okay with you, I'm not comfortable thinking about Zeke being naked."

"Probably for the best."

Andi had started to say something else when she noticed Boston's smile quiver—as if it wasn't as firmly in place as it should be.

Boston pushed the plate of brownies toward her. "Let's skip lunch and eat these instead. You'll feel better."

Andi reached for one of the frosted brownies and sighed. "Chocolate is truly magical, isn't it?"

"I've always thought so."

Deanna was tired of being the odd man out in her own home. Colin wanted changes? Fine—she would change. The girls wanted a fun mom. She could do that.

She waited until the twins were busy with puzzles in their bedroom, then went into the family room to get their dollhouse. They were always begging her to let them play outside with it. To spread out their dolls and tiny pieces of furniture on the lawn. She had consistently refused. The small pieces would get dirty or lost. It was one more thing she didn't need right now. Except if she wanted to show Colin she was trying, she needed to make an effort.

Not that she wanted to show him that. Not exactly. She wanted things to be back the way they had been. When he'd cared about her and she'd been more comfortable in her skin. So, as ridiculous as it was, she would take the twins' dollhouse out to the lawn and let them do what they would.

She picked it up and staggered slightly. It was heavier than she remembered.

"Sydney, Savannah," she called. "Come downstairs."

She walked toward the back door, then rested the corner of the dollhouse on the counter as she fumbled for the door handle. The house slipped but she caught it.

The girls came running into the kitchen.

"Mommy, what are you doing?"

"Letting you play outside," she said, focused on getting the door open.

It swung wide and she picked up the house again. She inched it through the doorway and started across the porch.

"Mommy, do you see Pickles?" Sydney asked.

Deanna sensed more than felt the cat slip past her. She shifted the house, trying to see the damn cat so they both didn't break their necks, only she moved too quickly. The house tipped, and then the center of gravity slid to her right. She shifted, holding on, but it was slipping and heavy. Her foot came in contact with Pickles, and the cat howled.

Pickles darted between her feet, she stumbled and suddenly the dollhouse was sailing through the air. It arced over the stairs and tumbled to the ground.

The crash was oddly silent as thin walls crumpled and miniature furniture and dolls were ejected onto the lawn. The roof cracked as the entire structure flattened.

"No!" Deanna breathed, lunging forward, knowing it was too late. "I was only trying to make it fun."

She looked at her daughters. Savannah's eyes filled with tears while Sydney looked at her with an expression so like Madison's loathing that she felt she was going to throw up.

"I'm sorry," she whispered. "I'm so sorry."

She reached for Savannah. Her daughter stepped back, brushing tears off her face. Then the twins joined hands and raced back inside together. Deanna stood alone on the porch, the broken dollhouse on the lawn, unable to fight the sense of dread that told her the toy wasn't the only thing shattered beyond repair.

"Can I take some to Madison when we're done?" Carrie asked as she carefully rolled out the dough for the sugar cookies. "I'll have to sneak them in. Slipping past enemy lines, like in an old war movie."

She grinned as she spoke, her dark eyes bright with amusement. Boston knew it was wrong to encourage her to help Madison break the rules. As an adult, Boston should respect her neighbor's particular obsession with homemade, organic and sugar-free foods. She should admire Deanna's determination to keep her children healthy. And she would, if Deanna weren't so sanctimonious about it.

"You may, but if you get caught, I've never seen you before."

Carrie laughed as she reached for the cookie cutter. She pressed the daisy shape into the dough, making sure to cut all the way through.

"Thanks for helping with the cookies," she said, glancing at Boston. "Dad said he was going to get to it, but you know how he is."

"A guy?"

Carrie nodded. "He tries, but it's not the same." She moved the cookie cutter and pressed again. "You remember her, don't you?"

"Your mom? Of course." Boston turned the question over in her head. "Are you having trouble remembering things, Carrie? About your mom?"

"Some. I have pictures and stuff. There are specific memories, but they all seem like a long time ago. I wish she was here, but that's different than missing her, isn't it?"

"Some." Boston touched her shoulder. "She loved you so much. She would be proud of you."

"Thanks. Do you think Dad will ever get married again?"

"I don't know. Have you asked him?"

Carrie rolled her eyes. "Like he's going to answer that question? He doesn't date much. At least not around here. I know what he's doing when he goes away for the weekend." She wrinkled her nose. "Okay, I don't know *exactly* what he's doing, but I know he's meeting people. Women. Sometimes I think it would be nice to be more of a family again, you know?"

"Losing someone you love is hard."

"Like when you lost Liam?"

Boston felt the stab clear down to her heart. "Like that," she agreed softly.

"Dad says parents aren't supposed to outlive their children, but I didn't like losing my mom, either. I don't think anyone should die."

"That would change things."

Carrie's eyes brightened. "The house would be really crowded if everyone who had ever lived here was still around."

"You'd have to share a bedroom."

"With a ghost. That could be fun." She peeled away the excess dough, then carried the cookie sheet over to the oven. "Andi seems nice. For Dad, I mean. But I can't tell if he likes her." She slid the cookie sheet into the oven and set the timer. "I mean, I know he likes her but I'm not sure if it's in a boy-girl way. Do you think Andi likes him?"

A question Boston happened to have the answer to, although she wasn't going to share the information with her twelve-year-old niece. "I think you should let them figure it out on their own."

"My mom's been gone half my life, Boston. That's six years. If my dad was good at dating, don't you think he'd have a girlfriend by now? Someone has to help him."

Boston laughed. "I think your points are excellent and still, I'm going to tell you to leave the poor man alone."

"Andi's really pretty. And a doctor, which is cool. Do you think she has a boyfriend in Seattle?"

"Carrie, stop meddling."

"Why? We could get them together, and then Dad and I would move in next door."

Boston put her arm around her niece. "I would like that, but people need to fall in love on their own."

"Like you and Zeke?"

"Something like that."

Carrie leaned against her. "It was love at first sight, wasn't it?"

"You've heard the story a thousand times."

Carried wrapped her arms around Boston's waist

and sighed. "Tell me just one more time. It's my favorite story."

Boston held her close and kissed the top of her head.

Holding this precious girl was as close to happiness as she'd been able to get in the past few months. If she held on long enough and tight enough, she could almost fill the hole in her heart. Almost.

"It was back in high school," she began.

Carrie scrambled onto a stool and waited expectantly. "And you saw him. He had on a letterman's jacket, right?"

Boston smiled. "Right."

Thirteen

"I can see my bedroom window," Lucy said, pointing.

Sydney and Savannah crowded close, wanting to look out, too. Raindrops rolled down the glass, obscuring the view.

"I like it up here," one of the twins said. As they were wearing different clothes than the last time they'd been by, Andi couldn't tell them apart.

"It's kind of snug, huh? Like a den or a cave," Andi said, then picked up the board game the girls had brought with them. "Candy Land? I love that game." She smiled. "I know. Let's take a bunch of blankets downstairs and we can sit by the window and play the game."

The girls agreed that would be fun. The twins took charge of the game. Lucy carried the cookies Andi had bought. Andi stuffed juice boxes in a shopping bag, then grabbed several blankets from her small linen closet. A few minutes later they were choosing markers. Andi shuffled the deck of cards, then put them facedown.

One of the twins smiled at her. "You can go first."

"That's very nice of you, but you're my guests. How about if Lucy goes first?"

Lucy beamed in surprise, then picked up the first card. The game was under way. Fifteen minutes later they'd completed the first game and started on a second. Andi let the three of them play so she could pass out cookies and get the juice boxes ready. Rain tapped on the windows. With new windows in place, plenty of light spilled into the room.

The space was coming together, she thought, glancing around. All the downstairs rooms were framed in. With the electrical and plumbing in place, insulation was next, followed by drywall. Talk about exciting.

Lucy moved her marker, then took one of the juice boxes. "Thank you," the ten-year-old said politely.

"You're welcome." Andi smiled at the girl. "School must nearly be out."

"Next week."

"That will be fun. Do you have any special plans for the summer? A family vacation?"

Lucy shrugged. "I don't know. Daddy travels a lot for work. He says he likes to be home with us when he can be."

"I'm sure he enjoys spending time with his girls."

"He loves us very much," one of the twins offered.

Andi studied the two of them, searching for some small difference. A slight pattern in the iris, the curve of an ear lobe. But there wasn't anything she could see.

"I'm stuck," she said at last.

The three girls looked at her.

"I can't tell you apart," she admitted. "I'm a doctor. Shouldn't I be able to find something?"

The twins giggled. The one on the left—in a lavender shirt covered with cartoon kittens—raised her right hand and showed Andi a tiny scar by the base of her thumb.

"This happened when I was a baby. So you can know I'm Sydney."

Andi wondered how many people were given the special secret of telling the identical twins apart. "Thank you for showing me that."

"You probably need to know," Sydney told her. "Because you're going to be our doctor."

"Am I?"

"Uh-huh. Mommy said so at dinner." Sydney frowned. "She wanted to know why you don't have kids of your own."

Because her ex-fiancé was an idiot, Andi thought, careful to keep her expression friendly and open. And she'd been just as idiotic herself. "I would love to have kids of my own. I hope to someday."

"You're not a lisbon?" Savannah asked.

Lucy flushed. "Don't say that."

"But I don't know what it is." She turned to Andi. "Mommy said it at dinner. We asked Audrey later, but she didn't know, either."

Lucy squirmed on the blanket. "Just play the game."

Lisbon? Andi tried to figure out what Deanna could have said that would make her children...

Lesbian, she thought suddenly, disliking Deanna more by the second. Talk about someone she didn't want for a neighbor. And just because she was in her thirties and not married didn't mean anything. She'd been in a long-term relationship that had ended. Would she be getting this much flak if she'd simply been married and divorced?

"I'm not from Lisbon," Andi said smoothly. "Which is, by the way, a city in Portugal. I've always wanted to visit, though. I hear it's beautiful. Lucy, is it your turn?"

Lucy smiled gratefully and reached for the next card.

Andi watched the beautiful girls playing on the blankets and wondered how on earth someone like Deanna had produced such great children. It must be their father's influence, she thought, hoping she didn't have to worry about a whole lot of contact with her less-than-appealing neighbor.

"And then she turns into a mermaid!" Sydney shrieked.

The high-pitched sound cut through Deanna's head like a laser. The low-grade headache she'd been fighting for most of the day cranked up a couple of notches.

Savannah pushed one of the bath toys under the water in the large master bathtub. "She has to be rescued. Hurry."

The girls giggled as they played, caught up in their imaginary world of water and mermaids. Deanna watched them from the master bedroom where she stood folding laundry. Her fingers were clumsy and she fumbled with the towels, unable to make the corners line up.

She was tired, she thought, her head pounding, her eyes gritty. She couldn't remember the last time she'd slept more than a few hours at a stretch. Every time she closed her eyes, she started to replay her and Colin's conversations. The uncertainty fed the fear and she ended up staring at the ceiling for hours at a time, her thoughts circling.

As she wasn't sure of the problem, she couldn't find a solution. When she wasn't terrified, she was furious. Colin was doing this to her and she didn't know why. Asking wasn't a possibility. When he called, he only spoke to the children. The way Madison was running to the phone when it rang, Deanna figured they'd set up prearranged times.

"Mom, I need help with my history project."

Deanna turned and saw Lucy standing in the doorway to the bedroom. "Not now," she said, her attention returning to the twins. "I have to watch your sisters."

"Then when?"

"I don't know."

"You said you'd help me. You said it this weekend and yesterday."

The pressure around Deanna's head tightened. "I'm busy, Lucy. There are four other children in this house. Not just you."

She picked up a towel, then let it drop to the bed when she realized her fingers were trembling. She felt the room sway a little. Low blood sugar, she thought. She hadn't been eating much. She should go downstairs and get a snack. Just as soon as the twins were out of the bath.

"Mom, I need to go to the library, remember? You said you'd take me tonight."

Audrey's voice joined the shrill laughter of her youngest.

"Not tonight."

"But you said."

"I have a project for history," Lucy said, holding out a worn book. "Mom, this is important. School's out in two days and it's due."

"Move, you two." Madison stepped between her sisters and pushed into the room. "Can Carrie spend the night this Friday? It's my turn to have her here."

"Mommy, the water's getting cold. Can I turn on the hot water?"

The room swayed again. The pain grew until it nearly blinded her. Deanna felt herself sinking, drifting. Everything hurt.

She sank onto the edge of the bed. The voices continued, the questions repeated again and again.

"Stop it!" she yelled, coming to her feet. "Stop it, all of you. Just stop. I can't take it. Go away. Go to your rooms and be quiet. Just be quiet!"

By the end she was screaming, her voice echoing off the walls. Audrey and Lucy reached for each other's hands and hung on tight. Madison's face hardened with loathing.

"You're such a bitch," she said clearly, before walking out of the room.

Deanna ignored her and the other two. She walked into the bathroom where the twins were shivering in the water, crying.

"Get up," she snapped.

They both stood. She wrapped towels around them and lifted them out of the tub.

"Go to your room. Dry off and put on your pajamas. Do it now."

Still crying, their eyes wide with tears and fear, the twins ran out of the bathroom.

She smelled it then. The stench of alcohol and dirt. Heard the skittering sound of roaches and rats, saw the piles of trash. She was back in her old house, her mother screaming like a crazy person.

"Stop it! Just stop it. You're sucking me dry. I have nothing left. Go away."

The house had been so tiny and Deanna hadn't had a room of her own. She remembered crawling into a corner and trying to make herself as small as possible. So the yelling would stop. So she wouldn't get hit. So the hits wouldn't turn into beatings.

"I'm not like her," she whispered, but when she looked

at herself in the mirror, she saw her mother. The clothes were different, as was the face, but the voice was the same.

She forced herself to breathe. When the shaking finally stopped, she pulled the plug in the tub, then walked over to the toilet. She raised the lid, bent over and vomited.

There was no food, just bile and self-hatred. When the retching was done, she sank onto the floor, wrapped her arms around her knees and began to rock back and forth.

Boston stood in the center of what would be the waiting room and tried to see walls where there was only framed spaces and subflooring. Over the past couple of weeks, she'd managed to come up with drawings of a half dozen animals and bugs for the jungle mural. Each time she sat down to draw, she became convinced she couldn't do it, but she managed. The cartoon creatures weren't anyone's idea of brilliant, but they were progress and she kept telling herself it would get easier with time.

She'd picked out her color scheme and had prepared a sample of the colors together for Andi to approve. Next up would be a painting-size view of the mural itself. Something for her to work from when she started on the actual walls.

Just the thought of putting it all together nearly made her break out in hives, but that was okay. Every time she got scared, she went back to her studio and drew pictures of her son until her heart stopped racing so much. The time to recover her equilibrium was getting shorter and shorter.

Andi's mural was a project designed to help her heal. Boston wasn't sure she liked that reality, but she didn't know how to avoid it. She supposed wanting to move on and wanting to stay stuck were equally understandable reactions. As long as she was in pain, Liam was still with her.

"Hey."

She turned and nearly dropped her pad when she saw Wade walk into the house.

"What are you doing here?" she demanded. "You were supposed to go to Marysville and talk to the cabinet supplier."

"I'm happy to see you, too," her brother-in-law said as he raised his eyebrows. "He rescheduled."

Boston pressed her lips together. "Sorry. It's just…" She glanced down at her pad, then back at him. "I didn't want you to know I'd come by."

Wade shook his head. "Why not?"

"I'm painting a mural for Andi's waiting room."

She didn't have to say more than that. Zeke and Wade were close. She knew they talked about nearly everything. So Zeke would have told his brother about the paintings of Liam and how he didn't think she was dealing with the loss of their son. Zeke would take news of her working on the mural as a good sign. She wasn't far enough along in the process to know if it was or not.

Wade smiled. "That's great. Why didn't you want me to know?"

"Because Zeke doesn't know and I'm not ready to tell him."

Wade held up both hands and took a step back. "I'm not getting in the middle of that."

"I know, which is why I wanted to come by when I thought you were gone. I didn't want to put you in the middle of anything. Can you pretend I wasn't here?"

Wade dropped his arms to his sides. "Sure, but I won't like it."

"Thank you." She studied him. "Andi's nice. I've seen her with Deanna's kids. She's really good with them. And she's pretty. Don't you love her curly hair?"

His dark eyes narrowed. "Boston, what the hell are you going on about?"

"I'm just saying, you're single, she's single."

"She's a client."

"Oh, please. Since when has that been an issue?"

"It hasn't. I'm saying I don't think it's a good idea to date a client while we're still on the job."

"So you'll date her when you're done?"

He groaned. "Are you torturing me on purpose? I thought you liked me."

"I do. You're my favorite brother-in-law. I'm simply pointing out that she's pretty and funny and single. You should take advantage of that."

"No way."

Boston stared at him. "Why not? You don't like her?"

"I like her just fine." He shrugged. "She's a doctor."

Boston waited for the rest of the sentence.

"That's it," Wade told her. "She's a doctor."

"You hate doctors?"

"She's well educated. Smart. I'm a guy who does construction."

"So?"

"I'm not her type."

Boston felt her confusion drift away. "You do realize you said you weren't her type, not the other way around. So you are interested."

Wade groaned. "Kill me now, I beg you."

"No way. So you like her. You should ask her out. I think she'd say yes."

He raised his head and stared at her. "How do you know that?"

"I'm naturally intuitive."

"Yeah, right." One corner of his mouth turned up. "She was asking about me."

"Maybe."

"Interesting."

She grinned. "Is this where I remind you it's not a good idea to date a client?"

"Shut up."

She laughed. "You're such a guy."

"It's one of my best qualities."

Andi leaned back in her chair and wished her office had a window. Then she could throw herself out of it. While the two-or three-foot drop to the grass around the office building wouldn't do any damage, the act would be nicely symbolic.

Instead she held the phone to her ear, her eyes closed, her psyche braced for the upcoming onslaught.

"You're settling into your house, then?" her mother asked.

"Most of my things are in storage, so there wasn't much to settle. The construction is moving along."

"I suppose that's a good thing." Her mother sighed. "Your father and I have made peace with your decision."

"At last I can sleep tonight."

"Sarcasm?" her mother asked. "I thought you'd out-grown being sarcastic."

"No. I'm going to be sarcastic to my grave. Sorry, Mom."

"I suppose you can't help it. As I was saying, we've decided that if you're going to waste your life giving vaccinations and bandaging scraped knees, you might as well provide those services in some little backwater town. I'm sure they need decent medical care there."

"I'm sure they do. So far the gratitude is very heartening. Some of my patients pay me with livestock. Just last week I got two chickens and the hindquarters of an elk."

Her mother sighed. "Really, Andi. Is that necessary?"

She opened her eyes. "Kind of. I'm a ferry ride away from Seattle. We have running water and cell service, Mom. Backwater? I'm living in a tourist nirvana."

"Fine. Your point is taken. I just hate to see you wasting your life. You could have done important work."

"My work is important to me."

"I heard about a fellowship," her mother began.

"No."

"But it's—"

"No. You're going to have accept the fact that I'm happy with what I'm doing."

"But you're a pediatrician."

And the family screwup, Andi thought. The one who never quite measured up. "Let it go, Mom."

"All right. You know there's talk of your sister and her research team being nominated for a Nobel Prize."

"Good for her."

"Your father and I are going to a medical symposium in British Columbia next month. Maybe we'll stop by on our way."

Ack! A visit from family. Why her? "That would be lovely," she managed, hoping she sounded at least vaguely sincere.

Her mother sighed again. It was something the esteemed Dr. Gordon did a lot when speaking with her youngest. "I do love you, Andi. As does your father."

"I know, Mom. You just wish I'd had a little more ambition."

"That would have been nice. You're a Gordon."

"Lucky me."

"I'll send you the information on the fellowship."

"I really wish you wouldn't."

A sharp beeping sound cut through the call.

"That's me," her mother said. "I have to go. I'll talk to you soon."

There was a click and the call disconnected. Andi put the receiver back in place, then glanced around for that elusive window.

Fourteen

Deanna hovered in her bedroom. It had been three days since her outburst. Three days of her children watching her warily and getting quiet when she walked into the room. The twins had forgotten what had happened, but the older girls remembered. They were afraid.

She recognized the symptoms because she'd experienced them herself. She knew what it was like to not be sure what to expect, to live with rules that always changed but punishments that were swift and harsh and often left scars. She'd vowed she would be nothing like her mother.

She wasn't, she told herself. Her house was beautiful. Clean. Perfect. There were regular meals of good food, and her children wanted for nothing. Yet their eyes were as shadowed as hers had been, and when she'd walked by Lucy that morning, her daughter had flinched.

Down the hall, Madison was in her room with her best friend, Carrie. Even though it was a weeknight, Deanna had agreed to a sleepover. Probably out of guilt. Now she wished Madison would go to the bathroom or something so Deanna could speak with Carrie alone.

Not that she had anything particular she wanted to say;

it was just that Carrie was so friendly and approachable. Most of the time Deanna had no idea what to say to her own daughter, but conversation with Carrie was easy. Right now Deanna needed to spend a second with a kid who didn't look at her as if she were the devil.

Determined to think up an excuse, she started down the hall, only to come to a stop when she heard Carrie's voice in a low, worried tone.

"Are you sure you're okay?"

"I'm fine," Madison told her. "Just forget about it."

"I can't. I'm worried. You need to talk to your mom."

Deanna pressed her hand to her chest. Talk to her about what? Was Madison sick? Had something happened at school?

"I'm not talking to *her*," Madison insisted, her tone low and angry. "I would never talk to her about this."

"But she's your mom."

"I can't help that, but I won't let her think she's important to me. I hate her."

Deanna leaned against the wall, her chest tight, her eyes burning. The absolute rejection cut her down to brittle bone and left her in pieces.

"You're wrong about her," Carrie insisted. "She's not so bad. Parents are supposed to tell you what to do. My dad does it all the time."

"He's different. He loves you. When he looks at you, he's so happy and proud. She only sees us as a mess she has to clean up. She cares about what other people think, not what we feel. She wants everyone to think she's so perfect. It's all about her."

"Even if that's true, you're still lucky." Carrie's voice was quiet. "I'd give anything to have my mom back."

"You can have mine."

Madison's dismissal, so cold and practiced, made Deanna start to shake. She turned and started back toward her bedroom. The walls seemed to be moving—closing in on her—and she didn't know how to make them stop.

"Mom?"

She stopped and blinked, bringing Lucy into focus. "What?"

"You never said if I could go to the party. I was hoping you'd say yes."

Her second oldest, as blond and blue-eyed as her sister, stared at her. The ridiculous glasses perched on her nose made her look like an owl. It was as if the other girls were in sharp relief while Lucy was slightly out of focus.

"Fine. Go."

Her daughter smiled widely and moved toward her, as if offering a hug. At the last minute, she took a step back and raced for her room. Deanna stared after her. She'd already lost Madison. Would Lucy be next? Then Audrey? One by one her children were drifting away, and for the life of her, she couldn't say why.

"I've saved the best for last," Wade said, leading the way down the hallway to the back of what would be her office.

Andi followed him, as interested in his butt as she was in the progress being made. Not only was there actual drywall, but the majority of her medical equipment had been delivered and was stacked in what would be the waiting room. The remodeling was coming together.

While the office would be finished in a matter of a few weeks, her living area was progressing more slowly. The second floor would house her kitchen and great room, along with a guest bedroom and bath. On that level, they were still at the "oh, look, there are new electrical wires" stage. From a layperson's perspective, drywall was a lot more exciting than a few wires. Probably because it defined actual rooms.

Once the second floor was finished, she would move into the guest room and Wade and his men would go to work on the attic. That level would be turned into a master suite, a home office and a third bedroom. The entire project was to be finished by sometime in September. From how things were progressing, her office level would be done in plenty of time for her to open her practice before school started.

Wade walked into the break room and stepped to the side. Andi looked at the beautiful wood cabinets. They weren't installed and there weren't any countertops yet, but she could see the rich finish and details on the molding.

"I have cabinets," she said happily, running her hands down the side of the closest one. "I love them."

"Good, because they're the same ones you're getting upstairs."

"They're beautiful."

Wade had suggested ordering the same cabinets for the whole house. One big order rather than two or three smaller orders of different types of cabinets reduced the costs.

"We'll move these out and lay down the flooring," he said. "But I had the guys put them in here first so you could see what they looked like."

"And the layout," she said, studying the placement. She could see where the sink would go. "You were right about the long countertop. That's going to be really practical."

Light spilled in from the big window that faced her

backyard. Even in winter, the break room would be bright and cheerful.

She turned to him. "I love it all."

"Good."

His voice was low and just a little bit sexy. Or maybe it was completely normal and she was reacting to being within a tight space with a handsome man. Either way she felt a distinct tingle low enough in her belly to make her want to squirm.

He leaned against the drywall. "How are you settling in to life here on the island?"

"I'm finding my way. Everyone is friendly." She thought about mentioning that she was getting the hang of her Pilates class, but didn't think he would find that interesting.

"You were asking Boston about me."

Andi felt her mouth drop open. Thoughts crowded her mind. That Boston was Wade's sister-in-law, so it wasn't completely surprising she'd said something, but still. Wasn't there a female code? That Wade's mentioning the conversation could either mean he was interested or that he wanted her to go away. In an emotional sense, of course. She suspected he didn't want her actually moving, as that would mean not getting paid.

"Yes, well, I wouldn't worry about it," she said, then cleared her throat. "Rumor has it I'm a lesbian, so you're safe."

One dark eyebrow rose. "Are you?"

"No."

"Good."

Good? As in…good?

He straightened. "I'm thinking safe is overrated."

Her gaze locked with his. She was tall, but he was

much taller and she had to tilt her head back as he approached.

"I have a daughter."

"I've met her. She's terrific."

"I think so."

He moved closer still. Not touching, but certainly invading her space. The girly bits volunteered for a full frontal assault, but Andi did her best to ignore the hungry pleas.

"We work together," he said, reaching up and cupping the right side of her face. "You and I. That's a complication."

"I'm very good at problem solving," she murmured, thinking this couldn't possibly be happening. Her muscular, charming, big-handed contractor was not really staring into her eyes with what even her inexperienced self recognized as interest, was he?

"I was going to ask you out to dinner," he said. "But I think I'd like to do this instead."

Then he lowered his head and pressed his mouth to hers.

Andi's last first kiss had been over a decade ago. What she remembered most about it was that she'd felt awkward and unsure. This time what she experienced most was a burning sense of need that came from being kissed by a man who obviously knew what he was doing.

His lips pressed against hers with a combination of hunger and tenderness. She felt both wanted and oddly safe. While sexual tension increased, her nervousness faded and she let herself relax into him.

Wade put his free hand on her waist and drew her against him. She went willingly, automatically wrapping her arms around his neck. He moved from her mouth to kiss her nose, then each cheek before touching his lips to hers again. Without meaning to, she parted her lips and he swept his tongue inside.

Desire exploded. There was no other word to describe the rush of hunger that burned through her veins. Her breasts swelled in a matter of seconds, aching for his touch, and between her legs she felt a heavy, almost cramping need.

He raised his head and stared at her.

Dilated pupils, she thought happily. He wasn't faking his interest.

"Unexpected," he murmured, then lightly kissed her again.

"Definitely."

"Repeatable."

"Very."

Somewhere in the front of the house, something crashed to the floor. Wade straightened and stepped back.

"I need to check on that."

"Right."

They stared at each other for a second, and then he walked away.

Andi took advantage of the cabinets and leaned against one while her breathing slowly returned to normal. Her whole body tingled and she knew she was grinning like a fool. Not that she cared. As far as she was concerned, life on Blackberry Island had just gotten very, very interesting.

"Spying on our neighbors?" Zeke asked.

Boston stepped away from the window and laughed. "I think Wade is interested in Andi, and I happen to know she's interested in him. It's fun to watch."

Her husband groaned. "Don't get involved. It's always trouble."

"I can't help it. Besides, I may need you to talk to your brother. He's cautious because Andi's a doctor. What's up with that?"

They walked into the kitchen. Zeke crossed to the refrigerator and pulled out two beers. He removed the tops from both and handed her a bottle. She settled on one of the stools and he leaned against the counter.

"I'd be worried if I were him, too," he said.

"Why? What does it matter?"

"She's smart." He shrugged. "She went to college and med school. He didn't. It's different."

"So? That gives them something to talk about."

"She probably makes as much as him, maybe more. Some guys have trouble with that."

"Then they're idiots. I did better than you some years. Were you bothered?"

"No, but that's different."

"Why?"

"I don't know. It was. You're an artist. You can't help being talented."

"But Andi chose to be a doctor?"

"Maybe. I don't know. It's just different. I'm not saying it wouldn't work, but it's something Wade's going to have to think through. We're raised to believe we provide for our family. What if you're not needed? Then what's the point?"

She stared at him. "Wanting to be married doesn't have to be about financial support. What about love and commitment? Can't that be enough?"

"Because most guys are so good at talking about their feelings? It's easier to provide a paycheck."

"Is this before or after you grab me by my hair and drag me back to your cave?"

He smiled at her. "Do I have to decide?"

Their gazes locked. She felt the slight uptick in tension between them, and her body responded. Longing swept through her.

Before Liam's death, she would have acted without a second thought. She would have put down her beer, walked around the counter and kissed him. He would have kissed her back and in a matter of seconds they would have started making love. There had been countless late afternoons they'd made love right in this kitchen. As it was, she couldn't remember the last time they'd been intimate.

She missed the sexual compatibility she and Zeke had always taken for granted. Now that it was lost, she wasn't sure how to get it back. She didn't know why he wasn't able to perform and didn't know who to ask about the problem. For reasons she couldn't articulate, they never discussed it with each other, either. Maybe it was because she didn't allow herself to feel emotions and he drank until his drowned.

Even as she wondered if she should approach him, his gaze slid from hers and the mood in the room shifted to something more neutral.

"I should probably go next door in the next day or so and see how things are going," he said. "Wade mentioned the cabinets had been delivered and that they were going to start laying floors."

"That'll be loud."

"Lucky for Andi, she works all day."

Boston ran her fingers up and down the side of the bottle. "Zeke, do you…" She paused, not sure what she was going to say. How to tell him she missed making love with him.

As she struggled to find the words, he waited. His shoulders stiffened, as if he had to brace himself for a blow. Defiance battled in his eyes, and his mouth straightened.

"I've been working on something," she said, admitting defeat and taking the easier path. "I didn't want to say anything because I wasn't sure I could do it, but I've nearly pulled it all together and, well, why don't you come see?"

She stood and walked toward her studio. He followed.

The pictures of Liam still dominated the room, but there were large pieces of paper tacked up, as well. Jungle images with a grinning jaguar and happy monkeys. Different kinds of leaves in a rainbow of greens filled several sheets, and there were at least five kinds of butterflies fluttering against a blue sky.

The bright, primary colors radiated energy. She'd avoided any muted tones, so that even on the darkest day, the mural would draw attention and distract young patients from any fears.

Her husband stared in wide-eyed amazement. His shock was so complete that she had to laugh.

"What?"

"You did this." He looked at her. "You did this, Boston."

He sounded thrilled and relieved, making her wonder how worried he'd been. She shrugged.

"Andi asked me to paint a mural in her office. Actually I think it might have been my idea, but she agreed. I know it's not real work, but I'm trying."

He smiled at her. "It's great. The kids are going to love it. I like the monkeys."

"They're very happy."

"They're going to be trouble. You can see it in their eyes."

She laughed. "I hope so."

He held out his arm. She stepped into his embrace. Her hands settled on his back and she instinctively raised her head for his kiss. His mouth moved against hers.

She closed her eyes and let herself be swept away. They'd done this a million times before. It was easy. They just had to remember how much they loved each other and how good it felt.

She reached for his hand and drew it to her breast. When his fingers brushed against her tight nipple, her breath caught in her throat. She slid her hand down his belly to his groin and rubbed her palm against his penis. But before she could begin the second stroke, he moved away.

The rejection was as stinging as it was complete.

"I'm going to go next door and check on the progress," he said. "Congratulations on the mural."

Then he was gone.

Boston stood alone in her studio. Her body still buzzed with sexual arousal, but her heart grew heavy in her chest. The truth she'd been avoiding for so long now seemed unavoidable.

She and Zeke had both chosen not to feel their grief. He coped with drinking and she'd lost herself in her painting. She'd known there were problems but had assumed they would come out the other side together. Because they'd always been together.

But while she'd taken the first painful step on the road

to being better, Zeke had not. They were out of sync and for the first time she began to wonder if they would ever find their way back to each other.

Fifteen

A good kissing could carry a woman for a while, Andi realized the next morning when her body was still doing the internal happy dance and she found herself wanting to break into spontaneous song. So far she'd limited the latter to her shower that morning, but she knew she would have to monitor herself closely. Most parents preferred their children's doctor to be serious and attentive. Not lost in daydreams and humming pop tunes.

Still, she was one happy camper. The brief kiss had made her wonder what taking things to the next level would be like. Sex with Matt had been adequate but far from inspiring. Just once in her life, Andi would like to be swept away by passion.

She grinned as she completed a file. Okay, maybe not just once. At least twice for sure.

Nina knocked on the open door, a file in her hand. Her eyebrows were drawn together in a look of concern. "We have a walk-in. Madison Phillips. She's twelve."

Andi nodded. "I know her. Rather I've met her mom and her sisters. She lives next to me."

"Right. Deanna has a permission-to-treat form on file,

so you can see her without calling, which seems to be an issue with Madison. She wants to talk to you without you contacting her mom first."

That was never happy news, Andi thought. She logged out of her computer and stood. "Okay. Let's go find out what the problem is."

There were generally only a few reasons a girl wanted to talk to her doctor without her parents knowing, and none of them were good. Twelve, Andi thought, hoping the girl wasn't pregnant. Although it was physically possible, it was never healthy for a child that age to be having sex. A supportive family was a must, and Andi's few encounters with Deanna didn't give her a lot of hope for that.

She took the file from Nina.

"Room two," her nurse said.

"Thanks."

Andi scanned the file. Madison had been treated for the usual kid stuff. Bronchitis, a sprained wrist. The rest of her visits had been for vaccinations and wellness certificates for trips or activities.

She closed the file and tapped on the door, then walked in.

"Hi, Madison," she said with a smile. "I'm Andi Gordon."

Madison looked like a slightly older version of her sisters. The long, pale blond hair and big blue eyes. She was pretty with coltish long legs and thin arms. Her mouth started to curve up in a smile, but didn't quite make it.

"Hi, Dr. Gordon."

Andi pulled up a stool and settled on it. She dropped the file onto the counter and prepared to listen. "You can call me Andi."

"Thanks." Madison glanced around the room. "Lucy

talks about you a lot. So do the twins. They say you're really nice. Carrie likes you, too." She looked at Andi, then away. "She's my best friend."

"Oh, right. Wade's daughter. Carrie's great." Andi's stomach twisted into a knot. If Madison was having sex, Carrie might be, as well. Oh, God, that was so not a conversation she wanted to have with Wade.

Madison cleared her throat for a second time. "Thank you for seeing me. I know I didn't have an appointment." She paused. "I'm supposed to be at a friend's house."

"I'm glad you stopped by." She kept her posture relaxed, determined to let the girl speak in her own time.

Madison stared at her hands. Finally she raised her head and drew in a breath.

"I got my period. It's my first time and I didn't know if I was supposed to tell anyone. Carrie said I should, and I thought of you."

Andi did her best to keep her expression from giving away the relief that flooded her. A period was easy. A normal part of growing up. Although shouldn't Madison be having this conversation with her mother?

Andi smile gently. "How are you feeling? Any cramping?"

"A little. I think. I just feel kind of weird, you know?"

"I do, believe me. Okay, I'm going to give you a quick recap on what's happening with your body right now and what you can expect to continue to happen. You probably won't get regular periods for a few months. Your body has to settle in to this stage of your development."

She talked briefly about the changes Madison could expect and how to manage the symptoms.

"You need supplies," she said. "Do you have those?"

Madison shook her head. "I took a few things from my mom's bathroom."

Andi glanced at her watch. "Okay. We'll go to the drugstore and get you what you need."

"I don't want to use tampons," Madison said quickly. "Not yet."

"That's fine. When you're ready we can talk about them. They're easy and safe, as long as you follow the directions." She paused. "You know, this is the sort of thing you might want to talk to your mom about."

Madison's expression hardened. "No, thanks," she said quickly. "I don't want her to know."

Andi's radar went on alert. "Is there anything I should know about how she treats you?"

"She's horrible. Selfish. She has a lot of rules that are so unfair. Sometimes I think she's sorry she had us. If we weren't around, she could have a perfect house and not have to worry we were going to mess up."

Madison bit her lower lip. "Sometimes my dad gets so sad. I've seen him look at her as if he can't figure out why she's not happy with him. She's always telling him what to do and then complaining he's doing it wrong. I wish he'd leave her and take us with him."

Madison's eyes filled with tears. "She's so mean. Last night the twins asked for ice cream and she just started screaming."

Andi knew there was a thin line between a parent losing it on occasion and crossing into emotional abuse. As a doctor, she was responsible for the safety of her patients. She also knew the danger of overreacting, reporting something that didn't exist and ripping a family apart.

She'd spent time with Lucy and the twins. None of

them had shown any signs of serious trouble at home. The girls were friendly and open, imaginative and stable.

Madison was smack in the middle of puberty and experiencing her first real hormone rush. That would make anyone emotional. Were Deanna's actions those of a woman who wasn't naturally warm or were they something more destructive?

"I'm sorry you're not comfortable talking about this with your mom," Andi told her. "As your doctor, I need her to know what's happening with you."

Madison crossed her arms in front of her chest. "I don't want to talk about it with her."

"I'll tell her that. I hope she'll respect your request, but I can't guarantee it. Madison, do you feel safe at home?"

Madison was quiet for several seconds. "I know what you're asking. It's not like that. She doesn't hit us. It's different."

"Okay. If you ever don't feel safe, come tell me, okay?"

Madison nodded.

"Then I guess we're going to the drugstore to buy you supplies." She stood. "Hmm, I'm thinking after that, we'll need to go to Starbucks. How does that sound?"

"Good." Madison rose. "Thank you. Carrie was right. You're really easy to talk to."

The preteen flung herself at Andi and hung on tight.

Andi was not looking forward to having any kind of conversation with Deanna. Her brief encounters with the other woman hadn't been exactly warm and fuzzy. Plus, the gossip at her staff lunch hadn't done much to make her anything but nervous.

She tried to convince herself to put off the conversation, but knew that was a bad idea. She wasn't going to talk to Deanna as a concerned neighbor, but as her daughter's doctor. This was important and her personal apprehension couldn't get in the way.

Fortunately her last appointment ended early and she was able to duck out at four. She drove home and went directly to Deanna's before she could talk herself out of it or get distracted by wishing for another kissing encounter with Wade.

She reached the front porch and pressed the bell. A few seconds later, Deanna opened the door.

"Hi, Deanna," Andi said. "I wondered if you had a minute."

Her neighbor stared at her for a second, as if trying to place her.

"I'm Andi Gordon," Andi said, and pointed to her house. "I live there. I'm the pediatrician."

"Of course," Deanna said, stepping back and motioning for her to enter. "Sorry. I've been distracted lately. Come in, please."

Deanna was as well dressed as she had been the last time Andi had seen her. The dark blue twin set was the same color as her eyes. Tailored khakis showed off her slim hips and long legs. She had on makeup, gold hoops and even lipstick. Andi felt disheveled by comparison. Her clothes were wrinkled from a day at work, and she was pretty sure her mascara had migrated to under her eyes, giving her that attractive raccoon look.

Deanna led her into a living room furnished in beautiful antiques. The tables were delicate, the fabrics traditional. Andi would guess the room looked much as it had a hundred years ago. She thought of her makeshift attic living space and the brightly colored mural Boston would be painting for her and knew she and Deanna had virtually nothing in common.

Andi settled on a small settee and tried to smile. There was no easy way to start this conversation.

Deanna sat across from her, perching on the edge of a chair, waiting expectantly. Andi drew in a breath.

"Madison came in to see me today," she said, then held up a hand. "Everything is fine. I don't want you to worry. But I do need to speak to you about something."

"All right." Deanna frowned. "You treated her?"

"No, although there is a permission-to-treat form on file. I actually just spoke with her. She had some concerns." Andi leaned forward. "Madison started her period a couple of days ago. She felt she had to talk to an adult, which is why she came to me. I went over all the basics with her and got her set up with supplies."

Deanna stared at her. "I don't understand. You're telling me that my daughter got her first period and told you rather than me?"

Her voice was low and strained, the words clipped.

Andi nodded. Her gaze dropped to Deanna's tightly grasped hands. To fingers that were chapped to the point of being raw. The flaking, angry-looking skin was at odds with the rest of Deanna's perfect appearance.

Not an issue for this second, Andi told herself.

"I felt it was important for you to know what's going on with your daughter. And I wanted to offer my support if—"

Deanna sprang to her feet. Her face flushed and her eyes hardened.

"How dare you come here like this! Who do you think you are? You had no right. You should have sent her home to me. She's my child. Mine. Not yours. I don't know what your problem is, but you're going to get out right now."

Andi stood. "Deanna, I wasn't trying to take anything from you. That's why I'm here. So we can talk about it."

"Talk about it?" Her lips curled into a sneer. "When it's too late? Is this what you do? Fill your pathetic, empty life with other people's children?" Her voice rose. "You got in the middle of something that doesn't involve you. You never had my permission to talk to her about her period. To be a part of that rite of passage. You overstepped your bounds, Doctor."

She stalked to the door and held it open. "You need to leave."

"I'm sorry," Andi said, walking past her. "Deanna, please, there's a bigger problem."

"Don't tell me how to raise my children. Don't tell me what's wrong. You don't know anything."

The last words were delivered in a scream. Andi felt her face get hot. Her stomach twisted and her hands were shaking. She hurried down the stairs, eager to get away before she did something really stupid like starting to cry.

When she reached the sidewalk, she turned toward her house, but realized she didn't want to go inside. What if someone had heard the screaming? She couldn't explain what had happened—as Madison's doctor, she couldn't discuss it with anyone but the girl's parents.

She stood on the sidewalk wondering why it had to be like this. Every time she started to think she could fit in, something happened to mess her up. Was the universe sending her a message? Should she simply admit defeat and pack her bags?

She knew the answer before she finished asking the question, but everyone needed a few moments of self-pity now and then. The trick was how to keep it from becoming a lifestyle choice.

Not knowing where else to go, she started for her house. Maybe she could slip upstairs without being seen. But before she reached it, Boston stepped out of her front door and motioned her over.

"Do I want to ask?" the redhead asked as she approached.

Andi sighed. "One of Deanna's kids came by to talk to me today. I was filling her in on the details."

"She obviously didn't like what you were saying."

"Not really."

Boston touched her arm. "You're trembling."

"I'm not good at confrontation."

Boston surprised her by hugging her. Strong arms held her for several seconds. Andi hugged her back, appreciating the show of support.

When Boston stepped away, she smiled. "Normally I'm a big believer in the power of tea, but right now I think a glass of wine is the better option. What do you think?"

Andi dropped her purse on the small table in the entryway and followed her into the kitchen. "Wine sounds perfect."

Deanna leaned against the closed front door of her house. She pressed a hand to her stomach to stop the roiling of bile and the small quarter sandwich she'd managed to get down at lunch. Hatred burned in her throat, the bitterness of it nearly making her gag.

That bitch, she thought viciously. *That raging bitch. So sanctimonious, so sure she knew everything. All smug with her education and her job. Bitch, bitch, bitch.*

But the pain deep in her heart had nothing to do with

Andi and everything to do with the news she'd delivered.
There was no escaping it. Madison really did hate her,
Deanna thought, barely able to grasp the truth, let alone
accept it. This wasn't teenaged rebellion or a stage. It was
loathing. The kind Deanna had felt for her own mother.

What she didn't know was why it had happened.
Where had her sweet baby girl gone? When had everything changed? Until a couple of years ago, she and Madison had been so close. It had always been the two of
them, working as a team. Madison had helped with the
younger girls, staying close, wanting to be a part of the
family. Now all that was gone.

Deanna drew in a breath. She glanced out the window
and saw Andi speaking with Boston. The two women
went into Boston's house. No doubt they were going to
talk about her. About what a shitty mother she was. How
her own daughter couldn't bring herself to share anything
intimate with her.

Madison had gotten her period and didn't want her to
know. How could that be?

The walls of the house seemed to move in on her. She
felt the familiar sense of urgency and knew that if she
gave in, if she walked into the bathroom and turned on
the water, she might never stop. She thought about driving away and not coming back. She thought about walking into traffic and letting the problem solve itself.

Instead she turned to the stairs. "Madison," she called.

She heard a heavy sigh and then, "Yes?"

"I have to run next door. Please look after your sisters."

Normally her oldest objected to taking care of her sisters. But instead of complaining, Madison simply said,
"Okay."

Deanna wondered if her complacence had anything

to do with guilt. She could only hope the girl still had enough caring left that guilt was possible.

She walked out of her house and started down the sidewalk. When she reached Boston's porch, she hesitated a second, before firmly ringing the bell. She heard footsteps, and then the door opened.

Under other circumstances, Boston's wide-eyed shock would have been comical. As it was, her neighbor's expression confirmed Deanna's worst fears. Everyone knew her daughter hated her and knew she was to blame.

"I need to talk to you," Deanna said. "I know Andi's here. I need to talk to her, too."

Boston held open the door and pointed to the rear of the house. Deanna walked down the long hallway, ignoring the fairies, the hideous color choices and telling herself she would get through this. That she would find a way and then she would stop feeling so afraid all the time.

In the kitchen, Andi sat at the counter. There were two glasses of wine, a plate of cheese and an open box of water crackers. When Deanna walked into the room, Andi's expression mirrored Boston's.

"Don't worry," Deanna told her. "I didn't come armed."

"Good to know."

Boston pulled out a stool. Deanna slumped onto it and then took the offered glass of wine. She gulped about half of it before sucking in a breath and wondering why they were both so blurry.

She touched her cheek with her free hand and felt the tears, then set down the glass and started to cry in earnest.

Harsh, ugly sobs choked her, making her gasp as her chest heaved. She struggled to stop, but couldn't. Embarrassment joined pain until she was nothing but a wound, bleeding and infected.

Tissues were pushed into her hand. She felt reassuring touches on her shoulder. Andi said something and Boston disappeared for a few seconds, then returned with a washcloth. She wet it and pressed it to the back of Deanna's neck.

Deanna had no idea how long she cried. The sobs slowed, then became hiccups. She was able to catch her breath and blow her nose. The pile of tissues grew as she wiped her face. Andi turned the cloth over, putting the cool side against her skin, then lightly held her wrist.

"I'm not having a stroke," Deanna said. "I'm fine."

"I'm not a doctor and even I can tell that's not true," Boston told her. She pushed the glass of wine closer. "Have some more. I think you need it."

Deanna tried to pick up the glass, but her fingers were shaking too much. Then she noticed her raw skin and tucked her hands under the counter.

Boston settled on a stool on the kitchen side of the counter. Andi took her seat next to Deanna. They were both watching her cautiously.

"I'm okay," Deanna said, then decided she didn't care enough to hide her hands and reached for her wine again. This time she managed to sip from the glass.

"Actually I'm not okay," she admitted. "Everything is wrong. Colin cheated."

The other women glanced at each other, then back at her. Deanna shook her head.

"No," she said quickly. "He didn't. I don't even know why I said that." She paused. "That's not true, either. I do know why. Because if he cheated, then nothing is my fault, right? He's the bad guy, I'm the victim and I win. How sad is that? How sad is it that I want my husband to have had an affair because then none of this would be my fault?"

Boston squeezed her forearm, but didn't speak.

Deanna looked at each of them. "They hate me. Colin, the girls. Madison, especially." She turned to Andi. "That's why she didn't want to tell me." She felt tears swimming in her eyes. "She didn't want to share that with me. I don't know if it was about keeping it to herself or punishing me. Either way, I get her point. She looks at me the way I used to look at my mother. But I don't understand why. I'm nothing like her."

Boston continued to hang on, her fingers moving against Deanna's arm. The touch was oddly comforting. For the first time in weeks, Deanna no longer felt completely alone.

"I take care of them," she continued. "I cook and clean and Colin tells me I'm rigid and controlling. He says he thinks I don't love him and I like his paycheck a lot more than him. That he only gets in the way. Madison says I'm more concerned with how things look than how they are. That I want everything perfect." She swallowed. "I do want perfect. I want my life clean and nice. Why is that so bad? Why don't they understand?"

She finished her wine. "My mom drank and there wasn't any food in the house and she locked me in the closet and I swore I would be different. That my children would never be hungry or embarrassed or afraid. Then they look at me the way I looked at my mom and I don't know what I'm doing wrong." She paused to breathe in what she'd been avoiding for weeks. "But the worst part is that I think maybe all the stuff they say about me might be true."

* * *

Andi could see the emotional cracks in Deanna without even looking very hard. For once, her neighbor was mussed, her face blotchy and swollen, her shoulders slumped. She was human and hurting, and in her pain, Andi felt empathy.

"Madison's confused by a lot of things right now," she said gently. "When parents are fighting, the kids get scared. That makes them act out."

"I don't want them to be afraid. I just want them to…" Deanna shook her head. "I guess I don't know anymore. What I want, I mean. I would say I want what we had before, but not if everyone thinks I'm horrible. I just wanted things to be nice."

"You can be a little intense," Boston told her. "I know it's your way of staying in control, but there are consequences to being so rigid."

Deanna stared at her. "I don't know how to be any other way."

Boston smiled unexpectedly. "None of us do. That's the point of life. Haven't you figured that out yet? All of this—" She motioned to her kitchen. "It's a facade to keep the demons at bay. Some of us are better at faking it than others, but we all have our issues."

Deanna looked at Andi. "You don't. Look at you. You're so beautiful and a doctor."

If Andi had been drinking, she would have choked. "I'm the screwup in my family. My mother's disappointed that I'm not a pediatric neurosurgeon or doing cutting-edge research. I just found out my sister's research group is on the short list for a Nobel Prize. I dated a guy for ten years who finally proposed. He left me standing at the altar, literally. We had three hundred guests, including his mother, and he didn't bother to show up. Later, when we finally talked, he said he wasn't sure and needed more time. Two weeks later, he ran off with his secretary. To make matters worse, I just recently figured out he was always trying to change me and even though I resisted, I never called him on it. Now I'm not sure I ever loved him at all."

Andi refilled her glass. "You can't make that shit up."

Boston drew in a breath. "I can't work. I haven't painted anything decent since Liam died." She turned to Andi. "That mural project is the most I've been able to do." She turned back to Deanna. "I haven't cried, either. Not once. I can't. Maybe I don't want to. Maybe if I finally cry, I'll have to admit he's really gone."

Deanna put her elbow on the table and raised her glass. "I guess this means we're all completely screwed up, doesn't it?"

Sixteen

By the following Monday afternoon, Andi was still feeling pretty good about her encounter with Deanna and Boston, and she was a whole lot happier with her decision to move to the neighborhood. It was comforting to know that everyone was completely messed up nearly all the time. That she wasn't the only one trying to figure out how to fake her way through the tough stuff.

Knowing what Deanna was going through put her actions in a different perspective. History defined a person, and from the little she'd shared, Deanna was dealing with more than most. Andi could feel sympathy for both her and her daughter. Madison only saw the results of old patterns. Andi hoped the two of them could find a way to break through and really connect.

She parked in front of her house and walked inside. Instead of battered subflooring, gleaming hardwood reflected the bright afternoon sun.

Wade walked toward her.

"I'm desperately in love," she said, reaching down to run her hand over the smooth surface. "It's beautiful."

"It'll be better when it's finished. We're going to have

to cover them to protect them while we complete the rest of the work, but I wanted you to see them."

She stood and sighed. "I have floors. Like a real person."

He chuckled. "You're easy to please."

"Which is different than being easy. Just so you're clear on that."

"I am clear." He glanced over his shoulder, as if making sure they were alone. "Which brings me to our other topic. About before. The kiss."

The kiss she'd been dreaming about for the past four nights? The kiss that had left her breathless and purring? That kiss?

"Do I need to apologize?" he asked.

"Did you want to?"

"No, but you're a doctor."

She tilted her head. "What does that have to do with anything? Do you think doctors take a no-kissing oath?"

He shifted his weight. The movement was subtle, but just enough to make her wonder if he was nervous. Wade? Nervous around her? It didn't seem possible, but she could read the signs.

"I'm a contractor."

"Yes. I know. That's why I hired you to fix up my house. It would be so awkward if you were an accountant."

"You don't see a problem with our career choices?"

"Not if you like what you do for a living. I happen to enjoy being a doctor."

She studied him. "I'm genuinely confused by this line of conversation. The doctor thing shouldn't be an issue. All that studying of anatomy means we know things. Isn't that kind of intriguing?"

He gave her a slow, sexy grin. One that made her usually sensible toes curl. "I hadn't thought of it that way."

It occurred to her that her mouth was writing checks her girl parts might not be able to cash, but that was a problem for another day.

"You're happy with the floors?" he asked.

"Very."

"And the kissing."

"That, too."

His dark eyes twinkled with amusement. "Want to do it again sometime?"

"I could be persuaded."

"How about dinner?"

"I could do that, too."

"Carrie has some school stuff going on over the next week, but right after that?"

"That sounds great."

Deanna carried the load of laundry into the bedroom and tossed it on the bed. Since her breakdown last week, she'd alternated between feeling slightly more hopeful and knowing if she disappeared tomorrow, no one would miss her. The constant mental back-and-forth wasn't restful, but it beat being miserable all the time.

She started folding the pile of towels, even as she wondered why she bothered. Her kids hardly cared that the linen closet was organized and color-coordinated, and she suspected Colin could use the same towel for weeks without noticing. No one noticed the effort she went to, and it was—

Deanna dropped the towel back on the bed and walked out of the bedroom. Once in the hall, she pulled open the door of the linen closet and stared at the neat stacks. They didn't notice. They didn't care. So who was she doing this for? Why did she take all the time and make the effort? If it was for herself, if it made her feel better, then fine. But if she was doing it to get credit, no wonder she was always disappointed.

She stood in the center of the hallway, half expecting a choir to start singing. Isn't that what happens in movies when characters have an epiphany? At the very least, there could be elevator music.

She started down the stairs. Lucy was on her way up.

"Honey, can you watch your sisters for a couple of minutes? I need to go ask Boston a question."

Lucy stared at her. "Me?"

"Sure. You're responsible and the twins are playing together. The three of you have played outside alone for hours. I think this is the next step. Come next door if anything happens, okay?"

Lucy grinned. "I can do it, Mom. I'll watch them."

"Good girl."

Deanna headed out her front door and hurried along the sidewalk. She raced up the porch stairs to Boston's house and rang the bell.

"I'm being a pain," she began when the other woman opened the door. "I know. But I need to ask you something."

Boston invited her in. "You're not being a pain."

"I'm showing up without an invitation. I would consider that being a pain." She paused, not sure how to ask the question delicately. Then figured this woman had seen her with snot pouring out of her nose. She didn't have much left in the way of pride.

"Do you think it's possible for me to seduce Colin

back? We haven't slept together in months. I'm not sure he still wants me, but I don't know what else to do."

She immediately wanted to call the words back, but was determined to stand her ground.

Boston's expression shifted from concern to surprise to something Deanna couldn't read.

"I'm not the right person to give you an answer," Boston told her.

"Sure you are. You've been with the same guy since you were what, twelve?"

"Fifteen."

"You're blissfully happy. I see you hugging and kissing all the time." What she didn't mention was how she generally found those PDAs annoying. Or she had. Now that she thought about the way Zeke looked at his wife, she felt a little envious. Had Colin ever looked at her that way?

Boston led her into the kitchen, where they each settled on a stool. "Is sex going to solve your problem?"

"I don't know. I'm not clear on what the problem is. I think it's that Colin doesn't like me very much. Or he thinks I don't like him."

"Do you like him? Are you happy in your marriage?"

"What's happy? I have responsibilities. I take care of them."

"Maybe he wants to be more than a responsibility."

Deanna did her best not to look impatient. This wasn't helping. There was no way she could get inside Colin's head and figure out anything. She wanted things back the way they had been. Which was exactly what he didn't want, she realized.

"He says I don't want him to be involved with the girls. That I need everything to be my way."

"Is that true?"

"Of course not."

Boston smiled at her. "Really?"

"Okay, I have my systems and it's annoying when he ignores them. There's a reason I fold the towels the way I do and fill the dishwasher with the plates facing the center. It's more efficient. It makes life easier later. I do my best to keep things organized and he drops in and messes it all up."

Deanna heard her own words and thought maybe they were part of the problem. But why did she have to be the one to change? Sex would be easier. If he was happy in bed, wouldn't he be happy everywhere else?

"He swears he's not sleeping with anyone else. So he's got to want to do it," she muttered. "I just don't know how to seduce him."

"How did you do it before?"

Deanna stared at her neighbor. "I don't understand the question."

"When things were good between you, how did you tell him you were interested?"

"I didn't."

Boston waited, silent, her green eyes dark with compassion. "Not ever?"

"No. He asked and I said yes." Most of the time. She glanced down at her hands, then wished she hadn't. "Some of the time." She glanced back at Boston. "Men are the ones who want it, so they should be the ones to ask."

"More rules."

Anger joined impatience. Why didn't people understand that rules were good? Rules showed a person where she stood. What the risk and dangers were and how to avoid them.

She stood. "I guess you don't have an answer."

"Everyone is different, Deanna. I'm not trying to be difficult, but there is no way I can know how to seduce your husband. If I did know, wouldn't that be a little scary?"

"I was looking for general information."

"Let him know you want him. Most men find being wanted a powerful aphrodisiac."

Which was its own problem, she thought as she left. She didn't really want to have sex with Colin. She wanted her life back. Still, she could do what had to be done and consider it a small price to pay for the ultimate goal. Maybe she could find some ideas on the internet.

Boston sat on the rocker, watching the sun slowly drift toward the horizon. It was nearly nine in the evening. The longest day of the year was only a few weeks away. Then the days would start to get short again. While she appreciated the beauty of fall, she didn't love the lack of sunlight. In the fall, the rains came. But until then, she basked like a cat on a windowsill.

Zeke lay stretched out on the grass. They'd had dinner on a blanket in their backyard and he'd yet to budge. His eyes were closed, one hand lay flat on his belly, the other held a beer. The air was still, the evening filled with the sounds of birds settling in for the night, a dog barking a few streets away, the sound of Deanna's girls playing in the front yard.

"How's the mural coming?" he asked.

"Good. I'll start painting in Andi's house next week."

"Looking forward to it or are you nervous?"

She smiled. "Both. I keep telling myself her patients won't be critical, and that helps." She pushed her bare foot against the grass to start the rocker moving. "I like Andi. She's dedicated and funny."

"We need to get more men on this street."

"What do you mean?"

"All three houses are owned by women. You and Deanna inherited your homes and Andi bought hers. Colin and I are outnumbered."

"That'll keep you in line."

"I'm a rebel at heart."

She laughed. "You've been with the same woman since you were seventeen. How exactly is this rebellious streak manifesting?"

"I haven't figured that out yet."

She watched him, enjoying the shape of his face, the curve of his shoulder. Back when they'd been younger, she'd done several portraits of Zeke nude. Because of his construction work, he showered when he got home. Sometimes, when she was in a playful mood, she put one of the nudes out in the bedroom. A not-so-subtle invitation. He would see it and then come find her. They would make love wherever she happened to be.

"Deanna and Colin are having troubles," she said quietly.

He groaned. "I don't want to know that."

"She wants to make things better."

"She's one scary lady."

"Why do you say that?"

"Everything has to be perfect with her. The house, the kids. Have you ever seen those girls in anything that didn't match? She won't let them watch regular TV."

"How do you know so much about her life?"

He turned his head and looked at her. "Carrie tells her

dad. Wade tells me." He frowned. "You've always disliked her. Why are you sounding sympathetic?"

"I didn't dislike her."

"Sure you did."

She drew in a breath. "I didn't exactly warm up to her before, but she's different than I thought. Vulnerable."

"Right. Just avoid the claws. She's the kind of woman who would go right for the soft underbelly. Or the dick."

"Does Colin think that about her, too?"

"I don't know. He and I don't talk. He's never around. The guy spends his life on the road. What's the point in having a family if you never see them?"

"Do you think he wants to leave her?"

Zeke groaned and closed his eyes. "Don't know, don't want to know."

His dismissal irritated her. "That's your style, isn't it? Avoid anything unpleasant."

He kept his eyes firmly closed. "Neither of us has the facts. What is there to discuss?"

She could think of a dozen things. Or just one. The one that was always with them, lurking. Rubbing at the edges of their lives like sandpaper. Leaving raw spots that never quite healed.

"You don't want to deal with your pain," she said softly.

"Neither do you."

"You drink."

"You paint." He opened his eyes and sat up. "At least I'm hiding from something. You're pretending there isn't anything at all. You get lost in your pictures of Liam. He's not coming back. He's never coming back. You can't paint him back to life any more than I can drink myself into forgetting."

"I want us to be different. I want us to talk."

He shook his head. "No, you don't. You want me to get over it. I'm trying. Every day, I'm dealing with my pain and yes, sometimes I drink to escape it. But it's there, with me always. Fix yourself, Boston. Then we'll worry about me."

She glared at him. "I'm trying, too. I'm doing the mural."

"Have you cried? Even once?"

"My lack of tears has nothing to do with how I feel."

"Right. Just like me being unable to get it up is unrelated. Face it, we're both broken."

"How do we fix it?"

"Hell if I know." He stood. "I'm going out."

To a bar. She rose and put her hands on her hips. "Don't you walk away from me."

"Why not? Neither of us is willing to be the first to bend. We're too afraid we're going to break."

"I'm bending."

"How?"

She opened her mouth, then closed it.

His gaze was steady. "Want to talk about how you felt when he died? How you screamed for help and there wasn't any? Want to talk about the way time didn't move right or how everyone said exactly the wrong thing at the funeral? Want to talk about the way—"

She raised her hands and pressed them against her ears. "Stop it! Just stop it. I don't want to talk about it anymore."

He nodded slowly, then walked past her. A minute later, she heard his truck start up, and then he drove away. She sat back down on the rocker and turned her face to the sun. There were no tears, she thought, pressing her hand to her stomach. There wasn't much of anything.

As had become their biweekly tradition, Andi and Dr. Harrington's staff went out to lunch at the Blackberry Island Inn.

"My daughter's pregnant," Laura announced after they'd placed their orders.

"Congratulations," Dawn said.

"That's great," Misty told her.

Andi and Nina agreed.

"Easy for you to say," Laura told them. "I'm too young to be a grandmother. And my daughter is only twenty-six."

"Weren't you younger than that when you had her?" Misty asked.

"Yes, but that was a different time. But she's excited and I guess I will be, too. She wants me to come stay with her for the first two weeks after the baby's born."

Laura sounded both proud and a little stunned.

"Where does she live?" Andi asked.

"Seattle. It's not far."

"It's nice that you're close." She couldn't imagine wanting her mother around after she had a baby. No doubt her mother would spend every second telling her what she was doing wrong.

Perhaps not the fairest assessment, she thought. Hers had never been the closest of families. Achievement was valued over emotional connections. From the outside, she would guess her family seemed successful. All doctors. Yet she couldn't remember the last time she and her sister had talked. She hadn't seen her brother in nearly ten years.

"Your mother still lives on the island, doesn't she?" Laura asked Nina.

"Oh, yes. My mom and her partner share a house." Nina's voice was a little strained. "They're interesting people."

"Is that shorthand for crazy?" Dawn asked.

"Sort of. The two of them were never poster children for responsibility. My mother defines flighty, but she has a good heart."

"Which left you to be the responsible one," Andi said, then wrinkled her nose. "Sorry. Every now and then those pesky psychology classes I had to take rear their ugly heads."

Nina laughed. "You're right. I do take care of her and everyone else. It's why I went into nursing. It's a natural fit for me. My mom wants to know when I'm going to get married again. One failed marriage is plenty. I'm not looking to take care of someone else, thank you very much."

Laura raised her glass of iced tea. "To our families. They make us insane and we still love them."

The four women touched glasses.

"How's work on the house coming?" Misty asked Andi.

"Progress is being made. I have floors and cabinets and the medical equipment gets installed in two weeks."

"We want to come see everything," Laura told her. "You should have a grand opening party."

"That's a great idea. I hadn't thought to do something like that."

"Make sure Wade is there." Laura winked. "Wearing tight jeans."

"Otherwise you're not coming?" Dawn asked.

"I'll still be there, but I won't be as happy." Laura leaned forward and lowered her voice. "Does he ever work shirtless? Please say yes. I'm going to be a grandmother and I need a little excitement in my life."

Andi thought about the kiss she and Wade had shared. One that, sadly, had yet to be repeated. Although they were still planning to go out. Just yesterday he'd confirmed their dinner date for Friday night.

"No shirtless working," she said.

"Bummer."

Before she could admit she and Wade were going on a date, a server appeared with their lunch. Then conversation shifted to the upcoming end of school and how hard it was to find good day care.

By one they were back at work. Andi went to check her schedule for the afternoon. Nina came into her office and closed the door.

"Can we talk for a second?"

"Sure." Andi motioned to the chair by her desk. "What's up?"

"I wondered if you'd made any decisions about staffing. You're going to need someone to run your office along with at least one nurse, maybe two."

"I know. I've been talking to an employment agency in the Seattle area. They specialize in medical office placements. I wasn't sure I could find anyone on the island. Unless you have some suggestions."

"I think you could find someone local to run the office. That's more managerial than medical. You could put an ad in the paper and do interviews yourself. I would be happy to help, let you know if the people you're talking to have any red flags in their past."

"I'd appreciate that."

Nina smiled briefly. "I would also be willing to come work for you, if you're interested. I like kids and I like how you are around them. Dr. Harrington is great, but I used to date his son and it will be awkward when he starts working here."

Andi leaned toward her. "I appreciate you letting me know. One of the things Dr. Harrington made clear when I came to work for him temporarily was that I couldn't poach any of his staff." She smiled. "He really used the word *poach*."

"That sounds like him." Nina shrugged. "He knows about me and Dylan. If you're interested in me working for you, I'll talk to him and get his okay. Trust me, Dylan doesn't want to be around me any more than I want to be around him."

"May I ask why?"

"We had a high school romance that went bad. We were engaged when he went off to college. His parents didn't approve. Not so much of me but because we were young. He discovered college girls were willing to put out and dumped me. It was all pretty humiliating. I got back at him by marrying the first guy who asked, which turned out to be a disaster. The rest is history."

"Don't take this wrong, but I'm really glad to hear I'm not the only one who picked a complete idiot to fall for."

Nina smiled. "You, too?"

"Oh, yeah. One night we'll go out for margaritas and I'll tell you the whole sad story."

"I look forward to hearing it."

Andi leaned toward her. "Nina, I would love for you to come work with me. You're great with the kids, organized and efficient. What's not to love? As long as Dr.

Harrington is okay with it, you're hired. We can talk about the details after I talk to him. How's that?"

"Wonderful. Thank you."

Nina rose and left. Andi wanted to jump out of her chair and do a little happy dance, but she contented herself with a chair wiggle and a silent one-handed high five. She had staff. Or at least the beginnings of a staff. Getting Nina was a huge coup. With a decent office manager and a couple of part-time nurses, she would have a real practice. One day she would even have a kitchen and then life would be pretty darned close to perfect.

Seventeen

Andi turned in front of the mirror, but couldn't see beyond her shoulders. First thing in the morning, she was going to check the plans for her master bath and make sure there was a full-length mirror somewhere. How was she supposed to fully obsess about her date when she couldn't see how she looked? A dating woman had needs, and seeing herself in a mirror was a big one.

She checked the digital clock by the bed and saw she had less than ten minutes until Wade was due to arrive. Which meant changing her mind again about what to wear was no longer practical. It wasn't as if she had forty-seven choices, either. Apparently there was a whole first-date-clothing protocol that she'd completely forgotten. Because from the second she'd stepped out of the shower over an hour ago until right this second, she hadn't been able to decide what to wear.

Jeans seemed too casual, trousers were too worklike, which left either a skirt or a dress. She wasn't really a skirt person. It came from her boyish hips. Dresses never hung right, so her selection was pathetically limited. She certainly didn't own anything remotely sexy.

She'd settled on a polyester wrap dress that felt like silk and didn't wrinkle. It was her all-purpose little black dress. Without the sexy, unfortunately. Then she'd decided the dress was too formal for a place like Blackberry Island. Plus, she looked as if she were going to a funeral. So she'd pulled out a purple cotton dress that was maybe twelve years old, but still pretty cute. It had capped sleeves, which she was probably too old for, but Wade didn't strike her as a fashionista, so he wouldn't know.

The scooped neck was nearly low enough to be flirty and she'd put on her best push-up bra to make the most of what she had. The slightly full skirt of the dress made it seem as though she had hips, which was nice.

"Forget it," she told herself, turning away from the mirror. Wade had seen her in shorts and a T-shirt more than once. He had a fair idea of what her body looked like. If he was only turned on by women with Scarlet Johansson–esque curves, he wouldn't have asked her out in the first place.

"I'm going to throw up," she muttered, pressing her hand to her stomach. "I should have dated more."

Not exactly practical advice, considering that she'd been in a committed relationship for over a decade, but true nonetheless. Going out with Wade? What had she been thinking? She didn't know how to act or what to say.

She gave her closet one more hate stare, then headed down the stairs. No matter what, sometime in the next couple of weeks, she was going to get her ass to Seattle and buy some new clothes. Fun, age-appropriate clothes she felt good in. She would go to a little boutique and put herself into the fashion-forward hands of one of the salespeople.

She'd reached the main level of her house only to

realize the whole place was under construction. There were tarps and cabinets everywhere. Tools sat on top of plastic-covered furniture. Pencil from the outline of Boston's mural covered the walls.

There was nowhere to sit, nowhere to have a casual conversation before heading out on a date. She also hadn't thought to provide drinks or appetizers. There were a couple of bottles of red wine upstairs, but where was she supposed to put them? Or glasses? And inviting Wade up to her makeshift attic living quarters seemed a little too weird.

"I can't do this," she murmured, even as she heard footsteps on the porch.

She walked to the front door and pulled it open before he could knock.

"I'm not very good at dating," she blurted, then winced. "Just so you don't expect this to go well."

Wade stood on her porch and looked at her. His not speaking gave her a second to take in the dark-washed jeans, cream-colored shirt and surprisingly nice loafers.

He looked good, she thought with appreciation. Sexy and masculine. He smelled good, too. All clean soap and temptation.

One corner of his mouth turned up. "You might want to try something more conventional. Hello works well. At least it always has for me."

She hung her head. "Kill me now."

"Not my style." He stepped into the house. "I like what you've done with the place."

She laughed as she shut the door behind him. "Do you? I have a great contractor. Want his name?"

He moved in front of her and put his hands on her

upper arms. "A guy, huh? I hear stories about women and their contractors. Any of them true?"

His thumbs moved against her skin. Just a slow up-and-down rubbing that shouldn't have been all that interesting, yet was. She found herself getting lost in his dark eyes.

"Not yet," she whispered, "but I have high hopes."

"Me, too."

He leaned in and kissed her. His mouth was firm, yet gentle, teasing even as he claimed her. Her arms came up and around his neck. His hands slipped to her waist. She took a step closer so she was pressing against him from shoulder to thigh.

She tilted her head. When she felt the light caress of his tongue on her bottom lip, she parted her lips for him. He deepened the kiss, and she met him touch for touch, sinking into the liquid arousal washing through her. Hunger burned, making her breasts tingle and ache. She wanted him touching her everywhere. Then she wanted to feel him inside her.

He shifted so he could kiss her cheek; then he pressed his lips to her jaw.

"I made reservations," he murmured. "For dinner."

"Okay." She was having trouble catching her breath, which made speaking difficult. "Dinner would be great."

He kissed along the side of her neck, then licked the sensitive skin behind her ear. She shuddered as her thighs began to tremble.

"We should, uh, probably get going," he said, before nibbling on her earlobe.

She gasped and arched against him. Her belly came in contact with something very hard and very thick. Her eyes flew open and he straightened. They stared at each other.

"Do I need to apologize?" he asked.

For having an erection? In her sadly chaste world, it was practically a miracle.

She shook her head.

There were a thousand reasons to smile politely and suggest they head out for their dinner. With Matt, sex had always been if not scheduled, then at least regulated. He didn't believe in spontaneous encounters or skipping dinner to get right to dessert. That was the world she knew.

There was also the possibility that Wade really had just wanted to go to dinner and that assuming anything else would lead to a new level of humiliation. But Andi suddenly realized she'd spent her whole life playing it safe. Buying this house had been her first really impulsive act. Maybe it was time to keep the trend going.

"Dinner would be very nice," she said, aware she was jumping off a cliff. She could only hope to find a nice soft net below, instead of jagged rocks and certain death. "Or we could go upstairs."

"What's upstairs?"

"My bed and condoms."

Something hot flared in Wade's eyes. He gave her a slow, sexy smile. "Lead the way."

There was no way she could do this, Deanna thought. It was impossible. Ridiculous. It was also all she could think of as a solution. Men liked sex. She had the working parts. As far as she knew, Colin hadn't been with anyone else. Surely he would be interested. If she could just get him back into bed, everything else would work itself out. At least that was her plan. She tried not to think about the disaster the dollhouse incident had been. Even though she'd replaced the broken one with a new, shiny house, the twins still flinched whenever she got too close to their toys.

She showered and shaved her legs, then went through her underwear drawer. She had a couple of thongs she never bothered to wear because they were too uncomfortable, but desperate times and all that. One blue-and-white pair had a matching bra. She'd never worn either, mostly because they were too trashy. As she fingered the lace, she thought maybe Colin had given them to her as a present.

She tossed both on the bed, then knelt on the carpet and pulled out the under-bed storage container on her side. After unzipping the top, she peeled it back and studied the contents. Mostly she saw her winter sweaters. The thick, heavy ones she put away for the season. But there was also a fair amount of lingerie. Short, sexy nightgowns, a couple of camisole sets with tap pants. A teddy. Most never worn, several with tags in place. All from Colin.

She'd meant what she'd told Boston earlier that day. She never initiated sex. If Colin asked, she mostly said yes. Well, some of the time. At least half. Lately he'd been asking less and less. She'd been too busy to notice. Or maybe she'd been gratful because sex with her husband confused her.

He was a patient lover, she thought, sitting on the carpet, staring at the pastel rainbow of silk and satin. Or he had been. While he hadn't been her first time, he'd been her first orgasm. She'd resisted letting him touch her "down there" and had claimed she would die if he ever tried to use his mouth. But he'd kept at her, gently teasing and touching until the magic of what he could do to her body had seduced her into giving in.

She remembered the first time she'd climaxed, mostly because afterward she'd felt exposed and terrified. She'd cried and he'd held her until she was still. Then he'd made love to her again and had told her that he loved her.

She'd wanted more, she remembered. She'd wanted the sensations they created together, even as she'd resisted the emotional intimacy that came with the act. Afraid to be that vulnerable, she'd withdrawn little by little. After a while she figured out that the less she participated, the less she wanted to. It was as if that part of her grew rusty with disuse. In an effort to keep herself safe, she'd guided their sex life to be about him.

He'd needed more, she thought, remembering him asking if she wanted him at all or if it was always going to be only about him. She'd dismissed the question because she was busy. A young mother with two children, then three, then five. Who had time for sex, let alone any interest? She was run ragged with the demands of her family.

What she hadn't admitted, even to herself, was that she'd chosen to withdraw. Because not connecting was so much safer than exposing herself. It wasn't the body part she worried about—it was her soul. What if Colin was able to see how damaged she was? So she kept herself safe, but at what price?

She tucked the lingerie back in the storage container. After zipping the canvas closed, she pushed everything back under the bed. But out of sight was not out of mind, she thought as she walked into the bathroom.

She put on the fancy bra and matching thong, then went into her closet. She pulled on a sleeveless dress with a plunging neckline. One that zipped down the back and would easily fall to the floor. Then, before she could stop herself, she walked out into the hallway.

It was nearly ten. All the girls except Madison and Carrie were asleep. The house was quiet. Deanna knew her oldest and her friend would stay in her room until the morning, and her girls slept deeply. So it was nearly like being alone.

She went down the stairs, her bare feet not making any sound. She paused outside Colin's study, then tapped once and went inside.

Her husband sat on the sofa, reading. His hair was mussed and the reading glasses he'd started using the previous year were perched on his nose. He'd changed into jeans and a T-shirt when he'd gotten home earlier that evening. His feet were bare.

He looked good, she thought in mild surprise. Younger than his nearly forty-years. Sexy. They'd both stayed in shape.

She tried to look at him as other women would. Not as a husband, but as a man. He was, she admitted, someone who still interested her.

He glanced up and saw her, then raised his eyebrows but didn't speak. Nothing about his body language invited, but she forced herself to smile anyway.

"I thought I'd come say hi," she told him. "We didn't get a chance to talk much at dinner. How was your week?"

He removed his glasses and put them on the small table next to the sofa, then dropped the magazine to his lap. "My week was fine. How was yours?"

"Busy." She inched closer to the sofa. "There were a lot of activities before school ended for the year. I've also had the final paperwork for everyone. Registering them for all their camps."

He watched her approach. She sat on the sofa, close, but not too close, then angled toward him. Feeling like an idiot, she leaned forward slightly, showing off her cleavage. The lacy bra did its thing, making her appear bigger. Not that Colin seemed to notice.

"Lucy's excited about the party she's going to tomorrow," he said. "I hope she gets a new best friend quickly. At her age, it's important."

"I agree."

He picked up his magazine. "Was there anything else?"

Deanna sat there, completely at a loss. What was she supposed to do now? She'd put on the stupid dress, was wearing a thong and a padded bra and nothing was happening. She didn't know what to say or do. Acting sexy had never been her thing. She didn't know the first thing about seduction. She might have been married to Colin for more than a decade, but she had no idea as to how to turn him on.

"I thought," she began, then had to stop because she had no clue what came next.

He stared at her expectantly. "Yes?"

Her cheeks heated. "It's been…"

He continued to look at her, either not getting it or wanting her to suffer. For a second something flickered in his eyes. Not interest, she thought. Maybe compassion, but she couldn't be sure.

Nothing about this was fair, she thought. Why was she the one who had to try? Why did she have to change? It wasn't as if living with him was any picnic and—

"Deanna?"

She stared into his blue eyes and tried to see some small hint of interest. Some flicker of what had been there before. There was only faint impatience, as if he wanted her gone.

Men were visual, she reminded herself. A factoid she'd probably read in a magazine while getting her hair done. Actions might get the point across more easily than words.

She reached her arm behind and grabbed the tab of the zipper. After giving it a pull she shrugged out of her dress and let it fall to her waist.

"You gave me this bra and panty set," she said, not able to look at him as she sat there more exposed than she could remember being in months. "I saw them tonight and thought…If you wanted, we could…"

He looked at her for a long time, his expression still unreadable. His steady, blue gaze made her uncomfortable, but she refused to pull up her dress.

"You're doing this because you think it's what I want," he said at last. "Not because you have any interest in me being in your bed."

Shit. She glanced at her lap, then back at him. "No, Colin," she lied. "I do want you."

His jaw tightened. "Right. I've seen it with the girls, Deanna. You're going through the motions, but you're not getting it. Any of it. We're still not real to you. We're still in the way."

She flushed, then forced herself to her feet. The dress fell to the floor. "So that's it?" she demanded, the shaking starting on the inside and working its way out. "You're saying no?"

"I'm saying no."

Her chin came up and she saw him picking up his glasses. He turned his attention back to the magazine.

"I'm pretty tired," he told her. "Good night."

She felt the slap as surely as if he'd struck her with his open hand. Her cheeks stung as heat burned through her. Anger joined shame as she pulled up her dress and then ran from the room.

But when she reached the hallway, the anger disappeared, taking all her strength with it. She sank onto the floor and dropped her head to her knees. She shivered, perhaps from cold, perhaps from the realization that whatever Colin had once felt for her had died long ago. She didn't know what he wanted from her, but it wasn't this marriage.

For the first time in months, maybe years, maybe ever, she longed to feel his warm hand on her shoulder. She wanted him to draw her to her feet and hold her the way he used to. Back when they still hugged. He'd always been the last one to let go. He used to joke that she couldn't break a hug fast enough. Now she wanted to experience that lingering hug again, only this time she wouldn't let go first. She might not let go at all.

But he didn't come out to check on her. She sat there alone, cold and shivering. Finally a cramp in her leg and hip drove her to her feet. She zipped up her dress and climbed back to her bedroom. Once there, she walked to the window and stared out at the night.

She didn't know what questions to ask, let alone understand how to find the answers. All she knew for sure was that she'd been so busy getting everything right that she'd lost something she hadn't even known she wanted. For all her love of planning and details, when it came to Colin, she'd offered too little, too late.

He was going to leave her, she realized. She'd thought that on and off for the past few weeks. But for the first time she was a whole lot less worried about living as a single mother with five daughters. Instead she was a woman who had realized too late she had lost the man she really did love. She'd taken him for granted for so long she'd reached the point where the relationship couldn't be fixed.

Colin didn't love her and when she finally gathered the strength to look deep inside herself, she had to admit she knew exactly why.

Eighteen

"He knows," Andi said.

Wade set the pizza box on the floor, then pulled her into his arms and kissed her. "He doesn't know."

"The pizza guy knows we just had sex. I could tell."

"He's jealous. Now, how can I get you to stop thinking about him?" he asked, and kissed her again.

She stepped into his embrace and raised her mouth to his. Even as he kissed her, he moved his hands against her body, pulling up the oversized T-shirt she'd slipped on so he could touch bare skin.

She was in big trouble. She had to accept the truth of the statement and figure out a way to deal with it. Because the man was a sexual god and she was in danger of having to quit her job so she could join a cult that spent all its time worshipping at the altar of Wade King.

They'd just made love in her small bed in her creaky attic with the cool night air around them. Wade had touched her and stroked her and done things to her body that had sent her spiraling into an orgasm that had fulfilled her on a cellular level. Even now, as his tongue tangled with hers and his fingers explored the curve of her hips and butt, organs were composing sonnets of adoration. Her kidneys had a mad crush on Wade and her pancreas never wanted her dating anyone else.

"We have pizza," she said, thinking they should probably eat, but not wanting to move away.

"It'll keep."

"I should get dressed."

"You are dressed."

"I'm wearing a T-shirt. Just a T-shirt. There's nothing under it." Wade had pulled on his jeans and shirt, but she had been too dazed by the aftershocks to figure out complicated tasks, like finding her underwear.

"I'm too close to naked to eat dinner," she told him.

He looked into her eyes. "Let's test that theory."

"What?"

He turned her in his arms so she was facing away from him, then slid one hand under her shirt so he could fondle her breasts and eased the other between her legs.

She wanted to protest they were still downstairs and there weren't any window coverings. Only it was still fairly light outside, so no one could see in. Besides, the feel of his fingers sliding deep inside her as his thumb settled over her still-swollen clitoris made speech impossible.

He'd done this earlier, she thought, closing her eyes and getting lost in the sensual ministrations. Touched her with a certainty that left her breathless. The hand at her breasts knew exactly how to tease her tight, aching nipples such that the nerve endings began to sing. Vibrations rocked her, a perfect pitch of need and arousal, linking her erogenous zones.

Wanting swept through her. She opened her legs more, now shameless and weak with need. Muscles tensed in anticipation as he moved in and out, going faster and faster, his thumb providing a steady, circling pressure that forced her closer and closer until she cried out, shattering in another orgasm.

When the last quiver had faded, he led her to the stairs and settled her on the second from the bottom. Even as he knelt in front of her, kissing her, he was fumbling with his jeans. He handed her a condom. She ripped open the package. They were both shaking as they jointly tried to slide it over his penis.

"You," she gasped. "You're the expert."

He finished, then plunged inside her.

With the very first stroke, she came again. She wrapped her legs around his hips and hung on, wanting, no, needing, more. Sex had never been like this, she thought, crying out her pleasure. This easy, this amazing. This spectacular.

She came over and over until there was nothing left. Wade shuddered and was still. They stayed where they were, both gasping and spent. Slowly he withdrew and stared at her.

He looked as stunned as she felt.

"I think I pulled a muscle in my back," he admitted.

She straightened her leg, feeling the first twinges of a muscle cramp. "The stairs might have been pushing it."

He staggered to his feet, then helped her stand. He cleared his throat.

"Is it usually like that for you?" he asked.

"No. I'm pretty boring in bed."

He gave her a rueful smile. "No, Andi. *Boring* is not a word I'd use." He shrugged. "I like sex as much as the next guy, but I have to admit this was a hell of a ride."

"I guess we have chemistry."

"That's one word for it. Be right back."

He ducked into the downstairs bathroom. She got the pizza and waited for him. When he reappeared, he'd fastened his jeans and his belt. He still looked shell-shocked. It was nice to know he was as rattled as she was.

She led the way upstairs. While she served the pizza, he opened a bottle of wine. "What time do you have to be back?" she asked. "Does Carrie have a sitter, or does she stay on her own?"

Wade handed her a glass of wine. "She's spending the night with Madison. I don't have to be home until morning."

Her girl parts cheered. "Oh. That's nice." Instinctively she glanced toward the bedroom.

Wade took the glass from her and set it back on the counter. "My thoughts exactly."

They reached for each other. By the time they got into the bedroom, they were both naked. The old bed creaked in protest as they tumbled onto the mattress. Andi gave herself over to Wade's magical touch and prepared to let the man sweep her away.

As a rule, Deanna loved her house. She owned it—her aunt and uncle had left it to her. More than an inheritance, she considered it something she had earned. When they'd taken her in, they'd made it very clear that she was expected to be the child they had always wanted. That any hint of her being her mother's daughter was unacceptable.

She'd done her best to be perfect. Be polite and clean, get good grades, cooperate. She'd learned the history of the house. She knew which pieces were antiques and which were reproductions. She understood the importance of always being ready for unexpected company.

That how things looked mattered so much more than how they were. The house was her kingdom. Or it had been.

For the first time since she first arrived when she was ten years old, Deanna felt out of place. She felt as if a shameful spotlight followed her, illuminating her humiliation.

She hadn't slept. Instead she'd made her way back to her bedroom, where she'd locked herself in her bathroom. From the darkest depths of her closet, she'd removed a long-handled scrub brush, then gotten in the shower and used it to scour every inch of her body in a feeble attempt to wash away her shame.

Blood had trickled down the drain and when she had finally stepped out of the water, her body had been covered with open wounds. She'd spent the night in pain. This morning, she'd dressed the worst of the sores. She wore a long-sleeved shirt to cover up the evidence, but even the constant ache wasn't enough to allow her to forget Colin's rejection.

She had laid herself bare and he'd turned his back on her. She'd offered all she had and it wasn't enough. She wasn't enough.

She never had been—she'd always known she was living on borrowed time. Being with him was like being with her aunt and uncle. She'd been aware that at any moment she could be sent back. But over time, she'd grown comfortable. Complacent. She'd thought being perfect was enough, but it wasn't. And she didn't know how to be whatever else it was he wanted.

"Mommy?"

Deanna turned and saw Lucy standing in the entrance to the kitchen. For once she didn't see the ugly glasses or the too-big eyes. She saw the fear in the way her daughter's mouth trembled slightly.

"What is it?"

"I have the party this afternoon. You remember you said I could go."

Her heart twisted. She heard her own voice, half begging, half reminding. The silent plea not to change the rules, not to be punished for having the courage to ask. Lucy was the age she had been when her mother finally snapped. That final beating, the one that had caused neighbors to call in authorities, had changed everything. Deanna supposed it had been worth a broken arm and bruised rib to finally be free. At least she'd thought that at the time. Now she wondered if she had ever achieved freedom. If she had simply exchanged one kind of abuse for another.

She managed a shaky smile. "Yes, Lucy. I remember. I'm glad you're going to the party. I know it's been hard for you, with your closest friend moving away."

Emotions paraded across Lucy's face. Hope, relief, then caution, as if she wasn't prepared to believe she would get what mattered most without paying a price.

"What time are you supposed to be there?" Deanna asked.

"Three. We're bowling and there's dinner." She flinched as she spoke.

Right, Deanna thought. Because dinner would be pizza and chicken fingers and God knew what other kind of processed food.

"There'd better be cake," she said. "It's not really a birthday without cake."

"And ice cream," Lucy said with a grin.

"Both are required." She drew in a breath. "We'll leave

at two-thirty. That'll give us plenty of time. You can take the emergency cell phone and call me when you're ready to come home."

None of the girls had their own phone, but she kept an extra around for trips or events like this.

Lucy nodded. "I'll be extra careful with it, Mommy. I promise."

"I know you will."

Lucy grinned, then flung herself at Deanna. Her bony arms came around and hugged tightly. Pain exploded as she pressed on the open sores and Deanna gasped.

Lucy jumped back. "I'm sorry. I'm sorry. Don't be mad."

Before Deanna could say anything, the girl turned and ran, as if chased by the devil.

Not the devil, Deanna thought. Her mother. In this house, those two people were the same.

"Emma said she and her mom were going into Seattle next Saturday and she asked me to go and I'm going to ask Dad later." Lucy barely paused for breath before continuing. "And then we had cake and we had teams for bowling and both Sarah and Emma wanted me on their team."

Bright blue eyes danced with happiness. Andi impulsively leaned over and hugged the ten-year-old. "I'm so glad you had a good time."

"Me, too."

They were in Andi's tiny makeshift kitchen up in her attic. The windows were open and the sound of soft rain provided background music to a Sunday afternoon of conversation and cookie decoration.

Andi had found already baked sugar cookies at her grocery store. They were part of a kit that included icing and sprinkles. Thinking she might have company in the way of the girls next door, she'd bought the package. She'd also stocked her small refrigerator, done her laundry, scrubbed the bathroom and generally tried to keep herself busy. Because the alternative was to obsess about Wade.

Their night together had been amazing. They'd finally gotten to the cold pizza sometime after eleven. Then they'd gone back to bed and made love until they were both exhausted. She'd spent yesterday tired and sore but happy. Every twinge had been a reminder of a very delicious night.

But this morning, insanity had reared its ugly head as her mind had started with the questions. Why hadn't he called? Shouldn't he have called? Was it just about sex? Did he think she was easy? He hadn't mentioned getting together again, so were they dating or what?

If they weren't dating, what were they doing? Was it friends with benefits? Did she want more? Did he? He'd been a widower for years. So was he like Matt? Would he string her along for a decade, then dump her and marry someone else two weeks later? And why the hell hadn't he called?

Lucy had provided a voice different from the one in her head.

"What are your sisters up to today?" Andi asked, hoping to continue the conversation and the distraction it provided.

"Dad took Audrey and the twins out on the duck boat." Lucy pushed up her glasses. "I like it but I usually get sick."

"Motion sickness?" Andi asked. "On long car rides and rides at the fair?"

"Yeah."

"That's a yucky feeling. I get carsick a little, too. I had it a lot when I was younger. I don't know if this will help, but you'll probably get better when you get older. I'm better than I was."

Lucy smiled at her, then passed over a daisy-shaped cookie she'd decorated. The petals were bright pink and the center was green.

"Beautiful," Andi told her. "Why don't we finish these? Then we can take some over to Boston. I know she likes cookies, too."

"That would be fun."

"I think so, too."

And when they left, Andi would deliberately leave her cell phone at home. If Wade wanted to reach her, he knew how. If he wanted to phone, he had her number. She refused to be one of those insane women constantly checking their voice mail or looking for a text message. She was strong. She was mature. She would get through this and everything would be fine.

Nineteen

Andi was going to have to kill someone. She accepted that by doing so, she would have to go to prison, but she wasn't afraid of the consequences. At least in prison she wouldn't have to worry about things like men who rocked her world with incredible sex and then didn't phone.

Men who smiled and looked all hunky in their work clothes, who grabbed her arm and pulled her into a quiet corner and whispered, "I haven't been able to stop thinking about you," only to get called away for some stupid work issue.

Because that's what had happened. On Monday afternoon, she'd seen Wade for exactly forty-seven seconds before they'd been interrupted. Then Carrie had walked in with Madison, and that had been the end of any possible private conversation. On Tuesday, Wade hadn't been there at all. Some end-of-term thing with his daughter.

It was now Wednesday morning, and Andi's day off because she was working Saturday, and she was honest-to-God going to have to kill someone.

It wasn't just the phone call, or lack thereof, she admitted to herself. It was the craziness that was growing in her obviously twisted brain. She'd moved from wondering about the status of their relationship to wondering if he loved her or planned to fall in love with her. She was inches from becoming a stalker or worse, although she didn't know what worse was.

At seven forty-five in the morning, Wade arrived. She watched his big truck park in front of her house, then saw him get out. She realized then she couldn't just stay in the house all day. She would end up doing or saying something they would both regret. She needed a distraction and very possibly professional help.

She grabbed her purse and headed for the stairs. After briefly waving at Wade, she raced out the front door, then paused. Boston was the more obvious choice. But going to her offered two potential problems. First, she might not be awake yet. Second and more important, she was Wade's sister-in-law and would probably discuss anything Andi said with him.

Decision made, Andi ran to Deanna's house. The five girls had already left for summer camp, which meant Deanna should be up and reasonably functional. With luck, she would be willing to talk Andi off the ledge, while not spreading her issues to the world.

She rang the bell, not once, but twice.

"Are you all right?" Deanna asked as she opened the door.

"No," Andi admitted. "I'm really not. Do you have a second to talk?"

Deanna looked at her cautiously. "What's the topic?"

"Man trouble."

"Good, because I can't take one more emotional hit. Let me grab my purse. We'll go get breakfast."

"Breakfast sounds great."

Ten minutes later they were seated at a window table at the Blackberry Island Inn. They both ordered coffee and stuffed French toast, and then Deanna raised her eyebrows.

"I'm braced."

Andi glanced around at the few businesspeople lingering over breakfast and the abundance of tourists planning out their day.

"You thought bringing me here meant I wouldn't start crying," Andi told her neighbor. "You think you can control me in a public setting."

Deanna smiled. "I thought it might help. Very few of us are comfortable making a scene."

"Good planning."

"Will it work?"

"I don't know." Andi drew in a breath, then leaned forward. "You know Wade King?"

"Sure. His brother, Zeke, is Boston's husband. They're the contractors working on your house."

"Wade's handling most of the work. He's funny, charming, sexy and single."

Deanna waited.

Andi grimaced. "We slept together," she said in a rush. "Friday night. It was supposed to be a date, but we never got out the door and he spent the night and now I'm going crazy. Seriously. He hasn't called. We've seen each other and he was fine, but I'm not fine. I dated Matt for ten years. That's a decade. Then he left me at the altar because it was all such a rush. So now I'm finding myself asking questions like, does Wade want to get married? It's been three days and I can't stand this."

"Breathe," Deanna said. "You have to breathe."

"Apparently not." But she did draw in a slower breath.

"I hate acting like this. I like Wade and sure, I want to see him again. But I don't want to be scary or a mess. I want to be normal."

"Let me know what it feels like."

The waitress stopped by and topped up their coffee, then left them alone. Deanna picked up her mug.

"What did he say on Monday?"

"That he couldn't stop thinking about me. Then Carrie walked in. I didn't see him yesterday and I was nervous about giving in to begging or something today."

"You don't want to beg," Deanna told her. "Trust me on that one."

Her tone was sad, Andi realized, really looking at Deanna for the first time since sitting down. As always, the other woman was well dressed with a pair of pink jeans and a tailored white shirt. She had on a scarf, chic loafers and dangling earrings. But the pretty makeup couldn't hide the circles under her eyes, and there was a sad twist to her mouth.

"Are you okay?" Andi asked. "Did something happen?"

Deanna lightly rubbed her left forearm, then shook her head. "I'm fine."

"I don't believe that."

"Are you making the decision as a doctor or my neighbor?"

"As your friend."

Andi figured using the *f* word was a bit of a stretch, but the more she spent time with Deanna, the more she liked her. The brittle, perfect facade had enough cracks to make her vulnerable.

The waitress appeared with their plates. A huge stack of stuffed French toast, covered in maple syrup and powdered sugar was surrounded by blackberries. Andi felt her eyes widen. The plate had to contain two days' worth of calories, and she honest-to-God didn't care.

"I'm eating it all," she said reverently.

"I might join you," Deanna said.

They each took a bite. The outside of the French toast was crisp, the filling both sweet and creamy.

"As good as that night with Wade?" Deanna asked.

Andi grinned. "Close. Very close." She sipped her coffee. "Tell me what's going on with you."

"Nothing that exciting. I'm fine." She stabbed her French toast, then put down her fork. "No, that's not true. I'm not fine. I'm a mess. Everything in my life is a mess."

Andi took another bite and waited.

Deanna shifted in her seat. "Things are going badly with Colin. My kids hate me."

"They don't," Andi said quickly.

"I scare them. I overheard the twins playing house yesterday. They were telling their dolls to clean their rooms and eat vegetables because there's no dessert." Deanna dropped her gaze to her breakfast. "I only let them have dessert on certain days of the week, and here I am, eating this."

"When was the last time you ate like this?"

"I think it was the nineties."

"Okay, then."

Deanna's brief smile faded. "I'm too strict. I see that, but it's hard to change. I'm so scared all the time." She leaned forward. "My mom was an alcoholic. The mean kind. When I was Lucy's age, I came to live with my aunt and uncle who owned the house we're in now. There were rules. Having rules made everything easier because I knew what was expected. Now, though, I think I've let the rules be the only thing that makes me feel safe. And Colin…I don't know what he wants."

Andi had limited experience with alcoholism in families, although she knew the damage filtered down through generations. It took someone extraordinarily strong to stop the cycle.

"What do you want?" she asked gently.

"I don't know," Deanna admitted. "I want to feel safe. I want to not be afraid. I want my family to like me."

Andi reached across the table and touched her hand. "What are you scared of?"

"If I'm not perfect, I have to go back."

The words came out so quickly, Andi knew Deanna hadn't thought through the answer. "Go back to your mom's?"

"Ridiculous, huh? She's been dead for years. The house isn't even there. I went and looked the other day. It's condos. I own my home. No one can take it from me."

"Maybe home isn't a location. Maybe it's what you said about feeling safe."

"Maybe." Deanna speared a blackberry with her fork. "They really don't like me."

"Are you someone they should like?" Andi reached for her coffee. "I think about my mom. I know I love her and she loves me, but do we like each other? I'm not so sure. I'm a chronic disappointment. In a family of success, I settled. Matt strung me along for a decade and then he dumped me. Why did I let that happen? Not the leaving-me part, but his inability to commit? Why didn't I walk away? Based on how I was pissed and humiliated rather than hurt, I'm not sure I was even in love with him anymore. So why did I want to marry him?"

Deanna smiled. "If you're trying to make me feel better, it's kind of working, so thank you."

"You're welcome. I'm really only pointing out that the family thing is hard. We all get messed up and then we have to find our way out of it. If my mom got off my ass, I'd probably want to talk to her more. But every conversation revolves around how I'm not living up to my potential and how great my brother and sister are doing. It's not something I look forward to."

She shook her head. "But hey, you're the one with five beautiful daughters and I don't even have a cat. So you probably shouldn't listen to me."

"I think I have to. You're making a lot of sense."

They smiled at each other and returned to their breakfast. A few minutes later, Deanna put down her fork.

"I think you need to try to back off with Wade. He's not Matt. From everything I've heard, he's a decent guy. His daughter is wonderful. I wish Madison were more like her. So don't assume the worst right away."

"But assuming the worst is so easy."

"How's that working for you?" Deanna asked with a grin.

Andi laughed. "Don't take this wrong, but I really didn't like you much when I first met you."

"Don't worry about it, no one does."

"But you're really nice and funny."

"Maybe you could write a letter of recommendation to my family."

"If you think it would help."

"No, but thanks for the offer."

Andi lightly touched her arm. "I'm here for you."

"I'm here for you, too. The next time you feel yourself slipping over the edge, come find me."

Andi nodded. "You promise the same."

"I will."

They smiled at each other. Andi knew the Wade-worry would return soon enough, but for right now things actually seemed okay. As for the rest of it, she had a friend. And with friends, she could survive anything.

Boston sat on her front porch and watched Deanna's daughters playing in Andi's yard. Carrie was with them, too, as was the long-suffering cat. While the girls ran and laughed, Pickles lay in the shade, grooming. Young feet came perilously close to his tail, but he didn't bother even looking to see if he was safe. She couldn't decide if the cat was fatalistic or incredibly trusting.

Sunlight spilled through the leaves on the trees. The whine of saws and hammers punctuated the laughter. Savannah circled around her sisters, shrieking that she didn't want to be tagged.

Summer had arrived, and with it childhood freedom. Long days with endless possibilities. Cool nights filled with stars and the magic of a full moon. Boston moved her pencil, quickly filled in the background, ignoring the reality of the grass and the house, instead placing the girls on a pirate ship. With a few quick strokes, Pickles had an eye patch and Carrie's waistband sported a cutlass. The twins wore hats, and beyond the edge of the ship, the angry sea threatened.

She finished and ripped off the sheet, then started drawing again. This time the girls were fairies with ethereal dresses and wings. Pickles became a butterfly cat, and Madison was their queen. And Carrie held a small baby in her arms.

Boston's fingers slowed as she gently drew in the

features. So familiar, she thought. So precious. Liam.
Baby Liam.

She filled in the curve of his mouth, the sweep of his
chin, then stilled as something unbearably heavy settled
over her entire body.

She could still breathe, still move, but only on the
outside. Inside, there was absolute stillness. And then
she knew from the colors. How the heaviness was dark
blue and purple with hints of green. Brown at the edges.
Brown fading to gray.

Sadness, she thought, almost afraid to acknowledge
the sensation. She felt like a flower in the desert, so close
to withering, yet unwilling to believe the storm clouds
brought life-giving rain.

She let the pencil fall to the grass and held her hand
palm up. She was open to receiving, she thought. She
welcomed the pain, should it choose to come. She had
lost her precious child. Held him as his heart stopped and
his soul left her.

The awfulness grew even heavier, driving her down
into the ground. She was anchored, unable to move. The
gray invaded the other colors until there was no color at
all. There was only absence.

Boston closed her eyes and prayed. Prayed for tears,
for the ache that came with loss. Prayed for any feeling
at all.

The grayness grew and she welcomed it. Welcomed
the burning in her eyes, the tightness in her throat.

And then it was gone. The sound of laughter returned,
the colors bled away and she could move again. The stairs
were just a seat and there wasn't a single storm cloud on
the horizon.

She stared down at the fairy drawing. She recognized

the faces, but it was as if it had been done by someone else. She carefully ripped the sheet off the pad and drew in a breath. Then she began to draw again, this time creating Liam.

There might not be sadness, she told herself. But as long as she could hold him inside her, there would at least be peace.

Twenty

Thursday afternoon Andi drove home at her regular time. She was doing a little better on the OMG front of her life. She could go entire minutes of time without panicking about Wade. She considered that improvement. They still hadn't had a conversation, something she was going to rectify that very afternoon. One way or another, they were going to talk about what had happened and he was going to explain why he hadn't called. If he thought they'd shared a one-night stand and now they were done, she would figure out a way to get through the rest of the remodeling without dismembering him and stuffing him in her trunk.

She pulled up in front of her house and stopped her engine. Before she'd made it halfway up the stairs, the front door opened and Wade stepped out. His dark eyes brightened when he saw her.

"Finally," he said with a grin. "I sent the guys home early, and Carrie's not expecting me for an hour. Come on."

He took her hand and led her inside. Once the door closed behind her, he pulled her close and lightly kissed her.

"Hey, I haven't seen you in days. How are you?"

She blinked, not sure how to take friendly Wade after four days of I'm-not-talking-to-you Wade. "I'm good."

"You spent most of yesterday avoiding me. I wanted to make sure everything was okay."

Avoiding him? She'd stayed away so she didn't humiliate herself in some way.

"As you said, we haven't really talked," she told him, liking the feel of his hands on her waist way too much. Leaning closer and kissing more seemed far more interesting than talking, but she had to do what was right, not what felt good in the moment. She took a deliberate step back. "I didn't know if you were being evasive or playing hard to get or what."

"What are you talking about? I sent you a text on Sunday. You never answered."

A text? "I didn't get it." Or at least she hadn't heard it, she thought.

She pulled her phone out of her purse and scrolled through the notifications. Sure enough, there was a text from Wade.

Thinking about you. Can't wait to see you tomorrow. Let's plan dinner for later in the week.

She looked at him. "Oh. I put my appointment schedule on my phone, so I keep the notifications turned off. Otherwise it would beep every thirty seconds. Since I moved, I don't get many texts and I never checked, so…"

She swallowed, feeling really stupid. "I thought *you* were avoiding *me*."

"So we were both wrong." He touched her chin, forcing her to look at him. "Let's start over. I had a great time Friday night."

"Me, too."

"I want to see you again."

"Me, too."

"We should go to dinner. And this time I mean dinner. Not that you didn't surprise the hell out of me before—in a good way. But let's get to know each other."

"Okay."

"Yeah?"

She nodded.

He grinned and kissed her again.

She let his mouth linger, then drew back slightly. "I need to tell you that I went a little crazy with the silence. Because of Matt and how he strung me along for so long. I thought maybe you were like him."

"I'm not."

She nodded. "I really want to believe you, but it's going to take a little time."

He rubbed his thumb against her cheek. "You're not the only one who worries. My wife was never happy with me and Zeke going into business. She used to bug me to go find a job in Seattle. To get off the island. We fought about it a lot."

Andi stared at him. "I didn't know that."

"It was a long time ago and we kept the fights pretty quiet. But it was a source of tension. So even though you're sexy as hell and funny and smart, the doctor thing has me worried."

"Why?"

"What if you try to change me? I'm kind of set in my ways."

She nodded in understanding. "Matt wanted me to

change, too. It didn't work and made for a lot of tension. For what it's worth, I like you just the way you are."

He gave her that smile she loved. "Yeah? I feel the same way."

"As for what you do for a living, I don't care what any man does. I care who he is. I want someone I can depend on, and who I can trust. I'd probably draw the line at chronic illegal activities, but otherwise, what you do for a living is really the least of my issues. I like that you're taking a sad, abandoned house and making it beautiful again. That's impressive. Besides, you have a really great butt."

He grinned. "You're shallow."

"Yes, and proud to be so."

"I can live with shallow." He stared into her eyes. "So we're going on a date."

"Yes. And this time we're actually leaving the house."

"Saturday night. Seven."

"I'll be ready."

He grinned. "Maybe you should let me honk and you come out. I'm afraid if I come inside to pick you up, I won't be able to control myself."

Andi sighed. She didn't even care if he was lying; that was so nice to say. "I don't mind you honking. It'll be like high school."

He put his arm around her shoulders and turned her toward the waiting room. "Now that we have that settled, let me show you what we did today."

Andi walked into Pilates on Monday afternoon. "Hey, Katie," she said to the receptionist.

"Hi, Andi." The twentysomething looked up, then frowned. "What happened?"

"Nothing."

"No way. Marlie, get over here. Doesn't Andi look different?"

Marlie, Andi's regular instructor, studied her for a second, then grinned. "I'd say it's a guy. She has guy-glow. And it's not just about sex. It's about being happy." Marlie plopped her size-zero dancer's ass on the edge of the desk. "Okay, start at the beginning and tell us everything. Who is he?"

Andi felt herself flush. "There's no guy," she began, but then couldn't help grinning. "Okay, there's a guy."

"I knew it." Marlie sighed. "I love it when relationships are new and there are so many possibilities. Plus the hot sex. Am I right?"

"You might be."

The other women in the class strolled in and greeted everyone. Andi escaped to put her purse and shoes in a cubby, then walked over to the mats.

As promised, she and Wade had gone out Saturday night. Dinner only, which had been both great and disappointing. The good news was, they'd had a chance to get to know each other a little better. The bad news was, all he'd done was kiss her at the door. The explanation that Carrie was home alone, waiting for him, had made his actions understandable, and his obvious disappointment had gone a long way to ease some of her own regret.

The other women settled on their mats, and Marlie walked over.

"Ready, everyone?" she asked. "Let's start with the hundred."

"Couldn't we start with sixty and do the other forty later?" Kathy asked.

"I like that idea," Andi said.

The other women laughed. Marlie rolled her eyes. "So you're going to all be trouble?" she asked. "It's a Monday, right? This always happens on Monday. Grab your handles and let's get going. The sooner we start, the sooner it's over."

Andi picked up her handles and stretched out on her mat. She raised her legs, making sure her heels were together and her toes apart. She tucked her chin and raised her shoulders off the mat, then started pumping.

The class moved from exercise to exercise. During the roll-down, Andi was careful to focus on her core and eased herself back onto the mat, bone by bone.

"Good form, Andi," Marlie called out from the other side of the class. "Slower, Kathy. One more, everyone."

By the end of the hour, Andi's muscles were exhausted and a little shaky. She staggered to her feet and walked toward the cubbies.

"You're doing great," Marlie said, falling into step with her. "I see lots of improvement."

"Thanks. I'm feeling better. Stronger."

"I'm doing a demo in the park in two weeks. There's a whole fitness program. My demo is from eleven to eleven-thirty. I was wondering if you'd be one of my students. There will be four of you. Just basic moves—all things you know how to do." Marlie pulled a business card out of her tote. "Here's my email address. Think about it and let me know if you'd be interested and are available."

"I should be free," Andi said. "But I don't understand. A lot of your other clients are way better than me."

Marlie laughed. "You're my star beginner student. I like to have all different levels. When I tell people you've been doing Pilates a couple of months, they'll be less intimidated by the classes."

"I'm hoping there's a compliment in there somewhere."

"There is. I promise."

Andi took the offered business card. "Let me double-check my calendar and I'll let you know if I'm available. I'm pretty sure I don't have to work."

"Great. I'd love to have you."

Andi nodded and left. As she walked to her car, she told herself this was how people started fitting into a community. One person at a time, one day at a time. Taking it slow, making connections. There were times when she missed her life in Seattle, but not that many. Since her breakup with Matt, she'd discovered that a lot of friends were more couple friends than girlfriends. Despite her invitations, no one seemed to want to visit the island.

She'd made the decision to start over in a moment of panic and impulse, but she was beginning to see that she'd been right about the island all along. She was making a home for herself here. Making friends, finding out the best way to belong.

As she walked toward her car, she glanced up to the three houses perched on the hill. The three sisters, she thought. She, Deanna and Boston weren't sisters, but they were well on their way to being friends. And wasn't that just as good?

Boston finished dressing after her afternoon shower. She was exhausted, but in a good way. She'd made good progress on the mural the whole week. She'd already sketched in her design on the two main walls of the waiting area. Now she was trailing a smaller version of the jungle scene down the hall. She would sketch different animals in the various examination rooms, then start painting.

Wade had offered the services of their best painter
to help her. Hal would fill in the background while she
worked on the animals, bugs and foliage. The good news
was Andi didn't plan to open her offices until late August, giving Boston plenty of time to finish the mural.
The bad news was she hadn't worked with a deadline in
nearly a year and was feeling the pressure. Still, it was
good to have a goal. It gave her purpose. She didn't want
to let Andi down.

She glanced at the clock and saw it was nearly five.
Zeke should be home by now. She made her way to the
kitchen to see if he'd left a message on the landline. She'd
barely reached the counter when she heard a crash from
the back of the house. What on earth?

She hurried down the hallway and walked into her studio. Zeke stood there, his arms at his sides, his fingers
splayed. Her easel lay smashed on the floor.

"What happened?" she demanded. "When did you
get home?"

"A few minutes ago." His face was white, his eyes
hard. He looked at her with a combination of anger and
disgust. "Look at this. Look!"

She glanced around her studio, not sure what he was
talking about. It wasn't any messier than it usually was.
She'd pinned up the various animals she was going to
paint. There were different versions of the monkeys and
jaguars. She'd wanted to get the positions right. She'd also
played with colors in the butterfly wings.

"What are you talking about?" she asked, bewildered
by his obvious emotion.

"Goddammit, Boston. Stop. You have to stop."

He picked up a drawing of Liam. One she'd done recently. Before she realized what he was going to do, he ripped it in half.

She gasped. "Zeke, no."

"This is wrong. It's been too long. Wade said you were working on the mural. He said you were doing well and I believed him. But look at this." He waved toward an oil painting she'd started the other day and then pushed the stack of sketches of their baby to the floor. Black-and-white images of Liam fluttered down.

"How many are there?" he asked, his voice thick with anger and maybe pain. "How many?"

Now she saw what he saw. Yes, there were a few pictures for the mural, but everywhere else, on every surface and inch of wall, were detailed drawings, paintings and quick sketches of their baby. Sleeping, awake, laughing, sitting. Liam in her arms, Liam in his bed, on the grass, by the fireplace.

"Hundreds," she whispered, not bothering to count. "Hundreds."

He picked up an oil painting and threw it across the room. Another stack of sketches went flying. He crumbled and tore and tossed, destroying her studio.

She stood by the door and let him. Not because he frightened her but because his anger was the first part of anything alive they'd shared since their son died. And maybe because she knew she needed this, too.

When he finished, he turned toward her. His chest rose and fell with each gasping breath. He radiated pain. His fingers curled into fists and she saw the sheen of tears in his eyes.

Deep inside her, emotion struggled to get out of the hard shell of her denial. It fought like a newborn chick, pecking for life. She took a step toward Zeke, wanting him to hold her. Wanting to cry with him. For them to share the pain. They'd started this journey together, and the only way to finish it was with each other.

He turned to her. "This is your fault."

She stared at him. "What?"

"It's your fault. You were there. You should have done something. You should have saved him. You let him die, Boston."

The accusations, the assumption, tore at her. She felt herself being ripped into pieces and had to hang on to the back of a chair to keep standing.

"No."

She tried to speak the word, but couldn't make the sound. Couldn't do anything but shake her head. He couldn't believe that. Couldn't.

"The doctors said..." she began. "It wasn't..."

His expression was as hard as his words. As unforgiving. And then she knew. What was wrong between them had little to do with the actual death of their son and everything to do with blame.

Logic didn't matter. Zeke knew in his head that Liam's death had been a cruel twist of fate. He'd been taken because his heart wasn't strong enough. But what he thought and what he felt were two different things. Maybe that's why she'd gotten lost in her art. Maybe she'd always sensed what he'd been unable to tell her until now.

"I can't be sorry for something I didn't do," she told him.

She saw it then—the chasm that opened up between them. It was as if they were on opposite sides of a canyon. There was no bridge, no way across. Only space and distance separating them. It was as if he looked at her from a thousand miles away.

"Zeke," she began.

He shook his head; then he walked away.

He'd left so many times, after so many fights. He'd gotten frustrated, he'd used her as an excuse to go. But this was different. This was quiet. Deliberate.

She stayed where she was, aware that this time he might not come back.

When the room was silent and she was sure the house was empty, she carefully lowered herself onto the chair. There were paintings and sketches everywhere. Brushes and paints lay scattered on the floor. But in front of her, a pad sat on the table. Next to it, a piece of chalk.

She picked up the latter and made the first stroke. The curve of a baby's head appeared and she began to breathe again.

Twenty-One

Deanna stared out her front window. It was nearly eight, and Zeke's truck was nowhere to be seen. While she didn't generally spend her life spying on her neighbors, she knew enough about the comings and goings of their lives to be aware that something was wrong.

She walked into Colin's study. It was rare for him to be home midweek, but he had a series of meetings in the office and hadn't traveled in several days. For all they talked, he could already have taken the office job and not bothered to tell her.

She paused in the doorway and waited until he looked up from his computer.

"Zeke hasn't been home in a couple of days," she said. "I want to go check on Boston. Make sure she's okay."

Blond eyebrows rose. "I didn't know the two of you were friends."

She shrugged. "I shouldn't be very long."

"All right."

She thought about reminding him to make sure the twins took their baths and that Audrey might need help with a craft project. But she didn't say any of it. Audrey was perfectly comfortable coming to her dad for help, and if the twins didn't get a bath, the earth's rotation would hardly shift.

She moved through the kitchen, grabbed a bottle of wine from the rack in the pantry, then walked out the front door. On a whim, she stopped at Andi's place and rang the bell.

She waited, knowing Andi would have to climb down two flights of stairs to get to the front door. When it opened, Deanna held up the wine.

"I haven't seen Zeke's truck in a couple of days. I want to make sure Boston's okay. Want to join me?"

"Sure." Andi joined her on the porch. "Now that you mention it, I haven't seen the truck, either. But I didn't put it together. You don't think anything happened, do you?"

"Wade would have told you if there was an accident."

"That's true."

Deanna glanced at her. "You're still talking to him."

Andi grinned. "Among other things. We've been on two real dates in the past couple of weeks and had a lovely sleepover this past weekend."

"You look happy."

"I am. The things that man can do in bed."

"So you're in it for his body?"

"I think focusing on the physical aspects of our relationship keeps me from wondering why he hasn't proposed, so yes. For now."

They reached Boston's front porch, and Andi rang the bell.

"I've never been someone who drops in," Deanna muttered. "I'm turning into a very needy neighbor."

Boston opened the door. She looked only a little surprised to see her neighbors.

"Hi. What's up?"

Deanna hesitated, not sure how to delicately ask if everything was all right. She'd never been very good at the friendship thing. All her energies always went into the impossible goal of perfection.

Fortunately, Andi took the lead. "We're worried. Zeke's truck hasn't been here, so we came by to see if you're okay. Are you okay? Do you want to talk? Deanna brought wine, which makes her a better person than me."

Boston bit her lower lip. "We had a fight and he's been gone ever since. I know he's staying with Wade, so it's not like he's roaming the streets, but it's tough."

Deanna felt the first flutterings of panic. Now what? What did that information mean? Were they supposed to try to help? Make her feel better? Leave?

Once again, Andi took charge. She stepped forward and hugged Boston. "Come on. We'll drink wine and tell lies about boys. How's that?"

"It sounds great."

Deanna followed the two of them into the living room. The eclectic colors and funky furniture couldn't have been more different than the perfect period pieces she had in her place. She'd always thought Boston was a hippie wannabe with delusions of grandeur. Now as she took in the bright colors and fairy painting, she wondered if maybe she'd been too judgmental. Deanna's living room wasn't a place anyone felt comfortable in. In Boston's living room, she could imagine kicking off her shoes or burning sage in celebration of the summer solstice, or whatever it was people did to celebrate that sort of thing.

"The wine opener is in the dining room hutch," Boston called. "I'm going to grab glasses and snacks."

Deanna followed Andi into the dining room and offered the bottle to her. "I'll help Boston carry everything," she said.

She walked into the kitchen to find her neighbor loading brownies onto a plate. She'd already piled on several kinds of cookies and had set three wineglasses on the counter.

"I never used to stress-eat," Boston admitted. "It's my new thing. If I get any bigger, I won't fit in my house and I honest-to-God don't care."

Deanna took in the dark red streaks in the other woman's hair, the feather earrings, the flowing tunic top and smiled. "You look beautiful."

"You're sweet and lying, but I'll take it."

They walked back into the living room and found Andi had already opened the wine. The merlot was poured and glasses passed around; then the three of them settled onto the sofa and chairs.

"Zeke and I are still dealing with Liam's death," Boston said, holding her wineglass in both hands. "He blames me for what happened. Or not being able to save him."

"No," Andi breathed. "He can't. You couldn't have saved him. No one could."

"I think he knows that, but he doesn't want to believe it. Or maybe he's just angry because I won't cry." She looked at them both. "I don't cry. I can't. I've tried. I don't feel much of anything these days. It's like my heart is in ice. Or stone."

"Grief manifests differently in different people. We all get through things in our own time."

"Maybe," she said dully. "He's drinking. Do I have to worry that he's an alcoholic?"

Andi blinked, then turned to Deanna, as if to ask. Her mouth opened, then closed and she turned away.

Because Andi didn't know how much Boston knew and didn't want to spill secrets, Deanna thought, grateful for the kindness.

"If he can get through most of the day without drinking, then he's not an alcoholic," she said with a shrug. "Was he drinking much before you lost Liam?"

"Just a couple of beers in the evening. Or wine. Neither of us drank while I was pregnant."

"Then I wouldn't worry. Well, except for how he's making this harder than it needs to be."

"Thanks," Boston said with a sigh. She shook her head. "What if he's right about me? What if I'm not getting through it? What if I'm hiding?"

"You can't hide forever," Andi said. "One day your grief will find you."

Boston didn't look convinced. "I'm afraid that will happen too late. That I'll have already lost Zeke." She paused. "You'd think that would be enough to terrify me into sobbing, wouldn't you? But it doesn't."

"He's not going anywhere," Deanna said before she could stop herself. "I've seen how he looks at you. That man loves you so much. I don't think Colin ever looked at me like that." She gave a strangled laugh. "I'm seriously jealous."

Jealous and maybe a little bitter, she thought. "Colin hates me. No, that's wrong. Hate would be better because at least there would be feeling left. He doesn't think anything about me. Zeke will be back because he can't live without you. Trust me. I've seen indifference, and he's not living it."

She felt her eyes burn. She cleared her throat. "I'll cry for both of us," she told Boston. "How's that?"

"I wish it worked."

"Me, too. Because I can't stop crying. I've screwed up everything and I don't know how to fix it. I don't know how to tell my family that I love them. I've lost Colin and Madison. Audrey and Lucy are probably next. And it's not like the twins need me. They have each other." Tears filled her eyes. "I'm a complete mess."

"Is the OCD worse?" Andi asked quietly.

Deanna stared at her, then glanced down at her raw hands. "You know?"

"I guessed. Your hands are always chapped, and for a few days you wore long sleeves, even though it was warm."

Boston looked confused. "I don't understand. What are you talking about?"

"When I get stressed I wash my hands compulsively. To the point where the skin bleeds. I can trace all the reasons back to my childhood. It's a way of feeling in control."

"I eat," Boston said. "I saw my ass the other day and nearly had a heart attack." She shook her head. "Is yours really bad?"

"Sometimes."

"There are medications," Andi said gently. "Therapy. I can get you some names, if you're interested."

"I don't know. Maybe. I'm not exactly trusting. Spilling my guts to a stranger seems an odd way to get help." Deanna looked at Andi. "What do you do when you get stressed?"

"I obsess. I bury myself in work. I impulsively buy houses on islands and then have to figure out how to fit into a brand-new life. My mother would tell you I have impulse control issues."

"You dated a guy for ten years," Deanna reminded her. "How is that impulsive?"

"She would also tell you that I have trouble making decisions."

"Can you really have both?" Boston asked, sounding doubtful. "Aren't they the opposite?"

Andi took a drink of her wine. "I'm a chronic source of disappointment to my parents." She raised her glass. "And they're coming to visit. They called earlier. They have a seminar in British Columbia and want to stop by. Do I look like I can't contain my joy? Because I feel it bubbling out all over."

Boston winced. "That bad?"

"It will be two days of them being critical and finding fault."

"Tell them not to come," Boston said.

"I don't know how to do that."

Deanna knew that if her aunt and uncle were still alive, she would find it difficult to refuse them anything. They'd been the ones to rescue her—she would always feel that she owed them.

She suddenly remembered a time from years ago. When she and Colin had first been married. They'd fought about something. She couldn't remember what about, but she did recall standing at the sink, washing her hands over and over. Colin had watched her, then muttered something about her aunt doing more harm than good. She'd yelled at him, saying he couldn't ever understand. But now, as she stared at her chapped skin and remembered how she'd scrubbed herself raw in the shower, she started to wonder if maybe he'd been right.

"What's that old saying?" she asked. "How do any of us get out of this life alive?"

Boston sighed. "None of us do."

"Damage is everywhere," Andi said. "We can only do our best, work with what we have and remind our parents that people can be happy even if they don't have a Nobel Prize."

Boston groaned. "You're a doctor. That's huge." She held up her hand. "I know, I know. Not in your family. Tell your mom I spend my day painting pictures of my dead son. That will make her grateful."

"Still?" Deanna asked.

"Mostly. It's better." She smiled at Andi. "The mural is helping a lot. I'm getting into butterfly wings. But when I start to get upset or anything is difficult, it's what I do." She turned to Deanna. "Maybe I should try admitting the truth every now and then as my own form of therapy. I'm sorry we weren't friends before. I don't know why that is."

"Because you thought I was a humorless bitch with a stick up her ass and I thought you were an undisciplined artist determined to show off her perfect marriage to anyone willing to watch."

Deanna slapped her hand over her mouth. "I can't believe I said that."

Andi glanced between them both. "I would say progress has been made."

"Me, too," Boston admitted, then started to laugh. "I'm going to paint you as the evil queen in *Snow White*. I think she's always been portrayed as a brunette, but in her heart, she's totally blonde."

Deanna waited for the flash of annoyance, the self-righteousness that came from being wronged, but all she felt was a little exposed and very accepted.

"What the hell?" she said. "I *am* an evil witch. No one likes me. Why should they?"

"I like you," Andi said. "And yes, that is surprise you hear in my voice."

"I like you, too," Boston told her. "You're impressive and scary, but I like you."

"I like both of you, as well." Deanna blinked against the rapidly forming tears. "And here I go, crying. I'm thirty-five. Is this menopause starting?"

Andi laughed. "No. It's stress and alcohol. Plus a feeling of connection. I'm as twisted as either of you."

"Maybe more," Deanna said drily.

Boston nodded. "Definitely the weakest link."

"Yeah, yeah. Pass me a brownie."

"Here are the tiles for the backsplash," Andi said. "They'll go up to the bottom of the upper cabinets."

Her mother nodded and walked around the still-under-construction kitchen. The floors were done and the cabinets had been put into the room, but not yet installed.

Leanne Gordon was a tall, willowy woman in her sixties. With her bone structure, her skin-care regime and judicious use of fillers and Botox, she could easily pass for a woman in her forties. When her mother made her completely insane, Andi tried to find comfort in the fact that at least she had inherited Leanne's good genes. Eventually that would make up for some of the other pain and suffering.

Leanne glanced out the window. "You have an excellent view from here. The windows are double-paned?"

Wade kept his arm around Andi's shoulders. His fingers squeezed gently, as if offering strength and support.

"They are," he said easily. "We took all the interior walls down to the studs and put in new wiring and insulation."

"Is there some kind of historic society you have to answer to?"

"The county has one," Andi told her mother. "The guidelines are very general. The house can't be torn down and the basic exterior must be kept intact. But I'm free to update as I'd like on the inside."

Andi's father asked about the plumbing involved with adding a kitchen to the second floor. Leanne linked arms with her daughter and led her out toward the stairs.

"He's doing a very nice job," her mother said. "I like the office downstairs. The mural is going to be...cheerful."

"I think my patients will like it, and I have a wonderful local artist doing the work."

"Do you?" Her mother glanced around at what would be the living room. "When you first told me what you planned to do, I thought you'd lost your mind. Perhaps some kind of chemical imbalance or blood disorder was clouding your thinking."

Which was just like her mother, Andi thought. "And now?"

"I can see the appeal."

"I doubt that."

"I'm trying to be supportive. You've certainly decided to settle in here. Moving back to Seattle would be difficult."

"That's okay with me," Andi said. "I'm staying where I am."

"But your career, Andrea. Don't you want more?"

"I'm happy, Mom. Can't you accept that?"

"I'm trying. Have you spoken with Matt recently?"

Andi instinctively glanced over her shoulder to make sure Wade wasn't anywhere nearby. "No. Why would I?"

"You were together a long time. It's so sad what happened."

"You mean him leaving me at the altar with no warning? In front of everyone?"

Her mother sighed. "He could have handled the situation better."

Andi thought about screaming, but what was the point? She looked at her mother. "But?"

"But what?"

"You're about to explain why it's really not his fault, or as bad as I think it is. You want me to know you're really on Matt's side in this, which is pretty astonishing because I'm your daughter. Shouldn't you be on my side?"

Her mother regarded her steadily. "The two of you had so much history together. It's unfortunate things didn't work out."

"So no blame for him at all? You don't want to call him the scum of the earth?"

"How would that help?"

"It might make me feel better. Or you could try a little righteous indignation at the fact that he never offered to pay even half of the bills he stuck me with."

"Do you need the money?"

Andi sighed. "That's not the point."

Her mother pressed her lips together. "I didn't come here to fight with you, Andrea. I'm sorry you think I'm not being supportive."

Which was completely different than saying she was sorry she wasn't *being* supportive, Andi thought, then shook her head. She would never win this fight. She would never be the famous specialist they wanted her to be. She would always be the screwup who couldn't keep her man.

"We should rejoin the others," Andi said, glancing toward the direction where her father and Wade had disappeared.

"Of course. Wade seems nice. I'm glad you found a handsome blue-collar man to sleep with. And he seems to do quality remodeling work."

Andi didn't know if she should laugh or throw herself over the stair railing. Not that either would change her mother. She looked toward the hallway, hoping Wade was out of earshot. No way he would take that comment well.

"You're right," she said wryly. "It's very handy to have Wade around."

"The sex is good?"

Andi stared at her mother. "Excuse me?"

"I want to make sure you're happy. You're not going to have much of a career to fall back on, so you'll need to be happy in your personal life."

Andi opened her mouth, then closed it. "As always, you leave me speechless, Mom. It's a gift."

"That wasn't a compliment, was it?"

"Not really."

"You never change."

Andi linked arms with her mother. "I get that from you."

Twenty-Two

Deanna stared at the painting propped up against her living room Queen Anne easy chair. The background of the portrait was a dark blue that faded to nearly black. The pose was straight out of the Disney movie, with the wicked stepmother Snow Queen holding out an apple. But instead of a dark-haired evil witch, this painting's villainess was a blonde, with blue eyes and a smug smile.

"I'm not sure if I'm flattered or insulted," Deanna admitted, staring at the uncanny likeness.

"Go with flattered. The painting is brilliant," Andi said.

"If you don't like it, I'll take it back," Boston offered.

"No, that's okay. I want to keep it. I feel like if I embrace the portrait, I might find redemption."

Of course that could just be the margaritas talking.

It was about eight-thirty on the Fourth of July. Colin had taken the girls down to the park to watch the fireworks. Rather than spend time in close proximity with her husband, Deanna had elected to stay behind. She'd noticed that not one of her children had asked her to join them a second time and that Colin had seemed more relieved than disappointed.

Rather than let the emotional reality of being unnecessary and unwelcome around her family bring her down, she'd gotten out the ice, margarita mix and tequila, prepared to spend an evening alone. Then Andi had called, saying she and Boston were celebrating the country's Independence Day together, and the impromptu party had been born.

Now they lay sprawled over the delicate furniture in the living room, sipping margaritas and trying to figure out when their lives had gotten so out of control.

"Still no Zeke?" Andi asked Boston.

"No. He's been by a few times to pick up clothes. I assume at some point Wade's going to throw him out, but he hasn't yet." She shrugged. "I'm okay. Determined to wait this out and then figure out our next step." She offered a shaky smile. "Another topic, please."

"Absolutely," Deanna said, understanding the pain of having a marriage in limbo. She turned to Andi. "You survived your parents' visit?"

"Barely. My mother managed to take my ex-fiancé's side while claiming to be supportive."

"Nice trick," Deanna said. "Did you hit her?"

"No. I realized she'll never change. I want her to be different, but that's not going to happen. We'll never be one of those mothers and daughters who are close, you know? The worst part is I want her to regret that, but I don't think she does. She would rather have me the way she wants me than meet me halfway. Or even a quarter of the way."

"That's really sad," Boston said. "If I had a daughter, I'd want us to be close."

"She said she was excited I'd found a nice blue-collar man to sleep with," Andi told them. "Dear God. Can you imagine if Wade had overheard that? Talk about being insulted."

The two of them continued to discuss the bond between mothers and daughters, but Deanna wasn't listening. She was thinking about her own daughters, wondering what they would be saying about her in a decade or two.

She'd never wanted to be their enemy, she told herself. She'd wanted to be one of those fun moms who played dress-up on rainy afternoons and had the cool house where everyone wanted to hang out. But somewhere along the way, she'd lost sight of the goal. She'd gotten so caught up in keeping her demons at bay that there hadn't been time for anything else. She'd been so busy trying not to drown she hadn't noticed the truck barreling down the road toward her.

"That doesn't make any sense."

Andi and Boston both looked at her. "What doesn't make sense?"

"My metaphor. Sorry. I was thinking about my girls. How I want us to be closer."

"You could make it happen," Andi told her.

"Really? Can you imagine that?"

"Yes."

"You're delightfully naive." She gulped her margarita. "I thought about leaving. It's what they all want. Me gone. I packed a bag and put it in my car, and then I sat there. Where am I supposed to go? I don't have a life outside of my family. I've done everything possible for them, and they hate me."

"Technically you've done everything possible you

want to do for them," Boston said, then hiccupped. "Sorry," she murmured, covering her mouth with her fingers. "I might be drunk."

"I've done things I haven't wanted to do," Deanna snapped, annoyed at the assumption that she was the center of the universe. "Now you sound like Colin. Do you think I love handling their laundry and cooking every damn thing they eat from scratch?"

"Then why do you do it?" Andi asked.

"Because it's the right thing to do. I don't want my kids eating all that processed food."

Boston leaned back in her seat and closed her eyes. "There's an ocean between eating healthy and baking your own bread. You don't let them eat dessert more than once a week, they're not allowed chocolate, they can't watch regular television."

Deanna drew her knees to her chest and wondered why everyone assigned evil motives to everything she did. "I'm being a good mother," she protested. "I want them to grow up right. Besides, how do you know all that?"

Boston looked at her. "Carrie tells me."

Deanna's cheeks got hot. "Does she also tell you Madison hates me? That she wants her dad to leave me and take her with him?"

Boston nodded.

Familiar, sucky tears spilled down Deanna's cheeks. "Dammit all to hell, I'm not a horrible person. I'm not."

Andi leaned toward her. "Being in control keeps you safe, right? And if you control everyone, then everyone stays safe."

Deanna sniffed. "Maybe."

Andi smiled. "I've got it! Stand up." She turned to Boston. "You, too."

Deanna reluctantly did what she said.

"Grab her wrist," Andi told Boston. "I'll take the other one."

They stood there, in the living room, each holding on to a wrist. Deanna was in the middle, waiting.

"Now what?"

"Now nothing. We're keeping you safe."

This was beyond stupid, Deanna thought. "I have to pee."

"Sorry, no. You might get hurt. We're going to hang on because it keeps you safe."

Deanna waited a couple of seconds, then tried to pull free. Both women continued to hold on. She tugged harder.

"Okay, okay. I get the point. Let go."

Andi shook her head. "No. You think you know what's better, but you're wrong."

Deanna felt the first wisps of panic. The need to run and hide. She wanted to duck into the bathroom, not to pee, but to feel the warm water rushing over her hands. She wanted the clean slickness of soap. She needed it. They didn't understand that—

"Let her go," Andi said, then stunned Deanna by pulling her close and hugging her. "It's okay," she whispered. "You're safe. We're right here for you. Whatever happens, you're okay."

The words were accompanied by a soothing pressure moving up and down her back. She was being comforted as if she were a two-year-old, she thought, slightly dazed and unsteady. Even more humiliating, it was working.

Andi drew back and Boston took her place. Her touch was less sure, but no less comforting. "I'm here, too," her neighbor said. "For you and for Andi. It's really okay you're a bitch. You're a good bitch."

Deanna started to cry. "Is that like being a good witch?"

"Kind of."

Boston released her.

Deanna sank onto her chair and picked up her margarita. She sipped, then wiped her face. "What was that?"

"I don't know," Andi admitted. "Obviously I wanted to show you what it was like to have someone making decisions for you, but then you went somewhere else. I'm sorry I nearly triggered a panic attack."

"It's okay," Deanna said, then sucked in a breath. "I got the point of what you were saying. As for the other thing, I guess I flashed back to what it had been like with my mom. How she monitored everything about me."

Deanna stopped talking. Well, shit. She'd worked her whole life to be nothing like her mother, and here she was—exactly where she'd started.

"I'm definitely a bad witch," she muttered.

"Acceptance is the first step in healing," Boston told her smugly.

"If I had something other than a drink in my hand, I'd throw it at you."

Andi leaned back and sighed. "I just love our girls' nights. They're not traditional, but they're very satisfying."

Deanna raised her glass. "To us."

Boston walked into her house close to midnight. She and Andi had stayed with Deanna until her family had returned and everyone else had gone to bed. They'd decided it was safer for everyone that way. Deanna was still figuring out the problem, which meant finding a solution was a ways off. Confusion and margaritas didn't make for a happy combination.

Now she walked through her dark living room, easily finding her way. She knew every inch of this house, knew every piece of furniture. Like Deanna, she'd lived here most of her life, had lost her parents early. They'd been so close physically, but had never become friends. Not until recently.

As a kid, she hadn't bothered to wonder. As a recently married twentysomething, she'd assumed Deanna looked down on her. Boston wasn't traditional enough, was too artistic, didn't care about being perfect.

For her part, Boston had decided Deanna walked around with a stick up her ass, and who needed that? But they'd each had their pain, and they'd concealed it in the corners of their lives.

Boston and Zeke had put off having a family—loving their "just the two of us" lifestyle too much to share it with anyone. But every time Deanna got pregnant again, Boston had felt guilt. As if her neighbor were better than her. Then she and Zeke had decided it was time.

What she hadn't told anyone was that when Liam was born, she'd been terrified of being punished for being selfish. Then his death had confirmed her fears. That she hadn't wanted him enough so he'd been taken back. Not that she hadn't loved him, but that she'd waited. She hadn't proven herself worthy.

Boston intellectually understood the insanity in that line of thinking, but knowing and believing were two different things. Having Zeke blame her for the loss of their son had brought all those old worries to the surface.

The weight of her emotions caused her to stumble.

Sadness surrounded her, pulling her down until she fell to her knees in the darkness. She welcomed the sensation, reached for it, wanting it to fill her until finally, finally, she could feel the pain, the ache, the missing pieces of her soul. She welcomed the battering to her heart, and the tears. Mostly she longed for them.

She huddled on the rug, hugging herself, waiting, hoping, eyes squeezed shut, breathing shallow. Longing for the first rip of agony.

Gradually the weight faded, as did the dread. Her breathing regulated and then there was nothing but the quiet rhythm of no emotion at all. Life was as it had been since Liam died. A kaleidoscope of gray. Empty and foolish. Only now she didn't have Zeke to show her what it was like on the other side.

Deanna glanced at the clock. It was barely after six, which meant it was morning. Monday, she thought. Her brain was fuzzy from lack of sleep. She'd heard Colin leave a short time ago. He was gone again, back on the road, leaving her and the girls.

For the past couple of days, she'd tried to make sense of what Andi and Boston had shown her the night of the Fourth. That by hanging on too tight, she was losing the very thing she sought to keep. She had reached the point where the words were clear, although she still didn't have anything close to a plan of action.

Colin was much harder, she realized. Mostly because she couldn't believe he cared about her anymore. Why would he? Although she hadn't stopped loving him, she'd acted as if he were the least important person in her world. She certainly never told him she loved him or wanted him. He'd been right—she'd seen him as little more than a paycheck to support her lifestyle.

Owning the house had made her feel secure when the truth was that without her family, the house had no value to her. Insights that would probably be more helpful if she could just get some sleep, she thought, and started downstairs.

She started coffee and got lunches ready for the girls. Although they were out of school and now in summer camp, she still had to provide them with lunch. As she sliced the loaf of bread she'd baked and frozen a couple of weeks ago, she thought about what Andi and Boston had said the other night. About having to control every detail of her children's lives. Maybe she should practice letting go.

She finished making the sandwiches and refilled her cup of coffee. It was nearly time to wake up the girls. Before she could gather herself, Madison walked into the kitchen.

Her oldest was so beautiful, she thought wistfully. Long blond hair, big blue eyes. From what Deanna remembered, she had an amazing smile, although she hadn't seen it in months. At least not on purpose.

On cue, her daughter glowered at her. "Is Daddy already gone?"

"Yes."

Madison sighed heavily. "I wish he didn't have to travel. Why do you make him? You could work more, you know. It's not fair he's the only one taking care of us."

Deanna clutched her coffee cup. The unfairness of the statement jabbed her like dozens of tiny needles. "I suppose what I do around here doesn't count?" She motioned to the kitchen. "All the cooking and cleaning, washing your clothes. That's nothing, right? I work, as well. What do you do to contribute, Madison? You complain about your father being gone, but you're the one who insists on having the latest style of clothing. Or should your sisters be the only ones who sacrifice?"

Madison flushed. "That's not fair."

"Isn't it?"

Madison glared at her. "I don't like that Daddy's gone all the time."

Deanna stared at her. "Neither do I," she admitted, then walked out of the kitchen.

She was back thirty minutes later, the four younger girls in tow. The stars had aligned because she'd managed to get them all up and dressed without anyone having a meltdown. They trooped into the kitchen and took their seats at the breakfast bar. Madison already sat there, but she hadn't bothered getting her own cereal.

Deanna thought about pointing out that kind of behavior was exactly what she'd been talking about, then shook her head. She'd taken on enough already that morning.

She got out two different cereal boxes, then stacked bowls. Audrey and Lucy started to pass them out.

"I don't want this," Madison told her. "I hate this cereal. Why can't we have something good for breakfast?"

Deanna turned to her. What had happened to the sweet little girl she remembered? Where had she gone?

"In a few years, you're going to look back on your behavior and you're going to be really embarrassed by it," Deanna said conversationally. "Eventually these memories are going to make you cringe and you're going to wonder how any of us could stand to be around you."

Her daughter flushed and jumped down from the stool. "I hate you!" she shouted.

"You're not my favorite, either."

Madison's eyes widened. "You can't say that to me."

"Why not? It's true. Would you want to be *your* mother? Would you want a kid like you in the house? What about you is pleasant or fun to be around?"

Madison's mouth dropped open. She sputtered for a second, then ran out of the kitchen. Deanna didn't bother watching her go. Instead she reached for a box of the cereal and looked at the picture on the front.

Healthy grains, the writing proclaimed. Honestly, it looked more like something raked off the forest floor after a big storm, she thought. Talk about disgusting.

She crossed to the refrigerator and pulled it open. Two pizza boxes claimed the middle shelf, leftovers from a dinner the previous night. A dinner Colin had walked in with. Not that he'd checked with her first. So the meal she'd prepared had mostly gone uneaten.

She pulled out the pizza boxes and set them on the counter, then grabbed several small plates.

Her four younger daughters stared at her.

Lucy spoke up first. "Mommy, are you giving us pizza for breakfast?"

"If you want it. There's the cereal, too."

Audrey was off her seat in a flash. She and Lucy put slices on the plates, then took turns heating them in the microwave. Deanna poured juice for everyone and then picked up her cup of coffee.

The smell of melting cheese mingled with pepperoni and mushrooms. For the first time in days, she actually felt hungry.

Lucy held out a plate. "Mommy, would you like a slice?"

Deanna smiled at her and took it. "Thank you, Lucy. That's sweet of you."

Her daughter beamed at her. "You're welcome."

Soon everyone was eating. For once there was plenty of chatter at the breakfast bar. The twins had everyone giggling over a series of knock-knock jokes. Deanna looked at the lone empty chair and wondered what Madison was thinking. No doubt Deanna would star as the villain of the piece.

She didn't know how to reach her oldest, she admitted to herself. But the younger girls were still accessible. She would start small. Find a way to be the mother they deserved. And maybe the mother she deserved, as well.

Twenty-Three

"Thanks for taking me," Carrie said, walking into the department store with Andi. "Boston's not feeling good. She said it was her tummy."

Andi privately wondered if Boston's upset stomach had more to do with the fact that Zeke was still living with his brother than anything gastrointestinal, but wasn't going to mention that to Carrie.

"I'm happy to help," she said instead.

Carrie grinned as they took the escalator to the second floor. "Dad would have brought me, but seriously. That's embarrassing."

"Bra-shopping is much more a girl thing. He'd be uncomfortable, you'd be uncomfortable. Why go there?"

"Exactly."

Carrie walked over to a rack of pretty bras especially designed for preteens. She fingered the various tags. "I'm pretty sure I'm an A cup now." Her eyes crinkled with amusement. "Have you seen a triple-A bra? Why bother? But last year Boston brought me and said it was time. That I was going to be a woman."

Carrie wrinkled her nose. "I told her I wasn't ready."

"The body has a mind of its own," Andi said. "Although I was a triple-A until I was about fourteen. I'd nearly given up hope of ever getting breasts."

"I'm not sure I want them," Carrie confessed. "I've seen the way boys stare at them."

"They are fascinated."

"Why? Their moms have breasts."

"They don't think of it that way. It's kind of a biological thing."

"I know. Sex, right? We've had the classes at school. Dad tried to talk to me about it, and that was horrible. He's really great and all, but it's not a conversation I want to have with him." She picked a couple of bras, then turned to Andi. "It's more a mom conversation."

"I know. I'm sorry."

"It's okay. I don't remember her very much." Carrie's smile faded. "I look at Madison and her mom. Madison is so mad all the time. I wonder if it would be like that with me and my mom. If I'd take her for granted."

"You would if you hadn't lost her. We all did it. You have a different perspective than most girls your age."

Carrie nodded. "I know. But now it's like I miss the idea of her rather than a real person." She waved the bras. "Let me go try these on and I'll be right back."

Andi wandered around while Carrie went into the dressing room. Fifteen minutes later, she'd chosen three bras and Andi had used Wade's credit card to pay for them. They went into the mall to find somewhere for lunch.

After they'd been seated, Andi looked at the pretty girl sitting across from her. "So boys are still stupid?"

Carrie laughed. "They're a little less stupid than they were last year. One of my friends at school had a boy-girl party when she turned thirteen. It was at a bowling alley just across the bridge. It was kind of fun. Mark Evenson kissed her, if you can believe it."

"On the mouth."

Carrie shuddered. "Yes. I'm not sure about the kissing. Sometimes I think it would be nice, but other times I think it's totally gross."

"You'll grow into it."

"You kiss my dad."

Andi did her best not to react physically. Flinching, squirming or shrieking would all be bad. "We've kissed, yes. It's nice."

Carrie held up both hands. "Don't tell me any more, please. I don't want to know."

"Not a word."

They looked at the menus and made their choices. When the server came, they placed their orders. Carrie wanted a burger and fries, while Andi chose a salad.

"I saw the mural," Carrie said when the server left. "I love what Boston's doing. The animals are awesome."

"I love it, too."

Over the past week, Boston had transitioned from sketching to painting. Every day there were more colors on the wall. The trees were nearly filled in, and two of the butterflies were done.

"I wish I could draw like her," Carrie said. "I've tried and she's shown me a few things, but I have no talent. I like knitting. I've taken a couple of classes at the store where Madison's mom works. It's fun. I made Dad a scarf for Christmas."

"I'm sure he loved it."

Carrie grinned. "I don't know if he loved it, but he wore it. He's that kind of dad."

A casual statement made in conversation, Andi thought. Information and a funny story. Even so, they touched her in a way she would guess Carrie didn't anticipate. Wade was a good guy. He'd proved it over and over again. He was funny and smart, generous and thoughtful. He'd done an amazing job with his daughter. All of which put her on alert. Given her history, it would be very easy to fall for someone like him.

She didn't object to the whole "love" thing, but she wanted to be smart about it this time. Not assume things. Not sell herself short by waiting for a decade for a man who then humiliated her without a second thought. She also didn't want to presume too much. Expect more than was right. Balance was a whole lot tougher than it should be, she thought.

"I think he likes you," Carrie said.

Andi frowned. "Who?"

"My dad. He acts funny before your dates and he talks about you a lot."

Andi smiled. "Thanks for telling me." She wanted to say more, or at the very least, start asking questions, but knew she couldn't say or do anything to make Carrie uncomfortable.

"I like him, too."

"I hope it get serious," Carrie admitted. "Although he's being totally weird, like dads get."

"What do you mean?"

Carrie shrugged. "You know, reminding me fifty times for thanking you for taking me shopping. You'll tell him I thanked you, won't you?"

"Promise," Andi said with a laugh. "I'll tell him you have very nice manners and he should be proud of you."

"Good. After all that, he told me not to get too attached, if you can believe it. I'm not a kid. I don't assume he's going to marry everyone he dates. Although I think you'd be a good stepmom. But he won't talk about that. He always tells me he's not interested in getting married and that I should stay out of his life. Not that he does the same for me, right? He's always asking about my day and my friends. Parents."

"They can be frustrating," Andi said, then smiled automatically as the server brought their drinks.

"Tell me about it." Carrie sipped her soda. "Last week after he hung out with your parents, he was all like 'we grew up pretty differently.' That's when I said you'd be a great stepmom, just so you know. I'm totally on your side."

"Thank you," Andi said, hoping her voice sounded stronger to Carrie than to her.

Carrie continued talking, saying something about a new movie that was opening Friday and how she and Madison wanted to see it. Andi hoped she answered appropriately, although it was hard to tell with the rushing sound she heard in her ears.

She'd accepted Wade's explanation for keeping Carrie out of their relationship. She knew it made sense not to bring children into dating until things had moved along. She could list all the reasons and believed they were right. But she'd assumed the shopping trip today was a way for her to start to get to know Carrie. If it wasn't that, then what was it? Free babysitting?

What had changed and when? Had something happened during her parents' visit to upset him? Had she said something she shouldn't have?

She told herself they'd only been seeing each other a month or so. That she wasn't interested in getting married anytime soon. That she respected Wade for moving at a steady pace. That he wasn't Matt. But the woman who'd recently been left at the altar in front of all her friends and family found it more difficult to be rational. Was he playing her? Was this a game for him? Had she just started seeing someone exactly like Matt—a guy who would string her along and then dump her in public?

She pressed a hand to her chest as she felt the muscles tightening. Was it her or was it hot in here? Suddenly she couldn't breathe.

It's only a panic attack, she told herself. *Or the beginnings of one.* She was focusing too much on herself. On a situation that frightened her. She needed a distraction.

She glanced around the restaurant and saw a college-aged guy with his girlfriend. "Look," she said, pointing. "Doesn't he looked like Zac Efron?"

Carrie turned and squinted. "Not really. Although maybe a little around the eyes. He's cute." She turned back to Andi. "Should I tell my dad you like Zac Efron?"

"He's kind of young for me, and when he calls I can't get him off the phone. It's kind of a pain."

Carrie laughed. "I wish that were true."

"I don't. He really is too young for me."

"What about Ryan Gosling?"

"Better. More age-appropriate. What about you? Who is your movie star crush?"

Andi picked up her soda and took a sip. She was breathing more easily now and able to focus.

Carrie chatted about the TV and movie stars she liked. Andi joined in as best she could. She would think about the Wade issue later, she promised herself. Figure out if she was overreacting or if he was a jerk. Then she would decide on a course of action. Or maybe swear off men forever. It was certainly the easier path.

But, as her mother had often told her, life wasn't meant to be easy. It was meant to be lived.

Deanna picked up the phone and dialed the number. She was shaking and she couldn't stop. Her hands were raw from the hundreds of washings and she'd had to throw her scrub brush in the outside trash to keep from taking it into the shower again.

"Dr. Gordon, please," Deanna said. "This is Mrs. Phillips."

"Of course," the receptionist said. "I think the doctor is between appointments. Let me see if I can catch her."

Deanna gripped the receiver as she waited for Andi to come to the phone.

"Deanna?"

"Yes, it's me. I'm sorry to bother you."

"You're not. What's wrong? Is it one of the girls?"

"No, it's me. I need help. It's not just the hand-washing. I'm scared."

"I know you are. I'm here. What's going on?"

"No. I use a brush in the shower. To feel clean."

There was a couple of seconds of silence. Deanna figured Andi was smart enough to put the pieces together.

"Let me get you a name. I'm going to call her and ask her to see you today, then I'll call you right back. All right?"

"Yes."

"Do you need me to come be with you?"

Deanna squeezed her eyes shut. "No. I'll be okay for a while."

"Give me five minutes."

The phone rang in three. "She'll see you at two. Here's her name and address."

Deanna wrote down the information. "Thank you."

"You're welcome. And don't be mad, but I called Boston. She's going to come be with you until your appointment."

"You didn't have to do that."

"I kind of did. I'm worried about you."

Deanna fought tears. "You're being so nice and I'm such a bitch."

"You're not a bitch. You're dealing with a lot and we all have coping skills that work and don't work. Talk to the therapist, Deanna. You deserve to feel better than you do right now."

"I don't know what to say," Deanna admitted in a whisper.

"You don't have to say anything."

Boston walked Deanna to her car. "You sure you're all right? I can come with you."

"I can drive myself the eight miles to the therapist," Deanna said. "She's right across the bridge. I promise not to steer over the edge between here and there."

Boston smiled, then hugged her. "And to think all this time, I never knew you had a sense of humor."

"I'm not sure I did, either."

Deanna waved, then got in her car. Boston watched her drive away, then turned back to Andi's house.

Progress was being made on the mural. She liked how the colors were happy and the animals charming. While it wasn't work that would win her any new customers, she was proud of what she'd accomplished so far. It nearly made up for the growing sense of unease that accompanied her every waking moment.

Zeke still hadn't come home. This was by far the longest they'd spent apart. The longest they hadn't spoken. She'd taken to sleeping in one of his shirts, so she would feel as if he were with her. She didn't know what she was supposed to do—wait him out or go talk to him. They'd come so far, she thought. She didn't know who she was without her husband. Was she really supposed to try to figure it out now?

She walked into the waiting area and studied the large, bright painting. It filled two walls and narrowed to only a couple of feet high as it trailed down the hallway. She had spent the past couple of days sitting on the floor, painting tiny bug families sitting together, watching TV. Surprises for the toddler set to find as they waited for their appointments.

"Hey," Wade said, stepping into the room. "Everything okay?"

She nodded. "I needed to ask Deanna something."

"You're getting friendly with her. I thought you hated her."

"Hate is too strong. I didn't really know her and I assumed the worst. My bad. How are you?"

"Good."

"You're seeing a lot of Andi."

Her brother-in-law gave a quick look, then glanced away. "Trying to distract me?" he asked.

"No. Just stating the obvious. She's great. I like her."

He nodded, but there was something about his expression. Something she couldn't quite read.

She waited, thinking there would be more, but he was silent. She thought about pointing out that Carrie liked Andi as well, but knew better than to spook him. Men could be emotionally delicate.

"I'm having a barbecue," Wade said. "On Saturday. Kind of a neighborhood thing. Your neighborhood, actually. I thought I'd hold it next door. At your place."

She wanted to believe this was Zeke's idea, but knew better. "Tired of your brother sleeping on your couch?"

"He's taken the guest room, but yeah, he needs to get back together with his wife. Unless you don't want him."

"I still want him. I'm not the one who left."

"He thinks you don't care anymore."

She thought about the long nights alone in their bed and how she ached for him. She thought about how she missed holding him and how he no longer needed her.

"I'm not the one who changed."

Wade shifted awkwardly. "Boston, I…"

She held up her hand. "I'll take pity on you and just say yes, we can have a barbecue. What time?"

"Three?"

"Great. Did you invite anyone else, or should I do that, too? So your plan is less obvious."

"If you could ask some people, that would be great."

"Food?"

"I can bring burgers and stuff."

"Buns?"

"I'll bring buns."

She knew she would have to provide everything else. Still, she didn't mind. Not if this gave her a chance to spend time with Zeke. They could talk and she would explain that she needed him here.

"Saturday at three," she said. "It'll be fun."

Darrelyn was in her forties, with dark hair and sympathetic eyes. She led Deanna to a comfortable sofa in a small office.

"How can I help you?" she asked when Deanna was seated.

Deanna drew in a breath. "I'm not sure. I can't go on the way I am. It's too hard." She felt herself shaking, but still held out her hands. They were chapped and raw from the frequent washings.

Slowly, shamefully, she rolled up her sleeves to expose the scabs on her arms—proof of her use of the scrub brush.

"I threw it out," she whispered.

"The brush?"

Deanna nodded. "Today. It's so hard. I hate myself for doing it, but it also makes me feel better. I don't know if that makes sense."

"It does. Do you know why you feel compelled to wash your hands so much?"

Deanna nodded. "Some of it is from my mom and some is from my aunt and uncle. My mom was an alcoholic. She was mean and difficult. The house was so dirty. I hated that. When I was little she used to lock me in the closet. I remember the smell of it and how dark it was. I remember things crawling on me."

The memories tumbled out, one after the other. Darrelyn listened without speaking, taking occasional notes. Deanna talked about her aunt and uncle, how she was finally taken away but had to promise to be perfect. How hard that was. How she was afraid all the time. Afraid of being sent back. Afraid of being turned out onto the street.

"I wanted to be perfect so they would love me," she whispered. "Then when I married Colin, I wanted to be perfect to keep him. But being perfect is what drove him away and I've lost my children, as well. At least I've lost

Madison. I might have a chance with the younger ones. I don't know."

She reached for the box of tissues. "I never wanted to be like this and I don't know how to stop. The only time I feel safe is when I control my world. I know in my head I don't really have control, but it feels like it and then I can't stop."

She started to cry. After wiping away her tears, she glanced at the woman sitting across from her. "Is it hopeless?"

Darrelyn gave her a gentle smile. "You are so brave, Deanna. So strong. I'm very impressed."

Deanna stared at her. "Excuse me? How can you say that? What about what I've done to my children? To my husband? He hates me. No, I wish he hated me. He feels nothing."

"If he felt nothing, he would have left a long time ago." Darrelyn leaned toward her. "Look at you. Look at where you started. Have you ever once hit your children?"

"What?" She stiffened. "Of course not. I would never do that to them."

"Do you have any idea how difficult it is to break the cycle of violence? You were beaten so hard your mother broke bones, yet you've never once hit your children. You turn any frustration on yourself rather than risk hurting them. Your need to control your world is because you're afraid of what you are inside. Of the emotions you feel. That's why you hold on so tight."

Deanna crushed the tissues in her hand. "It can't be that simple."

"It can, but it's not simple. You're going to have to figure out how to believe in yourself, and that's not easy. You're going to have to trust your children and your husband. You're going to have to break a lifetime of patterns. You're going to have to believe the world will keep on turning, without your help. It's a long road, but look how far you've come."

She flushed. "I didn't do anything."

"I hope you can come to see that's not true."

"So you can help me?"

Darrelyn smiled at her. "Yes. I don't usually say this to people, but I feel it's important for you to know. You're not anywhere near my most damaged client. You need a little tweaking. That's all."

Deanna thought about the compulsive need to wash her hands, of the blood running down the shower drain. "You need to work on your definitions."

Darrelyn laughed. "You'll see what I mean in a few short weeks. Now let's talk about a plan. I'm going to recommend a medication. You won't need to take it for long and we'll start at the lowest dose, but it will help with the OCD. Then you and I can come up with a plan to let you safely experiment with trusting the people around you. You'll start to give up control, a bit at a time. We'll role-play here."

"Are you any good at being the difficult twelve-year-old?"

"It's my specialty. What do you think? There's lots of work to be done, but you've already come so far."

"I want to do this," Deanna told her. "I want to be normal."

"Normal is highly overrated," Darrelyn said with a grin. "I'm just saying."

Twenty-Four

Andi had been doing a good job of avoiding Wade. She wasn't sure if that was something she should be proud of or not, but it was how she'd decided to handle the situation. Unfortunately Saturday morning, she literally ran into him.

She was coming up the stairs, he was going down and they collided. He reached for her with one hand and grabbed her overflowing bag of groceries with the other.

"You okay?" he asked, steadying her.

Just the feel of his fingers on her skin made her insides get all gooey. She wanted to melt into him, kiss him senseless, then lead him into her bedroom. Common sense and the crew working in her house stopped her. Sadly, more the latter than the former, but whatever worked.

"I'm fine," she murmured. "Thanks for the rescue."

He took the bag from her and started up the stairs. "Food for the barbecue?"

"I'm making potato salad. It's about all I can manage in my makeshift kitchen. I'll boil the potatoes in batches. I have an old family recipe."

"I look forward to it."

The words sounded right, but he wouldn't completely meet her eyes. Even as they were forced to walk close together in the narrow stairwell, she had a feeling he wanted to put more distance between them.

They reached the third floor. She followed him into the kitchen. He put the bag on the table, then took a step back.

"I haven't seen you lately," he said, stopping in the doorway.

She couldn't look at him without wanting him, but where a couple of days ago she would simply have walked up and slid into his arms, right now she couldn't. Not only didn't she want to feel the first stirrings of passion or the way her body fit so well against his; she wasn't sure how he would react. Something had changed between them. Something had gone wrong.

She supposed the right thing to do was to ask. To find out and then fix the problem. Only what if she couldn't? What if she'd lost Wade before she had the chance to really get to know him? Not mentioning there was a problem was so much easier than facing things head-on. Only look where that had gotten her with Matt.

Honestly, she told herself. She could handle whatever he had to say.

She studied him—took in the handsome lines of his face, the steadiness in his eyes. "We have to talk about it."

His expression went completely blank. "What do you mean?"

"What's going on between us. Or not going on. You told Carrie not to get attached. She mentioned it when we were shopping together the other day." Andi held up a hand. "Please don't tell her I told you. I don't want her getting in trouble."

"I won't say anything." He crossed his arms over his chest. "What would you have preferred I said to her? She likes you. She sees you a lot because she's always with Madison."

"So? She's a smart kid. She knows adults date and sometimes it works out and sometimes it doesn't. But to tell her not to get attached..." She moved to the other side of the table, needing distance and maybe something physical between them. "You're assuming this is going nowhere. I don't think I want that."

"Neither of us knows what's going to happen. It's been two months, Andi. We're still figuring things out. Why are you so upset?"

Because Carrie had admitted her father wasn't getting married. Because she felt herself falling for him and worried that she was once again putting her heart in the hands of a man who would abandon her.

"I was surprised," she said instead. "I thought we had potential. Obviously you don't. I'm going to have to figure out if I'm willing to be in a 'sex only' relationship."

He shook his head. "That's not what's happening here. You know that. Carrie's my kid. I have to protect her."

"I think the person you're protecting is yourself. You've pulled back. What happened to change things?"

He looked startled, as if she'd stumbled onto the truth. Which meant she probably had. But what truth? Why would he need to protect himself about her? She wasn't dangerous. She hadn't done anything that should worry him.

They stared at each other. One of the guys called from the base of the stairs.

"I have to go," Wade told her.

She nodded, hoping he would say they would talk about this later, but he didn't.

"That was a disaster," Boston said.

Deanna looked at her friend. "I'm sorry things didn't go better with Zeke."

"He didn't want to talk. He barely looked at me."

Deanna wanted to say that wasn't true, but it had been obvious from the first second he'd walked into the backyard that Zeke wasn't there to make friends. He'd kept to himself, sitting under one of the trees, steadily drinking beer. Deanna had kept herself on the fringes, so she'd been in a position to notice things like that.

"He looked at you when you weren't watching," Andi said. "He's in a lot of pain." She reached out and squeezed Boston's hand. "I know you are, too."

The three of them sat in Boston's backyard, the remains of the barbecue around them. The trash can was full, the cooler empty except for water and a few sturdy ice cubes. Bottles filled the recycling bin. Pickles sat on a nearby chair, washing his face.

"Poor Wade," Boston said, leaning her head back in her chair. "He wanted to make things right."

"I wouldn't spend too much time worried about Wade," Andi said.

Deanna nodded. "He put his foot in it, for sure."

"Men are stupid," Andi said. "And I'm even more stupid. Why did I think he'd be different? He's not."

Boston nodded. "I want to defend him, but I can't. Telling Carrie not to get attached is idiotic. What did he think would happen when you found out?"

"He didn't think I would. Damn, I wish the sex weren't so good."

Deanna surprised herself by laughing. "Seriously?"

"Okay, maybe I don't wish that, although it would make things easier." Andi sighed. "I know it's early. I know that because of Matt, I'm more sensitive to any signs of him not being committed. I accept that I have unreasonable expectations, but he didn't even try to convince me. A little groveling would have gone a long way." She sipped her beer, then turned to Deanna. "You're doing better. You seem less tense."

"I'm trying. The therapist helped and I'm taking the medication she prescribed. So far I'm not feeling any different, but it's only been a few days."

"Hope gets you through," Boston said.

A theory Deanna was willing to hang on to with both hands. "She told me that if Colin wanted to leave, he would already be gone."

"He was friendly tonight," Andi said. "He sat next to you."

Deanna had noticed that, as well. "I don't want to assume anything. I don't think there were any other places to sit."

"It was a picnic," Boston told her gently. "He could have sat on the ground with the kids."

"She's right." Andi raised her beer bottle. "But he sat next to you on the bench. Run with it."

"I'm not ready to run. I'll just sit here and breathe it in." She looked at the other two women. "Thank you for getting me through this. I don't know what would have happened if you hadn't been here for me."

"I'm glad to help," Boston said. "I need to help. It gets me out of my head." She grinned. "So thanks for being a mess. The timing is perfect."

Deanna laughed. "You're welcome. My mental illness is always here to serve."

* * *

Andi and Deanna left sometime after midnight. They'd both helped with the cleanup, so there was little left for Boston to do but make sure the doors and windows were locked, then head upstairs. She wasn't tired and doubted she would sleep, but she had to at least go through the motions. Maybe she would get lucky and doze off for a couple of hours.

She was halfway up the stairs when her cell phone rang. She hurried down and pulled it out of her purse. Her heart pounded as she fumbled with the talk button. No call at this hour was good news.

"Hello? Zeke? Are you okay?"

"Mrs. King?"

The voice was male and unfamiliar. "Yes."

"I'm Deputy Sam Anders. Zeke's been helping me with a remodeling on a house I'm buying. I'm getting married in a few months. Anyway, I know him and, well, I brought him in about a half hour ago. He was driving drunk, ma'am. He ran his truck into a tree."

Boston sank onto the sofa and closed her eyes. "Is he all right? Did he hurt anyone?"

"It was a single-vehicle accident. He's a little banged up, but he says he'll be fine. The truck's in bad shape."

"I don't care about the truck. So he's in jail?"

"I didn't arrest him, ma'am."

Right. Because the island was a small town and everyone knew everyone else. Which was why the deputy had told her the seemingly insignificant detail of Zeke working on his house.

"You can come get him and drive him home, if you'd like."

Home? Zeke didn't live here anymore. He didn't want her. He blamed her for the death of their son.

"I'll be right there."

She got her purse and drove to the sheriff's station. At this time of night, there were only a couple of people on duty. The deputy led her to a small room where Zeke waited.

Her husband sat in front of a table. He had a couple of bruises on his jaw and what looked like the beginning of a black eye. She could tell he was still fighting the effects of the alcohol.

The deputy closed the door behind her, leaving them alone.

"I guess you can't ignore me now," she said into the quiet.

Zeke looked up. His dark eyes were expressionless, his mouth a firm line. Although everything about him was exactly as she remembered, it was as if he were a stranger. She felt the distance between them. The sadness.

On the drive over, she'd planned what she was going to say. How she was going to tell him that there was no way she would enable his drinking. That he had to stop and if he couldn't stop on his own, he had to get help. But even though she had her speech prepared, what she said instead was, "If you really think I'm responsible for Liam's death, we're done. Because you can't forgive me for something I didn't do and had no control over."

Zeke continued to stare at her. Emotions chased across his face, none staying long enough to be named.

"Is this what it took?" he asked.

"What are you talking about?"

"I've been waiting all this time. Waiting for you to call

me on what I said. Waiting for you to stand up for yourself. For us. Is this what it took?"

Disbelief stole her breath. "This was a *game?*" she asked. "You were *pretending* to blame me?"

"I was trying to get your attention."

She didn't want to get any closer, didn't want to be near him, but she was having trouble standing. Her legs trembled and she seemed to be losing her balance. She crossed to the second chair and pulled it out from the table. After positioning it as far from Zeke as possible, she sank down. Betrayal coiled around her like a snake, squeezing tighter until it was impossible to breathe.

How could he have done this to her? Tried to manipulate her? Lied to her in such a hurtful way?

"No," he roared, coming to his feet. "No. I'm not the bad guy here."

"And I am?"

"No. Don't you see? I had to do something. I had to get through to you." He paced across the room, then turned. "You're gone, Boston. You've been gone since Liam died. I can't get anywhere near you. I've tried and tried and you're simply not there. I didn't just lose my son that day. I lost my wife, too. You're right in front of me and I can't touch you."

"You're not making any sense. I'm right here."

"No, you're not. I don't know what you think or what you feel. Does our marriage mean anything to you?"

"How can you ask that?" She fought tears. "I've loved you nearly all my life."

"You used to love me. I believe that. Do you feel anything now? You think I drink because I don't miss my son? I drink because I can't stop missing him. Because the pain is too big. I don't know where to put it, and when

I try to talk to you about it, you disappear into that damn studio of yours and paint."

"It's how I deal with what happened," she snapped.

"No. It's how you hide from it. It's how you feel nothing. I'm in this alone. I've been alone since the day we buried our son. I reached for you and you were gone. I don't think you're coming back."

She stood and glared at him. Anger gave her strength. "You're saying all this because I haven't cried. How I deal with my loss is my decision. You don't get to say what's right."

He shrugged. "Fine. Have you dealt with your loss? Would you say you're doing better? Moving forward?"

"I'm painting other things. I'm working on Andi's mural. That's progress. I'm showing up every day, Zeke. You're the one who's not home. You're the one not participating in our marriage."

She waited for him to yell at her. To tell her she was wrong, but instead his expression turned sad. The kind of sad that came from the loss of hope.

"You don't need me, Boston. You never have. You've loved me, I'll give you that. You're a brilliant artist. You have clients begging you to start painting their fabrics again. You have that house and your friends. You don't need me for anything."

"I don't understand," she whispered. "What have I done that's so wrong? Why are you doing this? Why don't we make love anymore?"

His expression hardened. "We haven't made love because you're not there. You're a shell. You look the same and you can say the words, but you won't let me in. I still love you, Boston. I'll always love you. But I won't be a part of this…denial."

He blamed her? He was judging her?

"Right. You're too busy driving drunk. You could have killed someone."

"I know. I was stupid. It won't happen again."

She gave an angry laugh. "Sure. Just like that. You'll stop drinking."

"Alcohol isn't the problem."

"Because I am? You're blaming me for everything. I didn't do anything wrong. I didn't kill him."

The words came out in a scream. They echoed in the small room, then grew silent.

She looked at Zeke. In their brief conversation, he'd become a stranger. She felt coldness inside. A wall of ice forming around her heart.

"You're right," she told him. "I don't need you. There's no reason for you to come home now, is there?"

She clutched her purse tightly to her chest and walked out. She made her way to her car and climbed inside. Once she was there, she waited for the enormity of what she'd done to crash in on her. She waited for the tears because now, surely now she could cry.

But there was nothing. No tears, no panic, not much of anything. Just the chill of the ice and the knowledge that nothing would ever be the same again.

Twenty-Five

Deanna placed forks and spoons on the table as she told herself she was going to be fine. She didn't believe the words, of course, but saying them over and over provided a certain level of comfort. Or maybe the illusion of comfort. At this point, she would take what was offered.

Darrelyn had told her to simply observe her children. To listen without judgment. That was her homework for this week. To take her medication, to count to ten before allowing herself to wash her hands and to listen. Which had all sounded so easy in the privacy of her therapist's calm office. In real life, it was a bitch of an assignment.

She glanced at the clock and realized that dinner would be delivered shortly. The table was set and she'd already put out the money by the front door. She'd taken care of all the details. She could go off duty for the evening and simply pay attention to what was going on around her. Easy, she told herself. Doable.

The doorbell rang.

She answered it and collected the two large paper bags filled with containers and paid the guy.

"Keep the change," she told him, then closed the front

door with her hip and yelled up the stairs, "Dinner is here, girls."

Audrey appeared at the top of the stairs. "Here? What do you mean?"

"We're having Chinese. The guy just delivered it."

The twins joined their sisters. Lucy followed. All four of them stared down at her with varying expressions of disbelief.

"Chinese?" Sydney asked. "From China?"

Deanna laughed. "No. From the new Chinese restaurant in town. I thought it would be fun to try."

"You didn't cook dinner?" Lucy asked cautiously.

"I thought this would be a nice change."

The girls moved as one, racing down the stairs. Audrey paused to call up the stairs, "Hurry, Madison. We're having Chinese."

They split up, the twins heading for the kitchen, the two older girls going into the downstairs bathroom, and washed their hands. Deanna set out the food, then waited until her children were seated at the big table in the kitchen before pouring drinks. Madison joined them last, obviously reluctant and sullen.

Observe, Deanna reminded herself. She wouldn't get on her oldest for anything tonight. She would watch and listen.

"I've never had Chinese," Lucy admitted, staring at the take-out containers.

"Me, either," Savannah said.

"It's no big deal." Madison sounded bored.

"I'm excited," Sydney told Deanna. "What does it taste like?"

"There are different dishes." Deanna started opening the containers. "This one is moo goo gai pan. Chicken and vegetables, mostly. We have sweet-and-sour chicken, beef with broccoli, fried rice and egg rolls."

Savannah turned to her. "Eggs for dinner?"

"They're not eggs. To be honest, I'm not sure how they got their names. Why don't you try a little bit of everything and figure out what you like? Then you can have more of that."

The twins nodded. Lucy and Audrey waited for her to help them, as well. Deanna smiled at her oldest. "I'm sure you already know what you'd prefer."

Madison shrugged and reached for the rice.

It took a few minutes to get everyone served. Deanna snagged an egg roll on her way back to her seat and took a bite. She realized her four youngest were watching as she chewed.

"It's good," she said with a smile. "Try it."

They all picked up their egg rolls and took tiny bites. One by one, they started to nod.

Sydney speared a piece of chicken and stuck it in her mouth. "This is good," she mumbled over the food.

Deanna started to remind her to chew with her mouth closed, but then remembered she was to observe, not judge. "I'm glad you like it," she said.

"We have to pick a country for camp," Sydney told her.

"We should pick China," her twin added.

"We could talk about the food!"

"That would be fun," Deanna said. "I could speak to your counselor about bringing in samples. I'm sure the restaurant could make up little pieces for the campers to eat."

"Mom, we're going horseback riding next week," Audrey said. "Can you sign my permission slip?"

"Sure. Where are the horses?"

"Marysville. There's a ranch out there. Alison's been riding before and says even though we're up really high, it's not scary."

"You're athletic," Deanna told her daughter. "I think you're going to do really well. The horses they'll use will be gentle. You'll have fun."

Audrey smiled with obvious relief. "I think so, too."

Lucy reached for the sweet-and-sour chicken. "Emma and I are going to the library on Saturday. For the reading hour. There's a sign that says in August an author is coming to speak!"

Madison frowned at her. "No author would come to Blackberry Island."

"The sign says," Lucy told her sister. "I want to go listen to her."

"Me, too," Deanna said. "Meeting an author would be very exciting."

"Mommy, can I have more rice?" Sydney asked.

"Sure." Deanna walked around the table and helped her. She checked on the other girls, then resumed her seat.

The dinner progressed. She kept reminding herself to listen without judgment. To ask questions and let her girls answer. As conversation flowed around her, she was reminded that Lucy was more earnest than her sisters and that Audrey had a shy sense of humor. That the twins finished each other's sentences and that Madison nearly boiled with suppressed rage.

Nothing for her to deal with right now, she told herself. That was for a later homework assignment.

They finished the meal and put away leftovers. The girls quickly cleared the table, and Deanna loaded the dishwasher.

"Maybe we can have Chinese for breakfast," Audrey joked.

Deanna laughed. "I think that would be very interesting."

The five of them walked into the family room. Madison stood by the stairs.

"I want to go up to my room," she announced.

"That's fine," Deanna said, and sat on the sofa.

Lucy reached for the TV remote and turned on the television. It was already set on the local PBS station.

"Tonight we'll learn how trash makes its way from your kitchen container to landfills across America."

Savannah and Sydney exchanged a look but didn't say anything. Audrey sighed. Lucy took a seat without saying anything.

Because there were rules, Deanna thought. Only PBS on weeknights. And only for an hour. Then the girls had to play games or read before bed. Movies and commercial television were a weekend treat.

Observe, she told herself. No judgments. Not even of herself. Because she'd established the rules with the best of intentions. Although at that moment, they seemed dictatorial and harsh.

Impulsively, she picked up the remote. "I'm not in the mood to see how trash gets into landfills," she said. "What else is on?"

She activated the guide and scrolled through the channels. One of the stations was having a *Family Ties* marathon.

"My aunt loved this show," she said, turning to the channel. "I used to watch it when I was growing up."

"What's it about?" Sydney asked, sitting next to her on the sofa.

"A family with two girls and a boy. The parents used to be hippies."

"What's a hippie?" Savannah asked, sitting on Deanna's other side.

"That's kind of hard to explain. Let's watch the show and you can see if it makes sense to you."

The familiar theme began and Alex P. Keaton walked into the family kitchen. Within a couple of minutes, all four girls were laughing. Lucy and Audrey had joined the twins on the sofa. By the end of the episode, Sydney and Savannah were snuggled next to her and the two older girls had inched closer.

Deanna had a thousand things she needed to be doing. Email and bills and a few lists. But instead of excusing herself, she stayed where she was—surrounded by her girls. Tears threatened, but she fought them back. Crying now would be too hard to explain.

This had been a good night, she realized. No fights, no orders, no "you have to." Just an evening enjoying time with her children. And for once, them enjoying time with her.

Wade's truck wasn't in front of her house when Andi arrived home from work, but she didn't think anything of that. He would show up later, or see her tomorrow. They didn't go more than two days without him bringing her up-to-date on what was happening with the house. But when she stepped inside, she found Zeke walking around with a clipboard.

"Hey, Andi," he said. "How's it going?"

Except for socially, she hadn't seen Zeke since before the job began. "I'm good. What's up?"

"Nothing. I thought I'd show you what we've accomplished today."

Andi shook her head. "I don't understand. Where's Wade?"

Zeke glanced down at his notes. "He's, uh, at another job." He mumbled something else that she couldn't hear, but it didn't matter what.

"No way," she said, glaring at Zeke. "You are not telling me that he didn't have the balls to show up."

Zeke winced. "Kind of. Look, Andi, I don't know what's going on between you two, but I want you to know that I'm going to make sure you're happy with the work we do."

"Uh-huh." She squeezed her car keys in her hand. "Where is he?"

"Wade?"

"Yes. Give me an address. We're going to have this out today."

Zeke only hesitated a second, then wrote down an address and handed it to her.

"Smart man," she said as she walked out.

"Don't hurt him," Zeke called after her.

"I'm not promising anything."

Andi found the address easily. Wade's truck was parked in front of a two-story apartment building. From the number of other vehicles in the driveway, she would guess the building was undergoing a major renovation. Nice to know she could find him easily if she decided she needed to attack him with a fork.

She followed the sound of demolition and found him talking to a couple of his guys. When he saw her, he excused himself and walked over.

Neither of them spoke as he led her out of the lobby and around the side of the building. She ignored the sight of his butt or anything else she might find appealing and instead focused on the fact that he'd chosen to disappear rather than face her. Shades of Matt all over again.

"Really?" she asked when he turned to her. "Really? You didn't show up? That was your solution? Not a conversation? Even an email? On *Sex and the City* Berger at least broke up with a Post-it."

"Who?"

"Never mind." She poked him in his very impressive chest. "So it's over?"

"I don't know," he admitted.

"You decided we weren't going anywhere," she told him. "That's what happened. But instead of delivering the message yourself, you let your daughter tell me. That's pretty crappy."

She held on to her anger because feeling anything else would mean crying, and he didn't deserve to know she cared enough to cry.

"Now you're disappearing. I never thought you were that guy. I guess I was wrong."

"I'm not the one sleeping with a handsome blue-collar guy. How convenient for you that I also do remodeling. Sort of a two-for."

Andi took a step back. "You heard."

Wade's gaze turned icy. "Every word. And you didn't disagree."

Andi flushed. "I'm sorry that upset you. But I wasn't going to go into detail about us with my mother."

He shook his head. "Yeah, why would you tell your family? I'm not the one who decided this wasn't going anywhere, Andi. That was you."

"No. That's not what I meant. I didn't want to say more because my mother has a way of twisting things around. If you heard that, then you heard her defending the guy who left me standing at the altar. She's not someone I trust with anything that matters to me." She touched his arm. "Is that what this has been about?"

He pulled free. "I get it. You're having your fun while you get settled in town. Now you're pissed because I'm ending things before you're ready."

"You're not listening, Wade. What I said or didn't say to my mother has nothing to do with how I feel about us. I like you a lot. I want us to be together. Because of Matt I'm a little stressed about you holding back, but I'm working on that. Don't end things because of my mother. You have to believe me."

His dark gaze was unforgiving. "No, I don't."

"Just like that?"

"Carrie's mother didn't like what I did, either. She wanted more than this life here. Than the island. She was always pushing me to be more. Well, I like what I do and I like who I am. I don't want to be different."

"I'm not asking you to change."

"You'd be happier with someone more like you," he said flatly. "And I'd prefer someone I could trust."

She felt that slap and took a step back. "So that's it? We're done?"

"I am."

She turned to walk away, then spun back. "You're wrong about me, Wade. And you're letting pride get in the way of something that could have been great."

"A chance I'm willing to take."

She wanted to tell him that he was letting his past define him, just as she let what had happened with Matt make her a little crazy. She wanted to point out that Carrie liked her and didn't every parent want his kid to marry a doctor? But what was the point? He'd already made up his mind. And she vowed that as long as she lived, she would never again beg a man to love her.

Twenty-Six

Deanna always considered Crock-Pot cooking a form of cheating. As if by not doing all the work, it didn't count. But she was trying to change, and as Darrelyn had pointed out, some rules existed simply because they'd never been questioned. Her assignment this week was to test one rule a day. On Friday, Deanna decided it was time to challenge her relationship with her Crock-Pot.

Colin had texted that he would be home at four. She picked up the girls from their various camps and returned to the house a few minutes after. His car was already in the driveway.

"Daddy's here, Daddy's here," the twins shouted. They barely waited for the minivan to come to a stop before scrambling out. Audrey and Lucy quickly followed. Madison was going home with Carrie and wouldn't be back until the morning.

Deanna got out more slowly, both anxious to see Colin and terrified that this would be the day he announced he was leaving. She went inside, careful to avoid him. Something she'd gotten good at. A few weeks ago, she'd done it because she was trying to show him she didn't care. Now it was because she did. More than she'd realized. Only she didn't know how to tell him…mostly because she was pretty sure it would be too little too late.

She checked on the pot roast, then collected berries she'd bought at the stand by the bridge. She would use them to make dessert.

She'd just finished rinsing the strawberries when Colin walked into the kitchen.

"Hello, Deanna."

She braced herself, then turned and smiled at him. "Hi. It's nice to have you back."

He studied her as he moved toward her, then leaned against the counter, his arms crossed in front of his chest. "You're using the Crock-Pot."

"Pot roast. It's cool and rainy, which seemed like Crock-Pot weather."

"You hate the Crock-Pot."

"We've had a troubled relationship until now, but we talked it out and I think we're going to be able to stay friends."

He raised his eyebrows. "Interesting."

"We agreed we'd been quick to make judgments about each other. The pot roast is going to be a test. I can report back on things tomorrow, if you'd like."

"Sure. How was your week?"

"Good. Yours?"

"Successful."

She waited. This was the point where he usually walked away. They didn't talk anymore. They hadn't talked in weeks. Before that they'd fought and before that…well, it hadn't been good.

"Is everything all right?" he asked. "You seem different."

"I'm fine. I've been busy with the girls. I've been thinking about what you said, about us needing more income, so I've been polishing my résumé. I took an on-line class. It was free, but helpful."

His blue eyes flashed with surprise. "You really like working at the craft store."

"I know, but it doesn't pay much. I need to take on more financial responsibilities. Besides, the twins will be in first grade, so they'll be gone all day. I should be working more. You're right, you're gone too much. The girls need you here."

I need you here.

The words lodged in her throat and her heart. The truth of them nearly drove her to her knees. She missed Colin. Not the cold stranger she'd created, but the man he'd been before. He'd adored her and she had loved him and they'd been happy. Why had she wanted that to change?

She cleared her throat. "I'm, uh, seeing someone."

He stiffened. His arms dropped to his sides as his mouth straightened. "Who is he?"

She frowned. "What are you— Oh, no. I'm—" She glanced over her shoulder to make sure they were alone, then lowered her voice. "I meant I've started seeing a therapist. About the hand-washing and the other stuff you and I talked about. She's very helpful. I'm making progress. There's nothing for you to do, I just wanted to tell you so when it came through on our insurance, you'd know what it was about."

He relaxed. "That's a big step."

"A necessary one. Given my past, I suppose it's not unexpected that I have issues. I want to make sure I'm not passing them on to my children. Break the cycle and all that."

She felt sort of tingly and hopeful inside. If Colin was jealous at the thought of her being with someone, that had to be good, didn't it? She didn't want to read too much into his actions, but maybe this was a start.

"How can I help?" he asked.

Hope fluttered a little bigger and brighter. "So far, all the assignments are mine, but if that changes, I'll let you know."

He glanced at the Crock-Pot and grinned. "Was that one of them?"

She laughed. "Technically I have not used my time in therapy to work on my Crock-Pot issues, but yes, using it does address my homework for the week."

"I can't wait to see what's next. An immersion blender?"

"Or a deep fryer. You never know."

"It's beautiful, don't you think?" Andi asked as she stood in the doorway to one of her exam rooms.

The painting was done, the examination table was in place, as was the counter and small sink. Boston had sketched in the happy monkey for the wall and would paint it over the next few days.

"I think everything is coming together nicely. I'll be able to open a couple of weeks early, which is very unexpected." She cleared her throat. "Dr. Harrington okayed Nina coming to work for me and we're holding interviews next week. She's been an amazing help."

Andi paused as she had to swallow back the need to burst into tears. "So, as you can see, I'm really getting it together."

Pickles shifted in her arms, as if pointing out he'd

been very patient for a long time but this was getting ridiculous.

"You're right," she said, putting him down. "I'm sorry. You have a family to get home to. I've been at loose ends this weekend, but I shouldn't take that out on you."

Pickles rubbed against the side of her bare leg, then headed for the open front door. Andi watched him go, aware of the emptiness of her house and the long evening that stretched in front of her.

Lucy and her sisters hadn't been by in a while now. Andi knew it was because Lucy had a new best friend and was busy with her. Which was how it was supposed to be. The other girls had always only trailed after Lucy to visit.

As for herself, Andi knew she'd done well in the few short months she'd been on the island. She had her work friends and her Pilates friends and her beautiful house. She loved her work and found it fulfilling. If she'd accidentally fallen for a complete asshole boyfriend, well, that happened, right? Maybe it really *was* time for her to give up on relationships.

"Knock, knock. It's me."

She walked toward the front of the house and found Boston standing in the waiting room of her office. Her neighbor glanced around and grinned. "Do I do good work or what?"

"You're gifted."

"Thanks." Boston shrugged. "I'm in hell."

"Me, too."

They hugged briefly, and then Boston grabbed her hand. "Come on. We're meeting next door. Colin is taking the girls out to the movies, and Deanna went to Arnie's to get us pulled-pork sandwiches. I have wine and we're going to make a night of it."

"Thank God," Andi said, following her. "I was going crazy in there. I can keep busy during the week, but the weekends are endless and Sundays are the worst."

"For me, too. Now."

Andi didn't know the details of what had happened, but was under the impression Boston didn't expect Zeke to be coming back anytime soon.

"Still no word?" she asked as they crossed the lawn and up the front stairs.

"Nothing. He said I don't need him and I'm thinking maybe he's right."

Andi shook her head as they entered the kitchen. "I don't accept that. You love him. You're wonderful together. Losing a baby is very stressful. You have to give it time."

"It's been nine months, Andi. Three months longer than we had him. At some point we have to heal and move on. I'm trying, but it's not enough for Zeke. He needs me to be over it on his schedule, in his way. He can't accept we're different and he blames me for disappointing him."

"You sound so rational," Andi said, not sure that was a good thing.

"Don't overrate being rational," Deanna said, coming in with bags of food. "I'm paying a lot of money to at least fake rational."

"There's nothing wrong with you," Boston told her.

Deanna smiled. "All OCD aside?"

"Everyone has quirks."

She passed out the food while Boston opened the wine. Andi arranged the stools around the breakfast bar so they could see each other and set out plenty of napkins.

"Talking about Zeke?" Deanna asked as they all took a seat.

"Yes, he's being a jerk," Andi said.

"Not as big a jerk as Wade."

Andi did her best not to flinch. "It must run in the family."

Deanna glanced between them. "What's Wade's issue?"

"I didn't defend him to my mother." Andi stared at the sandwich and wondered if she was really hungry. "She talked about him being a nice blue-collar man I could sleep with. I didn't bother to engage because there's no point."

Deanna grabbed a fry. "Didn't your mother also defend the jerk who left you at the altar?"

"Yes."

"Did Wade hear that?"

"Probably."

"So he knows she's an idiot."

Andi wasn't sure that was helpful information. "I know. Which makes me think he's using this as an opportunity to pull back. Not exactly news to make me happy."

"Sorry," Deanna said.

"Don't be. I hid from the truth for a long time. I don't want to do that anymore. I just thought…" She shrugged. "I liked him a lot. I thought we were going somewhere. I was working through my need to have a commitment after the first fifteen minutes. I was getting better. I like Carrie and there was potential. I guess the hardest part is I don't think I did anything wrong. I see my parents maybe once every two years. They wouldn't be a big part of our lives. So why not just go with the flow and then be relieved when the visit is over? But Wade doesn't see it that way."

Andi glanced at Boston. "Do we need to change the subject?"

"No. I'm okay. Wade's being stupid and I'm not sure why, either." Boston turned to Deanna. "You seem happy."

Deanna smiled as she picked up her sandwich. "I'm doing better. I think the medication is helping and I'm making peace with various kitchen appliances."

"Excuse me?" Andi asked.

"Sorry. Silly joke. It's better. Colin is being nice, which gives me hope but also makes me nervous. I don't want to think everything is going to be fine only to have him walk out. I don't think I would survive that."

She stared at Boston and Andi. "I'm sorry. That was insensitive."

Boston shook her head. "Don't you apologize. I've been smug about my relationship with Zeke from the day we met. I've had this coming for a while."

"Still, I didn't mean to…"

Andi leaned toward her and bumped shoulders. "Let it go. We'll change the subject. Have you guys seen the foreman of my landscaping remodel?"

Boston laughed. "Oh, yeah. He's adorable."

"He's twenty-four. Don't get any ideas, but yes, Thad is very pretty."

"I like that he takes his shirt off early in the day," Deanna admitted. "All those muscles rippling in the sun."

"Or the rain," Boston added. "He's one with nature. I respect that."

"You respect his six-pack."

"That, too. I've always enjoyed doing nude portraits. I wonder if he'd pose."

Deanna and Andi laughed.

Andi realized she was hungry again and bit into her sandwich. As long as she had her friends, she thought, Sundays weren't going to be that bad after all.

Boston sat on the floor of Andi's waiting room. As she waited for the paint to dry in the few animals she had left to paint, she spread out squares of paper in front of her, then looked at the samples she'd been sent.

Although she hadn't worked in nearly a year, interior designers continued to contact her, asking if she was ready to take a job. For the first time since her late pregnancy, she'd felt she could finally look at the various projects and perhaps even take one on.

She picked up a letter from a designer in Raleigh. "The woman loves blue. I've tried to talk her into accent colors, but she's resisting. So anything blue. If you could put in another color, I would love you forever."

Boston smiled, then looked at the fabric samples and paint swatches included in the box. There were also photos of possible furniture choices.

Her job was to pull it all together in a custom fabric design. She would paint a couple of different options onto small squares of fabric. The client picked one and Boston then hand-painted the length of fabric required.

It was an expensive decorating option. She charged a hundred dollars a yard for her work, and that didn't cover the cost of fabric or shipping. What the client got in return was a unique element in a room along with the ability to say her drapes had been hand-painted by Boston Flemming.

Boston Flemming, not Boston King. She used her maiden name for her work, something Zeke had encouraged. He'd wanted to keep their businesses separate, and she'd agreed. Now she wondered if somewhere along the way, her success had become a problem.

Wade walked into the waiting room and squatted down next to her. "That's a lot of blue."

"This from a guy who thinks beige is a color."

"It *is* a color."

"Not a good one." She glanced up at him. "What are you doing here? I thought you were hiding from Andi."

"My brother and I have a bit of a dilemma," he admitted.

"You don't want to be here when Andi's around, and he doesn't want to be here when I'm around."

Wade sat on the tarp covering the floor. "Something like that. You could give him a break."

"I could but I won't."

"Why not?"

"He gave up on us." She looked at him. "Giving up seems to run in the family."

His expression tightened. "I'm not talking about Andi with you."

"Not a problem. I can do the talking. You're wrong about her. She's sweet and funny and she cares about people. She likes you a lot, and with all your flaws, you should be grateful someone does."

"Ouch."

"This is not the time to be delicate. You know her mother is weird. All parents are. Why are you punishing Andi for what her mother said?"

"It wouldn't have worked."

"It would have worked just fine, and I think that's what scares you. You're so comfortable in your life. You have Carrie and your brother and me and your work. Getting involved again means putting yourself out there. Taking a chance. What if you make another mistake?"

He stared at her. "I didn't make a mistake before."

Boston sighed. "Sure you did. I know she wanted you to leave the island and you didn't. I know you guys were talking about getting a divorce when she died. I know you weren't happy." She lightly touched his arm. "I know about her affair."

Wade turned away. "Yeah, well, it doesn't matter now."

"Of course it matters. Andi's terrified that she's going to give her heart to a guy who won't commit. You're terrified you're going to give your heart to someone who secretly wants you to be different. You're both so damned sensitive you can't see that you're perfect for each other. So until you get your own issues worked out, stay out of my marriage."

She drew in a breath and braced herself for Wade to point out she didn't have a marriage. Not anymore. But instead he leaned in and kissed her on the forehead.

"It should have been you and me, kid. We would have gotten it right."

She laughed. "I know, but you never did it for me. I'm sorry to break your heart."

"You don't do it for me, either. But I still love you."

"I love you more."

He chuckled. "That might be true." His laughter faded. "Talk to Zeke."

"Talk to Andi."

He stood. "You're stubborn." He held up his hands. "I know, I know. I am, too. I'm leaving now."

Boston glanced at her watch and saw it was close to five. "Coward."

"I'm a man who knows the value of a strategic retreat."

Twenty-Seven

Audrey bit her lower lip. "Are you sure, Mom?"

Deanna smiled. "Yes. A thousand times, yes."

"But it's pay-per-view."

"Push the button, sweetheart."

The twins shrieked and Lucy hugged a pillow to her chest. Audrey did as requested and the movie appeared on the screen.

Just one more place where she'd been far too rigid, Deanna thought sadly, going into the kitchen to make popcorn for her girls. Okay, sure, a pay-per-view every night would get expensive, but once in a while was fine. Something she'd never believed until now.

She poured the larger bowl of popcorn into two smaller bowls and carried them into the family room. The girls were already mesmerized by the cartoon playing on the screen.

"Enjoy," Deanna said, and returned to the kitchen. She glanced toward the ceiling and thought about taking a bowl of popcorn up to Madison. What stopped her was that somehow her oldest would turn the gesture into something awful, and right now Deanna couldn't face another glare or eye roll.

She was doing better. She could feel it. She was less tense all the time and sleeping better. The girls were more spontaneous and happy. Except for Madison, of course. But it was the weekend and that meant Colin was home. While she liked having him around, it also made her nervous.

"The girls watching their movie?"

She jumped and turned to see the man in question lounging in the doorway of the kitchen. He wore jeans and a T-shirt. Casual clothes that looked good on him. Sexy. A wave of longing swept through, settling in her heart and okay, maybe a little lower than that, too.

She wanted to make love with him, but just as much, she wanted to be held. Held in a way that made her feel safe. Comfortable. She wanted not to worry that he was leaving. She wanted them to be married again.

"They're enjoying their cartoon," she told him. "Except for Madison."

"At twelve, she's far too sophisticated for that sort of thing," he said.

She nodded.

"We've both been so busy with the kids we haven't had a chance to talk," he said. "Why don't you join me for a glass of wine and we can catch up?"

Deanna wondered if she looked as surprised as she felt. "Um, sure. That would be nice."

She followed him into his study, where he had a bottle of merlot and two wineglasses waiting. She settled in a corner of the sofa, then wondered if she should have sat more in the middle. Or...

She sighed. She'd known Colin for nearly sixteen years. It shouldn't be this difficult. But it was.

He handed her a glass, then sat on the sofa, as well. He angled toward her. They were close, but not touching, and she knew how much she needed his touch. Just one kiss, she thought longingly.

"The girls are doing well," she said. "I can't believe how fast summer is going by. The school emailed their supply list already."

"We never did plan a vacation," he said.

"I know. It's been busy and with everything else happening…"

Colin sipped his wine. "I talked to my boss about taking over the sales department. He's ready when I am. Without the commission and overtime for travel, we're looking at about a fifteen percent pay cut. I've been running the numbers. It'll make things tight."

"That's okay," she said quickly. "I've sent out my résumé to a couple of places. I have an interview next week at the Blackberry Island Inn. They want a bookkeeper for about thirty hours a week. I don't have all the details, but it sounds like I could do some of the work from home, which means I could be around for the girls. It's a big raise and more hours, so I would make up the difference from your salary and cover what I was making before."

His blue gaze was steady. "Are you sure?"

"Very. We've talked about this, Colin. You need to be here with your girls. They miss you." She cleared her throat. "I, um, miss you, too."

He put his wine on the coffee table and reached for her free hand. "I'd like to be around more," he admitted.

His fingers were warm and strong. Familiar, she thought, but it had been so long since he'd touched her.

Her stomach flipped over a couple of times and she wanted to both throw herself at him and run away. She settled on putting her glass on the end table and steadying her breathing.

"I'll talk to my boss when I go in on Monday," he said. "The transition should only take a couple of weeks. Then I'll be home every night."

She risked glancing at him and found him watching her. "You won't know what to do with yourself."

"I'll figure it out. I should be able to take over some of the driving duties with the girls."

"That would be nice. The twins want to take a dance class."

Was it her imagination or was he moving toward her? He still held her hand in his, which was nice, but suddenly she didn't know what to do with her other hand. Or where to look. Or what to think.

"We could go skiing," she blurted.

Colin straightened. "What?"

"If we're not going to get a vacation this summer, we could go skiing over Christmas. Rent a house in Sandpoint. It's not too far. You and I haven't been skiing since Audrey was born. I'm not sure I even remember how, but that could be fun."

He smiled. "Skiing would be nice. Let's talk about it *later*. Right now I want to kiss you."

She swallowed. "You do?"

"Very much."

"I wasn't sure. I hoped you did, but with everything that happened I didn't know." She leaned forward, then drew back. "You bought me all that pretty lingerie and I never wore it. I'm sorry. I should have. It's just that sex was so good and that scared me. I felt vulnerable. But if I pretended I didn't want us to make love, I wasn't so scared. And after a while I kind of lost that part of me and I didn't have to pretend anymore."

Her husband looked slightly bemused. "Are you trying to distract me?"

"Not at all. I'm apologizing." She grabbed on to the little courage she'd managed to muster and said, "It would be really great if you kissed me now."

"Yes, it would."

He leaned in and his mouth settled on hers. His lips were firm, yet gentle, claiming her with just enough passion to make her want to squirm. Low in her stomach she felt an ache that had been absent for years.

His tongue gently brushed against hers. She met him stroke for stroke. He dropped his free hand to her hip and moved it up her side, across her ribs, to her breasts. Her nipples were already hard and tingled when he moved his fingers against them.

The door to the study opened. "Dad, I need to—"

Deanna jumped and drew back. Colin looked up.

"What is it, Madison?"

Deanna didn't know what to think. She was embarrassed and scared and aroused and confused. The combination didn't sit well on her stomach.

"I, uh, wanted to talk to you about a class I was thinking of taking."

Deanna glanced at her daughter and saw Madison still in the doorway. Her daughter glanced between them. The yearning and hope in her eyes quickly faded to resignation. As if she'd learned not to expect too much.

Deanna stood and smiled at her oldest. "It's okay, honey. This is a good time. Your dad can help you."

She escaped before either of them could say anything.

When she'd reached the safety of the bedroom, she sat on the edge of the chair in the corner and covered her face with her hands.

Madison might hate her, but it wasn't for the reasons she thought. Her daughter was terrified her parents were splitting up—that she would have to deal with a divorce. She wasn't pushing Colin because she wanted her father to leave, but because if it was going to happen, she preferred sooner rather than later. She wanted to know. She was her mother's daughter, and so for her, the worst thing in the world was uncertainty.

At five-thirty the next morning, Colin moved quietly through the bedroom to the bathroom. He carefully closed the door before turning on the light. Deanna listened to the sound of him shaving, then brushing his teeth. He turned on the shower. She hadn't slept much the previous night. She'd been devastated to realize how much she'd hurt her daughter and not sure what the next step was with Colin. She was pretty confident that if Madison hadn't walked in they would have made love.

He'd made his move and she'd run, which meant the next move was up to her. Sometime in the past couple of hours, she'd decided what it was.

She got up and went into the bathroom. She'd already used the restroom and brushed her own teeth about a half hour before. Now she stood by the shower and waited until Colin noticed her. He finished rinsing his hair, then opened his eyes.

"You're up early," he said over the spray of water.

She nodded.

She was wearing a nightgown with skinny straps that slid easily off her shoulders. She pushed them down and let the garment fall to the floor. His eyes widened slightly. She opened the door of the shower and stepped inside. Fear was there, but she ignored it. She wanted her marriage to work, and part of making that happen was being willing to take risks. Besides, the sight of Colin's naked body was a fairly heady turn-on.

"Good morning," she said, and put her hands on his shoulders. Then she raised herself on tiptoe and kissed him.

Water rushed over them both, making their skin slick. She moved her hands from his shoulders to his chest. He kissed her back, his mouth hard against hers. He thrust his tongue inside, his movements nearly frantic. His hands dropped to her butt and he squeezed. She arched against him, then moaned when she realized he was already hard.

The feel of his erection pulsing against her stomach sent heat pouring through her body. She rubbed against him, wanting more, wanting him to touch her everywhere. She was hungry. No, she was desperate.

He pulled back from their kiss and lowered his head to her breasts. He drew deeply on her right nipple, licking as he sucked. She dropped her head back and gave in to the heat burning inside her. As he shifted to her other nipple, she cupped his head to hold him in place. He eased his hand between her legs and slipped a finger inside her. Involuntarily, she clamped her muscles around him, wanting so much more than that.

He raised his head. "You're wet."

Really? They were going to have a conversation now? "We're in the shower. What else would I be?"

"Not that kind of wet. You want me."

She heard it then, the combination of relief and apprehension. Because he hadn't been sure that this was real. He hadn't known if he could trust her or not.

"I'm sorry," she whispered. "Colin, I'm so sorry. For everything."

"Me, too," he told her. "For turning you down before." He swore. "I needed to know you wanted to be with me, that you weren't just going through the motions. It nearly killed me."

Her, too, but she'd needed to know she couldn't pretend her way back into the marriage.

"It's okay."

His apprehension faded, replaced by passion. He turned and shut off the water, then pulled her out of the shower. They were both dripping, but she didn't say a word. She would deal with the mess later.

Her naked, soaked husband left her by the bed long enough to lock the bedroom door; then he drew her onto the mattress and kissed her as if he never wanted to stop. At the same time, he moved his fingers against her breasts, playing with her tight, aching nipples until she found it difficult to breathe.

When he shifted to kiss his way down her body, she knew what would happen next. What she had resisted for more reasons than she could remember over what felt like a lifetime. But instead of protesting or telling him she didn't want that, she used her fingers to part herself for him, allowing him to kiss her more intimately.

At the first stroke of his tongue against her clitoris, she closed her eyes. With the second, she found it difficult to breathe and with the third, she had to hold back the scream of pure pleasure.

He licked all of her, exploring, maybe remembering, playing her until her muscles were tight and shaking.

Only then did he settle into a steady rhythm designed to reduce her to begging and leave her completely in his control.

"Like that," she gasped, as she spiraled closer.

His pace faltered for a second. She smiled without opening her eyes. "Yes, that was me, speaking during sex." Something he'd asked for so many times, but that she'd been unwilling to do. "Pretty soon you'll be telling me to shut up."

She felt him smile, but he kept up the delicious movement of his tongue against her swollen center.

She lost herself in the sensation, wanting to hold back but unable to. Closer and closer.

"Colin," she breathed. "Almost. I'm so close. I—"

She came without warning, shuddering into her release. She knew she cried out, she might have screamed, but hoped she didn't. Mostly because she didn't want to have to explain the sound to the girls.

She kept coming as he gentled his touch, giving herself over to him and the pleasure he created in her body.

Before she was quite done, he shifted, moving onto his knees and pushing himself into her.

"Don't stop," he told her. "Don't stop."

He reached between them and rubbed his thumb against her center. She opened her eyes and saw him watching her. Something that always made her uncomfortable. But she couldn't hold back. Not with him filling her, pumping in and out. Not with his thumb rubbing her swollen clitoris. She pressed down and felt the rippling climax begin again.

She wrapped her legs around his hips and drew him closer. "More!" she told him, pulling him in and opening her thighs at the same time. "Please."

He did as she asked and she had to cover her mouth to hold in the cries of her release. Then he exploded inside her and his expression tightened. He kept his eyes open, watching her watch him, and for the first time in her life, she saw down to Colin's soul.

Andi arrived home on Wednesday night to find Carrie waiting on her front porch. She hadn't seen much of the preteen since their shopping trip—mostly because she hadn't seen Wade. Zeke had been handling the day-to-day work on her remodeling.

Last week the crew had finished with the first level and had all moved up to the second story of her house. In less than a month, she would have a working kitchen and bathroom and then she could move out of the attic. A thrilling thought, she told herself.

But it was hard to get excited about much of anything when she was missing Wade. Worse, she was spending way too much time telling herself she shouldn't be missing him. Talk about a lose-lose proposition.

Andi got out of her car. Carrie raced down the stairs and grinned at her.

"We've been waiting and waiting. You have to come see."

"Who's we?" Andi asked as Carrie led her back to the porch and then paused by the front door.

"Boston and Deanna. We can't wait anymore!"

She opened the front door and practically danced inside. Andi followed more slowly. Then she came to a complete stop as she took in the finished waiting room.

Boston's magical mural dominated the bright, well-lit space. Sunlight poured in through big windows, illuminating the various jungle creatures. The big leaves practically vibrated with life, and the butterflies looked ready to fly away.

There were several chairs and a sofa that she'd ordered but hadn't known had arrived. Tables, stacks of magazines for both adults and kids. A play area filled one corner of the room. A thick rug provided padding for her younger patients. In addition to the durable plastic toys she'd bought, there were several beautiful wood toys that looked old and handmade. A train set, blocks and several farm animals were stacked together.

"Surprise," Deanna said as she and Boston stepped into the waiting room. "We added a few things. I hope that's okay."

"It's amazing." Andi touched one of the small tables. "I didn't buy this."

"I know." Deanna shrugged. "It's a donation. I'm redoing my living room. It's too formal. This is a reproduction and sturdy enough to survive years of kids climbing on it. I brought in this rug, too." She tapped her foot on the beautiful rug underfoot.

"The toys are mine," Carrie said, picking up a carved pig. "My dad made them for me when I was little. He said I could donate them if I wanted, but I thought I'd like them to be here. So other kids could enjoy them."

She smiled at Andi. "I kept a couple of my favorites for myself," she admitted. "For when I have a family."

"I'm glad you did. And if you want these back, just let me know."

"There's more," Boston told her. "Come see your office."

Andi went down the hall and stepped into her office. The desk was in place. There were several lamps and comfortable chairs for consultations, along with two paintings. One was a seascape and the other was Deanna's daughters playing with Pickles under the tree out front.

Andi drew in a breath. "I don't know what to say," she admitted. "Everything is wonderful. You've all been so kind."

"You're one of us now," Deanna told her. "Whether you like it or not."

Andi laughed. Carrie moved in and hugged her, and then they were all holding on to each other. Andi absorbed the sense of belonging, knowing that in a few short months she'd managed to find a home here on the island. And that home had nothing to do with the house she stood in and everything to do with the women she'd met.

They released each other. Carrie started for the door.

"I'm going to go see Madison," she told them.

"Have fun," Andi called after her. When the preteen had left, she turned to her friends. "Seriously, you didn't have to do this."

"We wanted to," Boston told her. "You're starting a new adventure in your life, and we get to be a part of it."

Deanna nodded in agreement. "Everything turned out perfectly. The mural is brilliant, Boston."

"Thanks."

Andi started to say something, but found herself watching Deanna instead.

"What happened?" she asked.

Deanna looked at her. "Nothing. Why?"

Andi studied her. Everything was exactly as it always was—from the perfect makeup to the coordinated clothes. Yet there was a change. Maybe something in her eyes or the brightness of her smile.

"You're happy," she said without thinking.

Deanna grinned. "Maybe. Yes. I'm trying. Everything

isn't perfect, but it's getting better. At least I hope it is. I'm trying and Colin's trying, too." She pressed her lips together. "We had the most incredible sex the other morning. We haven't done that in I don't know how long. If ever. I know there's still work, but I'm hopeful."

"Good for you," Andi said. "I'm only slightly bitter."

"Still no sign of Wade?"

Andi shook her head.

"The King men are all idiots," Boston said. "I've accepted that. I don't like it, but I know I can't change it."

Andi sighed. "So no Zeke?"

"Not even a whisper." Boston's green eyes filled with tears. "I love him and I miss him, but I don't know what to do to make things right between us. Maybe whatever we had died with Liam. I don't know."

"It's not dead," Deanna told her. "You'll find your way back."

"I hope so," Boston said. "Because we're both really lost."

Twenty-Eight

Boston stood in front of the closed door, her fingers hovering over the handle. "Thanks for coming over."

"You're welcome." Deanna touched her arm. "You don't have to do this."

"I do. It's time. I put it off for too long as it is."

She grasped the door handle and turned, then stepped into the corner room.

The walls had been painted a pale yellow. The curtains were blue-and-yellow checks, and the longest wall had a big grinning train engine painted right in the center. A whitewashed crib and changing table added to the lightness of the space. Thick rugs covered the hardwood floors, and there was a rocking chair in the corner.

Boston stood in the middle of the room and let the pain wash over her. She welcomed the stabbing ache in her heart and prayed that this time she would be able to cry. Deanna moved next to her and put her arm around her shoulders.

"I'm sorry," her friend whispered. "This really sucks."

Boston nodded.

"When were you last in here?"

"A week after he died. I haven't been back since. I'm not sure Zeke's been in here at all."

Deanna went into the hallway and returned with several boxes. "We'll pack up everything and when Colin joins us later to help disassemble the furniture, we'll cart it all up to the attic. If you're sure that's what you want."

Boston nodded. "It is. Even if Zeke and I were to work things out, I'd never use this room for our baby. I'd want to move the guest room to here."

"I think that's for the best," Deanna said.

She set one of the boxes by the dresser and began opening drawers. "You don't have to stay. I can do this."

Boston shook her head. "I need to be here."

As Deanna emptied drawers, Boston walked over to the rocking chair. "This has to go."

"Colin's taking it to the women's shelter in Marysville this weekend." Deanna glanced up at her. "I knew you wouldn't want to keep it."

Boston touched the chair. The cool wood was beautiful. Hand-carved and in perfect condition. But she'd been sitting in this chair when Liam had died. She couldn't allow it to stay in her house.

She sank onto the floor and pulled her knees to her chest. There weren't any tears, and the pain had faded. While she was in the room, it was all happening from a distance.

"Do you think I'm broken?" she asked.

"No."

Boston turned to her. "That's it? Just no?"

Deanna smiled. "You're healing, Boston. It's going to take time."

"I don't cry."

"Lately I've been crying too much. You're being too hard on yourself. You'll get where you need to go."

Boston managed a smile. "That therapy is really working."

"It helps a lot. I'm learning to not hold on so tight. That everything doesn't have to be perfect all the time. The world will not end if I don't floss every night or if my kids wear clothes that don't match." She lowered her voice. "I've put on three pounds and I'm not sure I care."

"I put on thirty with the baby."

Deanna shook her head. "Don't change, Boston. You're beautiful just the way you are."

"Thank you."

Deanna returned to the dresser. Boston watched her pull tiny pants and shirts from drawers. There were socks so small they looked as if they'd been made for a doll. Her chest tightened. She opened her hands, as if letting all the pain in. It settled on her, crushing her.

She closed her eyes, willing the tears to come. She needed an expression of her grief. *Please,* she prayed silently. *Please.*

Deanna stood and moved to the closet. Boston opened her eyes and knew that she wasn't ready. Not yet.

"I'm sorry to have to tell you there are three sets of books," Michelle Sanderson said from behind her desk at the Blackberry Island Inn. "There's the inn itself, along with the restaurant and that damn gift shop."

Deanna sat straight in her chair, determined not to let the other woman know how nervous she was. "You're not a fan of the gift shop?"

"My business partner and I argue over inventory. Do you know how many things you can get that are covered with daisies?" Michelle, a pretty woman with dark curly hair and big green eyes, said with an exasperated smile. "Too many. They come on everything, and Carly swears they sell. Unfortunately for me, she's right."

Michelle sighed. "I'm actually a very nice person. Please don't let my unnatural hatred of daisies make you less interested in the job."

"I'm still interested," Deanna said.

"Good. As you and I discussed on the phone, we're looking for someone who can take over the bookkeeping of all three businesses. It's too much for Carly and me to deal with. You'd be responsible for accounts payable and receivable, along with payroll. Carly handles the inventory, so you wouldn't have to deal with vendors beyond paying them."

Michelle glanced at the notes in front of her. "We were thinking that having you in three mornings a week would work best. We can discuss what's going on and be around to answer any questions. The rest of the work you can do at your home. Honestly, we're tight on space. The inn is full nearly all the time, and while that's excellent, it keeps us busy. Now with Carly getting married…"

Michelle leaned back in her chair. "She wants a big wedding, if you can believe it." She waved her left hand. There was a plain gold band on her ring finger. "Why the hell she can't run off to Reno like the rest of us, I'll never know. But Carly is big on the rituals."

Michelle might be complaining, but Deanna heard the affection in her voice.

She was a few years older than Michelle and Carly. While they'd all gone to the same school on the island, Deanna had been a few grades ahead. She knew the other two had been close friends for years. Something had happened later, but she'd never heard the details. Whatever it was, it had obviously been resolved. They were business partners here at the inn, and business was good.

"You're familiar with the software we use?" Michelle asked.

"I am. I recently completed an online course to brush up on my skills." Deanna passed over the certificate she'd earned.

Michelle glanced at it. "Excellent. Carly knows you from the craft store."

Deanna nodded. "She and Gabby took a couple of knitting classes from me."

"Crafts," Michelle grumbled. "Don't get me started." She stood. "Come on. Let's take the tour. I want you to understand the madness before I make an offer. Do you like pets?"

"Um, sure."

"We have a resident dog and cat. The dog is mine. The cat, Mr. Whiskers, belongs to our cook. Just so you're clear, Mr. Whiskers thinks he runs the place. Some days I'm pretty sure he's right."

An hour later Deanna sat in her car. She pulled out her cell phone and pushed in a familiar number.

"Hey, you," Colin said, answering right away. "How did it go?"

"I got the job."

He gave a low laugh. "Congratulations. I'm not surprised, but I'm happy for you."

"Me, too. I start in a week. I'm nervous."

"You'll do great."

"Thanks. I hope so."

This was new—them talking. Colin had called the night after they'd made love and they'd spoken until nearly midnight. Now they talked several times a day. Mostly about nothing, but the conversation wasn't the point. She got that.

She looked forward to hearing his voice, to telling him about the girls and having him tease her. She felt young and foolish and happy. It was like falling in love all over again.

"I'll be home tomorrow," he said.

"I can't wait."

"Me, either." He paused. "So, what are you wearing?"

"Colin! I'm in a car, in front of the inn. I'll be working there."

"Is this your way of saying you're not naked?"

She squeezed her eyes shut. "I'm not naked."

"Damn." He lowered his voice. "But you will be tonight?"

She felt her cheeks heating. Over the past few days she'd discovered she liked talking during sex nearly as much as Colin liked listening.

"I will be," she whispered.

"Me, too."

"Here you go." Dr. Harrington handed Andi an invitation. "We're having a big welcome-home party for my son. He's moving back to the island."

Andi smiled. "I can't wait to meet him. I've heard so much about him."

"His mother and I are so proud." He glanced around the office. "He has plans for this practice."

"Good ones, I'm sure." Andi couldn't imagine going into business with her parents. She felt a twinge as she briefly wished things could have been different between them. But regardless of their feelings, she'd found a place to belong and that was worth a lot to her.

"You're all set up with Nina?" Dr. Harrington asked.

"Yes. Thank you again for letting her come with me."

The older man shuffled his feet. "Well, it's for the best. She and Dylan dated back in high school and it didn't end well. At the time we thought they were too young, but maybe we shouldn't have interfered." He paused, then shook his head. "Water under the bridge, right? People change and move on."

Nina had also hinted at her romantic past with Dylan. Andi wondered if she would ever hear the whole story.

Dr. Harrington smiled at her. "You're an asset to our community, Andi. If you need anything, you know where to find me."

"I do. Thank you."

The older man left her tiny office. Andi turned off her computer, then pulled her purse out of her desk's bottom drawer.

She was done for the day, and Friday was the end of her temporary assignment in Dr. Harrington's office. Two weeks from Monday she would open her own practice in her house.

She and Nina were meeting together Monday morning to get things set up, and they would start taking appointments. Several parents had already left messages on her new number, asking when they could start bringing in their children.

Andi walked toward the back door. Tomorrow they were having one last staff lunch together. Two teachers had been in touch, asking if she would speak to their classes about general health and what it took to become a doctor. She had her friends, her Pilates classes and she was going to take a beginning knitting class at the craft store where Deanna had worked. She had settled into life on the island.

She walked toward her car, only to come to a stop when she saw a man leaning against it. He was tall and good looking, in a blond movie star kind of way. He flashed her a blindingly white smile when he saw her.

"Andi, there you are. I've been waiting."

She came to a stop, unable to believe he was here. After all this time. "Matt?"

"You sound surprised."

"Because I am surprised. It's been months."

The last time she'd seen him, he'd been trying to explain why he'd left her at the altar. He'd been more concerned with explaining why it wasn't really his fault than admitting to humiliating her. She'd been hurt and furious. Ending things had made the most sense, but a part of her had wondered if she would be stuck loving him forever.

Now, as she approached, she realized she hadn't thought of him in weeks. He wasn't important to her anymore. He was someone who had taught her a good lesson in a really crummy way. A total jerk, she thought with a smile. Didn't nearly every woman have a jerk in her romantic history?

"How have you been?" she asked, then shook her head. "You know what? I actually would rather know why you're here."

"To see you."

He reached for her hand. She pulled it away, then took a step out of touching range.

"Why are you here?" she asked again.

He moved toward her. "We need to talk, Andi. Can we go somewhere?"

She didn't trust him. Given his previous actions, hardly a surprise. But more intriguing was the fact that being around him didn't stir up any memories, at least, not any good ones. She would rather be home right now, planning her dinner. Or hanging out with one of her friends.

"Just a drink. There has to be a bar on the island."

"I'm sure there are several, but no. Either tell me why you're here or I'm leaving."

"Wow. This is a new side of you. Remember, I always told you to stand up for yourself. It looks like you've taken my advice."

She rolled her eyes, then reached for her car keys. He quickly stepped between her and the vehicle.

"Fine," he said. "I'm here because I want to tell you that I'm sorry about what I did. Leaving you like that. It was stupid and thoughtless."

An apology? Who would have guessed?

"Okay. I'm glad you figured out you were the bad guy. Anything else?"

He studied her. "I made a mistake, Andi. That's what I'm here to tell you. Running off like that, I overreacted. Getting married to Lindsey was idiotic." He shrugged. "We're getting a divorce. We've filed the paperwork already. It didn't take me very long to realize I picked the wrong girl. You're the one I love. That's why I wanted to see you. To tell you that I'm finally ready for us to be together like you always wanted." He gave her his charming lopsided smile. "Marry me, Andi. I still love you."

Six months ago she would have sold her soul to hear those words. Four months ago, she might have been tempted to say yes. But now...

"No, thanks."

She hit the button to unlock her car.

He blinked at her. "I don't understand."

"I'm saying no. I have no interest in being with you. I think what you did was awful, but I can't complain about the outcome. I don't love you, Matt. I don't want to get back into a relationship with you."

"But we had ten years together. We were great." He hesitated. "I know I was a little insistent that you change, but I'm over that. I want you just the way you are." His gaze drifted to her scrubs. He opened his mouth and then closed it. "Please, Andi."

"No. It's too late, Matt. The woman you liked is gone. I have changed and not in a way you'd like. When you first broke up with me, I was devastated. Now all I can think is that I should have broken up with you years ago."

"You can't mean that."

She reached for the car door. "And yet I do mean it." She thought about all the time she'd wasted with him, how she'd stood in her dress, in front of everyone she loved, and he hadn't bothered to show.

"Is there someone else?" he asked.

"No." There was Wade, but he'd made it clear he wasn't willing to be involved with her. Which was a shame, because she thought they had potential. But she wasn't going to be the only one showing up again.

Matt reached for her. "Andi, you can't do this. I need you."

She opened her car door. "You should have thought of that before you walked out on me. You had ten years, Matt. Plenty of time. Now it's too late."

His eyes widened and she would swear he was about to cry. "But I still love you."

"I'm sorry."

"Andi, no."

"Goodbye, Matt."

She slid into her seat and started the engine. For a second she thought he might throw himself in front of the vehicle. Fortunately, he didn't and she was able to drive away.

As she turned into the street, she realized that not only wasn't she feeling guilty, but there was a new lightness inside. Freedom, she thought. She would rather be alone than be with Matt. She was done with him. Her only regret was figuring that out about eight and a half years too late.

Deanna waited until all five of her daughters were seated around the dining room table. As this was where all serious conversations took place, they looked apprehensive as they squirmed in their places.

"Don't worry," she began with a smile. "No one's in trouble. There are going to be a few changes around here, and I wanted to talk to you about them."

The girls looked at each other, then back at her. Worry tightened the expressions of her oldest daughters, while the twins looked more confused than apprehensive.

"I'm going to be starting a new job in a few days. I'll be a bookkeeper at the Blackberry Island Inn." She and Colin had talked about telling them that their dad would be home more. He'd said to go ahead and share the news, but she wanted to let him be the one to tell them. They would be delighted, and he deserved to be a part of the moment.

"I'll work at the inn three mornings a week and I'll work from home the rest of the time. So I'm going to need your cooperation during my working hours. Once you're back in school, I'll try to get all my work done when you're gone. But we'll need a system that keeps interruptions to a minimum."

Madison's mouth trembled. "Is Dad... Are you..."

Are you getting a divorce?

Madison couldn't speak the words, but Deanna heard them all the same. She smiled at her daughter. "Your dad is very excited about my new job. We're all going out to dinner this weekend to celebrate."

They would also be celebrating him staying home instead of traveling, but she wasn't going to say that just yet.

She softened her voice. "We're a family, Madison. That isn't changing."

If the concern had come from any of her other girls, she would have punctuated the statement with a hug or a touch. But things were still difficult with her oldest.

Madison looked at her, then turned away. "Okay," she whispered.

Deanna returned her attention to the other girls. "I'm going to be coming up with a chore list for everyone. We'll talk about what you're comfortable doing and what your dad and I expect you to do. I'd also like to start teaching you girls to cook. There's no reason why you can't help me with the jam I'll be making over the next few weeks. I was also thinking you could each learn how to make something."

The twins looked at each other, then at her. "Cookies?" they asked as one.

She laughed. "Yes, cookies are a good start. Maybe peanut butter."

They clapped their hands together.

She smiled at Audrey and Lucy. "I thought the three of us could figure out a few dinners that would be fun to make together. Maybe using the Crock-Pot."

"Or spaghetti," Lucy said.

"That could work. I'd want to be the one in charge of the pot of boiling water, but you could learn to make the sauce."

Audrey grinned. "Chicken parmesan."

"Ambitious, but sure. It'll be fun." Deanna turned to Madison. "I'm guessing that hanging out with me in the kitchen isn't your idea of fun. That's fine. As long as the chore list is relatively even, I don't mind if you choose something else."

Madison stared at her. Emotions chased across her face. The battle was clear. She wanted to have fun like her sisters, but how much fun could be had with her mother?

Sadness gripped Deanna. They'd been so close, she thought, aching with the loss. Madison had been her sunny little girl, so filled with love. Now she was a stranger who hated her. Her therapist had counseled patience. Deanna knew she was right, but waiting was so difficult.

The twins scrambled from their seats and raced around the table. They threw themselves at Deanna and hung on tight.

"Can we make cookies now?" Sydney asked.

Savannah nodded. "I want to start learning how!"

Deanna hugged them. "I think cookies sound like an excellent idea. Everyone who wants to can make cookies."

Audrey and Lucy ran into the kitchen, yelling that they were going to wash their hands right away so they could help, too. Madison rose slowly, then started for the stairs.

Deanna led her twins into the kitchen. She wanted to look back, to see her oldest hesitating, but seriously, what were the odds? When she'd been Madison's age, there was absolutely nothing her mother could have done to heal the breach between them. She wondered if that line had been crossed here, too. And if so, how she would bear the loss and go on.

Twenty-Nine

Boston smelled the paint the second she walked in the front door of her house. It permeated the air and made her want to sneeze. For a second, she couldn't figure out what it meant. She only painted in her studio, so why had someone been painting in her...

She froze, literally unable to move. She'd told Wade about packing up the baby stuff. How Deanna and Colin had helped. She'd mentioned the mural, the beautiful train and how she knew she had to paint it over but didn't know if she had the strength. He'd offered to help. She'd refused.

"No!" she cried, then ran to the stairs.

She climbed them two at a time, arriving on the second floor out of breath. She hurried down the hall, but knew the truth before she crossed the threshold. Knew what had happened. Knew what had been taken from her.

The room was empty. There were no curtains, no rug on the hardwood floor. The light switch cover was neutral plastic. The pleasing yellow walls had been painted a creamy white color. And the mural was gone.

She stood in the center of the room and felt the absence of all she had once loved. It was as if Liam had never lived here at all.

Her chest felt as if it were going to split open. She pressed her hand to the wound, expecting to drown in blood, but there was nothing but her T-shirt and the warmth of her skin.

That was wrong, she thought, *wanting* to bleed. Everything was wrong. Liam, sweet Liam. She couldn't…

She sucked in air, but couldn't breathe. Cried out to him, but there was no answer. Without being fully aware of her actions, she pulled her phone out of her pocket and pressed a button.

"Zeke," she gasped. "Zeke. He's gone."

Her body shook. The phone fell to the floor and she collapsed next to it, curling into herself, hanging on to keep from splitting apart.

When the tears came, they were harsh and ugly and made her choke. She cried for what had been lost, for the innocent child who had been everything to her. For the aftermath and the loss of Zeke, as well. For the first time she felt the pain of being alone. Of having no one.

She covered her face with her hands and continued to cry. Time passed, but she had no sense of it, no sense of anything but the growing crater that had been the very heart of her. Then something warm touched her arm.

She opened her eyes and found Zeke on the floor. He lay in front of her, drawing her against him, his body comforting, protecting. He drew her into his arms and hung on as if he would never let go. She put her head on his shoulder and let her tears wash over them both.

Deanna looked at the clothes she'd laid out on the bed. For the most part, what she'd worn to the craft store would work for her new job at the inn. She'd erred on the side of conservative when it came to her choices, which was good. She and Colin had a ski vacation to save for. She didn't want to waste precious dollars on something silly like her work wardrobe. Especially not when he'd emailed her listings for a couple of vacation houses that were available.

Her favorite was a three-story chalet with the master bedroom on the third floor. Not only was there a fireplace, but there was a double shower and a tub big enough for two. Colin's only comment had been "Think the girls are old enough to go skiing without us?"

Just thinking about spending long snowy nights in that bedroom with her husband was enough to make her quiver.

"Mom?"

Deanna turned and saw Madison standing in the doorway to the bedroom.

"What's up?" she asked.

"Could I talk to you for a second?"

"Sure."

Deanna pushed the clothes aside and sat on the bed, then patted the space next to her. She expected her preteen to roll her eyes and remain standing, but Madison actually took a seat and angled toward her.

Deanna looked at her daughter's face, at the melding of her features and Colin's. The big blue eyes, the radiant skin.

"You're so beautiful," she said, then smiled. "Sorry. I don't think that's what you came to talk about."

Madison shook her head, bit her lower lip, then started to cry. Deanna tried to figure out what she'd done wrong. She couldn't think of anything, so she waited a couple of seconds. When Madison continued to cry, she finally leaned in and lightly hugged her.

"What's wrong, honey?" she asked. "Are you not feeling well?"

Madison cried harder. Deanna pulled her close and simply held on. She was both uncomfortable and hopeful. If her daughter was reaching out to her, she didn't want to screw up. Indecision and confusion made her uncertain. The tingling in her hands nearly drove her to the sink. Because the combination of soap and water would make her feel so much better.

It never goes away, she thought. Her therapist had been telling her that for several weeks now. The urge, the need. It was more easily managed these days. It could be argued with, but it never disappeared.

Deanna reminded herself to breathe. She started counting in an effort to distract the crazy but before she got to ten, Madison straightened.

"I'm sorry, Mom," her daughter whispered. "About how things have been."

"Me, too. I know I've been difficult to live with. All those rules." She took her daughter's hands in hers and squeezed her fingers. "Plus, I know you were scared that your dad and I were going to split up."

Madison's eyes filled with tears as she nodded. "I hated not knowing."

"It's a bad place to be." She searched for the right words and wished she were better at this. "I love you, and your dad loves you. No matter what happens, that will never change. We're both committed to our marriage and this family. We're working hard. I want things to be different for all of us. I know you're angry. I hope you're going to try to let that go, at least a little."

"I'm not angry all the time," Madison said. "And sometimes I don't want to be."

"Sometimes you're scared, and being mad at me is easier than admitting that."

"Yeah." Madison wiped her cheeks and gave a shaky smile. "You're different lately."

"I'm trying to ease up on some of the rules." She leaned in and kissed the top of Madison's head. "Your dad is going to make the announcement when he comes home tomorrow, but you'll probably feel better if you know sooner rather than later. He's changing jobs. He's going to manage the sales force rather than be the head sales guy."

Madison's eyes lit up. "Daddy won't be traveling?"

"Not much at all. But please don't tell the other girls. He wants to surprise them."

"I won't say anything." She sniffed. "Is that why you're taking the bookkeeping job?"

"Uh-huh. I want to help bring in more money. We still have five girls to put through college."

Madison smiled. "Lucy has a good shot at a scholarship."

"I think so, too."

Her oldest pulled her hands free and shifted on the bed. "Mom, I have to tell you something." She glanced down, then back at Deanna. "I got my period a few weeks ago."

Deanna braced herself for the jab and managed to get through it without flinching. "Are you okay?"

Madison nodded. "I was scared, so I talked to Andi. I saw her in her office. She told me what to expect and went with me to the drugstore to buy supplies." She swallowed. "She wanted me to tell you and I didn't want to."

The twelve-year-old covered her face with her hands and started to cry again. "I'm sorry, Mommy. I'm sorry."

Deanna pulled her close and held on. "I know, baby girl. We were having a rough time. I'm so sorry about that. But you know what? You did the right thing. You talked to a responsible adult. You didn't go on the internet or let your friends tell you what to do. You got help in a very mature way, and I think that's pretty terrific."

Madison dropped her hands to her lap. Her face was flushed and her eyes were red. "You're not mad?"

"No. I'm sorry I couldn't help you through that." She was devastated to have lost a precious moment with her daughter, but understood how much of that was her own fault.

"I had a difficult relationship with my mother," she said quietly. "She drank a lot and she hit me."

Madison stared at her. "Grandma abused you?"

Abuse. There it was, in a single word. "She did. One day she broke my arm and the police took me away. I came to live here, with my aunt and uncle. They said I could stay if I was a good girl. If I did what they said and didn't make trouble. I was so scared of going back that I decided to be perfect. If I was perfect, nothing could ever go wrong."

"No one can be perfect," Madison told her.

"I know, but I tried. Eventually being perfect became the most important thing in my life. I didn't care how things were, I cared about how they looked. I'm still figuring it all out, but that's why I sometimes get weird about things being done in a certain way."

"You're not so bad," Madison said.

Deanna smiled. "I want to learn to let go. I'm trying

and sometimes it's really, really hard. So please be patient with me."

Madison flung herself at her. "I love you, Mommy."

"I love you."

"I want to tell you next time I get my period."

"That would be great."

She continued to hang on. "Will you teach me to cook something, please?"

Deanna squeezed a little tighter. "Anything you want."

Madison drew back and smiled. "Meat loaf. It's Dad's favorite."

"That's a good idea. Want to come to the store with me to get the ingredients so we can make it for him tomorrow?"

"Uh-huh." Madison bounced to her feet. "You know, Mom, Lucy's ready to start babysitting the twins. She's pretty responsible."

Deanna held in a protest. Lucy was only ten. But then, Madison was only twelve. Trust, she thought. Making a family work was about love and trust and knowing where to draw the lines.

"Thank you for sharing that," she said. "I appreciate your input. Let's go ask her if she's comfortable being in charge while we run to the grocery store."

They walked down the hall together. Madison reached for her hand and squeezed. Deanna felt a similar tightness close around her heart. Things weren't perfect and she and her daughter would have their share of fights, but they had found their way back to each other.

Andi sat on the front steps of her house. She had a meeting with her contractor to go over everything that had been done to date. She was going to sign off on the main floor work, then discuss the plans for the attic level. None of which was a big deal, only her appointment was with Wade, not Zeke.

She hadn't seen Wade in several weeks. If he came to the job site, he was careful to do it when she was at work. Although she didn't have any proof, she would swear there were times she knew he'd been in her house. It was as if the energy changed or something.

Now she watched as his truck pulled up and he climbed out. She'd been half expecting him to bring Carrie as a buffer, but he was alone. Tall and handsome. Muscled. A god in bed. He was also kind and loyal, a great father. He made her laugh. But he didn't trust her and she knew in her gut that was a deal breaker.

She waited until he reached the bottom of the stairs to stand. His gaze met hers.

"Hello, Andi."

"Wade."

He looked good. Her girl parts whispered that maybe just one more for the road would be nice. She did her best to ignore the suggestion.

"Ready to sign off on the work?" he asked, holding up a clipboard.

She nodded. She had a check in her jeans back pocket.

They walked into the waiting area for her medical practice. Wade started talking about what they'd done, bringing the electrical up to code and how great the insulation was. They confirmed that the switches worked, the floor was level and the windows were the ones she'd paid for. Twenty minutes later, they were still in the waiting room. At this rate, they were going to be here a week. She should have thought to provide snacks.

"You're not listening," he said.

"We both know you do good work. I live next door to your brother. If there's a problem, I'll go over and complain." She pulled the check out of her pocket and handed it to him. "This is the final payment for the office space and the next payment for the upstairs remodeling."

He took the paper and met her gaze. "Trying to get rid of me?"

She stared into his dark eyes and knew this was one of those moments she would remember for the rest of her life. A crossroads, so to speak. Where a decision made or not made would affect so very much.

"Matt came to see me the other day."

He raised his eyebrows. "Ex-fiancé Matt?"

"That's the one. He swears he realizes he made a mistake and is getting a divorce. He wants us to get back together."

A muscle twitched in Wade's jaw. "What did you say?"

"I told him that wasn't going to happen. I'd already wasted too much on him. I live here now. I'm making a home and I don't want to leave. More important, I don't love him. I'm starting to wonder if I ever did."

She folded her arms across her chest. "I like what I do. I want to be a part of this community. I want to help kids."

She squared her shoulders. "I'm smart, funny, caring and successful. We have a sexual chemistry that is illegal in several states, and you know what? You're beyond stupid if you let me walk out of your life. I'm not like my mother. I don't want you to be different. I want you exactly as you are." She paused. "Well, I want you to be less of an idiot about us, but that's it."

She'd never said anything like this before to anyone. Matt had always taken their relationship to the next level, which was probably a large part of the problem.

Wade put his clipboard on the reception counter. "You know I have a kid."

Not sure where he was going with that, she nodded. "I've met Carrie, yes."

"You're going to want more."

Andi's mouth fell open. He was going way beyond where she'd stopped. She'd been talking about them dating, and he was... Well, she had no idea where he'd landed.

"One," she admitted, her voice small. "Maybe two."

"You're a doctor."

That pissed her off. She dropped her arms to her sides and stomped her foot. "I am and you know what? I'm not going to apologize for it. I studied a lot and worked my butt off and yes, I'm a doctor. So what? Tell me what my being a doctor has to do with anything."

He grinned. "You rile up easy, don't you?" He took a step toward her. "I've missed you, Andi. You're right. You are funny and sexy and all those other things, and I would be an idiot to let you get away."

He cupped her jaw. "But I'll admit I'm terrified that you're going to suck me in, get me to fall in love with you, then run off with some stockbroker."

"Why would I run off with a stockbroker?"

"Hell if I know and that's not the point."

"Then what is the point?"

He lowered his head and kissed her.

Her eyes closed as she leaned into him. His kiss lingered and her girl parts sent up a cheer.

When he straightened, she had a little trouble catching her breath.

"I can't say I'm fond of your mother," he told her.

"Me, either."

"When we tell her this is serious, I'm going to sit her down and explain how things are."

Serious? Things were serious? "I can't wait to hear what you have to say to her."

His dark gaze met hers. "When I'm in, I'm all in, Andi. Are you ready for that?"

She wrapped her arms around his neck and smiled up at him. "I'm all in, too, Wade."

He gave her his best slow, sexy smile. "That's what I like to hear. Now, what do you say we find out if this waiting room sofa is as comfy as it looks?"

She started to laugh. "I thought you'd never ask."

Boston hummed as she cooked bacon in the pan. It was early, barely after six, and she hadn't slept at all the previous night, but she was filled with energy and a sense of purpose. She pulled eggs out of the refrigerator, then paused to jot down a few notes. Three of her designers had been begging her to take jobs. She'd reviewed the materials they'd sent and now found herself overflowing with ideas.

She managed to whip the eggs and add them to the pan before having to stop to write down a few more ideas. Zeke walked into the kitchen in time to rescue the rapidly browning eggs.

"Morning," he said as he pushed the pan off the heat, then crossed to her.

"Morning."

They stared at each other.

They'd made love last night. Their old bed had creaked happily in the familiar rhythm of their joining. After, she'd burst into tears again and Zeke had held her. He slipped his hands under her robe and cupped her breasts.

She leaned into his touch. At the same time she pressed her palm against his groin. He was hard and thick and pulsed against her.

She laughed. "Your eggs are getting cold."

He kissed her, then released her. "My eggs? Aren't you having any?"

"I'll have one but no bacon. I'm going on a diet."

"Why?"

The genuine confusion in his voice made her want to give him the world. "Zeke, I gained thirty pounds while I was pregnant and I haven't taken off an ounce."

"You look great."

"I need to get into shape. Start exercising. Andi takes a Pilates class she likes. I could try that. And walking. I want to eat better." She smiled at him. "I want to be around a long time with you. And I want you to be healthy, too."

Zeke looked her in the eye. "I think I know where you're going with this."

"I've always loved you, Zeke. If we're going to move forward from here, I need you to stop drinking."

Zeke took her hand. "I already have, which you're going to have to see to believe. That's okay. We can do this. We can do anything, as long as we're together."

Boston held on to the hope in his words nearly as tightly as she held on to the strong hands of her husband.

Down the street, Deanna strolled out to get the paper. She saw Wade's truck was still parked in front of Andi's house and smiled. That explained the frantic phone call the previous evening with Wade asking if Carrie could spend the night. She saw that Zeke's truck was parked in front of his house, as well. The old neighborhood had been hopping last night.

She walked into the kitchen, where Colin sat at the breakfast bar. He smiled at her over his mug of coffee. "I have something for you."

She raised her eyebrows. "Already?"

He chuckled. "That, too. But I meant this." He handed her a brochure for a hotel in Seattle, right on the sound and close to Pike Place Market. "Compliments of my boss. Two nights in their best suite." He leaned toward her and lowered his voice. "You'll be able to make as much noise as you want."

She blushed. "It's not my fault the sex is so good."

"I'll take that as a compliment."

"Good, because that's how I meant it." She picked up the brochure. "This will be wonderful. I'll ask Andi and Boston to take the girls. I'm sure they'll agree." She glanced at the clock on the wall. "Speaking of our children, I'd better get them up."

She started toward the door. Colin grabbed her and pulled her against him.

"Deanna?"

"Yes?" She gazed into his dark blue eyes.

"I love you."

Her throat tightened as her heart spilled over with emotion. She couldn't remember the last time he'd said the words. It had been years. Too many years.

"I love you, too, Colin. I'm sorry I got so twisted around with everything."

He shook his head, then kissed her. "No blame. We both got lost. Now we've found our way back."

"I'm never letting go."

"Me, either." He stood and put his arm around her shoulders. "Come on. We'll go wake the girls together."

Epilogue

Andi sat with tissue woven between her toes and her hands carefully splayed. "I'm not good with nail polish," she murmured, terrified she was going to ruin her manicure.

Her mother was next to her, in the same position, but slightly more relaxed. "The polish dries in layers. The key is to avoid being fooled by a seemingly set surface."

Boston, who had gone for a buffed shine, slid her feet into her shoes and grinned. "Layers, Leanne? Like in cake?"

"Exactly like cake, dear."

Andi instinctively braced herself, wanting to come between her mother and her friend, then had to remind herself that things were different now.

Oh, sure, she still regularly received applications to fellowships and updates on her siblings' successes, but ever since she'd announced her engagement to Wade, her parents seemed to have mellowed a little. She was pretty sure her lecture about backing off had helped some. The other game changer had been Carrie.

Wade's daughter had met Andi's parents over Labor

Day when the five of them had spent time together in Seattle. The preteen had been delighted to have step-grandparents-to-be. Leanne had treated Carrie to a day of shopping at the downtown Nordstrom, and both the older Gordons had escorted her to a Mariners game.

By the end of the long weekend, they'd announced they adored the girl and couldn't wait to spend more time with her. Carrie had shared the love, and a new, slightly odd detente had been born.

Shrieks of laughter drew Andi back to the present. As part of her bachelorette afternoon and evening, they'd taken over a nail salon. Boston, Deanna and her girls had joined Andi, Carrie and Leanne for mani-pedis. Once they were all beautiful, they would return to Deanna's house for pizza and movies.

Deanna passed the bottle of champagne they'd brought with them. "You're still on your first glass, Andi. It's not a bachelorette party if you don't at least *try* to get drunk."

"It's three in the afternoon."

"Chicken."

"Your children are present."

"I've seen you drunk. You're still perfectly well mannered. It's not as if I was going to tell them what was going on. Besides, we're walking home."

"You should at least have a second glass," Leanne said, holding out her daughter's glass for a refill. Deanna obliged.

"You're all freaks," Andi muttered, but she took a sip.

Leanne excused herself to go sit by the twins. Boston took her seat and glanced around. She leaned toward Andi and motioned for Deanna to do the same, then lowered her voice.

"I have something to tell you."

Andi looked at Deanna and grinned.

They'd already guessed the secret. In the past couple of months Boston had sworn off alcohol and caffeine. A few weeks ago, she'd started to glow.

"Spill," Deanna said.

"I'm pregnant. About four weeks along." Boston kept her voice low. "Zeke and I didn't want to say anything until after the wedding, but I knew I had to tell the two of you."

"Congratulations," Andi said, hugging her while still keeping her fingers splayed. "That's wonderful."

Deanna hugged her next and sighed. "I'm so happy. More kids on the block. It's great." She turned to Andi. "How long until you start trying?"

Andi nearly choked. "Hey, not even married yet. Give me a break."

"You want kids and Wade does, too. You're not getting any younger."

"Gee, thanks."

Deanna grinned. "You're welcome."

They leaned back in their chairs and watched as the girls finished their mani-pedis. Madison and Carrie giggled together. The other four laughed. Leanne helped the twins pick out a vivid pink for their nails.

Tomorrow Andi would marry Wade at the Blackberry Island Inn. They would take off for two weeks in Hawaii before returning home. Then Wade and Carrie would move into the house on the hill. A house she'd bought impulsively, with the idea that if she could fix the house, she could fix herself. From that day to this she had figured out how to let go of the past, she'd fallen in love, learned that maybe she didn't need as much fixing as she'd first thought and discovered that sometimes sisters were made, not born.

She'd found home, and that had turned out to be the very best thing that had happened to her.

* * * * *

Three Sisters – Readers' Discussion Guide

Visit www.BlackberryIsland.com for a wealth of bonus content about the quaint island and its inhabitants. You'll find a map of the island to print out for your book group, recipes, a history of the island and more.

Suggested Menu:
Grilled Chicken Sandwich with Blackberry Relish

Blackberry Relish:
1 cup blackberries, chopped (frozen blackberries are fine, but thaw them first)
1/2 cup green onions, sliced
1 small can of mild chili peppers, minced
4 cloves garlic, minced
1 jalapeño, seeded and minced
2 tbsp balsamic vinegar

For the sandwiches:
Boneless, skinless chicken breasts
Black pepper
Provolone cheese
Lettuce
Buns

Mix together all the relish ingredients and set aside. This can be done the day before. Grill the chicken until thoroughly cooked. Add provolone cheese to each chicken breast so that it melts. Assemble the sandwiches and carefully spoon a couple of tablespoons of relish on top of each.

QUESTIONS FOR DISCUSSION

1. The Three Sisters in the book are the three houses atop the highest hill on Blackberry Island. In what way does each house reflect its owner? Would you like to live in a Victorian home that is more than one hundred years old? Why or why not? Which house would you want to live in and why?

2. Andi was left at the altar by a man she'd dated for more than ten years. How do you think you would've reacted if this had happened to you? What do you think of Andi's decision to move to Blackberry Island, where she had no support structure in place because she knew no one?

3. With which of the three women did you empathize most strongly? Why? Did your feelings change as the story progressed? What did the women have in common besides geography?

4. Which character changed the most? In what way?

5. A lot of women have control issues like Deanna's, though not to the same extreme. Do you think she knew she had a problem before Colin confronted her with his unhappiness? Why or why not? Deanna's need for control stemmed from her childhood as the abused and neglected daughter of an alcoholic mother. From chapter eleven:

   They didn't understand, Deanna thought. Didn't have any idea what her life had been like. Locked in her room, beaten, cleaning up vomit after one of her mother's benders. The pain and humiliation lived inside her. All she wanted now was to have a good life. To not be ashamed. But apparently that made her the devil, according to her husband.

When do you feel that Deanna truly began trying to change, rather than going through the motions?

6. Many couples split up after the death of a child because they grow apart while learning to accept their new reality. How did Boston and Zeke react differently to their son's death? Did you feel that one of them dealt with the loss more appropriately than the other? Why or why not? Why did Boston continue to draw black-and-white portraits of Liam?

7. Wade was angry when Andi didn't defend him to her mother. Andi felt Wade was using the moment as an excuse to avoid commitment. Who do you think was right? Why?

8. Susan Mallery is known for tapping into the humor of even the most emotional situations. Which scenes in *Three Sisters* made you laugh?

9. Female friendship is at the heart of this story, and yet for the first half of the book, the women really didn't interact much. Deanna's breakdown in Boston's kitchen was a major turning point in their relationship. How do you think this single moment changed the women's understanding of each other?

How do you think their friendship changed each woman from that point forward?

10. Overall, do you feel this was a sad book or a happy book? Why? Did you like the way *Three Sisters* ended for each of the characters? Why or why not?

Turn the page for a brief visit to Susan Mallery's

THE GIRLS OF MISCHIEF BAY

Meet Nicole, Shannon and Pam in their quirky, beachy town by the ocean, where life is richer with friends by your side!

Pam walked through from the garage to the main house, Lulu keeping pace with her. In the mudroom they both paused. Pam fished her small handbag out of the tote, then hung the larger bag on a hook.

The open area served as a catchall for things that otherwise didn't have a home. There was a built-in storage unit with plenty of hooks, shelves and drawers. The latter were mostly filled with Lulu's various clothes.

Now Pam eyed the lightweight sweater her pet wore and decided it would keep the dog warm enough until bedtime. Like the rest of the family, Lulu wore PJs to bed. Pam didn't care if anyone laughed at her for that. She was the one Lulu cuddled next to under the covers and she wanted her dog wearing something soft when that happened.

They continued through the house to the kitchen. Pam pulled her cell out of her purse and stuck it on the side table by the hall, then checked on the Crock-Pot she'd left on that morning. A quick peek and stir confirmed the beef burgundy was coming along. She added the vegetables she'd already prepared and stirred again, then went out the front door to collect the mail.

The day had warmed up nicely. February in the rest of the country could mean snow and ice. In Southern California there was every chance it would be sunny and seventy. Today was no exception, although she would guess it was closer to sixty-five. Hardly reason to complain, she told herself as she pulled the mail out of the box and started back toward the house.

Mischief Bay was a coastal community. Tucked between Redondo Beach and Hermosa Beach, it had a small pier, plenty of restaurants, a boardwalk and lots of tourists. The ocean regulated the temperatures and the steady light breeze made sure there wasn't much in the way of smog.

She and John had bought their sprawling ranch-style home ages ago. Jennifer, their oldest, had been what? Three? Pam tried to remember. If Jennifer had been three, then Steven had been a year and she'd been pregnant with Brandon.

Oh, yeah. She *had* been pregnant all right. There'd been the charming moment when she'd thrown up in front of the movers. Brandon had been a difficult pregnancy and she'd been nauseous a lot. Something she brought up every so often—when her son needed a little humbling. As all children did, now and then.

She paused to wait for Lulu to do her business by the bushes and studied the front of the house. They'd redone much of both yards a few years ago, when they'd had the house painted. She liked the new plants that edged the circular drive. Her gaze rose to the roof. That had been replaced, as well. One of the advantages of having a husband in construction—he always knew the best people.

Lulu trotted back to her side.

"Ready to go in, sweet pea?" Pam asked.

Lulu wagged her feathered tail and led the way. Pam glanced down at the mail as she walked. Bills, a letter from an insurance agent she'd never heard of—no doubt an ad—along with two car magazines for John and a postcard from the local high school.

Pam frowned at the postcard and turned it over. What on earth could they…?

Lulu walked into the house. Pam followed and automatically closed the door. She stood in the spacious foyer, afternoon light spilling onto the tile floor.

But she didn't see any of that. She didn't see anything but the stark words printed on the postcard.

Class of 2005. Fellow Cougars—save the date!!
Your 10-year high school reunion is this August.

There was more, but the letters got blurry as Pam tried to make sense of the notice. A ten-year high school reunion? Sure, Jennifer had graduated in 2005, but there was no way it had been ten years, had it? Because if Jen were attending her ten-year reunion, that meant Pam was the *mother* of a woman attending her ten-year high school reunion.

"When did I get old?" Pam asked, her voice a whisper.

Involuntarily, she turned to stare at the mirror over the entry table. The person staring back at her looked familiar and yet totally wrong. Sure the shoulder-length dark hair was fine and the irises were still hazel-green. But everything else was different. No, not different. Less…firm.

There were lines around her eyes and a distinct softness to her jaw. Her mouth wasn't as full as it had been.

Ironically, just last November she'd turned fifty and had been so damned proud of herself for not freaking out. Because these days fifty was the new thirty-five. Big deal, right?

John had thrown a huge party. She'd laughed over the gag gifts and had prided herself for achieving the big 5-0 with grace and style. Not to mention a pretty decent ass, thanks to the three-times-a-week classes she took at Nicole's studio. She hadn't felt…old. But that was before she had a daughter who had just been invited to her ten-year high school reunion.

Sure, she'd had kids young. She'd married John at nineteen and had Jen when she'd turned twenty-two. But that was what she'd always wanted.

She and John had met at Mischief Bay High School. He'd been tall and sexy, a star player on the football team. His family had a local plumbing company. One that worked in new construction rather than fixing stopped-up toilets.

John's plans had been set. He was going to get his AA in business from Mischief Bay Community College, then work in the family firm full-time. He would start at the bottom, earn his way to the top and buy out his parents by the time he was forty.

Pam had liked how he'd known what he wanted and went after it. When he turned his blue eyes on her and decided she was the one to share the journey, well, she'd been all in.

Now as she studied her oddly familiar and unfamiliar reflection, she wondered how the time had gone by so quickly. One second she'd been an in-love teenager and now she was the mother of a twenty-eight-year-old.

"No," she said aloud, turning away from the mirror.

She wasn't going to freak out over something as ridiculous as age. She had an amazing life. A wonderful husband and terrific kids and a strange little dog. They were all healthy—except for Lulu's ongoing issues—and successful and, best of all, happy. She'd been blessed a thousand times over. She was going to remember that and stay grateful. So what if she wasn't firm? Beauty only went skin deep. She had wisdom and that was worth more.

She headed into the kitchen and flipped on the wall-mounted TV. John got home between five-fifteen and five-thirty every day. They ate at six—a meal she'd made from scratch. Every Saturday night they either went out to dinner or had an evening with friends. Sunday afternoon the kids came over and they barbecued. On Memorial Day they held a big party, also a barbecue. It was L.A. When in doubt, throw meat on a grill.

She automatically collected the ingredients for biscuits. Self-rising flour, shortening, sugar, buttermilk, baking powder. She'd stopped using a recipe years ago for nearly everything. Because she knew what she was doing. John liked what she served and didn't want her to change. They had a routine. Everything was comfortable.

She measured the flour and told herself that comfortable wasn't the same as old. It was nice. Friendly. Routines meant things went smoothly.

She finished cutting in the shortening, then covered the bowl. That was the trick to her biscuits. To let them rest about twenty minutes.

Lulu sat patiently next to her bowl. As Pam approached, the dog wagged her fluffy tail and widened her eyes in a hopeful expression.

Pam rolled out the biscuits and put them on the cookie sheet. She covered them with a clean towel and started the oven. She'd barely finished setting the table when she heard the faint rumble of the garage door opener. Lulu took off running down the hall, barking and yipping in excitement.

A few minutes later John walked into the kitchen, their ridiculous dog in his arms. Pam smiled at him and turned her head for their evening kiss. As their lips touched, Lulu scrambled from his arms to hers, then swiped both their chins with her tongue.

"How was your day?" John asked.

"Good. Yours?"

"Not bad."

As he spoke he crossed to the bottle of wine she'd put on the counter in the butler's pantry off the kitchen. It was a cab from a winery they'd visited a few years ago on a trip to Napa.

"Steven's working on a bid for that new hotel everyone's been talking about. It's right on the water. Upscale to the max. He said they were talking about the possibility of twenty-four-karat gold on the faucets in the penthouse. Can you believe it?"

"No. Who would do that? It's a hotel. Everything has to be scrubbed down daily. How do you clean gold?"

"I know." John opened the drawer to pull out the foil cutter. "It's a bathroom. They're idiots. But if the check clears, what do I care?"

As they spoke, she studied the man she'd been married to for thirty-one years. He was tall, just over six feet, with thick hair that had started going gray. The dark blond color meant the gray wasn't noticeable, but it was there. Being a man, it only made him look more appealing. A few months ago he'd asked why she wasn't going gray, too. When she'd reminded him of her visits every six weeks to her hair person, he'd been shocked. John was such a typical guy, it had never occurred to him she colored her hair. Because he thought she was naturally beautiful.

Silly man, she thought affectionately, as she watched him.

He had a few wrinkles around his eyes, but otherwise looked as he had when they'd first met. Those broad shoulders had always appealed to her. These days he claimed he needed to lose ten or fifteen pounds, but she thought he looked just fine.

He was handsome, in a rugged kind of way. He was a good man. Kind and generous. He loved his wife and his kids and his routine. While he had his faults, they were minor and ones she could easily live with. In truth, she had no complaints about John. It was the her-getting-older thing she found faintly annoying.

He pulled out the cork and tested it with his thumbnail, then poured them each a glass of cab. She slid the biscuits into the oven and set the timer.

"What are we having?" he asked as he handed her a glass.

"Beef burgundy and biscuits."

His mouth turned up in an easy smile. "I'm a lucky man."

"Even luckier. You'll be taking leftovers for lunch tomorrow."

"You know I love me some leftovers."

He wasn't kidding, she thought as she followed him through the kitchen. His idea of heaven was any kind of red meat with leftovers for lunch the following day. He was easy to please.

They went into the sunroom off the back of the house.

In the cooler months, the glass room stayed warm. In the summer, they removed the glass and used the space for outdoor living.

Lulu followed them, then jumped up on the love seat where Pam always sat and settled next to her. Pam rubbed her dog's ears as John leaned back in his chair—a recliner with a matching mate in the family room—and sighed heavily.

"Hayley's pregnant again," he said. "She told me this morning. She's waiting until three months to make a public announcement."

Pam felt her mouth twist. "I don't know what to say," she admitted. "That poor girl."

"I hope this one takes," John said. "I don't know how much more of her suffering I can stand."

Hayley was John's secretary and desperate to have children, but she'd miscarried four times over the past three years. This would be try number five. Rob, Hayley's husband, wanted to look into adoption or a surrogate, but Hayley was obsessed with having a baby the old-fashioned way.

"I should send her a card," Pam said, then shook her head. "Maybe not." She took a sip of her wine. "I have no idea how to handle this."

"Don't look at me. You're in woman territory."

"Where if you stray too far, you'll grow breasts?"

"Damned straight."

"I'll write a note," she decided. "I can say we're rooting for her without a you're-having-a-baby message. Did the doctor say she would be okay if she could get to three months?"

Her husband forehead furrowed. "I don't know. She

probably told me, but I barely want to know if she goes to the bathroom. Baby stuff is too intimate."

"You're not a complex man, are you?"

He raised his glass to her. "And that's why you love me."

He was right. She did love that he was dependable and predictable. Even if every now and then she wanted something different in their lives. A surprise trip to somewhere or a fancy bracelet. But that wasn't John's style. He would never plan a trip without talking to her and as for buying jewelry, he was more of a "go buy yourself something pretty" kind of man.

She didn't object. She'd seen too many of her friends endure surprises of the not very pleasant kind. Ones that involved other women or divorces. John wasn't looking for more than she had to offer. He liked his routine and knowing that gave her comfort.

"Jen got mail from the high school today," she said. "An invitation to her ten-year reunion."

"Okay."

"You don't think it's stunning that we have a daughter old enough to have been out of high school ten years?"

"She's twenty-eight. So the reunion is right on time."

Pam sipped her wine. "I was shocked. I'm not ready to have a daughter that old."

"Too late to send her back now. She's used."

Despite her earlier distress, Pam laughed. "Don't let her hear you say that."

"I won't." He smiled at her. "And you're not old, sweetheart. You're barely in your prime."

"Thanks." She heard the timer chime and stood. "That's our dinner."

He scooped up Lulu and followed Pam back to the

kitchen. As Pam went about serving the meal, she reminded herself she was a very lucky woman. That a bit of sagging and a few lumps and bumps didn't change who she was as a person. Her life was a blessing. If there weren't any tingles anymore, well, that was to be expected. Wasn't she forever hearing that you couldn't have it all?

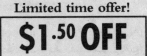

SUSAN MALLERY

31813 BAREFOOT SEASON	___$7.99 U.S.	___$8.99 CAN.
31324 ALREADY HOME	___$7.99 U.S.	___$9.99 CAN.

(limited quantities available)

TOTAL AMOUNT	$ _____
POSTAGE & HANDLING	$ _____
($1.00 for 1 book, 50¢ for each additional)	
APPLICABLE TAXES*	$ _____
TOTAL PAYABLE	$ _____

(check or money order—please do not send cash)

To order, complete this form and send it, along with a check or money order for the total above, payable to MIRA Books, to: **In the U.S.:** 3010 Walden Avenue, P.O. Box 9077, Buffalo, NY 14269-9077; **In Canada:** P.O. Box 636, Fort Erie, Ontario, L2A 5X3.

Name: _____
Address: _____ City: _____
State/Prov.: _____ Zip/Postal Code: _____
Account Number (if applicable): _____
075 CSAS

*New York residents remit applicable sales taxes.
*Canadian residents remit applicable GST and provincial taxes.

MIRA®

www.MIRABooks.com

MSM0215BL